# CAPTURE A HEART OF STONE

Books by

TERESA SMYSER

*Heaven Help Us!*

*The Warrior & Lady Rebel*

*In His Embrace*

# CAPTURE
## *a heart of*
# STONE

*Warrior Bride Series,* Book 3

# Teresa Smyser

*Capture A Heart of Stone*
Copyright © 2017 by Teresa Smyser, revised edition 2022

Cover design by Whitley Fleming
Cover photography by Boiko Olha/Shutterstock.com

ISBN 978-1981470112

**Scripture quotations are from the King James Version of the Bible.**

*To my loyal readers!*
*Without you, writing wouldn't be nearly as fun.*
*Thank you.*

# *1*

*1627 England*

"Gwendolyn, fetch my cape," Pippa whispered. She scanned her bedchamber and spotted the document on her desk.

"Please, oh please, do not do this terrible thing," Gwendolyn begged in a hushed voice.

Pippa didn't need to turn around to know her childhood friend stood near the door wringing her hands with worry. Ever since the death of Pippa's mother, Abigail, Gwendolyn had taken it upon herself to coddle the motherless girl. Pippa whipped around. "My cape, now!"

Gwendolyn teared up yet turned to do her lady's bidding. Pippa steeled her heart against the tears, or she might reconsider her actions. Riding well before dawn under the cover of darkness would be risky yet necessary. She had no other option to save herself and her people.

Across the room, Gwendolyn sniffed. "Ye risk much riding into the wolf's lair."

Strapping on her sword belt, Pippa rolled her eyes at her dramatic friend. The wolf's lair indeed. Being the lone child of

Lord Phillip and Lady Abigail Fairwick had left Pippa with few to call friend. As a child, she played with Gwendolyn and Merry even though both were children of castle servants. Unfortunately, there were times when Gwendolyn used their friendship to dissuade her decisions ... such as now.

With sword and knives in place, Pippa turned to face her friend. She took the cape and fastened it under her chin. "Help me attach my quiver and arrows under my hood."

Pippa was quite proud of the leather quiver she handcrafted with the help of her father. She had become rather proficient with her bow ... enough to feel confident in protecting herself. But her knife throwing ability is what grabbed her enemies by surprise.

"Oh, my lady, please reconsider this dangerous undertaking. Henry would be happy to do your bidding."

With a deep sigh, Pippa stopped her preparations and grasped Gwendolyn's hands. She peered into her friend's anguished eyes as tears threatened to fall. "I appreciate your offering your husband's services, but he has other tasks to perform to insure my journey. You mustn't worry so. I'll be safe in God's protective hands."

That should stop Gwendolyn's scolding. No one dare fault God's security. With one final squeeze, she released Gwendolyn's hands. "Shall we go over your part to play in my plan?"

Gwendolyn clutched her apron, her eyes wide. "I'm to leave your bedchamber locked and go about my duties as if nothing is amiss. If anyone asks for you, I'm to say you're not feeling well and decided to rest while writing your correspondence."

Pippa looked at Gwendolyn. "If you don't feel you can hide your anxiety from showing on your face, then stay busy cleaning the unoccupied rooms. I don't want anyone becoming suspicious."

Gwendolyn hung her head. "Ye have it aright." With a bowed head she peered up. "I worry I might break down if questions are asked."

Pippa gripped Gwendolyn's shoulders and gave a slight shake. "You must stand strong. Our very livelihood depends on making a powerful alliance ... and before you speak ... yes, he does have a somewhat scandalous reputation, but he is the wealthiest and most skilled warrior in our realm."

"But ..."

Pippa released Gwendolyn's shoulders and placed a finger across her lips. "No buts. Do as I say, and all will be well."

As a lone tear leaked from Gwendolyn's eye, she said, "I fear this will be the last time I see you."

For a moment Pippa pressed her eyes closed and inhaled a deep breath. With hurried motions she grabbed the document holder and attached it under her cloak. "We are wasting precious time. It will be daylight in a few hours. No more discussion about my plot." She studied Gwendolyn. "Carry out your part, and I will see you tonight or tomorrow morning." Pippa slipped behind the door which led to the passageway and waited for Gwendolyn to scoot out before she locked it.

Gwendolyn paused with her hand on the door latch. She placed her other hand upon Pippa's arm. "God's speed, my lady."

Pippa squeezed Gwendolyn's hand and offered a smile. "All will be well. You will see." Pippa hoped her performance had convinced Gwendolyn to carry out the reckless idea. The more it tumbled through her mind, the crazier it sounded.

She turned the key in the lock and dropped the safety bar in place. Giving herself a mental shake, she lifted the candle from her bedside table. Walking into her changing room, she placed the candle on a stool in the corner. Now to find the concealed handle to release the latch on the wooden wardrobe.

As she reached toward the wall, the candlelight flickered. Pippa jumped around to face the doorway expecting to see an intruder but found it empty. A tingle slipped down her back. She chastised herself for being spooked. No time to let her imagination play tricks on her. Her telling ghost stories to Gwendolyn and Merry resurrected to spook her.

Pippa sucked in through her teeth. As she puffed out her breath, it stirred a tendril of hair that had loosened from her braid. For her own peace of mind, she shut the door connecting the bedchamber to the changing room. Back to her task.

With steady hands, she ran them along the edge of the wardrobe until she felt the loose stone. She worked and wiggled the stone but couldn't dislodge it. Taking the knife from her boot, she slid the blade under the stone and shimmied it loose. With a little more effort her fingers grabbed the edge of the stone and pulled it out. Placing it on the floor, she reached for the candle to illuminate the hole. When she saw the iron ring, a small giggle escaped.

To keep from burning herself, she set the candle on the stool and clutched the ring with both hands. She placed one booted foot against the wall and gave a hearty yank. The well-greased mechanism began to grind as the wardrobe slid sideways. Pippa froze as the opening revealed the hidden stairway.

Her father, Phillip, had divulged this particular secret after an attack by a would-be suitor trying to capture Pippa. After the attack, her father had decided she should make this her bedchamber for the duration of her life at Fairwick castle. Until today, she had never traversed the tunnel.

As she stared into the dark abyss, her heart raced. The circular stairs disappeared downward into blackness. Her father had left two torches on the wall, ready for use. With her candle, she set one torch ablaze and blew out the candle. There was no turning back when she stepped onto the stone platform. Her father's trap door would slide shut, as if never disturbed.

In order to keep her spot secret, she replaced the stone in the wall. Leaving the changing room, she put the candle back on her bedside table. Unsure of the success of her mission, she glanced around the room that had served her for many years. Her possessions brought her comfort especially since the death of both parents. Would she sleep here again? It mattered not. She needed to rescue her people whatever the cost ... the mission couldn't wait.

Not wanting to become downhearted, she squared her shoulders and marched back to the stairs. With great determination, she stepped onto the platform and watched as her haven disappeared. Pippa picked up the lighted torch in one hand and the spare, unlit torch with the other. She hesitated ... unsure as to the length of her journey, she closed her eyes.

*Almighty God in Heaven. I place myself in Your protective hand. Be my shield against my enemies and my refuge in case of danger. I entrust You to defend my people in my absence. Guard them with Your angels of might. This I pray thee.*

Opening her eyes, she began her steps into the mysterious channel. The stones were damp and mossy. Not wishing to fall to her death, she placed each footstep with care. With only the sound of her boots to keep her company, she had ample time to reflect on her life.

As the first born of Phillip and Abigail Fairwick, they had christened her Philippa Emma Gail Fairwick. The name Philippa was for her father, Emma had been in honor of her aunt and Gail had been after her mother. It saddened her to think how little she remembered about her mother who died giving birth to a little boy. Unfortunately, her baby brother had died on that dreadful day as well. With vivid clarity she envisioned the pain etched on her father's face during that time. It had been more than she could bear, and she had run from the castle to her special hiding place. Just the thought of it now caused a pain in her chest.

*I need to stop these morbid thoughts. It profits me nothing.*

She was grateful to arrive at the bottom of the secret stairs. Ahead of her was a long walk through the gloomy passageway. She recalled her father saying the opening at the end of the corridor would place her far into the woods outside the castle grounds.

Her burning torch dimmed. She quickened her pace since it would not last the entirety of her journey. The unused torch in her hand brought a smile to her lips. Her father had thought of all her needs.

*I love you, papa.*

The further she traveled from the castle, loose stones from the wall gave her pause. Would she negotiate the slippery hallway and find her way blocked from fallen stones? Her loud heartbeat rushed faster.

*Mighty God, please keep my pathway clear.*

Onward she trudged. 'Twas but a matter of moments yet felt as if hours ticked away. Just as her second torch burned low, she saw the hidden door. A slow breath escaped as her tense body relaxed. Trapped in the dark unknown was no longer a fear.

Pippa dropped the dwindling torch to the dirt floor and grabbed the latch on the wooden door above her head. She hesitated. Once the hidden door opened, she would need to be ready for any situation.

*You better be waiting for me, Henry.*

With a fortifying breath, she shoved the door upward just to have it snatched from her hand. To her utter relief, Henry peered into the hole.

"Take me hand."

She grasped his extended hand and with great ease he hauled her aboveground. Henry placed her on solid footing before shutting the door and covering it with moss and dirt.

"Follow me."

The two crouched low as they disappeared into the dense forest. She had faith that Henry had prepared her horse for the treacherous mission. As children, his father had worked for her father. Not having a son, Phillip had permitted Pippa to train in weapons. She and Henry's companionship had solidified during those early years of training together. Now he was a trusted protector under her leadership.

It wasn't long until her horse came into view. The muzzle was still in place as well as the covers over his hooves. With a soft hand, she tugged his head down. "'Tis alright, my sweet." She stroked his forehead while making kissing sounds in the air. In a short time, a wolf appeared on the fringe of the trees.

Henry hissed. "I wish ye would wait until I'm away before calling the beast."

Pippa suppressed her smile. "Hold Romeo's head while I mount."

Henry held fast while she arranged her belongings. After she took the reins, Romeo pranced around until she forced him into submission. "I'll return posthaste. Keep my departure our secret."

"I'll do as ye say, but under protest. I should be the one to meet the wolf in his lair. Not ye."

Pippa could hear the agitation in his voice. "Wolf's lair ... you and Gwendolyn are quite the pair," she said in jest. "God is my defender and provider. Do not fear for me." On a serious note, she said, "I need your assurance that all will be well while I'm away. I want no worries to hinder my task."

"Ye have my word." He took hold of the bridle once more and looked at her. "Have a care, m' lady."

She nodded and turned to leave. "Come." With one word, her loyal wolf trotted after her. When she twisted around for one last glance at Henry, he had already vanished into the dark.

*Teresa Smyser, Warrior Bride Series, Book 3*

2

William once thought that weeping and gnashing of teeth was reserved for those dead who deserved it ... not so. As the oldest son of Laird Daniel McKinnon, he could scarcely grasp all that had transpired in the past two months. Standing in the ruins of the McKinnon castle, he kicked a charred log with his boot as he rubbed the back of his neck. The thought of his father in the hands of an enemy set his teeth on edge, but to think that he might have been murdered was not to be borne.

He had witnessed much carnage in his years as a mercenary, but nothing had prepared him for this. His father had called him home to escort his mother to Sanddown castle on the coast. She would winter there with her brother, Nicolas, and her sister-in-law, Isabelle. According to his father, he would join her before she gave birth to what his father hoped was their final child.

Daniel had sent his best warriors to help ensure the safety of his wife, Brigette, and William's four younger siblings, leaving less experienced men to accompany his father and guard the castle. William had sensed a flaw in his father's travel plans. Often his father was preoccupied with his all-consuming love for his wife. This time his distraction had cost him dearly.

*Why didn't I insist we all travel together?*

He blew out a frustrated breath and plopped onto the one blackened chair that remained in the shell of a room. After his father's capture, his father's enemies had returned to burn their castle to the ground. William put his head in his hands as he leaned on the scorched, wobbly table. The once massive table had served as his father's desk.

Tears filled his eyes as he thought of the castle folk fighting against their unknown enemy and suffering defeat. Some of the people had escaped into the hills while others were tortured before their deaths. He pulled his hair in agony. When he had stood before the castle ruins, a tight band around his heart had left him breathless and forced him to his knees.

He had hoped sitting in his father's chair would somehow bring them closer. As he lifted his head, his tear-filled eyes scanned the burned-out library. To his left, the crumbling stone fireplace sat cold and dark. Ashes from the countless books littered the floor like black snow. Creeping vines pushed through the gaping hole in the wall and slithered across the floor like a snake after its prey. His chest constricted at the sight before him.

"Oh, father. Where are you?" he whispered as he blinked back tears. At a shuffling sound, he turned toward the open space where a door had once stood. In walked his trusted guardian, Ross.

"Sir William, 'tis time to break our fast."

He leaned back from the table. "I'm not hungry."

"Ye canna think nor plan on an empty stomach. Coom away from this dreary room and back to tha warmth of tha tower."

He studied the salt-and-pepper haired man who had guarded him since infancy. Loyal to the McKinnon family, Ross often risked his own life to ensure William's safety. He was thankful Ross had accompanied the family to Sanddown Castle or else he, too, might have been slain during the surprise invasion. Instead, when his father didn't arrive at Sanddown castle in a timely manner, Ross had returned home to find the castle in ruins and the people scattered.

10

William realized rehashing the few facts he knew didn't aid his cause but instead kept his pain fresh. Rising, he stretched his arms above his head and let out a sigh as his stomach rumbled.

"Mayhap you are correct." He came alongside Ross and draped his arm around his shoulders. William had long ago surpassed his companion in stature. "Come, my friend, we will eat and strategize together."

The two men trudged through the debris littering their path. Much of their walk existed outside in the elements. Few solid walls remained for protection which left a passageway fraught with dangerous rubble to pick through. William saw evidence where Ross had cleared away large stones for a safer route to the lone tower which stood majestically against the gray sky.
There the men had taken refuge.

They walked along in silence. When Ross had returned to Sanddown castle with the devastating news, the image he painted lived forever etched in William's memory. He had feared his mother would die from grief. She had collapsed against him when Ross had walked in without his father. After Ross had reported the horrible facts, the shocking news had caused her to go into labor. Thankfully, she had delivered a healthy baby boy. Not even the new babe had lifted his mother's spirits. Only William's promise to find his father had brought her a small semblance of peace.

When the men stepped into the tower, warmth from the fireplace seeped into William's aching bones as the smell of gruel permeated the air.

"Sit, and I wilt serve ye," Ross offered.

William eased onto a rug covering the floor near the fire. The mesmerizing flames danced in the draft which filtered under the closed door. Ross handed him a bowl as he sat beside him.

"I've found a few more items for ye to sort through. I spread them out in tha next room."

"Thank you, Ross. I'll examine them after our meal."

"They are from yer parent's room."

William closed his eyes in torment. After a short moment, he captured his brittle feelings and began his meal. The sound of

11

clinking utensils against the bowls was the lone man-made sound in the room as they ate. The whistling of the wind under the door grew louder with the threat of an approaching storm.

"Thank you for the meal, my friend." William slapped the back of Ross's shoulder and looked at him directly. "I shudder to think my state of mind if you hadn't been here by my side."

Ross's eyes softened. "I wish there was more I could do to lessen yer grief, m' lord."

William stood to his feet. "Let's reserve that title for my father. I feel certain he is still alive ... or at least it's what I desire."

"Of course. 'Tis my prayer as weel." With unhurried movements Ross collected their dishes for cleaning.

William walked a few steps and stopped before opening the door. "You stay here and rest while I shuffle through the items you found. You have earned a respite from your labor."

Through eyes of understanding, he met William's gaze. "As ye wish, m' ... ere ... Sir William."

William drew the door closed and stood with his back against it. He pulled up his hood as the cold wind whipped around his neck. Everywhere his eyes touched, devastation reigned. Collapsed walls, ruined vegetation ... utter destruction. He grew angry with himself. He knew nothing was gained from his gloomy thoughts. Thankfully, he had missed the task of burying their dead. It had taken place before he had arrived—a sad business indeed.

He pushed away from the door and with a heavy tread made his way to what was left of the next room. As he stumbled over a tree root, the loud flutter of birds startled him. With rapid speed he whipped out his sword. Once he ascertained the noise came from foragers, he sheathed it. He needed to stay alert even in the midst of the wreckage. His father's enemies could still be close at hand.

He knelt on one knee before a pile of objects. Laying his sword on the floor next to him, he lifted what appeared to be a broach. Surprised it hadn't melted in the fire, he ran a finger over the intricate design. Tears threatened. He couldn't waste valuable time indulging his volatile emotions.

Removing a cloth from his belt, he stretched it out on what appeared to be a charred footstool. There he laid the precious broach. He was pleased to see several pieces from his father's marble chess set. Also in the heap was a couple of iron candle holders, a small dagger, and some gems that survived. However, what intrigued him most was the small, locked chest. Surprised, yet delighted that it had endured the blaze. No doubt it had resided under the floor planks.

He tried to force open the lock to no avail. When he reached to use the hilt of his sword, thunder rolled across the sky. Not wanting to get wet, he decided the secrets of the chest would have to wait. He wrapped his treasures in the cloth and picked his way back toward the tower. Just as the first plops of rain fell, he looked to see Ross in the open doorway.

"Hurry, Sir William."

William jumped over debris and ran toward the beckoning refuge. He tumbled through the doorway with his bundle in tow. Ross closed the portal just as the storm picked up in intensity.

"Take off yer damp cloak before ye catch yer death. 'Tis risky to get wet this time of tha year."

He reverently laid down his prized parcels before removing his wrap. On his knees he spread out the objects. "You have a keen eye, Ross. I'm happy to see some of mother's jewels withstood the fire and the plunderers. No doubt much of their valuables were pillaged before the castle was torched."

"Aye. I'm sure ye have it aright. Yer mither will be moost displeased when she sees this dismal place."

Sitting back on his haunches, William rubbed his brow. "I believe my mother could bear anything if my father returns to her side."

Ross placed his hand upon William's shoulder. "Ye are right in yer assessment. Love of anither can help ye endure much. Yer mither is a strong one."

A small chuckle escaped William. "That she is Ross, that she is. I dare say she would blister my ears if she knew of our living conditions."

13

A smile spread across Ross's face. "Indeed."

William rubbed the soot off a chess piece to reveal the white marble knight. "Can we capture enough rainwater to clean these valuables?"

"Och, I forgot to mention I prepared a wash bowl of water for juist such a task." Ross dragged a small table to where William knelt.

William jumped to his feet. "Here allow me to carry the water bowl." As he picked up the bowl from under the window, a movement caught his eye. He ducked into the shadows and peered through the ragged shutters.

Ross sank to the floor. "Whit is it?" he whispered.

"I'm not sure. Something caught my eye, but now 'tis gone."

"A person?"

"I can't be certain." William eased the bowl to the floor and drew his sword. He stared at the group of trees ... waiting.

## 3

William remained by the window watching for another sighting, but nothing materialized. "Do you think I imagined it?"

"I know not. Let me go aboot my business as usual and see if anything is amiss."

William's eyes met Ross's. "Nay. We will go together. My conscience couldn't bear if you met with tragedy while I remained ensconced in this tower." William grabbed his other weapons and hooked them to his belt. "I will stow away our treasures while you prepare for departure."

Once Ross was ready, William opened the door with great care. With a tight grip on his sword, he peered around the edge before venturing out into the open. Both men stopped outside the closed door to listen. The storm had passed but the remaining wind caused raindrops from trees to pound the earth. With no unusual sounds detected they proceeded forward.

William was keenly aware of each step they took knowing a wrong placement and tumbling stones could alert their enemy to their location. They worked their way all around the castle ruins and saw nothing out of the ordinary.

Not willing to let down his guard, William gave a hand signal for Ross to go to the kitchen ruins while he scanned the library. The men parted company, each keeping a sharp eye on the landscape.

William crept into the room but found nothing but birds. He shooed them away and walked to the gaping hole in the wall. There he pulled back the vines and stared at the damaged land.

*Where are you, my enemy? Show yourself.*

Not sure how long he remained by the opening, he heard Ross talking with someone. He jogged over to the doorway and edged his head around the corner. Moving his way was Ross, conversing with a man. Measured by the horse he led, the man was of slight build. The man didn't appear to pose any danger, but William knew it was possible all was not as it seemed. He inched backward and strode over to the table. There he sat and propped his feet up. Let his enemy think him unconcerned about the intrusion.

He didn't have to wait long when Ross appeared in the opening. "Ye have a visitor, m' lord."

William cringed at the salutation. Old habits were hard to change it seemed. "Send him in." No sooner had the words left his mouth when the man emerged from the darkness with his horse in tow.

Ross gave a slight bow and left the two alone.

The stranger gripped a bow in one hand and the reins in the other. The hair stood on William's arms. William wasted no time on pleasantries and made his distaste evident with his curt remark. "State your business."

The small warrior remained unmoving and speechless. William knew he could talk for he had heard him speaking with Ross. He wondered at the man's tactic. His identity remained hidden under the hood of his cloak while he stayed mute.

Now William was agitated. "Speak up, man." He watched as the man released the lead line and with a delicate hand pushed off his hood.

William sucked in air. *A woman?* A tight braid of hair fell out of her hood and across her shoulder. William's feet hit the floor

16

with a thud as he straightened in his chair. Her piercing blue eyes bore a hole through him with unnerving precision. "What game do you play, madam?"

"No game, William," she rasped.

Her voice sounded vaguely familiar. "Do I know you?" he demanded.

She cleared her throat before speaking. "I am Philippa Emma Gail Fairwick of Fairwick castle."

His eyes widened. "Pippa?" he mouthed. Before him stood a woman full grown, not the young girl he remembered. With both hands placed flat on the table, he leaned forward. "What do you here?"

She squared her shoulders. "I need your help."

He gapped at her before a harsh laugh erupted. Rising to his feet, he threw his arms wide. "Look around you foolish girl. Me help you?" A forced laugh boomed out. "If you haven't noticed, I'm a bit understaffed, not to mention, lacking in shelter, weapons, fighting men, food ... shall I go on?"

Other than a slight blush, she appeared unaffected by his little speech.

"Who travels with you?"

"No one. I travel alone."

"That's preposterous. Your father would never allow it." Before she had time to respond, he marched past her and looked out amongst the rubble and the surrounding land. He turned and stalked over to the opening in the back wall and peered through the vines. "Where is your escort hiding?"

She huffed. "We are wasting time with this line of questioning. I'm alone. Now may we proceed?"

William whipped his head around to stare at her. "I don't believe you."

"It matters not."

With slow, deliberate moves, he walked over and plopped in his chair. He leaned back in the chair and propped his feet on the charred table. Placing his sword on the tabletop, he kept a firm grip on it while his other hand rested in his lap. In the stillness of the moment, he stared at her. She didn't even flinch but remained stoic in her demeanor. Her eyes followed his as he ran them down and back up her form. She had matured quite nicely if one liked a rugged woman which he did not. Her cobalt eyes came from her father's side of the family—an unusual, but beautiful blue. Her diminutive stature and fiery hair were from her mother's side.

He noticed she stood as still as a warrior poised for battle. Waiting. Anticipating. Ready to pounce. Obviously, his discourteous manner hadn't deterred her. Mayhap he should hear her out before sending her on her way. First, he would send Ross to look for her guard.

He felt certain Ross was close at hand. "Ross," he bellowed.

In a matter of seconds, Ross's head popped into view. "Aye, m' lord?"

William motioned for him to come to his side. Ross rushed to do his bidding but flashed a smile at Pippa as he passed her by. William refrained from rolling his eyes with annoyance. Instead, he maintained a hardnosed expression. He whispered instructions for Ross to search out her men and report back to him.

He watched as Pippa nodded her head in acknowledgment to Ross as he left the room. She quickly swung her eyes back to William. "Will you allow me to speak?"

He released his sword and crossed his arms over his chest. "Does your father know you are here?" He noticed a pained expression pass right before she masked it.

"You must not have heard. My father was murdered."

His arms flew apart and again his feet hit the floor. "Murdered? Are you sure of this?"

This time she did struggle with her reply. He watched as she tried to blink away her tears. After a couple of deep breaths, she answered.

"His wrecked carriage was found in a deep ravine. Two guards traveled with him that night. Evidence of their struggles were all around. The bodies were torn to pieces by the enemy or from scavengers—I know not which." She licked her trembling lips

18

before continuing. "My father's shredded clothes were among the remains."

Now it was his turn to feel pain. He regretted causing her to reveal the distressing news. His curiosity peaked to know details, but he couldn't afford to show interest for he had no time to come to her aid. He had his own father to find along with a mountain of obstacles to overcome.

"Of this I am sorry. Your father was well respected and valued in this realm."

"Without my father, it has been difficult to run the castle while fighting off would-be suitors."

William's brow raised. "Oh?" If he hadn't been observing her, he would have missed the slight shrug of one shoulder.

"They want the land, not me. However, they have caused much damage to my castle."

"Why don't you call upon your Uncle Nicolas? He should still have an interest in the family property."

"Suffice it to say it is not an option. I know you worked as a mercenary and have great skills. 'Tis you I need."

Her reference to his past days riled him. Most people saw mercenaries as greedy soldiers who worked for the highest bidder no matter the cause of the battle. That had not been the way William functioned. He had chosen his battles with care and made sure to fight for the family in the right. Of course, no one seemed to care about his moral standards. They judged him merely on their own explanation of a mercenary.

Not liking the guilt she resurrected, he went on the attack. "Mayhap you should call upon the special powers of your Aunt Isabelle. Some say she is a witch."

Unblinking, she stared at him. "It matters not what you think of my family. The question remains. Will. You. Help me?"

He stood. "Nay. A thousand times, nay!"

She caught the reins as her horse threw his head back. Stroking his nose, she calmed him while whispering in his ear.

Ross chose at that time to enter the room. He hurried to William's side and spoke close to his ear. William reared back and looked unbelieving at Ross.

"Thank you, Ross." He watched Ross exit the room and then eased into his unsteady chair. Sitting forward with arms on the table and hands clasped, his nostril's flared. "I see you are still foolish when it comes to your safety— traveling alone with no protection. If I had a woodshed, I would take you there and beat some sense into you."

No sooner had the last words left his lips when a hurtling knife stabbed the top of the table next to his sword. He jerked in surprise. When he glared at Pippa, he found an arrow aimed at his heart.

"What's the meaning of this?" he roared.

"I have spent enough time listening to your excuses. Now you will listen to me."

His eyes narrowed to mere slits. "How dare you come to my home, asking for my service, and then threaten me." He slowly rose to his feet.

"Do not test me."

When he made a move toward his sword, she released her arrow. It found its mark next to the hilt of his sword—inches from his hand. He was shocked to see another arrow ready for flight in such a short span of time. "You will regret this strike," he said with deceptive calm.

"I told you it is my turn to speak. You may take a seat." She motioned with her arrow for him to sit.

Even though furious, he decided to allow her this small victory, for he would win the day. Of this he was certain. Without a word, he plunked down and leaned back in the chair as if unconcerned with her display of power. He would wait for an advantage and then ...

"I need you to live at my castle and help me make repairs to the walls and gates. The repeated attacks have done much damage. I will even permit you to enlist the help of your mercenary friends if need be. We are also in great need of food which I know you can purchase."

It took William's many years of training to sit idly by while she spouted off her ludicrous requests. He had no intentions of helping her much less abiding under the same roof with her. Foolhardy woman.

"With you staying at my castle it will afford us an opportunity to plan our strategy to find those who murdered my father and who captured yours."

William straightened at those words. "You know who abducted my father?"

"I have gathered information along those lines."

"You don't know who's responsible," he spit out. "You just want my assistance. The fact you would use my father's disappearance to bend me to your desires is appalling. You just made a tactical error in judgment."

"I did not wish to trouble you with my line of reasoning, but you are being most difficult. I had hoped our past friendship would inspire you to agree. But that is not the case." She lowered her bow. "I will give you a fortnight to reach a decision."

Unbelievable. If he didn't know better, he would think she was daft. He observed the sadness in her countenance but hardened his resolve. When he saw her back toward the opening and reach for the reins, he seized the opportunity to pounce. He scrambled over the table and launched.

His actions caught her unaware. She attempted to jump away, but his body weight took her to the ground. Her horse reared and bolted from the room barely missing the two on the ground. They scrambled and fought, but his bulk overpowered her small form. She ended up on her back with him straddling her while holding her arms pinned to the ground.

"You will regret your actions this day. Release me at once!" Her eyes threw daggers as she snorted with rage.

"I think not," he huffed. He eased closer to her hair. "For such a wild and untamed woman, I find your aroma quite pleasing." He tightened his hold on her wrists as she bucked from renewed fury at his words. "Woman, stop resisting. You cannot win."

"You are mistaken." She gave a deafening whistle. In less than a heartbeat a wolf's snarling fangs were within inches of Williams' throat.

He froze but held fast.

"I wouldn't move if I were you," she sneered. "You were correct; I didn't travel alone. I brought Wolf." She gave him a satisfied smile that provoked his already hot wrath.

"What would you have me do ... give you a kiss?" he whispered. Those words produced favorable results as he had suspected.

"No, you swine. You need to release the grip of your left hand without moving your arm."

His brows rose.

"I need to give a hand command to Wolf," she said calmly. "It's best I do it soon. I don't wish to lose my only choice of a redeemer." She followed her words with a deceitful smile.

William had no choice but to obey her request even though it chafed. He unclasped his fingers surrounding her right wrist but didn't move his arm in the process.

Still on the ground, Pippa turned her head toward the wolf and raised her right hand, palm out. "No," she said. She kept her hand in place as the wolf inched away two feet and sat on his haunches. His fangs were no longer in sight, but his eyes were ever watchful.

Her gaze swung back to William. "All will be well if you but ease backward onto your buttocks and then scoot over to your chair. This will allow me to sit up which will please Wolf."

"Such foul speech is unbecoming a lady." Again, her mocking smirk nearly caused him to kill the wolf first and then take out his frustration on her backside. In addition, where was Ross when he needed him? No doubt standing just around the corner stifling his laughter. As William eased into his chair, he wondered how his day had gone so horribly wrong.

He watched as the mangy wolf crawled toward his master and licked her outstretched hand like a pup. How had she tamed the wild animal? After their affectionate reunion, Pippa rubbed her wrists. He could see the bruising left from his tight grasp. Of that, he was regretful. Mentally, he shook his head. One moment he saw a vulnerable young girl, and in lightning speed she became a mighty warrior—one he would not underestimate again. Her knife throwing abilities were fresh in his mind.

She rested her arms on her bent knees. When she directed her attention his way, he said in a quiet voice, "Now, you will listen to me. Your plight is unfortunate; however, I have no time to devote to your cause, imagined or otherwise. I will escort you home where I will leave you ... alone. If you cause me any more trouble, I will put my hand to your derriere."

Her face reddened. "You are not my father," she said through tight lips. After a brief moment of thought, her upturned face wore a smug expression.

"But you *are* my betrothed."

# 4

"That's preposterous!" William jumped to his feet. His chair crashed to the floor.

Wolf bounded into attack mode at the sound of his booming voice. "Stay," Pippa commanded without taking her gaze from William. "I need him alive and well." She wanted to laugh at his look of horror but dared not. All that she held dear depended upon his acquiescence. "I have proof."

He released a coarse laugh. "I would know if I was betrothed, and I am not!"

Ashes swirled as William stomped back and forth through the room. He pounded his fist in his palm and mumbled obscenities that blistered her ears. He whirled to face her. "I want to see the proof of which you speak."

While William fumed, Pippa wondered at the wisdom of withdrawing her document. If his father's matching contract had burned in the fire, he might attempt to destroy her evidence. She studied his face. At one time he had adored her. In fact, at age five, he had been the very one to give her the nickname of Pippa when he found Philippa too hard to pronounce. Surely, once he viewed the written record, he would fulfil their fathers' wishes in the matter.

Eyes trained on William, she laid aside her bow. Long ago her father had taught her never to assume she was safe in the presence of an opponent. With one arm she lifted her leather pouch from around her neck. She felt secure with Wolf on guard. Any move by William, and he would regret it. "I have the signed contract between our fathers." She untied the end and turned it upside down.

"You spout nonsense."

She glanced to see his face turn multiple colors. Her hand lingered. "It would seem your father didn't mention this arrangement." She tilted her head. "How odd. My father told me of it when I was but twelve years of age."

"Mayhap my father changed his mind once he observed your behavior as a grown woman ... or should I say warrior?"

Pippa lowered her head as the contract slid into her open hand. His words stung. Other men had ridiculed her warrior-like conduct, but it hadn't mattered until now. As a little girl, William had been her champion. Growing up, she had amused herself with thoughts of marriage to him which had helped vanquish her loneliness. Alas, a woman in her station had few options outside of an advantageous marital contract. From his response, her future looked bleak.

With a reverent grip on the agreement, she held it close to her heart. "I will allow you to read the contract if you promise not to destroy it." She eyed him for a moment. "Do I have your word?"

His hands clutched and released several times. When she thought he would not concede, he gave a brief nod. She didn't want to relinquish her hold, but knew she had to trust him if they were to proceed. With head held high, she walked to the table and presented him with the document.

He snatched the parchment from her hand. "I'll judge the authenticity of this document. I know my father's signature well."

It took all her concentration to stand unmoving while he read the marriage contract. She held her breath and prayed he wouldn't tear it asunder. No doubt the hurt she saw travel across his face was from the betrayal of his father for not sharing this life-altering agreement. The anger, she felt certain, was directed at her for bearing the fateful tidings. Even though cold air swirled around her legs and raced up her neck, her palms sweated. Her heart pounded in her ears ... yet ... she waited.

"As you can see there are two seals at the bottom."

When he failed to respond, she pointed them out. "One made with the Fairwick signet ring, and one made with the McKinnon ring."

He scowled at her. "I can see what appears to be my father's signature and seal, but that doesn't make it authentic. How do I know for certain that you didn't fabricate this for your own purpose of trapping me into giving you my assistance?"

Pippa glared at him. "If you believe that, then you don't know me at all."

"Here!" William flung the paper which hit her chest.

Pippa flinched and Wolf growled. She grabbed the paper as it fluttered toward the blackened floor and frowned when she saw how his tight-fisted grasp had crinkled the edges. Stepping away from the table, she rolled it up while her gaze stayed on his face. Wolf stood between her and William as she slipped the contract back into its holder. "What say you?"

Standing tall, he said, "It could well be a forgery. I will search for my father's copy."

"Sear ... search for your father's copy?" Now it was Pippa who threw her arms open wide. "Look around you, William. Be reasonable. All is lost here. His contract would have burned unless he had it stored in an iron box hidden from the sight of his enemies."

"I said I would find his copy if one even existed."

She huffed. "As you wish. There is nothing further for us to discuss."

Saddened that he had to find out about the betrothal in this manner, she steeled her heart. In fact, after years of silence between them, their meeting would have flowed more smoothly if his father had divulged the truth.

"I will provide food for your journey and escort you home."

His dispirited countenance caused her pause. Should she try to comfort him or leave him to his thoughts? Her training won out. Never poke what appears to be a docile bear. "'Tisn't necessary. Wolf will protect me." She was relieved to see Ross had returned her horse—no time wasted hunting for Romeo amongst the ruins. "Come, Wolf."

Without a backward glance, Pippa tramped through the debris. Just before turning the corner, she looked over her shoulder. "A fortnight."

"Or what?" he taunted.

"Do not press me. You will not like the outcome." With that she left him standing with fisted hands once again.

As she picked through the rubble, a sunbeam raced through the trees and stabbed her eye. Welcoming the light, she turned her face toward the sun and allowed her weary body to soak up its warmth. She had been cold and without hope for too long. After following God's prompting to talk with William, she could but wait for the outcome of her labors. When she opened her heavy eyes, her hand flew to her knife without thought.

"Ross, you gave me a fright!"

"Forgive me, m' lady. I wished to talk with ye afore yer departure if it pleases ye."

"Yes ... I welcome it. Oh, and thank you for retrieving my horse. Romeo can be mischievous when he takes a notion."

"I am glad to be of service. Follow me. I have prepared a repast afore yer journey."

"Thank you, kind sir."

He walked in front while Pippa trailed along. With so much debris, there was but room for a single line. Wolf trotted along at her heels while searching the area for danger. After a short time, they arrived at a crude kitchen area. A pot hung over a small cook fire bubbling with a delicious aroma.

Ross indicated for her to sit on a dry stump. "Allow me to serve ye."

Pippa slid her tired body down. Not only had she slept little the night before, but hours had passed since her last meager meal. Her mouth watered on the thought of such a luxury—food for her alone. Sustenance in her region was sparse; not to mention, she gave much of her portion to the young ones at the castle.

Ross handed her a bowl of gruel and a hunk of dry bread. Blissful. She felt lightheaded with anticipation. "My gratitude, Sir Ross. Won't you join me?"

"Nay. I have eaten, but I dost wish to converse if ye don't mind, m' lady."

"Tell me what's on your heart," she said after swallowing a mouthful of delicious bread dipped in her liquid oatmeal.

He knelt before her and scanned the area before leaning close. "I wish to explain Master William's disposition."

With an understanding smile, she said, "That's not necessary. I didn't take his bad temper personally."

In a soft voice he began. "The disappearance of his fither hath shaken him to his very soul. They were ... err ... *are* verra close. Lord Daniel means tha world to young William." He shook his head in sadness. "Not knowing if his fither lives hath caused him tha deepest of grief. Moreover, he promised his mither he would find his fither. All of this coupled with his childhood home's being burned to tha ground hath caused him to be most disagreeable at times. Please understand."

His pleading eyes nearly brought Pippa to tears. She looked back at her bowl and sopped up the remainder of her gruel before answering. "There's no need for explanation. I, too, have lost my father and comprehend the agony of such adversity. I hold no ill will toward William. However, I must tell you that I presented him with our marriage betrothal written by our fathers."

"Och? His fither never mentioned such an arrangement."

"Yes. That's what William said as well. It matters not. My father owned an original document that I now have in my possession. It is legal ... and binding."

29

"Och, dear. This explains William's earlier outburst."

Her brows came to a point. "Do you believe his father had no plans of carrying out this contract?"

Ross's eyes snapped back to hers. "Oh no, m' lady. If Lord McKinnon signed such a document, he had every intention of seeing it through. I'm just a bit baffled why he didnae entrust William with this knowledge."

"I'm not sure. What I do know is that I was content to live my life with no man lording over me. Then when I heard William had become a mercenary ... well ... ." She allowed her sentence to die away. "Nevertheless, desperate times have caused me to rethink my desires. My castle has gone into disrepair due to repeated attacks after my father's death. I have not the money nor the resources to feed and care for my people. Hence, my trip here."

"And traversing this dangerous territory alone was not wise." He threw up his hand when she opened her mouth to defend her actions. "Nay. Ye know 'twas reckless. Yer fither would not have sanctioned such an outing."

Pippa had the courtesy to duck her head. In fact, his concern for her welfare warmed her heart. For over six months she had shouldered the demanding responsibility of running the castle and seeing to the wellbeing of her people. At times the task was daunting as well as burdensome. How refreshing to be on the receiving end of another's sensitivity.

"You might be right, my friend." She handed back the empty bowl and rolled her tight shoulders. "I have been gone overlong and must be away." They both stood. She placed her hand upon his arm. "Thank you for your kind hospitality. I will not soon forget it."

She led her horse into an open area and mounted. Adjusting her weapons for easy access, she waved farewell. "Until we meet again."

Ross watched her disappear into the forest.

A voice floated from the shadows. "Is she gone?"

"Aye."

William sauntered over to Ross. "Did she divulge her ludicrous claims?"

"Aye."

He twisted to face Ross. "Is that all you have to say?"

"Aye." Ross raised a brow. "Except ... where are tha manners yer fither taught ye ... m' lord?"

William stiffened. "She didn't want my escort."

"Did ye not reveal to me juist the other night that ye wished to repair how people viewed ye? That ye didnae want to be thought of as a heartless mercenary? If all ye said is true, ye have an odd way of going about the task."

Angry, William spun on his heel and left.

He grumbled to himself while riding to intercept Pippa. Why he allowed Ross to goad him into going after her, he couldn't fathom. Now he found himself riding after a woman who would not think twice about shooting him with an arrow if he provoked her ... or stabbing him with a knife. He had to confess, she was an excellent marksman. Of course, he didn't plan to admit that to her, but he did admire her skills.

His horse plodded along. Pippa was but one year old when he tried to convince his mother to bring her home to live with him. She had been such a cheerful baby. Her round cherub cheeks had captured his fascination, but it was the depth of her blue eyes that had held him.

After his Scottish father had married Pippa's English aunt, the two young ones had played together at family gatherings. However, those assemblies were once a year at best. With him five years her senior, the picture of her tagging after him still brought a grin to his face.

"You best watch your back."

William stopped his horse and gritted his teeth. Unbelievable! He had allowed her to catch him unaware. He pulled his horse around to face the little minx. There sat Pippa hidden in the brush with an arrow poised and ready for flight—directed at him no less ... again! If Ross had been present, he would have asked him to kick his backside.

Blowing out his breath, he asked, "Might you aim your arrow elsewhere?"

"I'm not sure what you have been contemplating, but I have followed you for over a mile. You really must be more alert." She lowered her bow and disengaged the arrow. "I thought I was clear; I don't need your escort."

"I didn't want guilt heaped on my head if you had succumbed to an attack ... so here I am."

"Ross made you come."

"Aye."

She nudged her horse closer to his. "I'm perfectly safe. Wolf is a superb protector. I dare say you didn't even hear him. He strikes with deadly accuracy after stalking his prey."

"I'll ride along. Mayhap you have stories to entertain me."

"Suit yourself, but I plan to ride hard. See if you can keep pace." With that her horse burst from the brush and onto the road.

William seethed. It seemed she had honed her arrogant attitude to perfection. *Keep pace, indeed. I will overtake you.*

# *5*

Chained to the wall of an abandoned castle, Daniel bristled at his predicament. He had been preoccupied when he set out for Sanddown castle to see his family. While home repairing his castle, all he dreamt about was his beautiful wife, Brigette. The last time he had seen her she was big with child. He glanced at the stone wall where he had scratched sixty-three marks with a small rock. A wave of sadness hit him. The babe had delivered long ago, and he had missed it.

All of his anger he directed at himself. His warriors trained to avoid this type of dilemma by always staying alert; yet, here he sat, guilty of the worst kind of blunder. With his back against the cold wall, his chin rested on his chest while he mentally chastised himself. The rattling of keys dashed away his thoughts. His head popped up. Perhaps he could get some information today.

The rusty door screeched open and in walked a young lad with a skimpy meal on a broken plank. With Daniel's left hand and left foot chained to the floor, there was little danger of his overtaking his keeper. The boy had learned how far he could venture into the room without having the prisoner overpower him. It had taken one mishap when he had grabbed the boy's arm and pulled him off balance. Unfortunately, the burly guard stepped in and knocked Daniel senseless. He hadn't repeated that action.

"What have ye brought me to eat this time? Is it pheasant, or wild boar, or mayhap hog?"

The boy didn't respond.

"Oh wait ... could it be succulent deer meat?"

The boy placed the tray on the disgusting floor and nudged it closer to the captive with his foot. He ventured a peep at Daniel before scurrying out the door. Once he cleared the threshold, the door shut with a deafening crash which echoed around the empty cell. The key turning in the lock caused a pain in Daniel's heart. Unsure if his men had survived the surprise attack, rescue seemed improbable, if not impossible.

After the ambush on the road to Sanddown castle, his enemy had slipped a cloth hood over his head and bound his hands to the saddle. The tightness of the rope had caused his hands to go numb from the hours in the saddle. After several days travel, they had placed him on a ship to an unknown destination, secured below deck for the duration of the trip. Based on the position of the sun that filtered through the narrow window, he determined the ship had traveled north.

He needed to garner more information.

"Guard ... guard," he shouted. "I can't reach my meal."

The guard peered through the small window bars in the door.

"The boy failed to push it far enough." He watched as the guard contemplated if he should open the door or not. "I can't possibly attack you. I'm chained to the floor."

Clanking keys hit against the door as the man shoved the door open wide. "Ye don't deserve to eat," he grumbled.

"Now why would ye say that? I've done ye no harm. I've never seen ye before yesterday, nor do I know yer name." One fact irritated Daniel ... his captor was intelligent ... abandoning him with no explanation of why he had been taken. In addition, he changed out the sentries every two days to avoid familiarity. Familiarity might garner significant exchange of information between Daniel and the guards. Clever and torturous.

The man picked up the food and laid it beside Daniel's leg where he sat upon the stone floor. "'Tisn't me ye've 'armed, but me master."

"Interesting. I don't even know your master. How can I make amends when he hasn't shown himself to me?"

"Ye are to suffer."

When he turned to leave, Daniel called out. "Wait." The man looked over his shoulder. "I wish ye to stay. Tell me about your family. Do ye have a wife or children?"

"Nay."

"Nay, you have no wife or children; or nay, you won't remain?" Daniel sighed as the man exited without a word. "You could talk to me through the door. Ye wouldn't have to fear me then."

The man's face appeared at the bars. "I fear ye not."

"Can you at least tell me if there are others like me? I've heard screams in the night."

The man's footsteps faded away the farther he walked from Daniel's cell. Even though the conversation was short, it encouraged Daniel. Until this point, no one had even talked with him. Progress.

"What say ye, mouse?" Daniel threw a piece of molded bread to the small mouse in the corner of the room. It scampered over and snatched the bread before scurrying away. "I wish I could fit under the door like you."

His eyes closed with intent. *Oh, God, my help in ages past. Hear your servant now. I'm in need of rescue. You are my greatest hope. I put my trust in Your provision as I await my Redeemer. Keep Your protective hand upon my family while we are apart. Thank You for my daily bread, but deliver me from mine enemies, and I will give You all the praise and the glory. Amen and amen.*

With hooded eyes, he looked at the broken plank once more. His chewing stopped. An idea began to form. He smiled.

*Thank You, Father.*

"The horses are lathered, we should slow our pace," William shouted.

Pippa pulled back on the reins bringing her horse to a walk. He followed suit.

The brisk ride had blown away his earlier agitation. As they rode alongside one another, he took notice of her appearance. The dark circles under her eyes stood out against her alabaster skin. No doubt the burden of caring for her people, in addition to her father's death, had taken their toll. Young women were not supposed to handle such an undertaking.

She glanced at him. "What are your thoughts?"

He had to smile at her straightforwardness. Just like a warrior, she wasted no time on extra words. "I want to apologize for my earlier behavior at your unexpected arrival. With my own troubles fresh on my mind, your announcement caught me unaware." *What an understatement.*

Preoccupied, she scanned for danger. "I didn't take it personally."

"I'm pleased to hear it. However, I must reiterate, I can't help solve your problems." When her anguished eyes turned his way, he almost relinquished.

"For now, that discussion is forbidden. Might we talk of other things? Tell me of your mother and siblings."

Inwardly, he sighed, but welcomed the change in topic. From the corner of his eye he glimpsed Pippa's rigid back as she rode tall and proud—more soldier than lady. Her conversational skills needed perfecting. It appeared training in warfare had been her focus growing up, not womanly decorum.

"As you know, Emilia is the oldest of the girls. She's an submissive young woman who obeys my every command." He chuckled. "Before I left home to pursue other endeavors, she fancied herself much in love."

Pippa stared at William. "With whom?"

36

He could feel his face heating. "With me."

She gasped. "But you're her brother!"

"This I know well. She believed father would allow the union since I am a mere half-brother. Needless to say, my mother delivered a much-needed discourse on the subject."

"Dear me," she said shaking her head.

"Next are the ten-year-old twins, Helen and Gillian. Each day they awaken with evil intent."

She arched one brow. "I find it hard to imagine those sweet girls being evil. Merciful heavens, how can you say such a thing?"

William snorted. "You have no idea what they are capable of devising. I believe Gillian instigates the devious plans, and Helen is all too happy to comply."

"I presume their evil is directed toward you?"

"Precisely. I never know when a prank will befall me. Father is too lenient with those girls."

Pippa grinned. "They sound delightful."

"No doubt," he muttered. "Now, my brother, James, turned seven this year. Mother is convinced his antics will make her hair fall out."

"Oh?"

"He's all boy—climbing trees, jumping off the stable roof, hiding when mother calls him. Those are but a few of his irritating qualities my mother grumbles about. I think James will grow into a mighty warrior."

"Why would you say such a statement when he is but seven?"

"He fears nothing."

Pippa remained silent for several heartbeats as their horses plodded onward. She twisted sideways in her saddle to face him. "Is that what it takes to be a mighty warrior—to be fearless?"

William looked at her perplexed. "Why do you ask it?" There it was again ... her slight shoulder lift ... a delicate, yet sensual movement from his viewpoint.

"It matters not." She rotated back around and nudged her horse into a trot.

He watched her ride ahead while her wolf kept pace at the forest edge. She might need lessons in speaking as a lady; nonetheless, her body actions spoke volumes. Acceptance as a warrior seemed important to her. Her sharpened skills told of her need to flourish in a man's domain. But why? What disruption had altered her upbringing?

For the remainder of their journey, both stayed silent until they crossed onto Fairwick land. There Pippa left the path and headed into the dense forest. William followed, unsure of her intent. When he came close to his antagonistic companion, he asked, "Why did you leave the road?"

"The people are unaware I left the castle. My battle commander and his wife were the only two I informed of my plan. I wish to keep my excursion a secret. My men already worry about the possibility of my capture by our enemies. No need to burden them further. Their energies are best served bolstering our defenses and holding our foes at bay."

William couldn't believe his ears. No wonder her people were concerned; she had no common sense. He reached out and grabbed ahold of her horse's bridle. The action caused both horses to dance in a circle.

Indignant, she tried to disengage his grip. "What are you about?"

The growl of her wolf didn't deter him. "Your people have good reason to fear for your safety. Wisdom seems to be lacking in your decision making," he said low and forceful. When he thought of the danger she might have encountered on her outing, his protective instincts flared. "You could have been captured or tortured ... or even killed ... all while your men went about their duties. Do you know what your imprisonment or, heaven forbid, your death would have done to your people? Did you even consider their feelings when you hatched this foolish plan?"

Her eyes reddened—hurt or anger—he couldn't decide.

"Are you quite done with your tirade? As you have told me numerous times, I'm not your problem. Now, release Romeo at once."

His lips pinched tight as his eyes narrowed. He threw the bridle from his hand as if it were a snake. "As you wish, m' lady," he said tongue-in-cheek. In his estimation, a lady she was not.

For a short span, they stared at one another and fumed until her wolf barked. At that point, her head lurched sideways as her eyes grew large. "There's trouble afoot." She took off through the trees with Wolf in fast pursuit.

*We've been reacquainted a few hours, yet, she has irritated me at every turn.*

His cheeks puffed out as he exhaled. Expecting her to run straight into danger, he followed her like a hound chasing a fox—bushes smacking his face.

Not far ahead, he noticed that she crouched low on her horse with an arrow secure in her bow. *Now what?* He slowed his pace and came alongside her. "What is amiss?" he whispered.

Without taking her eyes from the scene before her, she motioned for him to look. He could not believe his eyes. There were four mounted men with a catapult aimed at the gate of Fairwick castle. A burning mass sat ready to launch. Too far away to hear their words, he imagined they were taunting Pippa's warriors on the parapet.

"Why would they attack your castle?"

"I venture to guess they are would-be suitors coming to claim my hand in marital bliss," she murmured.

"With a war machine?"

"I'll aim for the one manning the catapult."

Before he had time to respond, she prodded her horse forward. With careful aim, she released her arrow. The soldier ready to hurl the fiery ball, tumbled from his horse as her arrow found its mark through his neck. With no delay, she burst through the trees with a war cry.

*Heaven preserve me. She's going to get herself killed!*

# 6

With another arrow loaded for flight, Pippa galloped headlong toward her enemy. Her war cry alerted her men of her presence, as well as those opposing her. At once, Henry raised the portcullis. Ten Fairwick warriors erupted through the gate ready for battle.

With the adversary aware of imminent danger, one soldier dodged her second arrow. Without a thought, she withdrew a dagger from her boot and hurled it as the man prepared to fling the fireball over the castle wall. The blade pinned his hand to the wooden release on the catapult.

"Pippa, watch out!" William yelled. As she twirled Romeo, she saw another foe fall to the ground within three feet of her horse—an arrow through his heart. She glanced around. Ross gave her a salute from the forest border. Smiling with relief, she returned the gesture.

She lost count of the enemy as they emerged out of hiding. More of her warriors rushed through the gate to join the fight. From her viewpoint, her men held the upper hand in the fray. Swords clashed and horses screamed. The stench of bloodshed rose to her nostrils. From her enemy's sword skills, they appeared poorly trained. She pulled Romeo around in circles. "I need one of them alive," she shouted.

A swift kick to her ribs knocked her sword to the ground. "How about me?" one snarled with his raised sword poised to strike. With no defense, her eyes remained focused on her opponent awaiting the strategic time to evade a lethal blow. Without warning, another blade blocked the downward slice as she lunged to the side. William.

He pointed his sword at her. "To the castle!"

"Aye!" Henry hollered from behind.

Her head swiveled between the men. Torn between pride and wisdom, she consented to their request but under protest. Anger bubbled up practically choking her. Heavy footed against Romeo's side, she was almost unseated. Humiliated, she guided her horse inside the castle gates.

Before her horse came to a complete stop, Pippa kicked free from the stirrups and jumped off. She hit the ground, rolled, and struggled to her feet. A moan escaped her lips as she ran up the outside stairs to the barbican while notching an arrow along the way. A thumping heart against her ribs reminded her of the solid jolt from her enemy.

She positioned herself at the furthest station on the barbican fighting against the nausea that came with such heights. With an arrow full drawn and resting at the corner of her mouth, she waited. Her eyes roamed to and fro among the men watching for an opportunity to slay her enemy. None came. Afraid of striking one of her own, she relaxed the bow string. The fight neared an end. Bodies littered the ground. How many of her own men tasted death? *Oh, Papa, I'm failing at my task to protect.* Tears pricked her eyes. A shaking hand rubbed the tears away.

She looked on as her men checked for survivors. Off to the side, two men sat tall in their saddles—William and Ross—as they rode toward the castle gate. Their impressive skills saved countless lives. They had fought unyielding in the face of great danger. Each had rushed to her aid. She leaned against the wall as the realization sank in ... death had nearly claimed her. If those two men had hesitated one moment, her people would be mourning their lady. William's chastisement came to mind. *I see you are still foolish when it comes to your safety ...*

Her eyes closed, shutting out the devastation. Without a sound, her lips moved in prayer. *Father in Heaven, thank You for my deliverance. Keep Your protective watch over my life as I seek to serve You and You alone. Today I offer up my praise for this victory granted by Your Hand. Give me wisdom as I search for answers to our plight ...*

"Lady Fairwick?" Henry shouted.

Her eyes popped open to see Henry looking at her as he waited for her direction. She straightened to full height. "What of our men?"

"Seven injured." His voice hitched. "One dead."

The stab to her heart caused her to gasp. Her friend might still live if she had not carried out her plan this morning.

*Oh, papa, how I need you.* "How many captured?"

"One lives," Henry offered as he stood with his sword at the throat of the man.

"Make ready his new accommodations." She turned on her heel and made her way down the stairs. The throb in her side intensified with each step. No doubt her ribs were injured. She couldn't show weakness. Her people depended on her strength and fortitude.

When she reached the bottom of the steps, William waited. "Are you hurt?"

"Nay." When she attempted to walk on by, he grabbed her arm. She winced in pain.

"Just as I surmised." Not releasing his hold, he leaned close to her ear. "You will see to your wound upon entering this castle."

"Or what?" she seethed. "You have no say on my conduct."

He used the previous words she had spoken to him. "Do not press me. You will not like the outcome."

Her squinted gaze traveled from his face to his grip around her arm. "Release me."

With reluctance, he released his hold. She resisted the urge to rub her arm and instead marched toward the castle steps determined not to show her pain.

A frowning Henry met her at the entrance to the keep. He nodded toward William. "Shall I deal with the man?" Glancing back, she made eye contact with her betrothed. "Nay." The two walked inside shutting out William's judgment.

"Lady Fairwick is quite a handful," Ross said.

"Precisely. I have no need of such an entanglement." Turning toward Ross, he said, "Come. Let us care for our horses and then see if any food awaits her two brave protectors."

When the door closed behind her, Pippa's tread became sluggish. It hurt to breathe, and her legs felt shackled with a heavy chain. She decided to meet with Henry to determine the approach to their prisoner and exchange other pertinent news. Afterwards a hot bath and a meal.

Pippa and Henry convened in the war room, the first space on the right after entering the keep. A large table sat in the middle of the room surrounded by chairs. A cold fireplace graced one end of the chamber. As she stopped at the threshold, memories assailed her. Her father and uncle often strategized and discussed important castle matters here. Their laughter still rang loud in her ears. She eased down the two steps leading into the room. Loneliness seized her.

"I cared not for the way that man clutched your arm. Is he Lord William McKinnon?" Henry asked.

Pippa blinked from her daze. She laid her bow and quiver on the table before answering. "Yes," she said while unbuckling her sword belt. "'Twas nothing." She slipped into the padded chair facing the door and ignored Henry's scowl. "Sit. Sit. Tell me which of our men fell today."

"'Twas Pierson."

Her hand flew to her mouth. "Oh, no," she groaned. Pippa hung her head and rubbed her eyes. How would Patrick receive the news about his twin brother? What about his wife? Oh, how she dreaded meeting with his family ... their anguish ... "Who's responsible for this outrageous act?"

Henry growled. "They slithered out of the Elliot Clan."

Pippa's eyes shot open wide. "Surely not!"

Henry banged the table with his fist. "Aye. A small fraction that survived the battle with the Fairwick's and the McKinnon's."

Pippa's mind reeled. Aware that William lounged at the doorway, she kept her voice low. "A revenge attack?"

Henry followed her eyes. With a voice just above a whisper, he answered. "I know not at this time. Do not fear; the prisoner will break under Duff's methods. Have no doubt; I will acquire yer answer soon."

"I have guests to attend. Keep me informed." She rose gingerly from her chair.

"Henry, did ye notice yer lady is injured?" William leaned against the door post with his arms crossed over his chest.

Henry's gaze looked from William, back to Pippa. "M' lady, does he speak truth?" Worry etched his haggard face.

"'Tis naught of which to concern yourself. The usual soreness brought on from battle which a hot soak will alleviate. Lord McKinnon oversteps his authority. Go about your business." She flipped her hand in dismissal—an action she learned from her Uncle Nicolas.

As Henry passed, William whispered in his ear. Henry nodded in agreement. Pippa's mouth tightened into a straight line. "As you so eloquently said, I'm not your concern. Please retire to the grand hall where a meager, yet satisfying meal awaits you. If you plan to endure the night here, I will see a room is prepared for you and Ross."

"Why is it you remain by your chair without retrieving your weapons and sweeping past me?" He pushed away from the door frame and sauntered to where she stood. "I wonder?"

His boldness made her temper flare. She refused to allow him the satisfaction that he assessed her correctly. "While you reside within these castle walls, I am in command. You have no say about

45

my behavior or decisions. You will cease to attempt to influence my men or try to usurp my authority. Am I clear on the matter?"

He moved within inches of her body. "Perfectly," he whispered.

A tendril of hair swayed from his breath. It took all of her self-control not to shiver. "Please excuse me. I have much to attend." She left her weapons upon the table and exited the room.

Ross joined William in the war room. "How bad is it?" William continued to gaze through the opening Pippa had just vacated. "I suspect a broken rib, maybe more."

"She is a tough one."

"Stubborn is the word I would choose."

Ross laughed. "Coom, my friend. Let us break bread together."

Pippa slipped into her hot bath. Ahh. Delightful. She refused Gwendolyn's offer of help knowing that Henry would hear of her bruises from his wife. After taking note of Henry's exhaustion, she refused to add to his burden. He already performed the work of two. There was naught he could offer to ease her pain.

She resisted the urge to linger as if she could wash away her burdens. What a luxurious thought. Nonetheless, men awaited her word on the prisoner, maids needed direction about the guest rooms, warriors needed plans for retaliation ... decisions ... never ending. Sinking under the water, she stayed until her lungs burned. A poor idea. When she popped out of the water, her side pulsated with pain.

Panting, she struggled not to cry out. Her shorter breaths brought the ache to a tolerable state. There were times when she didn't want to be strong and shoulder a heavy burden—like now. She longed to share her rule with another. A lone tear slipped to her chin as she remembered her father's words. *My problems are halved when I share them with your mother. It makes life more bearable.*

Afraid to allow her emotions an escape, she splashed water in her face and grabbed a towel. Sorrowful thoughts served no purpose. After drying off, she reached for her trousers ... her hand stopped in midair. William resided below in the grand hall. A dress might be more appropriate for the occasion.

She rummaged through her trunk and drew out a rumpled blue dress. Smoothing her hand over the wrinkles, she decided it would suffice. With caution, she searched for her slippers under the bed. Unable to reach them without causing herself pain, she crawled to the broom in the corner. Using the wooden handle, she dragged them out. Not wishing a spider bite, she tapped each one free of dust and any lingering bugs.

Raising her arms to arrange her hair was out of the question. Instead, she leaned over with care and gave her head a hearty shake while holding her arm tight against her ribs. She flipped her head backward causing her hair to cascade down her back. When she peeped in the mirror, she saw the activity had flushed her cheeks. At least she appeared healthy. A circlet around her head completed her attire. Now to entertain the man-wolf.

## 7

Trying to maneuver the stairs in a dress caused Pippa trepidation. Awkward came to mind several times during her quest. Each foot she placed with caution as she held her dress above her ankles—unladylike, but she cared not. As she rounded the last curve in her path, a great commotion erupted in the grand hall. "Now what?" she muttered.

Henry met her at the foot of the stairs. "M' lady, there are travelers requesting entrance for the night."

Her back stiffened. "Who's doing the asking?"

"Lady Hamilton and her escort."

"Matilda Hamilton or her mother?" she asked in a hushed voice.

Henry looked uncomfortable. "Lady Matilda Hamilton."

"Heaven preserve me. Can this day get any worse?" Her agitation filled the air. "How many are in her party?"

"At first glance, I wager twenty-five or so. I suggest we tell the majority of her men to camp outside our gates and house the rest."

Not only did her ribs ache, now her head joined in the game— the soothing bath forgotten. With eyes closed, she pinched the bridge of her nose. She looked up and sighed. "Allow her maids and two guards to enter. Send Gwendolyn to me at once."

"Aye."

Pippa shook her head as she watched Henry hustle away. She looked upward. "Help me," she whispered. When her face tilted down, there stood William with arms behind his back.

"I couldn't help but overhear. More guests to add to your home this night?"

"Yes. You heard correctly. Is eavesdropping one of your specialties?"

He offered the crook of his arm, ignoring her question.

"Allow me to escort you to the dining room. The fare is quite tasty. A bit of meat on your bones would serve you well."

She placed her hand through his arm. "Are you always rude to your host?"

He shrugged. "Truth. Nothing but truth."

All eyes latched onto the pair as they entered the grand hall. Clinking of bowls and mugs came to a quiet end as they stared at the two shuffling toward the dais.

William leaned next to her ear. "If our entrance causes such a stir, it would appear your people lack amusement."

She smiled sweetly. "No, your reputation precedes you. They're waiting to see if I stick one of my knives in you before we reach our destination."

His hand covered his heart. "You wound me, m' lady."

"Truth. Nothing but truth."

"Touché." He steadied her hand as she stepped up to take her place at the high table.

The peasants returned to their meal. After the short performance of their lady, whispered words floated through the room. She could well imagine their thoughts. Her eyes followed William as he returned to his seat next to Ross. Even though he had refused to believe their betrothal was sound, it appeared as if he laid claim to her while present. Pippa blew out a puff of air. She didn't understand men—such mysteries.

After a few bites of her meal, a small girl ran to her chair. She stood there giggling and waiting. Pippa handed her a slice of meat and watched as she scampered away.

*Oh, my Father in Heaven, how we need more food. Please hear my deepest prayer for the people.*

When she glanced outward, William held her gaze. Not understanding his expression, she looked away. She had no time for a diversion. Matilda was close at hand.

"I see why she is thin," William mumbled to Ross.

"Aye. She cares for her people."

"What good will her concern do if she succumbs to a disease from lack of nourishment?"

Ross coughed behind his hand. "I'm sure ye are correct. Are ye done?" Ross asked surprised as William stood.

"I have no wish to watch as she feeds everyone but herself. She has told me more than once. I have no say here. Finish your meal. You'll find me at the stables."

"Aye."

Pippa feigned indifference as she overheard their conversation. From under her lashes, she saw William exit the room. Her tense body reminded her how his presence causes her uneasiness. One moment he despises her, another, he acts as if he cares. Troublesome, indeed.

Gwendolyn rushed to the dais. Out of breath, she asked, "How many rooms should I prepare?"

"Prepare all the rooms in the east wing."

"All of them?"

"Yes, Gwendolyn. You heard me aright."

Pippa wished she could erase the anxiety from her friend's face, but not today. Her compassion for Gwendolyn flew like an eagle after its prey at the sound of Matilda's voice. How could one woman exasperate her with one spoken word? She stood when her childhood acquaintance entered from the passageway into the great hall, on the arm of William no less.

Pippa's vision narrowed as her teeth ground together unaware of why the scene annoyed her. Like mortar, her fake smile never wavered. She extended her hand. "Lady Hamilton, your presence is such a delight. Please join me on the dais." It took great strength not to cross herself and offer a prayer for the lie that rolled from her lips.

"Philippa," Matilda gushed as she sauntered forward. "'Tis so good to see you again. It's been far too long."

Pippa thought she might throw up the few morsels of food that had made it into her empty stomach. Leave it to Matilda to act as if they were long, lost friends when, in reality, they seldom socialized together. Even during those times, Pippa never fit into Matilda's world of influence.

She watched as Matilda hesitated and looked around. No doubt wanting all to view her with her handsome escort. At long last she made it to the platform. "I see you have made the acquaintance of one of my guests."

Matilda fluttered her lashes at William. "Lord McKinnon insisted he escort me into your presence."

Pippa blinked in rapid succession to keep from rolling her eyes at the absurdity of the comment. With her smile frozen, she looked at William. "Thank you, Lord McKinnon, for your gallantry." His aggravated look assured her he understood her insincere comment even though it skipped past Matilda. "Won't you both join me?" She wanted to laugh at William's look of horror as he extracted his arm from Matilda's grip.

"I will leave you two alone to get reacquainted. I have matters to attend."

Pippa raised her brow. "Oh?"

Matilda's pout was immediate. "I hope we have other opportunities to converse. I do so enjoy intelligent company."

Knowing that William scurried away from Matilda's presence gave Pippa a small bit of satisfaction, but then she was left to entertain the brash woman. In the past, Matilda had made it her mission to belittle Pippa at every turn. Perhaps, she had changed. One could hope.

Matilda hesitated at her chair. "Philippa, you look quite peaked. Are you ill?"

A small sigh escaped Pippa's lips. "Fear not. Supervising matters around the castle each day can be draining. Today was exceptionally long and arduous." With a light touch to Matilda's arm, she added, "You are safe in my presence."

Her hand fluttered to her chest. "Well, I would certainly hope it. I'm on my way to the king's court and cannot entertain the chance of contracting a dreadful disease in your castle."

Pippa clamped her mouth tight. At the sight of Henry, her mood shifted. "I'm sorry Lady Hamilton, but my presence is required. Please, make yourself comfortable in my chair so you can rest as you partake of the meal. I trust you'll provide great entertainment for the castle folk. Why, gazing upon your beauty will surely be a boon for them." She watched as Matilda's countenance brightened.

"Of course, my dear. You go on along. I'm more than capable of providing amusement for these simple peasants." She all but shoved Pippa aside to plop into the cushioned high-backed chair.

"When you are ready to retire, anyone here can escort you to the east wing. Your room will be awaiting you."

Matilda grabbed Pippa's sleeve before she could escape. "Can you be a darling and provide a steaming bath?"

The tug on her sleeve caused Pippa to flinch in pain. She gripped her hands together against her stomach. "By all means. Now if you will excuse me ..."

"Oh, one more thing."

"Yes."

Matilda motioned with a crooked finger for Pippa to come close. "Will the fetching Lord McKinnon be housed in the east wing? I might need his strong arm for added protection."

If Pippa didn't leave soon, she feared she might chip a tooth. Her irritating guest didn't know how fortunate she was that Pippa had worn her dress slippers instead of her boots with hidden knives. "All of my guests have rooms in the east wing. However, you will have no need of Lord McKinnon's assistance, for I provide excellent protection inside my castle walls. Armed guards will line the passageway."

With a stiff back, she hurried from Matilda's presence before she did bodily harm to the infuriating woman. It would seem her night could prove to be excruciating. *Deliver me, Lord ... deliver me.*

William made himself scarce. Darkness had overtaken the sky long ago while he hid in the stables. At first, he rubbed down his horse and then Ross's horse. Once completed, he sat propped against the stall door to rest.

He awoke with a start. It took him a moment to recognize his surroundings.

"Surely, she is abed by now."

William jolted at Ross's voice and scrambled up. "Of whom do you speak?"

"Tha one ye fear," he said with laughter in his voice.

William brushed the hay from his trousers. "Ahh, yes, Lady Hamilton. In the king's court, women like her can eat an innocent with one gulp. Pippa's survival is at risk as long as Lady Hamilton is about."

"I daresay, Lady Fairwick wilt hold her own. If she grows weary of inconsequential chatter, she can pin Lady Hamilton to tha wall with one of her knives."

William chuckled as he shut the stall door. He smacked Ross on the back. "Well said, my friend. Well said."

"While ye hid, I found tha location of our rooms."

"I'm offended by that remark," he said with humor. "Did you say rooms? We're not to share accommodations?"

"Nay. Lady Fairwick provided splendid rooms. She even offered a tub in which to bathe."

"Ahh. She need not think she can entice me with her womanly schemes. It won't work. I have no intentions of softening my stance on the betrothal she presented. It could well be a forgery. However, I will avail myself of the opportunity to wash away my filth."

Ross stayed quiet as they walked toward the castle. "Ye are wrong aboot her."

William looked surprised. "What mean you?"

"She does not scheme to get her way. Her methods are straightforward ... refreshingly so."

William stewed over Ross's observation. In his opinion, Ross was a bit naïve when it came to calculating women. His kind heart clouded his judgment. Grateful for his father's guidance, William wasn't blinded by a soft touch or a kind word from the fairer gender.

"It matters not. On the morrow, we travel to Sanddown Castle. I need to report our findings to my mother ... and see how she and the babe fare."

"Ye wish to ask her if tha betrothal is official."

"Aye."

## 8

William and Ross rose before dawn. William wanted to avoid a chance meeting with Pippa or Matilda. Guilt gnawed at him. He knew it was rude to leave without thanking his host for her hospitality. Yet, he couldn't suffer through another false performance from Matilda. Her self-importance shouted louder than her whisper of humility. Escaping Matilda far outweighed the anger Pippa would direct his way. He believed a future apology to Lady Fairwick would suffice.

Bumping into Henry at such an early hour proved informative. He defended his lady's choices and all but dared William to disagree. From the looks of Henry's stature, defeating him would be a challenge. It was good Pippa had a champion. Even though Henry held a low regard for William, he instructed Gwendolyn to provide supplies for their travels. Truth be told, they would not go hungry on their journey.

The breeze slapped their faces as William and Ross rode for several hours. The fast pace didn't allow for conversation. With his father's fate still uncertain, William's foul mood was a smoldering fire.

"Look there. A place to rest the horses." William pointed out a babbling brook lined with shade trees not far from the road. The sun had risen and burned off much of the early morning fog, creating an ethereal setting.

They left the horses free to graze while the two propped against mossy tree trunks. William laid his bow and arrows to his left and his sword within reach of his right hand. He leaned an arm on his up-drawn knee while his head rested against the tree. He savored his food while he examined Ross's profile through hooded eyes. The sound of birds chirping high above their heads broke the long stretch of stillness.

"You've been rather quiet since our departure. Are you troubled?"

Ross whipped his gaze from the landscape. "Ye know tha answer."

William's body tensed. "Ross, an accidental meeting with Matilda, or Pippa for that matter, would have caused a delay. I did what was necessary to speed our departure."

"Ye express how ye want to improve yer damaged honor, and then ye add to tha problem with yer actions."

William sprang to his feet and tossed his last bite of bread to the birds. He walked to the water's edge. With hands on his hips, he ground his teeth. What Ross said was true which irritated him further. His efforts were better served searching for his father, not pleasing people. Nonetheless, he pictured his family's disappointment if he dragged a ruined reputation in his wake. Thinking like a mercenary was no longer a choice.

He blew out a frustrated breath. He couldn't stay mad at a friend who spoke with honesty when oftentimes people lied and deceived at will.

With hands by his side, he turned around to find the food packed and Ross ready to ride. "You are correct in your assessment." He looked away and then back at his defender. "I've spent years doing as I wish without regard to other's opinions. I tend to forget how my selfish actions reflect poorly on my family." He walked over to Ross and grinned. "That's why I keep you around. I know you will speak truth into my life with no thought of the consequences. Keep taking me to task. Perhaps one day, the lessons will persevere." He grabbed his horse's reins. "Come my friend. Let us be away."

Ross graced him with an easy smile. It reminded William of his good fortune to have Ross as his protector. His father had chosen wisely. A pang hit his chest like a boulder. His father ... was he suffering? Had he been tortured? The visual images in his mind's eye caused great torment. One didn't serve as a mercenary soldier not to have horrific pictures left to blur one's perception of the present.

As he mounted his horse, his tears nearly caused him to miss the stirrup. Many of his acquaintances would say tears showed weakness ... he disagreed. Those men who killed with no conscience developed an iron casing over their hearts. For him, his watery eyes revealed he still had a heart.

"My lord. If I am not deceived, there are men oop ahead."

"Rein back." William scrubbed his eyes clear and darted into the brush off to the side of the road. Hoof beats thundered behind them.

"Follow me," he whispered. He headed back toward the stream. Once there, their horses lunged into the icy water and headed upstream at a quick pace. At intervals, William and Ross rode into the brush and then back into the water. They used the cover of the thick foliage when possible. Hidden from sight they climbed a steep hill to get a better vantage point.

They dashed behind a boulder, and William jumped from his horse. Ross instinctively grabbed the reins and held fast. William crawled along the forest floor and hid among dense undergrowth. He counted five unkempt men. They shouted at each other as they beat the bushes below.

"Have ye lost 'em?" one asked with anger.

"Nay. They are here."

"Dinna kill tha mon. We are to take 'im alive," another said.

William watched from his concealed place. What a bunch of galoots. The five were trampling his and Ross's tracks as they circled the area for clues. He wished he could hear all they said but suppressed the notion to sneak closer. They were such easy targets. He placed his forehead on his arm. What to do? He raised his head with a huff. He dared not risk an encounter for fear it would impede his progress to Sanddown castle. There were more pressing matters than to slay foolish thieves.

After scooting backward, William rolled down a small embankment. Crouched low, he made his way to Ross undetected by the robbers. "We will not waste our time on those dunderheads." He pointed over the ridge for their escape route.

Ross nodded in agreement.

The two led their horses over the ridge under the protection of low tree branches and flourishing vegetation. Once clear of the knoll, they mounted and kicked their horses into a gallop leaving behind the senseless five.

For several miles, William directed their flight through the forest. When he surmised they were not followed, he veered toward the road. They stopped just short of the road and listened. Both surveyed the surroundings.

"I hear naught of our enemies," Ross spoke softly.

"Neither do I. Let's take to the road."

The men stayed alert as they continued toward Sanddown castle. Not wanting to overtax their mounts, they stopped one other time to allow the horses to drink water and rest. Both rode stout war horses who required less fuss than a pleasure pony; nonetheless, William didn't wish to overburden them.

After a brief respite, they rode at a brisk walk for over an hour. "It shouldn't take us much longer. I expect we'll arrive within the hour."

"'Twill be good to take me leave of this horse," Ross added.

"Aye. Visions of a hot bath and a soft bed swirl before me."

"Darkness wilt be upon us soon. 'Tis good to arrive beforehand."

"True, my friend." A tingle raced up his spine. William glanced behind them but saw no one. "Let's increase our pace."

Ross complied.

Not long after they broke into a trot, distant hoof beats rumbled from the rear. William whipped around and groaned. "They're back." They kicked into a full gallop in hopes of outrunning their enemy.

"The castle is not far," William shouted. "Keep low and press onward." From his estimation, the adversary was a half mile back. If they maintained their pace, all would be well.

William could feel the fatigue in his horse. It became more evident with every mile. On occasion, he looked under his arm to gauge the distance of their foe. When an arrow whizzed past his shoulder, he received his answer.

"Faster," he yelled. The horse's muscles bunched under William's leg as he lunged to obey his master. His sides heaved with each breath. Just when William feared his horse would slow, the castle came into view.

As they raced onward, William shouted, "Ross and William. Raise the gate! Raise the gate!"

Guards on the catwalk leapt into action. Arrows in long bows readied for flight. The portcullis creaked as the chains pulled the iron gate upward to allow entrance. Followed by his protector, William ducked low to clear the iron spikes that were not open to full capacity. Arrows from the enemy struck the stone wall all around them. Once in the clear, the iron spikes dropped to the ground.

William launched off his horse and ran up the outside stairs to the parapet. When he reached the protected walkway, he saw his enemy stop out of reach of the archers. Their ponies' sides heaved from exertion as they pranced in agitation.

"What is this about?" Braden demanded.

"I know not. These men have pursued us most of our travels."

"From where do they hail?"

"I plan to find out," William fumed. Without taking his eyes from his opponent, he said, "Direct me to the postern gate and send five men to accompany me. We will skirt behind the menace and take them by surprise."

"You need not put your life at risk. I will see to their capture," Braden instructed.

"Nay!" Fire brewed in his belly.

"They are after me, and I want to know why. If they choose to fight, I want to make sure I'm close at hand to question one before his death."

Braden's lips thinned. "As you wish." He sprinted down the stairs. "Edward, Hansen, Dalton, Kiplin, Lyonel ... come!"

Relieved, William followed close behind. The men strapped on their weapons as they hurried to the postern gate. Braden selected large young men with bulging muscles.

Ross ran to William. "Dinna go."

Without breaking his stride, William said, "I must go."

"Yer mither willnae be pleased to know ye survived yer journey only to have ye slain at tha gate."

He looked sideways at his guardian. "Ross, your dramatic tactic will not dissuade me. You may remain within the castle walls, but it is vital I speak with one of these men. Mayhap they are the very ones who took my father."

Ross kept in step with William. "I willnae face yer mither alone."

William smiled. "Ross, you do have a way with words." Turning to Braden, he said, "Keep them occupied with questions. Don't approach them, and by all that is holy, don't let them escape."

Braden left the men at the hidden gate and ran back toward the front of the castle.

William divided the men into two groups: one to go along the eastern side of the forest and one to go along the western side. They would circle wide and come behind the culprits. All conversation ended once they exited the castle. Hand motions guided their movements. Even though deep in the forest, William could hear Braden conversing with the would-be thieves.

"Send out tha mercenary."

"You are mistaken. We house no mercenary," Braden shouted. William cringed. His past hounded his steps. Mayhap his mother would not overhear the exchange. She vehemently opposed his livelihood when he demanded to be free to choose his own path. No matter, her husband, his father, gave the final say and allowed it. William stumbled at the remembrance of his father's tear-filled eyes when he left home in pursuit of riches.

"Do ye think me daft? Tha one called McKinnon."

"You are at Lord Nicolas Fairwick's castle."

"Ye fool. We tracked 'im here. We juist wish a word."

"Hold fast," Braden suggested. He turned as if to fetch William.

William's men stepped out of the cover of darkness and onto the road behind the five ruffians. "Are ye lookin' for me?"

All five whipped their ponies around to face men with loaded bows aimed at them. The leader of the group roared with laughter. "Ye think ye can best me while a foot? Ye are as brash as yer fither."

William bristled. "What do you know of my father?"

"More than ye it would seem."

"Do you know who holds my father?"

"Och, young one, ye get no such answers. One thing is for certain, ye both are foolhardy. No doubt yer fither will die afore ye find him."

Kiplin released his arrow. It plunged into one of the offenders causing him to fall sideways on his mount. Commotion erupted. William and his men bombarded the five with arrows as the outlaws barreled toward them with shields high and swords drawn. Three arrows found targets, but that didn't hinder the enemies' quest.

The Fairwick guards split apart and dashed toward the forest for protection. William seethed. Kiplin reacted without thought. Now chaos ruled. Each guard pulled his sword ready to do battle. Nonetheless, the advantage belonged to those on mounts.

The leader of the five chased after William who weaved in and around trees. He was searching for an advantage point from which to do the most harm while separating him from the others. He trusted Braden would send reinforcements.

63

"Ye canna hide from me, ye weakling. Coom to me. I decided nay to take ye to me commander. Instead, I wish to kill ye." His eerie laughter filled the air.

William dove under a low bush and curled tight ... waiting. He peered through plant blades. His enemy slashed nearby undergrowth with his sword. William's hand searched around until it latched upon a thick branch on the ground. With a club in one hand and his sword in the other, he planned his attack.

"Yer fither widnae approve of yer spineless actions."

As the pony walked past his hiding place, William placed the club between his back legs causing him to stumble. The man collapsed onto the pony's neck. At that moment, William vaulted from his hiding place and slashed the man's sword arm. He screamed in anguish as his sword crashed to the ground with his hand still attached.

William punctured the man's side with his blade. Blood gushed from the wound as he crumpled to the forest floor and rolled to his back.

With his sword tip pointing at the man's throat, William demanded, "Who holds my father?"

Blood and spittle spewed from his lips when the downed man coughed.

"Speak and ye might live. From where do you hail and why were you seeking my death?

"Ye weel ne'er find 'im." His eyes grew wide with fear as his labored breathing increased.

William knew his foe had little time. He knelt and grabbed the man's ragged tunic with his free hand. "Who are you?"

The man's narrowed gaze glared at William. "Clan Elliot," he sputtered.

William threw the man's head against the ground as he fell backward. He staggered to his feet. When he looked again, his enemy's eyes were fixated on the sky.

## *9*

Pippa's shoulders were as tight as a bow string. Not only had William left before sunup without a by-your-leave, but Matilda had informed her last night she needed to remain for five days. Her womanly flow had arrived, preventing her from travel.

Rising early, Pippa had Merry prepare her hair and then donned a dress for William. All for naught. He had left far before dawn. She stomped her way down the hallway. Precious time wasted on her appearance made her teeth grind. With much to accomplish on the castle wall repairs, she had counted on the help of William and Ross. Her hands knotted at her side.

When she came abreast of Matilda's bedroom door, she heard screams from within. Not waiting a moment, she burst through the door. "What is the meaning of this?"

There lounged Matilda upon the bed with her hair a tousled mess. She threw her hand over her eyes. "Oh, Lady Fairwick, I'm so glad you're here to take this servant to task. She is unqualified to serve me."

As her anger bubbled to the surface, Pippa clasped her hands over her stomach. "Sweet Merry, please go below and see that my breakfast is ready."

Merry hurried from the room without a backward glance.

Matilda sat up with wild eyes. "This is outrageous! Now who will see to my requests?"

Pippa forced her lips into a smile. "Do not fret. Merry was not suited for your care. I'll fetch Helga. She's quite sturdy and very wise when it comes to womanly matters." She watched as her spoiled guest flopped against the pillows.

Matilda's mouth puckered. "I would hope so. I'm feeling poorly, and that woman ... well ... she's deplorable with her attention to my needs."

Pippa walked up to the bed and patted Matilda's arm. "All will be set aright. You rest. I'll send Helga post haste."

With eyes shut, Matilda groaned and curled onto her side. Pippa whipped around and left the room before the thorn pricked again. She didn't relish dodging Matilda and her demands for five days.

Marching straight to the kitchens, she found Helga mixing herbs. She sidled next to her. "Helga?"

Helga glanced up. "Yea, m' lady."

She murmured near Helga's ear. "I have one ailing who needs your assistance. Please mix a *long-lasting* sleeping potion with a bit of catnip and caraway for Lady Matilda Hamilton. Apply a heated brick to her stomach until she falls asleep."

"At once, m' lady."

"A strong arm of persuasion might be needed. She disparaged Merry this morn, and I won't tolerate such treatment of my people."

Helga grinned. "I understand. Leave her to me."

"Thank you, Helga. I trust your wisdom in the matter." Pippa grabbed a hunk of cheese and bread on her way out. She had no time to partake in a leisurely meal. Instead, she walked up the back stairs to her room in hopes of avoiding contact with anyone. A couple of times, she ducked into a darkened alcove to sidestep guests strolling toward the grand hall.

After they passed her hiding place, she darted into her room. She latched the door and leaned her head against the frame. With eyes closed, she inhaled a deep breath. A blanket of despair engulfed her. She forced her eyes open and gazed at her grand bed wishing she could curl up and sleep the day away like Matilda.

She offered William two weeks in which to make a decision about their betrothal. The days stretched out before her like an eternity with no end. Would he honor his father's wishes or challenge the authenticity of the document? She slid down the door and laid her head upon her knees. *Papa ... oh Papa ... I need your wisdom.*

Lost in the darkness of her own self-pity, the knock on the door gave her a jolt. She scrambled to her feet. "Yes?"

"I'm sorry, m' lady, but there is trouble in the stables. Henry asked me to fetch you," Gwendolyn said.

"I'll be there in a moment."

Pippa pulled at the ties of her dress as she rushed to her trunk. She left her dress in a puddle. After wrapping a tight cloth around her ribs, she pulled on pants and a shirt. Once she stepped into her leather boots, she strapped on her sword. Her time of acting a lady ended as she stormed from the room.

Helga emerged from Lady Hamilton's room as Pippa strode down the passageway. "She's asleep, m' lady."

"Praise the saints above. At least one problem is at rest." Pippa didn't linger. She ran down the stairs and out the front door of the keep. When she rounded the corner of the castle, there stood a group of knights clustered at the entrance to the stable. Her light blanket of despair just became a full set of heavy body armor.

"Back to work," she snapped. At the sound of her voice, the group of men dispersed like grease in water. She heard Henry before she saw him.

"Don't move or I will slay you." Henry stood with his sword tip touching a man's chest.

"Henry?"

With his eyes steady on his prey, he spewed, "This man is a traitor."

Pippa gauged the situation. Henry was ready to run a man through with his sword while the stable master, Malcom, fidgeted off to the side. "Malcom, fetch me a rope with which to tie this man."

"I didnae do anything."

"Cease," Pippa barked. "Malcom, my rope!"

"Aye, m' lady. Here ye be."

Pippa snatched the rope and proceeded to bind the man's hands behind his back and then shoved him to the floor. "Another rope, Malcom."

Once the man's feet were secure, Pippa was ready to hear the tale. "Henry?"

"Yer father instructed me to place a watch over this man when he first arrived. He is from the defeated Elliot Clan and pledged his allegiance to Lord Nicolas Fairwick after our conquest of the entire clan. None of the Fairwick brothers trusted this man and for good reason. After yer father's disappearance, his suspicious activities increased. Without his knowledge, I enlisted men to trail his goings and comings. Following the attack yesterday, I decided to track him myself. I caught him attaching a sack of documents to a saddle."

"Bring it to me."

Henry turned to Malcom who held up the sack. "Here, m' lady." He handed her the cloth bag tied shut with a leather strap.

She knelt on one knee in front of the man gripping the pouch in her hand. "Before I open the satchel, I wish to hear your name and your side of this story." Her face remained expressionless while she waited.

"His name is Errol Elliot."

Pippa raised a brow. "A relative of the Elliot clan?"

"A cousin, or so he claims," Henry spit out.

"I dinna do anything amiss."

"That's a lie straight from ... ."

Pippa held up her hand before Henry finished his sentence. She kept her gaze on Errol watching his eye twitch. "Hold fast, Henry. I need to hear this man's account. Again, I ask you, what is your part in this?"

Silence answered her. "If I open this rucksack and find important documents stolen from me, you will rue the day you were born. Traitors are beheaded."

His eyes grew wide. "I had nay choice."

"We always have a choice."

"Nay. He threatened to murder me kinfolk."

"A name!"

"I canna tell."

Pippa grew weary. "Malcom, send Gilbert for the neck and ankle chains. Our friend has need of them." She stood to her feet making the man strain to see her. "You have sealed your fate and that of your family. Henry, round up Errol's wife and children. Malcom, send word to Duff to prepare the dungeon for more guests."

Errol's red face twisted in anger as he squirmed. "Ye canna imprison me bairnes!"

Pippa kicked the bottom of his boot. "Your wife and each child will reside in a cage just like you. For every day you withhold the name of those behind this traitorous act, one finger will be severed from each child's hand."

"Ye canna do this barbaric deed to me babes!" he screamed.

"I'm not committing a barbaric act on your children. You have chosen their destiny with your silent tongue." She turned away before he could witness the anguish she felt. "Henry, away with this man."

"Nay, please, nay!" he cried.

Pippa marched out of the barn into the bright sunlight. She kept her head averted and walked straight through the keep door and into the war room. With a flip of her wrist, the sack skittered across the floor. She smacked her hands flat on the table and hung her head. Traitors without a face or a name lurked about unseen, yet deadly. The dilemma was crushing. *Dear God in Heaven, I've threatened innocent babes.* In place of her heart sat a stone.

At the threshold Merry asked with a soft voice, "How may I serve ye, m' lady?"

Without lifting her head, she said, "Tell Henry and Walter to come to the war room."

"Aye, m' lady. Might I also bring ye drink and food?"

"As you wish." Once the door latched, Pippa scooted a chair out from the table with her foot. She plopped onto the cushion and laid her head on her crossed arms. If tears could solve the present danger, she would produce a waterfall. Oh, how she longed for a helpmate. She tried to bolt the door against her scattered thoughts and instead listen to the comforting sounds of the castle life. Not sure how long she sat there in turmoil, her head raised at the sound of heavy boots.

Henry and Walter burst through the door grumbling amongst themselves.

"Leave the door ajar. Merry is bringing refreshments to bolster our weary bodies. Let's take our seats at the far end of the table." Pippa picked up the unopened sack and laid it on the table.

The three knew the importance of secrecy. All lives were in peril as long as a spy was in their midst. Merry placed trenchers of food and tankards of ale on the table. No one spoke until she closed the door on her way out.

Each man snatched a meat pie while they waited for Pippa to give direction.

"Is Errol secure?"

"Aye. He was crying like a babe when I left his cell. I chained him to the floor and the wall. He will be most uncomfortable." Henry grinned.

Pippa sipped her watered-down ale. Watching her men eat with gusto, her stomach churned with uneasiness. She would listen to their suggestions for finding the enemy; however, the ultimate decision would be hers alone. The overwhelming force of her quandary made it hard to breathe.

*Father, God in heaven, fill me with Your wisdom.*

While the men ate, oblivious to her plight, she untied the infamous sack of secrets. What she withdrew alarmed her ... maps ... maps showing the inside layout of her castle with markings to show the freshwater well, the location of the boiling oil holes, the entrapments located in the barbican, among other important defensive plans. Her eyes grew wide. An adversary planned to invade and capture her home!

"What is it, Lady Fairwick?" Henry asked.

"We have a great threat from within who must be stopped. Errol stole the layout to our castle which included a replica of our secret defense areas."

Walter banged his fist upon the table. "He should die for his treachery."

"Aye," Henry said.

Pippa's frown was fierce. "Nay! He is but a hatchling in this bed of vipers. We must find the ruler of the nest and crush him!"

Enraged, both men shouted their ideas of revenge. If she hadn't been so distraught, their fierce loyalty would have warmed her heart. After they exhausted their obscenities and graphic details of what they wished to inflict on the betrayer, Pippa held up her hand.

"I have a plan."

# *10*

"William!" his mother exclaimed. "Come to me."

He kissed her extended hand and knelt beside the bed. "Mother. You are well?"

"Yes, my sweet son." She traced his face with her fingers. "Your eyes tell me of your grief. You couldn't find him."

William watched his mother's tears spill over and run down her face. He held fast to her hand. "Mother, fear not. I will prevail. In fact, I just had an encounter with one of our enemies who spoke of father."

Brigette's expression brightened. She pushed into a sitting position. "Tell me all. Did he say who is at fault or where Daniel is being held?"

"No, but 'tis only a matter of time. I have a few leads that Ross and I will pursue." His words didn't bring her solace as he had hoped. "I will find him."

"Only if God will allow it. I'm in constant prayer for my Daniel and his safety, as well as for your search. God will hear and answer in His perfect timing. Of this I have no doubt. It's God's response that terrifies me."

Her utterance caused grinding of his teeth. God indeed. It was he who would find his father. If God cared about mere humans, his father would not have been abducted by a scoundrel. Instead, he would be enjoying his wife and new babe. William couldn't voice his opinion for fear of alienating his mother. An important question needed an answer, and he desired no hindrance to her response.

"Mother, I'm sure you are correct." Her sad smile pierced his heart.

She placed her hand against his cheek. "Oh, my son. Turning your back on God is dangerous. If you would but ask Him, He would direct your steps."

William covered her hand with his own. "Mother ... ," at that moment, his baby brother cried out. He turned toward the cradle in the corner.

"Will you change his swaddling, and bring him to me?"

William groaned aloud. "It's been years since I've had to change a nappy. I might need help."

Through her sadness, she chuckled. "One never forgets how to swaddle a baby."

"What is my brother's name?" He struggled with the soaked child. When she didn't answer, he looked over his shoulder to see her dabbing her eyes.

"I'm waiting for your father. He will want to help name his precious baby boy." A tiny laugh escaped. "Daniel warned me to have a boy, or he planned to cut Gillian's hair and train her in warfare." She shuttered. "Imagine!"

William could imagine it all too well when Pippa came to his mind's eye. He finished wrapping his little brother in a blanket and brought him to his mother's bed. "Might I ask you a question?" She received the bundle. He snuggled close and drifted to sleep while she rubbed his back. She half grinned. "Of course. I hope I have an answer."

William dragged a chair to the bedside. With his head down, he rested his arms on his legs and dangled his clasped hands between his knees. He mulled over the best approach.

"William, stop agonizing over it, and ask it."

His head popped up to see his mother's probing stare. She was right. No need to delay. "Did father enter into a betrothal contract on my behalf?"

She tilted her head and looked sheepish. "He might have."

"Mother," he yelled, "either he did or didn't!" His outburst startled the baby who began to cry in earnest.

"William, you have upset your brother." She tried to quiet his sobs but to no avail. Annoyed, she said, "I will need to nurse him. Pull the bed curtain and turn around."

William yanked the curtain closed and plunked his chair backwards. With a huff, he plopped down and crossed his arms over his chest. Certain he would not relish his mother's reply, he fumed. At long last the rustling bedcovers and crying babe ceased. His brother's hiccupping sobs escaped in-between suckling his dinner. His mother's snorting breath told of her displeasure. William did have a tad of remorse for his eruption, but not much.

After a few stressful moments, his mother began to sing to her young son. Her voice pleased him. William's tense shoulders relaxed with each new verse she sang. Often, she had sung to him and his siblings, but today was different. Today he heard the words, not just the tune. Her song told of her love and the love of God for his life ... how precious he was in God's sight ... and how God would guide his life if he would but love God.

*Do You love me, God? Even after all my wrong choices?* William pondered those and other life questions as his mother's voice soothed him ... almost to sleep. When he thought he would doze off, she spoke.

"Your father told me he would see you wed to a beautiful young woman when the time was right. When I asked who he was considering, he refused to divulge a name. He said I couldn't keep a secret. I suppose he was correct. I do love to tell what I know."

"Mo-ther," William said quietly.

"I'm sorry. I was remembering the day we talked about it. Daniel looked resplendent in his clan uniform and I in my beautiful dress. We were so happy."

William heard her sniffle. He closed his eyes in torment. How would any of them endure if his father never came home? Who would care for his siblings? His eyes popped open. It would fall to him. Helen and Gillian ... his insides rolled like the sea.

"If your father signed a contract, he would have stored it in our bedchamber in the trunk at the foot of our bed. Our clothing trunk has a hidden bottom. Release the latch by pressing the two top hinges at the same time." The bed linens rustled. "You can turn around."

His mother placed the sleeping babe on the blanket beside her. William secured the bed curtain and looked at his mother. His mind whirled. Should he tell her about the castle ruins or wait? Would the news cause her more harm?

"William, what troubles you? Do you fear your father has attached you to an unsuitable woman?"

He blinked. "It's not that ... it's ... well ..." He threw his arms wide and said, "I don't wish to be encumbered by a bothersome woman. I need to find father and make things right again." His arms dropped to his sides as a frown formed.

"Bothersome wo ... woman? William! That is preposterous!" Her bright eyes snared his own. "Wedlock is a delightful journey."

His hands came to his hips. "Perhaps ... if you were included in the choosing."

A giggle escaped his mother's lips.

How could she chuckle at such a time? Did she not understand his anger or how he wanted to take charge of his own life? Could childbirth alter one's mind?

She patted the bed. "Come close. I have something to tell you."

William couldn't resist his mother's pleading eyes. His love for her was strong. When she married his father, he had been almost six years of age; and she had treated him as if born from her own body. Her love for him—boundless.

As he eased onto the bedside, she reached for his hand. She rubbed his rough hand with her smooth fingers. The action reminded him of another place in time when she had returned home after a horrific kidnapping. He had feared her bruised and broken body would never heal. Many days he had sat by her side stroking her face and arms with his small fingers in hopes it would bring her joy. No doubt it had pained her more, but she had never scolded his acts.

And now? Now, she comforted him. He gazed at her wondering how she exuded beauty and grace after giving birth while grief stricken. She had the fortitude of a warrior.

"You were so young. You might not remember this. I didn't want to marry your father. My brother, Nicolas, gave me no choice." She smiled. "All three of my brothers made me furious. It felt as if they were conspiring against me. I struggled to think of an escape, but fear kept me from trying."

William tilted his head and frowned. "I thought you wanted me as your son."

"Oh, I most certainly wanted you in my life ... but not your father." As she peered over his shoulder, he saw her stare into the past. "I had a tainted history, and Nicolas feared I would forever live with him and Isabelle. Out of six possible suitors, only one was brave enough to enter into an agreement with my brother." She glanced back at William. "Daniel," she whispered. "At the time, I thought my life had ended. I would be a slave in your father's castle without any freedom. Needless to say, I entered our marriage with an intolerant attitude."

"I had no idea of your dislike for our family."

"Oh, no! I loved you! You were the one bright light in what I perceived as a dismal life."

"What changed?"

"For one thing, I grew up. Your Aunt Isabelle was such an inspiration to me. She helped mold me into the woman I am today by pointing me toward God. After my near-death experience ... I spent much time on my knees in prayer. From my daily talks with God, I realized He had a plan for me and had intentionally joined me with the McKinnon Clan."

William rolled his eyes. "Mother. Your circumstances were different than mine. I don't need to wed."

She shook her head. "I'm not making myself clear. What I want to convey is how God has a plan for your life. Even when you think man directs life's occurrences ... as I thought Nicolas controlled mine ... it's a Heavenly Father wanting the best for you who orchestrates the events."

The longer he mulled over her words, the angrier he became. "If I hear you right, no matter what I do, I have no control over my life?" He yanked his hand back. She grabbed for him as he stood to his feet. "If that's what your God does, I want no part of Him!"

"No," she said with panic in her voice. "I'm not explaining it properly. Please, please don't get upset with me. If Isabelle were here, she could help you see. It's all for your good!"

As her eyes filled with tears, William looked away. He wouldn't listen to any more of her gibberish about God. How could she believe such nonsense? His father believed in praying and being reverent toward God and had raised him with Godly principles. However, his mother ... she took things too far.

When he heard her whimper, his resolve melted. Knowing he had caused her pain speared his heart. What kind of a selfish creature would add to her despair? He knelt beside the bed and gathered her in his arms. "Oh, mother. Forgive my outburst and disrespect." He buried his face in her shoulder as her arms wrapped around him.

She sniffed. "'Tis nothing to forgive."

William relished in his mother's embrace as he remembered his happy childhood. Ready to play with him at a moment's notice, they had shared countless great adventures. Nonetheless, he was no longer a child. He was a man full grown and needed to show it through his actions and the words he spoke. Remorseful, he pulled from her arms, but remained seated.

She laid her empty arms upon the blanket. "Much has been thrust upon you in recent days with your father's unexpected abduction. We are all doing our best to persevere during these uncertain times and sometimes tempers flare."

"Thank you for your understanding." He offered a half grin. "Between you and father, I could always count on you to offer mercy first."

She raised forward and imprisoned his face in her hands. "Know this, my son. No matter what decisions you make in this life, I will always love you. There is nothing you can do to change that fact."

Their heads touched and William closed his eyes.

Her voice was but a whisper. "Also know how God loves you more than I, and He will move mountains if it brings you closer to Him. Unlike your father who allowed you to go off as a mercenary, your Heavenly Father will chase after you when you go down the wrong path."

William released a loud sigh as her hands fell from his face. His mother never gave up her fight ... but then it was a quality he admired about her. The more he refused to accept her words about God, the harder she would pursue the subject.

From the weariness he saw in her eyes, he knew he had overstayed his visit. "I must be away. You are over tired."

"I'm never too weary to spend time with one of my children."

He leaned close and kissed her head. "Take care, mother."

"And you, my son, have a care. There is evil about, ready to devour a good man such as yourself."

After reaching the door, he turned back. "I hope to have good news at my return."

"Make sure to call upon your siblings before you leave. The girls have missed you sorely."

"I'm sure they have," he said with sarcasm. Noticing her wicked grin added to the tightness in his back. Shaking his head, he left her with a low bow.

After easing the door shut, he looked up and down the passageway. No sign of his sisters or James. He felt safe to venture to the grand hall. The need to talk with his mother had outweighed his need for a meal. Sharp pains darted around his middle to remind him of his choice.

His head swiveled to and fro as he traveled the murky hallway. No doubt his sisters heard of his arrival and planned a special *welcome* of sorts. The stairs were within sight when he heard a giggle from a darkened alcove. When he twisted around, his feet entangled with a rope stretched across the passage causing him to stumble to his knees.

The loud squeals and cries came from both sides as three sisters and a brother jumped on his back pushing him to the floor. Legs and arms flew all about. He didn't even try to struggle against them. Instead of annoyance, their laughter and glee over his return made him smile.

Slaying his dragon would have to wait.

# *11*

Two weeks had passed and not a word from her betrothed. With his silence, William had forced Pippa to resort to drastic actions. She sorted through her gowns looking for ones appropriate for her journey. It had been two years since her father had commissioned the dresses sewn for her. Aware they were not the current style didn't deter her from her undertaking.

On her knees, Gwendolyn rummaged through drawers of the armoire. "This blue brocade would look lovely over your navy kirtle." She turned and twisted it in her hands. "The neckline would need to be adjusted to the existing fashion."

Pippa pulled her head out of the trunk to see what Gwendolyn had discovered. With her arms on the edge of the trunk holding a linen chemise, she sat back on her haunches. "What's wrong with the neckline?"

"The peddler said the ladies at court have plunging necklines surrounded by lace to provide a bit of modesty."

*Gasp!* "Why did you ask such a question of the peddler?"

Gwendolyn shrugged. "I try to modify your clothing to the current design. To accomplish it, I must know what the ladies are wearing in London society."

Pippa stared at her friend. She had no idea Gwendolyn even thought about fashion. "I do thank you for altering my gowns, but I don't find it necessary at this time. I'm going to court for one reason, and it's not to be seen in the highest fashion or to find a wealthy companion."

Gwendolyn walked over and stared down at Pippa. "M' lady, if you are seen in an unfashionable gown, you will draw much attention ... attention you say you do not want. I fear what might be said about you ... and your people."

Her words gave Pippa pause. She didn't want to have unfavorable speech directed against her family or the people under her care. Commissioning new gowns was too costly. A heavy sigh escaped her. "Alter my gowns as you see fit. I'll trust your judgment. However, please keep me modest."

A huge grin split Gwendolyn's lips. "I will not disappoint you."

The two kept to their task until the mid-day meal. "Why don't you go to the kitchens and have our meal brought to my solar. We'll eat and discuss which items we want to include in my trip," Pippa suggested.

"Yes, m' lady."

She watched Gwendolyn hustle from the room. The morning had been long and tiring. Sorting through her clothes brought back buried memories leaving her emotionally drained. Not to mention, the thought of wearing elaborate gowns repulsed her. They were uncomfortable and cumbersome. Men's attire was her preference.

The room was a disordered mess. Clothes strewn around rested on chairs, trunks, the bed, and the floor. Overwhelmed, she picked her way around them and went into her sitting room.

She plopped onto her divan located under a window. Lounging in her solar often brought her peace and contentment ... not today. Her jumbled thoughts added to her turbulent heart. Peering out the small window, she twirled her hair. Certain William had gone to visit his mother to find out the truth about their betrothal, she wondered why he hadn't contacted her. Did he hope she would release him from his obligation to her family?

"You don't know me at all if you think that is true," she spoke to no one. Agitated, she jumped up and began pacing the room. With hands behind her back, she pondered her actions for arrival at court. When the social *witches* found out her real reason for coming to London, the gossip mill would turn. If her manly behaviors had reached judgmental ears ahead of her arrival, she was in grave trouble.

She would be thrust into the devious realm of high society with hateful women and wicked men—people with personal gain as their goal. Not understanding their ways, caused her stomach to sour. One fact prompted her to stop in the midst of her pacing. Lady Hamilton would be in attendance. After she took advantage of Fairwick hospitality for nigh onto a week, surely, she would aid Pippa in her time of need.

"Merry is preparing our meal and will bring it soon," Gwendolyn said as she entered the room. "Henry wishes to speak with ye. He said he would await yer presence in the war room."

Pippa's heart sped up. She had been waiting for news about their prisoner. For two weeks Duff's methods applied to Errol Elliot had failed to give them any pertinent information. His silent tongue had provoked her to take aggressive action. "Continue sorting through my clothes, and I'll return shortly."

With no one about, Pippa ran down the back stairway and cut through the busy kitchens on her way to the war room. Her firm expression warned others away. She skidded to a halt just before turning the corner into the grand entryway. With determined poise, she glided into the war room and shut the door. What she saw caused her great concern.

Taunt muscles threatened to burst Henry's shirt seams while his fist pounded against the stone fireplace mantle.

"Henry?"

At the sound of his name, he jumped around to face her. He ceased striking the hearth. "Come close. We know not the location of listening ears."

Pippa's heart seized with apprehension. On unsteady feet, she stumbled toward Henry. She arranged two chairs facing each other.

"Sit here," she whispered, "and tell me what you have learned."

He plunked into his chair. Still fuming, he scrubbed his face with jerky motions. Pippa laid her hand upon his tense arm.

"Whatever it is, God will help us." After a slight squeeze she released her hold. At sixteen, she was eight years his junior, but there were times when she felt his equal ... such as now.

"Ye are right. It's just ... well ... ." He closed his eyes and gulped two deep breaths. "Of course, ye are right." A slight smile creased his leathery face. "First, I want to commend you on your war tactics. Duff tried mild torture to no avail. Today, I applied your strategy. When we put his screaming children close to his holding room, his chains began to rattle."

Pippa wanted Henry to get straight to the point of what he had discovered, but she knew he loved to expound on grisly details. It took great restraint to remain patient.

"I told 'im I planned to cut off his wife's finger first and then follow it with a finger from each child until he answered our questions. Of course, he called me names I can't repeat in yer presence."

"Of which I am grateful. Continue."

"Walter told the woman she needed to scream at the exact moment he told her to do so, or her children would suffer. Her bawling was genuine. We didn't have to prompt her. She even cursed her husband with great gusto. 'Twas a nice touch."

"Henry, please."

"Duff waited outside Errol's door in case he decided to betray our enemy before his wife lost a finger. Would you believe the no-good, filthy animal allowed her to lose a finger?"

Pippa gasped. "You didn't really cut off her finger, did you?"

"Naw. We did what ye said. Walter cut off a couple of fingers from our dead enemies before we threw them in the burial hole. Then he dipped 'em in animal blood from the kitchen and wrapped 'em in a cloth. The ruse worked. The repulsive man started wailing as soon as he saw the bloody finger."

"Did any harm come to his children?"

With a grim expression, he shook his head. "Ye know me better than to think I would do such a terrible thing to innocent babes."

"Yes ... yes, I do. Please hurry this along. I'm anxious to hear the whole of the report."

"With his children and wife caterwauling, he had to shout to be heard. Me and Duff went inside his dungeon chamber so others might not hear what he had to say."

"Henry, out with it!"

"Yea." He lowered his voice and spoke with urgency. "He is a cousin to Brodie Elliot. You remember, the man your uncle Nicolas burned to death during the raid on the Elliot castle when he helped rescue your aunt Brigette?"

"Yes. I've heard the story told numerous times. William's father, Daniel, instigated the rescue."

"Exactly. Both Lord McKinnon and Lord Fairwick were responsible for the destruction of the Elliot castle and the scattering of their clan."

Pippa jolted upright. "No doubt, these ruffians are the ones who kidnapped Lord Daniel."

"I daresay, ye are correct in your assessment. The leader of this Elliot remnant terrorized Errol's family. If Errol didn't obtain those maps, his children would be fed to wild boars while Errol and his wife stood by unable to rescue them."

Her eyes shut on the image. "How awful," she moaned.

"There's more. He swears on his wife's life that he is the lone spy in our midst who is to deliver the maps this very night." He paused. "With added persuasion, he revealed their location and time of the exchange. Our men prepare as we speak."

"Did he give a name?"

"Nay."

She stood to her feet. "I'll postpone my journey. I'm going with you."

Henry rose. "You will not," he said with authority.

His sureness rankled. Her body stiffened as her eyes narrowed. "You overstep your bounds."

"Ye are not considering all. Our people won't survive without you. You are the one who gives hope and direction to this weary band of castle folk. Ye can't wager with your life. Too many depend upon ye."

She bristled at his words even as they convicted her of the truth. Her irritation grew hot. Not to participate in the battle and possible capture of the despicable Elliot clan was vexing. Henry held her stare as she chewed on her lower lip. "I like it not."

"Ye have a significant task to accomplish, as well as I—different, yet both vital to our existence. Will ye be satisfied if I tell ye what we plan to do tonight?"

To miss the raid was maddening, but Pippa accepted his olive branch and agreed to hear his plans. They resumed their seats, and she leaned close to catch his quiet, yet eager voice.

"The men are camped five miles east of the castle near Deadman's caverns. According to Errol, he expects about ten mounted and heavily armed men. One element in our favor is the fact their weapons are inferior to our own. Wisely, your Uncle Nicolas seized their weaponry at his victory over the sorry clan. His action left them with the need to form spears and swords from scrap metal."

Henry's wicked smile didn't go unnoticed by Pippa. He rubbed his hands together with glee of a boy receiving his first sword. Grateful her father and her Uncle Nicolas had trained Henry in the art of battle and strategy, she had full confidence his men would be victorious. If she didn't know him so well, though, his excitement would be disturbing.

"What is the plan of attack?"

"I will take fifteen men at arms. Two will serve as scouts to determine the location of the camp guards. Once they have reported back, Walter and Edward will slay the watchmen while we silently surround the camp. We wait until they have guzzled much ale. I expect the leader to become agitated when he thinks Errol deceived him. At my command, our soldiers will release arrows and eliminate the easy targets while they're in a state of upheaval. Catching them unaware, the battle should be quick. We will show them no mercy, as is the Elliot way."

She jumped up. "You must spare at least one!"

He rose to his feet. "Do not lesson me. I comprehend the strategy of war and extracting information," he said through tight lips.

"Do not ignore who is the ultimate authority," she shot back. They stood nose to nose, both seething with restrained anger. "Though you are eight years my senior, you are not lord over me."

His tightly clenched fists stayed by his side. "It is as you say, Lady Fairwick. Ye remind me oft enough, I'm not soon to forget it." He stalked from the room.

Pippa's eyes burned as tears threatened. It was uncustomary for her to treat Henry with such disregard. If it hadn't been for his watchfulness, her life would have been forfeit many times over. Lack of food for her people and shortage of materials for castle repairs had put her in a quandary which had allowed her emotions to rule her head. She rubbed her brow in thought.

Her head popped up. *This is all William's fault. If he had stood by the betrothal, I wouldn't be in this mess alone.* Her imagination raced with ways to punish William. Each one more devious than the last.

For now, she would apologize to Henry. With a long ride ahead, she had ample time to hone in on the wisest cost for William's betrayal. On that happy thought, she left the room wearing a smirk.

———⟶———

Before the cock crowed, Pippa and her men readied for their journey to London. Rain dripped from the trees like hammer taps. As she walked up to her horse, she pulled on her riding gloves. Walter held the horse's bridle for his lady and awaited her final instructions.

Their heads bent close. "Walter, I leave you in charge of the castle. Keep the gates closed unless absolutely necessary. Keep our prisoner well fed but uncomfortable in his accommodations. We don't want him to get cozy while locked up."

"My lady, I would be relieved if I were riding by your side. Henry will be here to see to the everyday dealings."

"Nay. I would rest easy knowing you both are protecting my home."

"Wait! I'm coming along." They both turned when Henry shouted from the stables.

"Why wasn't I informed that Henry had returned?" She didn't wait for an answer but strode toward him. He met her in the middle of the courtyard. "Why didn't you deliver your report when you returned?"

"Forgive me, m' lady. There was no time. I returned within the hour."

"And ...?"

"We did not arrive in time. Our enemy had fled the area."

"Do you think the information provided by Errol was false?"

"Nay. The campfire still smoldered. We combed a several mile radius of the camp. I could not risk man and horse to pursue further. With the blackness of night, I called off the search."

Pippa stewed while her eyes roamed the sky. She looked back at Henry. "Stay here and expand the hunt."

"After the rain last night, all tracks will have vanished. Taking up the hunt will be futile. My time is best served accompanying you to London."

Distraught, Pippa closed her eyes. Was it too much to ask for one thing to go as planned? She looked back at Henry and exhaled. "Very well. We will wait for you to collect your belongings."

"Thank you, m' lady. It will take but a moment."

Pippa watched Henry run toward the castle. It took great restraint to appear unruffled from his news. Frustration snaked through her body. Enemies were afoot, her people lacked sufficient food, and the damaged castle cried for help. What she needed was a helpmate. Once again, her thoughts went to William and the dilemma his absence caused.

*I think when next I see him, I'll snatch him by the hair while my knife rests on his throat.* As that vision took root, a smile stretched across her face. *Beware my intended. I'm on my way.*

# *12*

In Brigette's solar, Emilia played the harp while her family lounged around her. William scanned the scene before him. He noticed Gillian lacked interest in her sister's music. She lay on an animal rug in front of a roaring fire while twirling her hair. Her eyes danced back and forth across the ceiling. Undoubtedly, she planned her next attack upon his person, while Helen watched Emilia with great concentration.

In the past few days, he had noticed a change in Helen. To him, it appeared she desired to be more like Emilia than her twin. He noticed Helen distanced herself from Gillian's antics when possible. Alas, Gillian's strong personality overrode Helen's more docile demeanor. In his opinion, Gillian deserved the lash to help curb her waywardness before she ruined her status in society.

While James dozed in his lap, William sprawled in a high-back chair that flanked the fireplace. Facing him in the other chair was his mother. She cradled her newborn as she hummed along with the tune. For him, the reality of his father's absence turned the music into a dreary dirge—robbed of his joy by an unknown assailant. His stomach churned with hot anger.

Gillian puffed with agitation. "Can this be over?"

Emilia stopped mid-strum.

"Gillian!" Brigette snapped. "You are rude."

The outburst woke James who rubbed his bleary eyes. He rolled out of William's lap. "Can I go to bed?"

"Mother," Emilia whined.

"You girls have upset the baby," his mother reprimanded as the infant wailed at the disruption.

What should have been a tranquil setting deteriorated with each utterance. His father could have calmed the volatile situation with a spoken word. William decided to take charge of his ill-disciplined sister.

"Cease!" he bellowed. All eyes swung his way. "Gillian, you owe Emilia an apology for your discourtesy." His eyes drilled into Gillian's defiant stare.

She vaulted to her feet. "What I do is not your concern."

"In father's absence, the discipline falls to me," he said with controlled anger. Instead of intimidation, his words provoked an unexpected clash. Gillian launched her body at him with arms flailing. Her fist smashed his lip before he trapped her arms.

Brigette jumped to her feet. "Gillian! What is the meaning of this outburst?"

With her back against his chest, William's tight grip detained the squirming fireball. If he had his way, he would give her ten blows across her backside.

"William, release her."

He hesitated before complying with his mother's request. As his grip loosened, Gillian whipped around and poked his chest. When he grabbed her finger and twisted, she screamed in agony.

"William!" his mother shouted.

He threw Gillian's hand aside and stepped away.

"Gillian, come to me this instant."

It pleased William to hear authority in his mother's voice. He watched Gillian scoot toward their mother. When she got close, she crumpled at their mother's feet and wailed.

"William hurt me."

He rolled his eyes at her theatrics. Surely, his mother wouldn't fall for such an obvious display of false injury. Her refined performances in deception frightened him. He shook his head. She was headed toward grave trouble if she continued down her evil path. Even though he knew Gillian had never attended court, she acted like a professional charlatan. Where had she acquired such skills?

Brigette handed the sobbing babe to Emilia. "Please comfort your brother."

What his mother did next was beyond comprehension. She gathered Gillian into her embrace and began to stroke her hair. Unbelievable! He bit his jaw to prevent choice words from spewing forth toward his spoiled sister.

"What has caused this volatile frenzy?" Brigette cooed.

Gillian sniffed and muttered, but William was unable to understand her.

"Mother," he huffed. "Gillian does not need to be coddled. She needs a beating for her disrespectful treatment of the entire family."

His mother frowned at him. "William, you are not helping the matter."

Gillian ducked her head under her mother's arm and glared at William. "He can't take father's place," she whimpered. "He's hardhearted since returning home, and I don't like it."

Incredible! William's eyes cut to his mother. Did she view him in the same manner? Did the family? "Mother, I'm not trying to take father's place, but you are blinded to Gillian's manipulation because you see her through biased eyes." He watched his mother's spine stiffen.

When his mother opened her mouth to respond, a knock came on the bedchamber door. Spared from his mother's tongue lashing, William opened the door. Fiona stood with clasped hands and frightened eyes. William stepped from the room and pulled the door closed. "What is a miss?"

"One of the king's men requests an audience with ye in the grand hall."

William's eyes closed as he scrubbed his forehead. After a short time, he looked down at Fiona. "First, I'll speak with mother and then come down. Offer him a repast and tell him I'm on my way."

Fiona bobbed a curtsey and hustled away. William frowned as he watched her retreating back. *What does the king want with me?* He went back inside to face his mother. Pleased to have a legitimate reason to escape the family debacle, he remembered why he left home in the first place. The constant bickering and childish antics of his sisters were best received in small doses.

To look grave would serve him well with his mother. She might forget their previous interplay and shift her concern away from his sister. Gillian's performance would vanish in light of the king's messenger waiting below. He smiled inwardly.

"Is anything wrong?" Brigette asked.

"I must take leave of the family. The king's messenger awaits me in the grand hall."

His mother gasped as her hand flew to cover her heart. The atmosphere took on a somber mood as the girls looked on with alarm. "What is the significance of his presence?"

"Mother, I know not. I will report to you once I have ascertained the reason of his visit."

"Mayhap he brings information about father." Emilia said as her eyes rounded with hope.

Brigette left the girls and approached William as he stood at the doorway. She laid her hand upon his arm. "Report to me. I'll break any news to the girls and James." A sheen of unshed tears filled her eyes.

William covered her hand. "Of course, mother. Have faith. All will be well." He imparted a crooked grin and left the women staring after him.

As he stalked down the passageway, his stomach flipped a few times. In his experience, it was never good news when the king sent a messenger. Perhaps, accusations arose from his mercenary days. He began to question himself. Had he ever killed one of the king's men by mistake? Ought he to bolt from Sanddown castle, never to return?

"Coward," he murmured.

He hesitated at the entrance to the great hall and looked about. Off to the side sat the messenger drinking his ale. William squared his shoulders and strode up to the man. "I am William McKinnon. How may I be of assistance?"

The man stood and reached into his bag. "I have news from our king." He handed the sealed parchment to William. "Ye may wish to read it in private. I'll await ye here."

"Thank you. Enjoy your meal, and I'll return shortly." William left the room and took the stairs two at a time. He intended to read the missive in his room—away from prying eyes. Upon reaching his room, he dropped the security bar in place and hurried to the table near the window.

For a moment, he held the document in his hands. His heart pounded in his chest as he dreaded the content. Sitting down, he broke the seal on the scroll and unrolled the paper on the table. Enough sunlight filtered through the glass to illuminate the words. It was short and to the point. He re-read it again for clarity, but the message didn't alter. The king required his presence at court— immediately. God help him!

———⟨———————⟩———

Daniel's head jerked from his dozing. A noise startled him awake. His eyes strained to cut through the darkness while his head tilted toward the unusual sound. An item scrapped along the corridor outside his prison door. Most nights his enemy left him unattended. Whoever crept near was not the usual guard.

A light pierced the blackness as a torch settled into the wall holder. After a short time, a small head popped up at the bars. It was the young boy who brought him food.

"What are ye about?" Daniel whispered.

The boy's eyes squinted. "I have some questions for ye."

"Oh, do ye now?"

"Aye."

"I have nowhere to go; ask away." Daniel kept a serious face. He didn't want to convey he thought the boy foolish by smiling at his behavior. It could discourage the young one's bravery.

"Why 're ye here?"

"I know not."

"'re ye evil?"

Daniel chuckled under his breath. "Nay."

"They say ye 're."

"Who says I'm evil?"

"The wicked mon."

"Do ye know his name?" Daniel became more hopeful with each question asked. Maybe the information he gained could work to his advantage.

"Nay. I stay far away from him. 'e eats little boys."

Daniel saw the boy's eyes grow wide with fear. If this was an indication, his enemy served up cruelty to everyone. To think he frightened little boys made Daniel's anger simmer.

"I have a young son about your age."

"Dost 'e have food to eat?"

"There is an abundance of food where I live. When I escape, you can go with me and live at my castle. Would ye like that?" He heard the boy shifting from foot to foot.

"Can me mither coom too?"

"Aye. Anyone who wishes to escape this evil man and offers me aid will be welcomed." Daniel watched emotions of fear along with hope cross the boy's face. "What shall I call ye?"

"All call me boy." He shrugged his boney shoulder. "'Tis good enough for me."

"Ye are such a brave lad, I plan to give ye a warrior's name. 'Twill be our secret. What say you?"

"'Tis a sound plan."

Daniel tapped his chin in thought. "From hence forth ye shall be called Sloan. 'Tis a Scottish name meaning fighter or warrior."

"'Tis a fine name."

"Now, Sloan. We need to be cautious with our meetings. I wish no harm to come yer way. Will anyone miss ye this night?"

"Nay ... weel ... mayhap me mither."

"What is your mother's name?"

"Woman."

Daniel cringed at the reference. Evidently, his mother was no better than a slave herself. "How many women reside at this castle?"

"Me mither, an old cook, and one more."

"How many men are aboot?"

"They coom and go."

"How many have swords or weapons?"

"Six. The others have clubs."

"What about my guard? He doesn't appear to have a weapon."

The young boy giggled. "'e dinna need any. 'e can kill ye with 'is bare hands."

Daniel could well imagine that as a fact after his altercation with the man. "I came here on a boat. Do ye know if we're on an island or on the mainland?"

"Nay."

"Is there a name for this castle?"

"Nay. 'Tisn't a real castle. More like ruins. Me and me mither sleep in a lean too with a leaking thatched roof."

"When the sun rises, is it over water or over land?"

Sloan's head tilted left and then right. "I'll see when morning coomes."

Fearful for the lad's safety, Daniel decided he had gained enough information for one night. "Ye have stayed overlong. Ye must return to yer mother's side before ye are missed."

"I can bring ye more food."

Daniel perked up at those words. Strength is what he lacked, and nourishment could improve his condition. "That would be most welcomed, but I don't want ye to risk getting caught and punished on my account. It's essential ye use great care, and do it under the cover of darkness. Douse yer torch and be on yer way ... and Sloan?"

"Aye."

"Ye are a fine warrior, but ye must be watchful."

95

He nodded and jumped from his stool. From the sound of it, Sloan dragged his stool back where it came from. The light disappeared as he scurried into the black of night.

Daniel offered up a prayer of thanksgiving and one for Sloan's protection. He hated using such a wee lad to aid his escape, but perhaps God provided him for such a purpose. Until God showed him otherwise, he would be grateful and continue to bathe the child in prayer. He knew his heavenly father had a plan and had provided a glimpse of freedom to lift his spirits.

"Thank ye, Father. Ye are a good, good Father." He shifted around for a small bit of comfort and with a lighter heart, shut his eyes for rest. He would need mighty power when he escaped and escape he would.

# *13*

Pippa's dress flapped in the wind as she tramped from the shelter of the trees to the road. She and her guards were on the outskirts of London waiting for Henry to return from town. He had gone to secure rooms for their stay; and in her opinion, he had been gone overlong.

"Stomping to the road every few minutes will not make Henry appear," Robert said.

Pippa shifted her eyes to Robert who had come alongside her. "This I know."

After her father's death, Robert had stepped in to give fatherly advice when needed. He had served her family since before her birth and was a trusted friend.

"Pacing to and fro will rumple yer fine clothing. Come back to the shade and rest while ye have the opportunity."

Pippa closed her eyes on a sigh. She knew Robert was right, but her insides jumped too much to rest. The two turned in unison as they walked toward shelter from the sun. "What delays him?" she asked in agitation.

"Now, m' lady, the ways of Londoners are not our ways. No doubt, he's using his haggling skills to procure a safe haven, as well as the best price. The town is bustling with people making his task more difficult."

She glanced at the faithful warrior. His calm wisdom somewhat eased her tension, but no words erased the dreaded mission. "I wouldn't be in this mess if William had honored the betrothal."

"*Tsk, tsk*, m' lady. With the recent capture or possible murder of his father, he has had much to consider." He paused. "Mayhap another will capture your attention at the king's court."

She stopped and faced Robert. With hands on her hips, she snorted. "I have no desire to find another. I don't even wish to wed William." Her arms flew out from her sides. "The only reason I am here is because we need funds and younger men to rebuild our damaged castle."

With hard swinging arms, she stalked away. The tunic sewn by the loving hands of Gwendolyn, restricted her every step. Whomever had invented women's clothing had been demented; of this she was certain.

Plopping down on the blanket provided by her guards, she rested her chin on her upraised knees. She yanked on her clothing to hide the trousers underneath. No need to get a scolding from Robert about the unseemliness of her attire. 'Twas bad enough she traveled without her maid. Henry and Robert were furious with that decision. No matter.

"Henry returns," Robert called out.

She scrambled to her feet as Henry rode up to the clump of trees. He hopped off his horse and threw the reins to a waiting page. "We have accommodations—not what I preferred for yer visit—but 'twas all I could acquire. The township is teeming with people from all walks of life."

"How close are we to the king's location?" she asked.

"A few blocks away. The nearer ye get to 'is residence, the thicker the people. It's like nothing I've ever seen before and hope never to experience again!"

"I'll prepare for departure."

Henry looked at Robert and back at Pippa. "Ye're required to ride sidesaddle the rest of the way."

"Sidesaddle? I think not!"

Henry lowered his penetrating gaze. "Then we're not going any further."

"You overstep your authority," she said through gritted teeth.

"He has it aright, Lady Fairwick. Ye must be above reproach in all things, or our journey is for naught."

Pippa grunted. Her tight jaw caused a tic in her cheek as she looked toward London. After a short pause, she said, "As you wish." She turned to mount her palfrey.

"And store the trousers in your pack," Henry added.

She spun around with eyes wide and nose in the air. "What?"

"Ye heard me. I know what's hiding under yer dress. Off with them."

Pippa's eyes narrowed into slits. When Henry stood firm without a flinch, she marched away and went behind the dense bushes to remove her pants. She grumbled and huffed as she snatched them off. Her men chuckled as her unladylike words floated in the air. After a short time, she emerged with her trousers hanging from her outstretched finger.

She walked up to Henry and tossed them into his chest. "Here." Her eyes went between Robert and Henry. "I see your smiles behind your hands. Stop it at once." She then flounced up to her horse. With one foot raised and hands grasping the saddle, she waited.

Robert came up behind her. "Allow me, m' lady." With a firm hold on her boot, he gave her a gentle boost into the saddle. Both men walked away as she tugged on her attire to cover her legs.

When she looked up, the mounted men waited at the roadside. She was thankful to see their backs. How humiliating to ride thusly. The men knew she was no lady, yet they were gracious enough not to mention it. She nudged her horse forward and took her place in the middle of the procession. Protected on every side, she trotted toward London where the vultures awaited.

They made good time until reaching the edge of town. There she experienced what Henry had mentioned. The press of such a crowd of people suffocated her while the stench stole her breath.

She held a handkerchief over her nose and tried to take in the sights of the city. More than once she offered a prayer of gratefulness for having Henry and Robert to escort her through the maze of streets. At long last they arrived at the Boarshead Inn. She hoped the interior didn't resemble the name.

Henry sprang from his horse and came to help her dismount. "Don't allow the name to fool you. The inside is quite nice. I think you will be pleased."

"'Twill be sufficient." Sweaty and tired, she would be satisfied with a barn stall if bathwater came with it.

Once inside, Henry and Robert bracketed her as they went upstairs to their waiting rooms. "Robert and I will share the first room. Your room is next door. Since you traveled without a lady's maid, one of us will sleep outside your doorway at all times."

Pippa was relieved when Henry refrained from chastising her for the foolishness of her decision. It was obvious why they had both insisted she bring a maid to attend her needs. Now, they would suffer for her stubbornness.

Henry opened the door and scanned the room before allowing her to enter. She almost squealed with delight. A steaming tub sat in the middle of the room. What a welcomed sight!

"We take our leave. If you have need of us, a tap on the connecting wall is all that is required."

With her hands clasped over her stomach, she said, "Thank you both." She didn't add more for fear she might tear up. She placed the blame of her fickle emotions on fatigue.

"There is little daylight left; but if you wish a tour of the city, it can be arranged. Otherwise, rest and dinner are all that is scheduled."

"I will take advantage of the time alone to prepare for my audience with the king. Please send up a laundress to press my clothing."

"At once, m' lady." Robert withdrew while Henry hesitated at the doorway. "I almost forgot to mention; I saw Lady Hamilton when I entered town. Would you wish a meeting with her?"

It was hard to comprehend, but knowing Matilda was nearby provided comfort to Pippa. "Splendid." Her eyes softened. "I truly appreciate all you have done to protect and provide for my needs."

"My pleasure, m' lady." Henry stepped into the hallway and spoke through the closed door. "Lock yer door at all times."

Pippa turned the key and placed the safety bar in its place. When she went to remove her dress, she understood another reason to have a lady's maid attend her. She might have to bathe in her clothing. Oh, bother ...

Her short nap and soothing bath had revitalized her sore body. She was now prepared to face her next obstacle—eating alone among strangers. After wrestling with several outfits, Pippa decided to wear a simple tie-in-the-front day dress. It wasn't stylish but perhaps her cloak would conceal the fact.

Emerging from her room, Robert stood ready to escort her downstairs. "Ye look rested."

"Yes. The lodgings are comfortable." Looking down the deserted hallway, her heart danced inside her chest. No amount of deep breaths eased her qualms. *Why did I ever think this was a good idea? Foolish!* She was thankful Robert had the wherewithal to remain silent the rest of the way. Making idle conversation was not her expertise.

Stopping at the dining room archway, a pleasant surprise awaited her, for there in a small nook sat Lady Hamilton. Remarkable. Henry had arranged for the women to dine together. When Matilda saw her, Lady Hamilton's eyes grew round. Unsure of what troubled her dinner companion, Pippa weaved her way past occupied tables to reach the back corner.

"Lady Hamilton, what a nice gift to see you all wrapped in your beautiful gown. May I join you?"

"Yes, and hurry," she hissed.

Pippa sat without delay and glanced behind her. "What is amiss? Is there danger about?" she whispered.

Matilda rolled her eyes. "No, child. 'Tis your clothing ... it's quite unsuitable. Please assure me you have more appropriate dresses to wear."

Pippa ducked her chin self-consciously and allowed her eyes to roam around the room. "I realize my dress is last seasons, but really ..."

"Last season? Try two or three seasons old. It's just not done." Matilda flipped open her fan and whipped it back and forth with force. No sooner had she generated a gale storm, she snapped the fan shut. "We must eat in haste. There is much work to do to make you presentable. Henry said you are to see the king. Is that not so?"

Aggravated at Henry, her lips pinched shut.

"Well? Is it so?" Matilda persisted.

"Yes. That is correct information. Yet I don't see ..." Before she completed her comment, Matilda's hand was in the air calling over a waiter.

"Sir, we wish our meal sent up to room ...?" She looked to Pippa to provide her room number.

Pippa glared at Matilda. She lowered her head and mumbled, "Room 205."

"Excellent m' ladies. I will see to it personally."

After he left, Matilda said, "Of course, he's so inclined. He will expect a coin for his troubles."

Alarmed, Pippa's head jerked up to stare at Matilda.

Rolling her eyes again, Matilda said, "I'll provide the coin. From the looks of your gown, you are short on funds."

Pippa hated the accuracy of Matilda's guess. With great reluctance, Pippa stood. No sooner had she stepped back from her chair, Matilda grabbed her arm and started tugging her onward. The fullness of her companion's elaborate skirt jarred cutlery as they swished past the diners on their way to Pippa's room. There was no help for it; her idea of a relaxing meal to settle her nerves vanished.

As she trailed behind, Matilda chattered something about Pippa *eaten alive* if she didn't intervene. Unsure how her senseless ramblings had anything to do with a lady's clothing, one thing was certain ... Pippa had a new advocate ... but at what cost?

*Teresa Smyser, Warrior Bride Series, Book 3*

# 14

In the wee hours, William and Ross trotted into London. That no rooms were available at the late hour forced them to sleep with their horses in the stable. Neither complained when they laid their weary heads upon clean straw.

"Time to arise, Lord William," Ross said. When he didn't respond, Ross rattled the stall door.

William groaned as he turned over. A sunbeam sliced across his face causing him to squint. "I'm quite sure 'tisn't time to rise; I just closed my eyes."

"I'm sairy, m' lord, but we need to find a bath house to wash away our stench before ye meet with tha king."

Sprawled in the hay with his arm across his eyes, he said, "Don't remind me. I have no desire to complete my task today."

"But complete it ye moost. Now coom." Ross gathered up their travel bags. "I've given coin to tha stable master. Our horses weel receive excellent care while ye are aboot tha king's business. I promised him additional coins if ye found all to yer liking when we return."

Pushing into a sitting position, William rested his arms on his up-raised knees. "Again, I say—what would I do without you?" He shoved to his feet and accepted his saddle bag from Ross. "Could you be persuaded to inquire of the king on my behalf?" William asked with a half grin.

Ross shook his head. "I think not. Shall we?" he asked as he swept his arm out before him.

William's grin disappeared as he exited the stall. He knew no one could take his place. No harm in wishing it so. "Mayhap we'll find a vacant room or two this morning."

"I inquired earlier and have two possibilities."

As they walked side by side, William looked at Ross perplexed. "Did you obtain any sleep?"

"I had adequate rest. Follow me." Ross looked in all directions. "Stay close and be alert." He proceeded to lead William down a narrow alley, across a street busy with early morning vendors and into another backstreet.

William didn't question Ross, but kept his knife concealed in one hand with his other hand upon the sword hilt. His eyes darted about until they emerged into the bright sunlight at the end of the alleyway.

"There ..." Ross pointed to a building. "... tha better of our two options. I put down a deposit to hold a room. If it meets with yer approval, we'll reside there. "

"The Seven Stars Inn," William read aloud.

"Tha outer building is not impressive, but tha inside 'tis clean."

"I'll have to trust you on this one."

The men weaved around fellas on horseback as they vaulted to the other side of the street. "'Twas built in 1602 and hath been well maintained," Ross explained.

They entered the inn and found themselves in a common area where several men talked and drank their ale. Off to the left stood a long counter which doubled as a check-in point and a bar. "The room is listed under yer given name," Ross said.

The two men approached the counter.

"How may I assist you?" the clerk asked.

William stood with shoulders back and head high. "There should be a room retained for Lord William McKinnon."

With his nose elevated high in the air, the clerk looked down at William. "Allow me to check my registry." To establish confirmation, he had to lower his nose. He sorted through several before asking, "Did you put down a deposit to hold a room?"

"Aye. In fact, it happened earlier this morning. Have ye already forgotten the fact?" William asked in his haughty voice. "If ye can't seem to locate the transaction, mayhap I need to speak with the proprietor."

"That will not be necessary." He pulled another set of papers from under the counter and sifted through those.

"I also require the services of a runner. The king needs to be informed of my arrival."

The clerk's eyes grew round with concern. "I will send a reliable man to your room once you've settled in. He will relay your message to the king's secretary." He reached behind him for a key. After clearing his throat, he said, "Lord McKinnon, room 15 awaits your arrival. Your key, my lord. I will provide a guide if need be."

"Nay. I don't think we'll get lost with only two floors." After accepting the key, William asked, "Do you offer baths in this establishment?"

"We furnish barrels on the first floor in the rear of the breezeway; or I can arrange tubs sent to your room."

"No need for special treatment. All I want is fresh, steaming water and two tubs reserved. We will be down in half an hour." William and Ross looked at the main room on their way to the stairs. Simple tapestries decorated the walls, yet there were no floor coverings.

Silence reined on the second floor as William inserted the key. The door opened into a large room with three beds along one wall. He turned to Ross. "Will we have to share with another?"

"Nay. Ye paid for tha third bed," he said with a smile.

William grinned.

Ross shrugged.

William and Ross walked through part of London shopping for the proper clothing. Neither wanted to offend the king in their native wear. It seemed the style of the city dwellers was far different from a Scotsman's garb. After making their purchases, they enjoyed their mid-day meal at the Fountain Inn Tavern near Temple Lane. In the tavern, no matter whether a Scotsman or an Englishman, common ground brought them together. All men relished a tasty meal with hearty ale.

Following their satisfying repast, William said, "I want to buy a trinket or two for my mother and sisters. Shall we stop in The Old Curiosity Shop we passed near the Piazza?"

"Aye. 'Tis a noble plan."

"Perhaps there will be a toy suitable for young James, as well."

Feeling uncomfortable among numerous women patrons, Ross offered to wait outside with their clothing merchandise. William agreed and made quick work at the shop. He picked out bright ribbons for his sisters' hair, a jeweled broach for his mother, and wooden animals for James. While he waited on the wrapping of his items, he noticed two young women staring at him. When he turned away from their glare, he heard them giggle. Women were strange creatures who baffled him.

William stumbled into Ross as he hurried from the shop. He grabbed Ross's arm to keep him upright. "Excuse my clumsiness."

"'Tis a scary place, is it not?" Ross asked as he glanced back at the door.

"Aye. Let's be away from here. 'Twill be the right amount of time to dress for the kings court if we hurry."

After a quick change, the men rode their horses to the king's residence. They stopped in a long line of arrivals waiting their turn for the groomsmen to take their mounts. From the numerous carriages and people bustling about, it appeared the king was entertaining this evening. Lighted lamps graced the building to give light for the procession of couples walking up the steps. Men and women in elegant clothing gave evidence of the wealth surrounding the king and his constituents. William's stomach plummeted.

"I weel remain with our horses, lest ye have need of me services," Ross said.

"Nay ... unless ye wish to take my place?"

Ross chuckled.

"If I fail to resurface by midnight, come and rescue me," William said with little humor.

"Perhaps tha king wishes to bestow upon ye an award for ridding his country of evil men."

"Or perhaps the king wishes to put me in the stockades for ruffling the feathers of his allies or plans to order my beheading."

"Either way, ye look quite grand in yer new clothing."

William shook his head at Ross. "There are times when your truthfulness ..." He stopped mid-sentence when they arrived and a groomsmen caught hold of their bridles. Both men dismounted—William with reluctance.

"I weel attend our mounts if ye weel but point me where I may dwell for tha evening," Ross said. The man handed him the reins and pointed to a holding area already filling with men and horses. Ross smacked William on the back. "Be yer usual charming self, and all weel be well."

William stood like a fatherless child as he watched Ross walk away.

"Your name sir?"

He turned to another man who held a list. "I'm Lord William McKinnon."

After a moment, the man checked his name on the list. "The king received your missive and is expecting you tonight. You may enter the grand ballroom and enjoy the festivities while you wait for your escort."

"Thank you." William's legs wobbled as he walked up the stairs. He had conquered three enemies at a time, wrestled wild animals, and stared at death; yet he had never felt as unsure of himself as he did at present. The king retained the power to change his life forever with one word. Would this be a confrontation as he thought or recompense for his good works as Ross suggested?

When he reached the top step, another guard asked his name. He verified William's admission and ushered him into the majestic hallway; he stood dazed from the beauty.

"Follow the crowd as they advance up the grand stairway and proceed into the ballroom," the doorkeeper said.

William came out of his stupor and shuffled forward. With back straight and head held high, William glanced around to see if his evening attire were proper. *Thank you, Ross.*

From his observation, this season the women's dresses had plunging necklines which might keep certain men entertained. His mother would be appalled at the indecency of it. Confident she would not allow his sisters to dress thusly, he would remind her to keep his sisters far from London.

Before reaching the second floor, he stopped midway up the stairs. A spokesman announced each person or couple who entered the ballroom which slowed down the procession. He progressed one stair at a time as he worked his way toward the threshold of the merrymaking. A drop of sweat rolled down his back. Moisture formed above his lip and along his hairline.

Not wanting others to witness his discomfort, he removed his kerchief to dab away the sheen. When they announced his name, he heard a gasp from his right. His eyes darted to a clump of women. As he descended a few steps into the room, his gaze fixed on a rather buxom woman from whom came the sound ... did he know her?

When he reached the bottom step, she edged next to his side. As he turned, his eyes widened ... Lady Hamilton!

# *15*

Ever the gentleman, William received Matilda's outstretched hand and bowed low. Still holding her hand, he straightened. "Lady Hamilton, what an astonishing wonder to find you here."

She batted her eyes as she withdrew her hand from his grasp. "Thank you. As I recall, the last I saw you, you were scampering away from me and poor, unfortunate Lady Fairwick. Not well done of you to leave us without a word of farewell." She flipped open her ornate fan and began to generate a cool breeze which tickled his face.

"I do hope you forgave me for my urgent, and shall we say, unchivalrous parting. In no way did I mean to slight either of you fine ladies. Pressing responsibilities needed my immediate attention. You understand, do you not?"

""Twas more of a retreat than a mere leaving." She slid her hand through the crook of his arm. "Holding a grudge against such a fine specimen of a man is not in my nature."

"Lady Hamilton! Please choose your words with care." Uncomfortable, William looked about to see if anyone overheard their exchange.

"Oh, fiddlesticks." She peeked around before proceeding.

"We're not babes in nappies any longer. Coy is not in my vocabulary," she whispered. "I prefer to speak my mind and for you to act likewise. Can we at least agree on that?"

"If you desire it. Nonetheless, discretion must be heeded."

"Of course." Her smile was genuine. "Escort me around the room while I inform you of the strange activities taking place."

Even though Lady Hamilton was a tad brash for his tastes, her company kept his mind off his own problems. The hearsay she planned to share might prove entertaining. The expanse of her language impressed William. No harm would come from indulging her; he might gain valuable news.

As they strolled along, Matilda pointed out the latest styles for women's hats, dresses, shoes, gloves, and fans. Hoping her chatter would turn less frivolous, he listened with one ear while scanning the crowd for other acquaintances. He made eye contact with several men who turned away. Pompous men full of self-importance—William had little use for such people.

"I'm parched. If you will be so kind as to acquire us a drink, I will await you over there."

"Indeed, my lady."

After weaving through the horde of guests, he retrieved a cup of wine for his companion and a tankard of ale for himself. Matilda commandeered two chairs along the outer wall. He perceived it as a strategic place to observe the festivities while conversing. William juggled their drinks hoping not to spill them on his elegant suit. As he crisscrossed the room, he decided to ask her a few questions with the hope of changing her tedious exchange from fashion to another topic.

He handed her the drink before sitting beside her. "Does the king offer such gatherings often?"

"Oh, my, yes. It's an honor when chosen by the king to attend his celebrations. My father arranged for my attendance in hopes I'll find a suitable, wealthy husband."

William choked on his ale at her bluntness. With haste he withdrew his kerchief to wipe his mouth. "Lady Hamilton, I'm unused to your candor."

Her eyes twinkled. "You should be relieved I have no designs on you for my mate. I'm afraid your reputation doesn't measure up to my father's standards. No disrespect intended of course."

He winced. As he feared, his reputation preceded him. He returned her smile. "None taken."

"Now," she murmured, "the main reason I sought you out ..."

As he waited for her to divulge her secrets, he spied the profile of a woman standing alone against the far wall—breathtaking. Her copper hair lifted from her swan-like neck with long curls falling over one shoulder. Perhaps Lady Hamilton might arrange an introduction. Even if the woman wasn't a conversationalist, at least he could enjoy her beauty for a time while he awaited the king's summons.

Matilda covered her mouth with her open fan and leaned close to William. "It's about Lady Fairwick."

William's hand jerked so hard he sloshed drink on the floor. Not wanting to make a further mess, he sat the tankard under his chair. "What say you?"

"You'll need to listen well. Come near, I don't want any to eavesdrop."

Against all reasoning, he leaned his ear closer.

"Lady Fairwick arrived here nigh onto a week ago. You should have seen the gown she planned to wear to her meeting with the king. Deplorable! If I had declined to come to her rescue, I shudder to think of the slaughter that would have ensued ... like a lamb eaten by wolves."

"I'm not sure I understand. Was she in danger from a pack of wolves?" His heart sped up. Even though angered at Pippa, he wanted no harm to befall her.

Matilda rolled her eyes. "There are times when you men are senseless. The wolves to whom I refer are the elite women and men who ruin one's social status with a few well-placed comments, words from which Lady Fairwick would never recover."

William's body tensed. Pippa had no business coming to London. "Who traveled with her?"

"The one named Henry. Not having a proper escort wasn't the worst of it; it was her clothing, I tell you. I supplied her with two of my older dresses reworked to fit her. Otherwise, the king might have dismissed her straight away. Even though I provided her with a maid to fix her hair ... can you believe she traveled without a maid?" Matilda shook her head. "She brought no one to arrange her hair! Preposterous! After all I bestowed upon her, she insisted on carrying her leather holder which sorely detracted from her appearance."

William bounced from annoyance to anger to outrage. "She journeyed without a maid?"

"Yes, it's as I said."

Irresponsible described her actions. A burning developed in the pit of his stomach. "You say she brought a leather holder. Capable of holding a document?"

"I suppose."

His head swiveled back and forth. "Is she here tonight?"

"She arrived earlier, but I haven't seen her as of late."

"Please, peruse the room, and advise me of her whereabouts." William sprang to his feet and pulled Matilda along. "What is she wearing tonight?"

"Stop squeezing my arm so tight." Matilda tugged her arm free. "Your agitation confounds me. You're not responsible for her impulsive, or should I say, reckless decision to arrive in London ill-equipped."

"I need to find her. Please?"

"Oh, all right. Once I find her, you are on your own. I have a prospective husband to discover, and you cease to be pleasant company."

"Forgive me, Lady Hamilton. My apologies for my abrupt behavior; however, it's vital I uncover her whereabouts. Has she spoken with the king?"

"Yes. The unfolding of the event proved quite odd." Her gaze scanned the room. "The king brought her into his inner sanctum on her second day of waiting. Most wait weeks to be summoned before the king." Matilda flipped her hair over her shoulder. "She failed to divulge the substance of their encounter. At least after their business, she no longer carried her leather holder which improved her appearance twofold."

In the middle of the room, he whirled Matilda around to face him. "Did the king take her document holder?"

"Stop raising your voice," she hissed. "I have no idea what became of the leather pouch."

He rolled his shoulders and tried to ease his expression. "Tell me the color of her clothing, and I'll release you from the hunt."

She snorted. "Very well. Her midnight blue-velvet gown sports a bum roll to show her striped petticoat. The low bodice includes a square neckline with silver embroidery. The tight half sleeves end with lace at the elbow. I'm not responsible for the changes she made to the gown after her arrival."

His brows came to a point. "What mean you?"

"She added a hideous lace insert to hide her bosom which I didn't recommend. Her shabby lace failed to match the lace on the dress. Tasteless." She shook her head in disbelief. "Interwoven with ribbons, her long curls flow from the crown of her head. She refused a head piece; at least she permitted my maid to apply red dye to her cheeks and lips ... unless she wiped it off. Lady Fairwick grew quite troublesome ... much like you." She fixed him with a glare. "Since you have become a tiresome companion, I'll take my leave." On her final words, Lady Hamilton turned her back on William and glided over to an unsuspecting chap.

William remained rooted to his spot. The blow Lady Hamilton delivered was lethal. His body burned while his hands grew clammy. The buzzing in his ears caused him to sway with dizziness. To clear his muddled head, he gave it a hearty shake. As his eyes bumped around the room, the music increased to signal couples to the center of the dance floor. If he stood at the fringe of the dancers while they swirled around the room, perhaps he might catch sight of Pippa.

His head twisted back and forth trying to catch a glimpse of a familiar face. At one point, he stepped back to avoid a collision with the couples. After several frolics around by the duos, he realized Pippa was not on the dance floor. If Ross had been present, he would have banged William's head against the stone wall. It wasn't Pippa's nature to dance in this public setting— valuable time wasted. He sauntered toward the tables laden with food and drink in hopes of spying her when one of the king's messengers approached.

"Are you Lord McKinnon?"

"Aye."

"King Charles awaits. Follow me."

William's mind whirled. What had transpired between Pippa and the king? Was the king about to reprimand him or confiscate the wealth he acquired during his mercenary days? He headed into battle without any weapons—a deadly encounter. As he approached the lion's den, were all eyes upon him? He kept his gaze straight ahead not wanting to witness anyone's judgmental stares.

"Wait here." The messenger knocked once and slipped through the door. William stood facing the closed entrance not liking the results as thoughts dashed through his mind. His heart thumped hard against his chest. When he believed he might collapse, the door opened.

"You may enter."

Hesitant, William walked over the threshold. He looked behind when the assistant closed the heavy door and bolted it. With slow movements, he turned to face the king. The cool, dark room was quiet. Two lighted torches graced the sides of the throne chair upon which King Charles sat.

"Come forward, Lord McKinnon," he boomed.

On shaking legs, William trailed along the oriental carpet runner. His eyes traveled around the room noticing the extravagant tapestries, paintings, and golden fixtures. There were lush pillows and divans scattered around the enormous room. Silk curtains divided the room into sitting areas. From his observation, no one else graced the room except the two guards who flanked the throne.

When William arrived at the bottom of the steps descending from the throne, he knelt upon one knee with his head bowed and fisted arm across his chest. "My King, Lord William McKinnon at your service." He heard the king rise and start down the stairs. With one step remaining, the king's boots came into his view.

"Arise."

William looked up and saw the king's extended hand. He kissed the back of the king's hand and rose to his feet. He found himself face to face with the king even as the king stood on a stair. The rumors about the king's short stature appeared true.

"Join me for a drink."

"Thank you, my liege."

The guards lit the candles on the table and the surrounding area before backing away to allow privacy, yet close enough if needed. William and King Charles walked to the elaborate table filled with fruit, finger pies, wine, among other items William couldn't name, each cradled in a silver cup or spread on a decorative platter. Fragrant flowers graced the table along with stuffed peacocks—feathers included.

"Let us sit over here." The king led William to a set of satin and velvet divans. He sprawled upon one and indicated for William to take the other.

William made himself comfortable for the king was in no hurry to make his wishes known. They sipped their wine and eyed each other. King Charles gave nothing away by his behavior which proved to heighten William's distress. It took great willpower not to fidget.

"Your father remains missing?"

"Yes, my lord."

"You search for him?"

"Yes. I'm gathering information in hopes of tracking his location ... praying he still lives."

The king nodded in agreement. "And your mother, how does she fare?"

"She grieves yet trusts God for his safe return."

"Ahh."

William wondered why the king chose this line of questioning. Perhaps a trap? Or did he truly care what happened to his subjects?

"I received a report where your father's enemy burned the castle. Can you confirm this?"

"Yes, my lord." With each sip of wine, he became more relaxed in the king's presence. It didn't take long before the wine began to jumble his thinking. Since he preferred alertness, his wine consumption needed to cease. Instead of finishing it, he swirled it in the cup.

"Where dwells your wife and family?"

William chuckled. "I own no wife; nevertheless, my mother and siblings reside with Lord Nicolas Fairwick at Sanddown Castle."

"Hmm. You are a man without a home?"

William sat up and leaned his forearms on his legs. "True, but it has not concerned me. Finding my father consumes my time. Combing through the castle ruins for clues left by our enemy takes precedence over my own comfort. In addition, uncovering any family objects that survived the fire is important to me. I hope to find enough keepsakes to bring my mother comfort when I inform her, she may never return home. My guardian and I follow all leads on our adversaries. The lack of a place to call home is not pressing at this time."

"Ah, I can understand it. Your mother is unaware of the destruction?"

"Aye. This I regret but deem it best for all concerned. Dealing with my father's absence strains her. No need to add to her burden."

"You sound like a sensitive, as well as an honorable son."

William calmed a bit and grinned. "I try, my lord."

King Charles set aside his cup and clasped his hands together. "It is your honor and loyalty I depend upon."

"I am your humble servant, my liege lord."

The king steepled his fingers and stared into William's eyes. "It was brought to my attention you possess a betrothal contract to honor."

William's jaw clinched ... that little vixen. The king's questioning made perfect sense. She ran to the king crying foul before he confirmed the authenticity of the betrothal. "You must be referring to Lady Fairwick's possible forged betrothal."

A frown formed on the king's face as he leaned forward. "I take exception with your accusation."

"Forgive me, my king," William said without delay. "My words were poorly chosen. My mother neither confirmed nor denied the betrothal. A search is planned to find my father's copy to verify Lady Fairwick's claim."

The king's stern expression lessened, and he flopped back against his divan. "No need. I personally verified the two signatures and seals."

At a loss for words, William sat dumbfounded. His mind raced. How could he refute the king without stirring his anger? William seethed. Ensnared by a sixteen-year-old girl.

"You are without a home or a wife. Lady Fairwick can provide both. You need an heir; again, she can produce. Your tattered reputation ... well ..."

William's eyes snapped wide.

"... yes, I know all that transpires in my kingdom. Fairwick castle needs a strong leader since the death of Lord Phillip Fairwick. As an offspring of a valiant knight, I trust you can be an accomplished ruler. Your wealth can buy the materials to fortify one of my border castles in disrepair such as Fairwick Castle. Knowing my borders are secure pleases me. You do wish to please your king, do you not?"

"At all cost, my lord king." William sank deeper into the grave dug by the king. Every word he spoke acted as a shovel of dirt heaped on his head. The king's words rang of truth even though not what William wanted to hear.

"Is there any reason to prevent honoring your betrothal?"

William cleared his throat. "No, my king, but ..."

"Splendid!" He clapped his hands with delight. "Lady Fairwick, come forth."

Stunned, William looked about. Pippa emerged from a darkened corner of the room as she parted the sheer curtains. Without question, all he and the king had spoken touched her hearing. When the light shone upon her face, he sucked in a quick breath ... the woman he admired in the ballroom!

"Come, come!" The king's grin covered his face as he watched Pippa.

William's rage blinded him from her previous beauty. He hoped his flaming stare scalded her as she approached. With her face averted, her temperament remained hidden. No doubt, she gloated over her victory.

She stopped at the edge of their curtained area. Her hands remained clutched in front of her with her face cast downward.

King Charles strode up to her and took her hand. "Fear not, my young one. Since you have no one to represent you, I will step in as the surrogate." He released her hand and turned. "Guards, find the priest," he bellowed.

When Pippa lifted her head, a path of tears glistened in the candlelight. Her tears could not erase what she achieved this day. William's heart hardened. Woe to the lassie who captured her wild wolf, for she plunged into unknown danger.

# 16

William had a firm grip on Pippa's arm as they made their way down a palace hallway. Confused at his behavior, she questioned their future. During the ceremony, he had not acted improperly in front of the priest and king. His expressionless face had given nothing away. Now, as they followed a servant to a room offered by King Charles, her wariness increased.

When she noticed no others stirred about in the massive passageway, she whispered, "Release your tight hold."

"I think not, wife."

She pulled against his secure grasp, but to no avail.

Without looking her way, he asked, "Is there a problem with this arrangement?"

"Yes, and you know it," she said through tight lips.

He ignored her request and continued striding along. With his furious gait, she ran on her toes to avoid losing her slippers. Her free hand tugged on the bodice while trying to keep the pace. She feared her bosom might burst forth. The lace insert had long ago fallen and wedged in her corset. Her head pounded, and every muscle screamed with agony born from her strenuous week.

Unsure of her new husband, Pippa stayed silent for the rest of the trek. She regretted that they had been unable to converse before the king sprang the wedding idea on William. At least a short exchange could have paved the way for William to warm to the notion of marriage. Not surprised he disapproved of her scheme to ensure his compliance. She found his quiet calm frightening.

Lightheadedness from an empty stomach threatened to overtake her. She hoped not to swoon forcing William to drag her the rest of the way. The thought brought a cheerless smile to her dry lips. When she pictured his enjoyment of the act, it strengthened her resolve to endure.

At long last the servant stopped at an open door. "King Charles wishes you both great happiness on your wedding night and beyond. If you have any needs, please pull the bell rope and a servant will appear." He placed the key in William's hand, offered a slight bow and scurried away.

After hearing the words *wedding night* Pippa's heartbeat thumped hard against her ribs. Her breath came in short spurts. *God help me!*

William yanked her into the room. He released her arm causing her to stumble a couple of steps before falling against the bed. She grabbed the post to steady herself. When William shoved the door closed with his boot, it shook the walls.

Her narrowed gaze assessed her new husband. He stood near the door with hands on his hips and feet apart. As his nose flared with each breath, she waited to see if fire spewed forth. With the ridiculous picture lodged in her mind, she bit her lip to keep a nervous giggle from escaping.

"You have sealed our fate for all eternity!"

Pippa let go of the post and straightened. She let her arms dangle by her side and tried to appear unfazed by his outburst. Her chin lifted. "Our fathers composed the contract."

He soared across the room and grabbed both of her arms. His face inches from her own. "You rushed to the king before I had time to verify the document. You and you alone created this mess today."

Her back stiffened at his outburst. "How dare you place the blame at my door? I afforded you two weeks to fulfill your duty. 'Twas your delay which prompted my actions. I had no other choice."

"There is always another choice." He shoved away and stalked to the door. "You will stay here. I have matters to attend."

"I will not! My men await my return for further instructions."

His eyes became mere slits. "You will dwell here until my return."

"You have no right to force me to linger here while you go about your business."

"You relinquished your rights when you said, 'I do.' To guarantee your compliance, I will lock the door."

She rushed toward the door, but not before he pulled it closed. The key turned in the lock as she lunged for the handle. "Unlock this door at once!"

His cynical laughter floated under the threshold and faded away.

"Come back here this instant." Pippa kicked the door, and then yelped. She sank to the floor as her eyes burned. The slippers failed to protect her foot causing her toes to throb. She snatched both slippers off and hurled them against the door as tears of frustration trickled down her cheeks.

"How dare you treat me thusly, William McKinnon." For a moment she indulged in her tears. When crying failed to soothe her frustration, she pulled her sleeve across her sniffling nose and peered around the room. If she wished to have victory over their next verbal confrontation, she needed sustenance and a fortifying nap.

She hobbled to a draped table. Underneath she found a variety of tasty morsels to satisfy her growling stomach. With a half-eaten meat pie in her hand, she roamed the room looking for suitable attire in which to change. The one clothing item she found was a white gown and cap.

"I think not." She snatched them off the divan and stuffed them under the bed. "There will be no wedding night with me." While

123

on her knees, she noticed a fancy chamber pot sitting in the corner. Her face warmed at the implication. *Oh, dear.* Standing up, she dusted off her hands.

She eyed the large four-poster bed and shook her head. Walking over to the fireplace, she added more logs to the already roaring fire and curled up on the bear rug spread before the hearth. The smell of wood burning brought comfort as it reminded her of home. The warmth settled over her like a blanket providing security from a cold night. She tucked her hands under her cheek. *Beware, McKinnon. You will not find a submissive wife at our next encounter.*

William stormed down the palace footpath in search of Ross. His anger knew no bounds as his arms slashed to and fro by his side. When he passed a stable boy, he asked where to find his horse and guardian. The boy happily led him to one of the waiting areas.

"Ross, where are you?" William shouted. He had no patience to be a gentleman and wait for the boy to locate his man. He tramped along and continued to yell until Ross dashed from the third stable.

"Whit is amiss?" he asked out of breath.

"Get our horses. It's imperative we leave at once."

With no further explanation coming, Ross hurried to saddle their mounts. William remained outside pacing back and forth smashing his fist into the palm of his hand—grumbling. Servants scampered past with uneasiness.

He poked his head in the doorway. "Hurry, Ross."

At long last, Ross led their two mounts outside.

"Whit happened with tha king?"

William snatched the bridle from his hand. "I'll explain later." After swinging into his saddle, his horse responded to a strong nudge and bolted away from the palace. Ross followed close behind.

William's horse galloped until the road narrowed forcing him to slow to a walk. Peasants crowded the streets in celebration. It appeared that when the king resided in town, merry making took place in the city of London. Men draped over their ladies staggered while the women tittered in amusement. A revolting scene to William.

The two men meandered through the crowd and alleyways until reaching The Seven Stars Inn. They left their steeds in the capable hands of the stable master with specific orders for their horses' care. Ross remained silent until reaching their room where he bolted the door. "Tell me of the king."

William seized his haversack and threw it upon the bed. He whirled to face Ross. "The king compelled me to wed!"

Ross's eyes grew round. "To whom?"

His fisted hands went to his hips. "To the little lass you think so innocent."

Ross cocked his head. "Lady Fairwick?"

"Aye, *Lady Philippa Fairwick!* She is evil, Ross. She went behind my back and showed her betrothal to the king, and implied I had failed to honor the contract between our fathers."

He stalked over and grabbed his clothing from the wall peg and stuffed it inside his bag. Each repeated motion was jerky and uncontrolled. "Now I am saddled with the whelp for all eternity."

Ross walked over and placed his hand upon William's arm. With clothes scrunched in his hand, William's actions stilled, but his eyes stared at the bed. Hot breath snorted from his nose.

"Might I offer a word?" Not waiting on a reply, Ross removed his hand and asked, "Is it yer highest wish to find yer fither?"

He looked sideways at Ross. "Ye know it is."

"Will ye not follow every lead to make it happen?"

"Aye."

"If ye knew a mon had tha information that would lead to yer fither's whereabouts, would ye pursue him until he relinquished it?"

William began to calm amid the questioning by Ross. "You know 'tis true. Why this query when ye know my heart?"

"Ponder it. 'Tis tha same with Lady Fairwick. Her highest wish is to provide for her people and rebuild her castle. She knows a mon who can save all that she holds dear, and she pursued him to make it occur. The difference between ye two ... she had a legal bond to back up her demands."

William turned away from Ross. He abandoned his gear and walked to the window. Pressing his face against the cool pane, he looked down at the people mingling about. He bit his jaw.

"Even though ye hoped to find yer fither's document to confirm her claims, yer knight's honor is enough to direct yer path."

Each word spoken convicted William of his dishonorable behavior. If a man treated his sisters with such disrespect, he would call him out and settle it with swords. Yet, Pippa had no one to champion her cause or defend her honor. His jaw loosened as his eyes closed against his shameful actions.

"Where is yer bride?"

"I left her at the palace."

"Och?"

The one word condemned. The memory of the key turning in the lock made his stomach quiver. William left the window and came to stand in front of Ross. "The palace will be where I lodge for the next few days. I'm not sure what other surprises the king has in store for me, but I will send word when possible."

Ross patted his shoulder. "All weel be well. Ye must have faith. Once we're away, we'll resume our hunt for yer fither."

"Thank you, Ross."

"Allow me to pack yer bag while ye freshen up for yer bride.

William groaned. "Please, Ross."

Ross laughed and went about his task. "I'll meet ye at tha stables."

William jumped down the stairs to the first floor to scrub off the road dirt in the Inn's wash tub. He changed into clean clothes. No need to parade around in his wedding attire. Refreshed, he met Ross at the stable to gather his belongings and be on his way. Atop his horse, he offered a weak smile and waved farewell to his friend.

The hour had grown late which meant more drunkards wandered the streets. With his hand on his sword, he used his boot to push several men aside so he could pass through. The city lamps lining the streets were a welcomed sight. The glow chased away the darkness leaving less of a chance to encounter unsavory men. The closer he came to the palace, the safer his route. Palace guards were interspersed along the way. Their presence provided protection letting him relax his watchfulness and allow his mind to wander. Of course, his thoughts darted to the red haired, blue-eyed beauty now his wife. She appeared shorter than he remembered but no less fierce.

As he approached the front landing of the palace, a groomsman caught the bridle. "Good evening, sir."

William swung down and unlatched his travel bag. "I'm a guest of King Charles tonight."

"Give your name to yonder fella. He'll direct you."

"Thank you. Please see to it my horse receives excellent care." He presented a coin to solidify the request. The man graced him with a toothy smile before leading his horse away.

William repeated his name to the next man who assigned a messenger to lead him inside. With a raised brow he said, "We weren't aware you had vacated the premises, Lord McKinnon. Is your wife with you?"

'Twas obvious William's departure was unacceptable. "No, she stayed in our room. I had business to conduct before retiring for the evening."

"I see."

To avoid the throng of party goers they wove their way around the gardens and entered a side door. The entrance was no less grand with its marble foyer and grand staircase.

"If my memory serves me, you are assigned a room on the second floor in the west wing."

A simple shrug was William's reply. After his wedding vows, he had been in such a state of anger, he failed to observe how many flights of stairs they ascended. This trip his mind recorded each twist and turn.

"I trust you have the key in your possession?"

"Aye. Thank you again for your assistance. I can manage from here."

"I'm sure you can."

His sarcasm wasn't lost on William. He watched the servant strut around the corner before he turned back to the closed door. With his free hand, he fished the key from his pocket. He stared as it lay in his palm. The weight of Ross's words caused his shoulders to stoop. Honor. He sighed and turned the key.

# 17

A stream of light caressed Pippa's closed lids alerting her to the arrival of morning. The smell from the smoldering hearth tickled her nose. She stretched. Every bone ached from her place on the floor.

'Twas obvious her groom never returned during the night to perform his husbandly duties of which she was thankful. A slight noise from behind caused her to jerk upright with eyes wide open. There in the wing-backed chair sat William with one boot resting on his knee and his hands folded in his lap—watching her.

"'Tis time to be up, wife."

During the night pieces of hair worked loose and now dangled in her face. She pushed the offending strands behind her ear and stared at William. Was he still angry with her? Would he attempt to consummate their marriage this morning? His matter-of-fact tone hid the answer while his emotionless eyes touched each part of her body. A quiver slithered down her spine.

He rose to his feet, towering over her still seated form. "Will you remain on the stone floor all day? Get up." He extended his hand. "I'll request a tub and hot water. You have one hour to make yourself presentable."

Hesitant, she placed her trembling hand into his warm, calloused palm. His grasp was firm making her feel protected in some way. He pulled her up and stepped back as he released her hand. "Don't dawdle. We have much to accomplish this day."

On his way to the door, she found her voice. "What must we achieve today?" She cringed at her pitiful question as if already relinquishing her fate to her new husband. He might think her weak.

"We'll talk in one hour." The door closed with a quiet click.

Rattled from their exchange, Pippa stood staring at the door. William was a mystery. Last night he yelled and stomped like a child, and this morning he appeared calm. "What are you planning, William McKinnon?" Noises from outside shook her out of her daze.

She walked to the window and looked out on the palace gardens. Groundskeepers dug in the soil while others trimmed the ornamental hedges. The flower beds burst with fall blossoms that edged the walkway. Such a lovely sight; yet it seemed a waste of manpower and coinage when she compared it to home. At Fairwick castle there was no time for such luxuries. Their resources filled hungry bellies and kept the fortress secure. A loud knock upon the door caused her to flinch.

She turned to face the door and realized she had done nothing to make herself presentable. "Enter."

William stormed in. "Never tell one to enter when you know not who is on the other side."

His tone set the mood. "I'm in the king's palace. No harm will come my way."

Two strong wills met in the middle of the room. Within inches of one another, William said, "You will have a care. As my wife there is protocol to follow."

His warm breath smacked her face. "Just as repeating a vow does not change my character, acquiring a husband doesn't make one daft unless he ..."

Someone cleared his throat. Their heads whipped around to see men holding a tub while others awaited with buckets of steaming water. Pippa was mortified yet responded first. "Please excuse our rude manners. You may place the tub before the hearth." She walked around William and halted by the door.

While waiting for the servants to complete their tasks, William added logs and stoked the fire. He wiped his hands on his trousers and stood.

After emptying the buckets, the men filed out with their heads averted. "Thank you, gentlemen, for your service," Pippa said to each one.

The last man shut the door.

She looked at William. "That was not well done ... *husband*."

He stalked to the door. "Do not lesson me on decorum. You have one hour."

This time the door slammed and locked. With fisted hands by her side, she stomped her bare foot. "Do not lesson me!" she yelled. With eyes fastened on the door, she willed him to return. No sound arose from the hallway. "A challenging future looms ahead of us, Lord William McKinnon ... however ..." She leaned her head over and flipped her hair back with the snap of her neck. "... I'm up for the challenge."

"Do not lesson me on decorum," she mocked as she made her way to the steaming tub. Sitting on the floor, she rolled down her stockings. The fluffy rug felt soft against her wiggling toes. Not wishing her water to cool, she stood and began the arduous task of shedding her dress and underclothes. Her discarded clothing lay in a puddle as she stepped into her bath.

*Mmm ... what a luscious treat.*

The long tub proved less cramped than the round one she used at home. She stretched her legs out, leaned back, and closed her eyes. Not often did she partake of such a luxury, and she planned to enjoy every moment of it. Her arms floated as her mind rehashed the last few days.

No matter how often she revisited her past decisions, she found no fault in what took place. She sighed, confident William would grow accustomed to the situation and make the best of it. Of course, he need not think he would dominate her in all things. She controlled a castle, trained fighting men, fought battles, buried friends, bandaged hurts, among other unpleasant activities. *I am a warrior!*

No man would control her. She dunked her head under the water and held her breath. When she thought drowning imminent, she burst forth spraying water all about the tub. Her fingers raked her hair aside and spied a bar of soap—what a delight. At home she only possessed a slither of soap. She lathered her hair and her body before dunking several times to rinse.

The water grew tepid. She dared not waste more time for fear William might surge through the door and catch her bare as a newborn. The oversized soft towel was like velvet against her skin. She dawdled while rubbing dry dreaming of what it would be like to live in such a place. What a frivolous thought.

What a pity she must don the same clothes from yesterday. Before picking up her dirty clothes, she glanced around the room in hopes of seeing another option. With the towel wrapped tight around her body, she padded through the room. Nothing stood out until she rounded the huge four-poster bed. There hanging outside the wardrobe was a new dress. Was it for her?

Sneaking up as if it might disappear, she stroked the silky material. She had never caressed anything so fine. Opening the door on the wardrobe, she discovered new stockings, chemise and bloomers. *Oh, dear. Who placed these here?* No matter whether ordered by the king or if William provided them, heat rose in her neck. As her father used to say, joyfully receive what is freely given.

The downy towel fell to the floor as she gathered up the clothing and laid them upon the bed. Each item slid on her body as if made especially for her which gave her pause. Who knew her measurements? Shaking her head, she continued.

Once fully clothed, she twirled around and giggled. In her exuberance, she failed to hear the door open.

"Well, I see you found your new garments."

Pippa stumbled to a stop to see William leaning against the closed door with arms crossed. Her eyes traveled from his face to her saddle bags draped over his arm. Those had been in Henry's care. She straightened and smoothed her hands down the front of her dress. "Yes. Of whom do I owe my gratitude ... you?"

He pushed away from the door and walked up to her. "No gratitude required." He twirled his finger around one of her damp curls. "You are my wife, after all."

She caught her breath. How was she to respond? She stepped back and curtsied. "Thank you, kind sir." When she looked up, his expression was most peculiar. Had she blundered?

He tossed the saddle bags onto the bed. "Gather your belongings. The king delivered his blessing on our marriage and has granted our leave. Let us make haste."

The gentle moment was lost. As she scurried around the room scooping up her clothes and shoving them into the bags, she said, "I must speak with Henry and my men. They await my instructions."

"That is no longer your concern. I have made all necessary arrangements. The men and horses await us."

She paused. With her back to William, her eyes closed, and her lips pinched . Now was not the time to define their roles in this marriage. She would have plenty of opportunity to clear up his misunderstanding of the position she planned to maintain. She inhaled a calming breath. "I'm almost ready."

After completing her task, she longingly scanned the lavish room. What a pity to leave it practically untouched. Her one night residing in a room of grandeur—wasted. Even the bed remained intact. She trudged to the door and her impatient husband. With a last glance over her shoulder, she sighed and thought of what could have been.

---

Seeing Fairwick guards next to Ross dredged up the distasteful events of the past few days. Fuming, William set a reckless pace out of London. No matter how he visualized it, his destiny had snapped shut. He teetered between reluctant respect for Pippa and anger at a young girl who snared him. His thoughts whirled with all that had taken place. In the beginning, fear of the king's rebuke for his mercenary days twisted his gut. Relief flooded his soul when it was not the case for his summons. In its place, a forced wedding in the midst of his family crisis received precedence in the king's agenda. 'Twas a worse outcome. The fate of his father weighed heavy on his mind; yet, instead of searching for his father he rode toward Fairwick Castle. The blame of this debacle belonged on Pippa.

He purposefully placed her in the middle of their entourage. It provided her extra protection; but truth be told, with his state of mind, he didn't want her close at hand.

"Sir William?" Ross shouted.

"Yes, Ross."

"Shall we rest our mounts? Tha journey's speed has been brutal."

William squirmed at the reprimand.

Ross rode closer. "In addition, ye have a bride to consider."

Once again Ross brought him to task. Up to this point, he had refused the idea of caring for another. "As you wish." William signaled. Several hundred feet from the road they found shelter under a clump of trees.

Pippa's guards surrounded her. She hopped from her horse and dashed for the bushes. Henry rushed to catch up. "Lady Fairwick, allow me to search the area."

"Stay back. All is well," she squeaked. Wearing a frown, Henry waited on the fringe as he inspected the grassy field for danger.

William glanced at his guardian. Ross raised his brow. The silent rebuke hit its mark. William had much to atone for where his new bride was concerned.

"Robert, spread a blanket for your lady upon which to eat her repast." It pleased him when Robert obeyed even though he belonged to the Fairwick Family.

With slow, stiff moves, Pippa emerged from her hiding place to find William and Henry staring at one another. Ignoring them, she stretched and gauged her surroundings.

"Come, m' lady. Food awaits your pleasure," William said. He indicated the blanket where bread, cheese, and meat pies rested.

Pippa looked about. "Is everyone partaking?"

The men looked down and scuffed their boots in the dirt.

"I shall neither rest nor eat unless all are permitted the same courtesy." Concern etched her face while her eyes darted to each man.

William's mouth pinched. Did she not understand men rebuffed coddling? Ross's glare changed his view. "Of course. Men, alternate ones who eat with those who keep watch until all are satisfied." William grasped Pippa's hand and led her to the blanket. She tripped over a stump and nearly plunged face down except for William's quick action.

"Thank you." With speed she righted herself and claimed her hand. "'Twould seem I have legs made of feathers."

"I fear my thoughts wandered during the journey. Our lengthy travel has left you saddle weary. I'm unaccustomed to a woman's delicate nature. Please forgive my shortsightedness," he said with formality. Her head whipped around so fast, he feared her neck might break. He watched as her back stiffened and her eyes narrowed.

"Do not fear; I am made of stronger substance." Plopping down, she presented her back—dismissing him.

William observed as Henry knelt and offered her drink. Her quick smile and kind *thank you* provoked his ire. How did a tiny girl irritate him so? He apologized for his negligence; and instead of gratitude, it annoyed her. He stomped away shaking his head.

Ross fell into step with William. "What puzzles ye?"

William glanced toward Pippa and kept walking. "That woman ... she creates turmoil."

"I see."

William snorted and stopped in the middle of the field far from his bride. "Ross, if you have more to say, then say it."

"Ye have a young warrior bride. No doubt, she recoiled at tha comparison to one of a delicate nature."

William's hands went to his hips. There were times when he detested Ross's accurate assessments. After a moment his hands dropped, and he turned to see Pippa's head close to Henry. "Look. She speaks with her commander as if he were her husband. Mayhap they are closer than we surmised."

*Tsk. Tsk.* "Dinna allow yer imagination to create trouble ahead of its season. She is but talking with one she trusts. Give her time to adjust. She will coom to trust ye."

*Humph.* "Mark my word, I won't be deceived." While he watched Henry and Pippa converse, two of her men mounted up and trotted down the road toward her home. *What are ye about, Philippa Fairwick McKinnon?*

"Did ye witness that? Two of her men sprinted north toward her home! This leaves us shorthanded for protection." He turned toward Ross. "Do ye see what I must endure? She irritates me at every turn thinking she retains power and rules."

Edmund, one of Pippa's men, galloped into the area from the south. "Riders approaching. Take cover!"

"How much time?" William asked.

"Sixty heartbeats."

Without thought, each person launched into action. When one said to take cover, they knew danger was forthcoming. William rushed over to Pippa and grabbed her hand. As he pulled her toward safety, she lunged backwards to retrieve the blanket.

"Quickly. Quickly." William's heart surged in his chest. Each man and horse ran for the thick foliage. "Pippa cover your dress with your dark cloak. I'll handle your horse." He barked orders as he ran. "Men, no glinting weapons!"

They voiced no other words as they rushed to hide. With so few men, to engage an enemy meant possible death to all ... or worse ... capture of Pippa. William shuddered at the thought.

Once her cloak was fastened, she freed William of her horse and weaved through the underbrush. Henry accompanied Pippa deeper into the forest. With a horse in tow, each crouched behind a large tree. As one hand held the bridle close, the other hand cradled the horse's lips in hopes of preventing them from crying out.

William signaled for Edmund and Peter to remain hidden with him at the forest edge. Robert seized the McKinnon horses and urged them deeper into the woods. In a short time, thundering hooves approached. As the traveling men came into view, William gulped. He recognized the leader—a former mercenary. A man who showed no mercy.

When the fifteen riders bolted past the hiding place, William released his pent-up breath. He and the leader had crossed words in the past, and he knew nothing good would have come from an encounter. In silence they all held their positions. Fear that one adversary might double back kept them hidden a few minutes longer.

William motioned for the front line of defense to scoot back into the woods. Once they cleared a line of trees, they stood and went to reclaim their mounts. As William approached Pippa, an atrocious smell accosted his nose.

Momentarily, he ignored the dreadful scent. Instead, he allowed his wrath to spew forth. "You sent two of your men north, alone. They are surely in danger when those rebels overtake them. Not to mention, it has diluted our forces to protect you." He grabbed her arm. "Don't ever give an order again without my consent."

Her eyes glistened with a film of tears as her hand covered her mouth. "My men," she whimpered. When William loosened his grip, she plunged to her knees in agonizing prayer.

# *18*

"What's that offending odor?" William demanded. "It smells of death."

The horrendous smell no longer affected Pippa. Thoughts of her men in danger caused her to rock back and forth as she prayed. *Protect them, Mighty Lord. Hold Patrick and John in Your powerful hand. Hide them from the enemy. Walk alongside them as in days of old with Daniel in the lion's den. I beseech Thee, Oh, Holy God and Creator of life, don't allow my decision to bring the deaths of my trusted servants.* She covered her face as tears leaked between her fingers. *I couldn't bear it, Father ... I couldn't bear it!*

"Ross ... Henry ... help me search out from whence comes this stench. I fear what we might uncover."

Pippa scrubbed away her tears and stood on shaking legs. She observed the men as they beat the bushes with their swords searching for the source which reeked. With no desire to find anything dead, she decided to accomplish an important chore. She led her horse away from the slashing noise to a dense area of bushes. There she secured his bridle to a tree branch and rummaged through her saddle bags. With a powerful tug, out came her trousers and shirt.

"Peter ... Edmund," she called out. "Assist me."
Both men ran to her position.

"Hold this blanket high and face away. This dress is a nuisance," she fumed.

"M' lady do ye not wish to wait until ye reach the castle?" Peter asked.

"No," she mumbled as the dress engulfed her head. "I can't fight or be of use when this irritating garb assaults my ankles with every step. It'll be but a moment. Hold fast."

She heard the two men shuffling their feet. Few wanted such a mundane duty when finding a dead animal remained an option. Men—their notions confounded Pippa. After she laced up her final boot, she peeked over the blanket. On the other side of the blanket stood her husband wearing his usual scowl.

"What's the meaning of this?"

Pippa stepped around the men. "I'm prepared for travel." She dismissed Peter and Edmund. "You may join the search."
Expecting William's frown to deepen, he surprised her.

"'Tis a sound tactic. I feel confident you can defend yourself without the restrictions of a dress. Make sure your knives are secure."

"Do you expect further trouble?"

"We must be prepared for all possibilities. I like it not those mercenaries are close at hand."

She sucked in a quick breath. "You know those men?"

"Aye. The leader is a man of no mercy. I never trusted him out of my sight." As they walked side by side toward the rest of their party, Henry came running.

"Ross uncovered a grisly scene. Come quickly."

William broke into a run. Pippa followed close on his heels. The closer they came to Ross, the stronger the smell. She pulled her tunic over her nose as her eyes watered.

Henry's arm prevented her from going further. "Ye don't wish to see what's been uncovered."

She watched as William crashed to his knees and cried out as if a wounded animal. "What is it?" she whispered.

"Three men from the McKinnon clan. Ross seems to think they traveled with Lord McKinnon when he disappeared."

"Oh, no." Sadness squeezed her heart. Ignoring Henry, she walked to the grim scene. The fiery words flying from William's lips scorched her hair. She saw the reason for his curses. Secured to a tree were three decomposing bodies with arrows through their hearts. Pippa closed her eyes and hung her head—executed! The odor ceased to affect her eyes. Instead, her fresh tears sprang from the deep well of grief.

She waited while William and Ross grieved their fallen comrades—William on his knees. Ross's hand rested upon William's trembling shoulder. Each day brought survival difficulties, but the murder of defenseless men ... cruel.

When William stood, he turned her way. His tear-stained face— ravaged with misery. "Do you wish to take them home for burial or shall we bury them here?" Pippa asked softly.

He rubbed his face with both hands. "I fear their bodies are too fragile for transporting them such a distance. We will scout out an appropriate resting place close by."

"I'm familiar with this area. Tell me what you need, and I'll suggest a location."

"Is this your land?"

"No, but I traversed this range often as a young girl. We are a little over a day's ride to the castle. A few hours down the road there is luscious grass surrounded by huge shade trees. Would this be to your liking?"

William glanced down at his former companions. "How will we secure them?"

"We can wrap each in a blanket and tie them to my horse. I'll ride pillion with another." She didn't wait for him to answer. "Henry, bring three blankets."

To allow William and Ross more privacy, she walked to the horses where Henry had commandeered three coverlets. "Take them to William." The rest of her men waited for instructions.

"Peter ... Edmund, please guard our camp until the bodies are ready. Robert, you may give assistance to the task. I'll remain with the horses." She watched them head out, eager to do her bidding. Robert was a seasoned warrior and acquainted with death. He could handle the gloomy mission. Peter and Edmund were strong and fierce young men with sharp eyes which made them outstanding guards. Pippa gave thanks for such fine men in her service.

She leaned against a tree and propped one foot at the base. For a while she listened as birds tweeted a soothing tune until the men's grunts and swear words interrupted the song. Her heart ached for their sorrow. She knew all too well the wretchedness brought on by death. Oh, how she longed for days of peace ... no enemies to vanquish.

She looked heavenward and closed her eyes. "O Lord God, Who is the beginning and the end of all things, I beseech Thee, remember the pain these men didst suffer and endure. Their enemies surrounded them like furious lions ready to devour. Thou, Who holds the earth in the palm of Thy hand, be mindful of their loved ones engulfed in bitter pain. And forget not the entire McKinnon clan who grieves even now with no knowledge of their loved ones' whereabouts. Oh, Father, bring peace where there is chaos, bring comfort where distress abounds. And My Mighty Warrior and Savior, if I may be so bold, bring fire and destruction upon the heads of those who committed this cowardly act! Amen and amen."

Engrossed in her prayer, she failed to hear the men approach.

"Ye pray with such power. Think ye, Lady McKinnon," Ross said.

"I covet your prayers," William said through a strained voice. "Come, we are prepared for our journey. You will ride with me."

Henry whistled to alert the guards. Pippa looked to see three small bundles tied to her horse. Exposed to the elements and scavengers for nigh on to three months, their bones scarcely held together. 'Twas not difficult for one horse to bear the burden. Atop his horse, William extended his hand to Pippa. She looked up. His dark eyes beckoned her. When she offered her hand, his firm grip snatched her upward with little effort. She settled behind him and wrapped her arms about his waist. Oftentimes, she had ridden like this as a girl; today it was awkward. He was her husband, yet still a stranger.

She issued instructions. "Robert, lead us to the grassy meadow northwest of the castle. You remember the spot of which I speak?"

"Yes, m' lady." Robert seized the lead, followed by Peter, Ross, William, Henry, and Edmund. Henry held the bridle of the horse containing the bodies. The somber pace meant a prolonged journey.

---

The party arrived at their destination as the orange sun hid among the forest. William gazed at the final resting place for the deceased warriors—a small valley several hundred yards from the road, cradled a lush meadow. The tall grass swayed in the breeze as if dancing to a lively tune. Trees touching the sky offered shade and protection from any harsh elements. Pippa was correct— unspoiled landscape.

"I will dismount first," William said.

After his feet touched ground, his hands wrapped around His wife's tiny waist. He lifted her down with ease and met her gaze. Her solemn face didn't diminish the depths of her blue eyes. Their allure was like that of a polished sapphire.

A small frown formed on her face. "Is something wrong?"

William's wandering mind snapped back as his hands fell away. "'Tis naught. My mind drifted out to sea." He shook his head. "Where do you suggest we dig?"

"Over there." She pointed to a recessed area in the dark shadow of the forest edge. Walking toward an old tree with droopy limbs, she said, "To me, this sheltered spot is serene." Her arms spread wide as she turned around.

He rubbed his chin and made a slow perusal of the site. "'Tis good."

He left Pippa and strode over to their companions. "Lady McKinnon has chosen a peaceful resting place. Find a sturdy branch with which to dig."

Henry led the horse bearing the dead bodies to Pippa. She secured the reins to a low bough. Together they untied the men and placed them on the ground with care.

"'Tis a dreadful business," Henry muttered.

"Yes. These poor men didn't have a chance to defend themselves."

"Do ye believe yer new husband to seek vengeance?"

"I would expect nothing less."

On horseback, Robert and Edmund guarded the area while Pippa gathered stones to cover the grave. William and Ross used their swords to cut the soil and peal back the top layer of grassland. The others prepared the burial site by digging a large hole. William had decided to bury them as they had died—together.

For over an hour, the pounding of the ground echoed through the valley. To dig without the proper tools required immense effort. When completed, Ross and William placed the three in the large dirt opening. Peter and Henry shoved the loose soil into the burial pit and rolled the layer of sod over their bodies to shield them from predators. In the end, the party circled for last words.

William paid tribute to the fallen knights ... their importance within the McKinnon clan ... their courage and valor in the face of their assassins—not one soldier had closed his eyes as he waited for death. He expounded on each man's finest attributes; but when he spoke of their families, his voice choked. Ross stepped up and offered a prayer for their souls and for wisdom on how to proceed. At the conclusion of the burial, each person placed stones around the grave. As they shuffled back from the site, the subdued group looked to William for direction.

William regarded his diverse group. Ross and Robert were near the age of his father. Yet, they were men of wisdom and tremendous skill born from long years of experience. Henry, Peter, and Edmund ... their brute strength and fighting prowess made them excellent warriors at one's back. Then his eyes landed on

Pippa ... his wife. That gave him pause. In his opinion, she was a warrior child—young yet deadly accurate with her weapons. As she held his stare, the dark circles under her cobalt eyes were the catalyst for his decision.

"This day has proven quite draining. Not to mention, with dusk upon us, I don't wish to risk injury to our horses by pressing onward. We will camp nearby."

"A hollowed-out hillside residing over this ridge will provide protection from the elements," Pippa said. She looked about and gaged the area. "Peter and Edmund, gather the digging sticks for our cook fire."

"No." William said. "There will be no fire. It would serve as a beacon to our enemies."

"Do you think the mercenaries will return?" she asked with round eyes.

"I know not, but we can't take the chance."

"Agreed," Ross added.

"We will need to eat what's left of our earlier provisions," William said.

"Of course." She offered a slight nod. "When you are ready, I will lead you to the new location. A nearby stream will deliver cool water for our flasks. It's best done before the sun hides for the night."

"Mount up," William commanded. "Lead on, Lady McKinnon." As Pippa led the small party, William turned in his saddle for one last look. All day he had allowed his emotions to wreak havoc on his soul ... but no more. As he replayed the events surrounding the death of his father's men, the sadness of his heart turned to stone.

*I will avenge you, my friends. Have no doubt! I will avenge you!*

# *19*

While Peter, Robert, and his wife filled the water bags at the stream, William helped Ross prepare their horses for the night. As he lifted off one saddle, he thought about Pippa. He knew she deserved recognition. Her correct assessment of the land produced an ideal place to spend the night.

Burrowed out in the hillside was an indention with three sides. There was room for the men and a place to house their horses far enough away, yet still sheltered. The slight elevation of their refuge afforded them a good view of their surroundings. No enemy would catch them unaware this eventide.

"She is resourceful," Ross commented.

William smiled to himself. "Yes, she is." Over the years, his love for Ross had grown. He never failed to see the good in everyone—an admirable quality. As far as Ross was concerned, even his enemy or the local reprobate owned one redeemable quality.

Ross stroked his horse's nose. "I admire yer wife. Tha lass might be young, but she overcooms her youthfulness with wisdom and cunning; and dost not forget, she has tha ability to throw knives with accuracy. Wouldn't ye agree?" He looked sideways at William.

William sighed with force. "Is there more?"

"Nay." He walked his horse over to the rope line leaving William alone.

There was always extra when it came to Ross's lessons. He never said anything without a purpose. William leaned his head against his horse and breathed deep. This is what William knew—horses, swordplay, and warfare. What to do with a wife—he had no idea. Her voice floated on the breeze while she conversed with her men at the stream. He hoped she wasn't devising some plan without his involvement.

He tied his horse's reins to the rope line stretching between two trees. Attaching the bridle to the rope secured the horses for the night. He dared not remove their halters. Having their saddles on the ground was risky at best. If an enemy appeared, they would be at a disadvantage.

Edmund laid out three small cheese chunks, four meat pies, and one loaf of hard bread for dinner while Henry perched high above keeping watch. William and Ross joined Edmund as the three others returned from the stream.

"Peter, take a meat pastry to Henry and then join us. We'll divide the rest of the food amongst ourselves," Pippa suggested as she dropped to her knees next to the fare. She broke off a piece from the loaf of bread and snagged a bite of cheese.

William refrained from speaking out against Pippa assuming control. He supposed it was a natural response for her to command her men. Instead, he said, "I want two men guarding the camp tonight. We will each rotate the watch. First, Henry and Peter, followed by Ross and Edmund. Last will be Robert and me."

"What about me?" Pippa asked as she stood.

All eyes swung between Pippa and William.

"You will not take a watch."

"Why not?" Her voice grew in strength.

William recognized that tone. He had heard it often enough from his sisters. If he allowed it to continue, there could be an explosion, of sorts. His face grew serious. "I wish for you to saddle our horses the last hour of my watch. It will prove helpful if the horses are ready to ride as the sun rises. This allows your men a longer reprieve."

She stared at him. No one moved or spoke while they waited. When he thought she might refuse, she said *as you wish* and then sat down. Unconvinced the subject was settled, William decided to accept her response.

Darkness enveloped the group as they ate the meager meal. Not a feast by any means, but sufficient to curb their growling stomachs. Peter grabbed his water flask, food, and Henry's meat pie before trudging up the embankment.

Edmund and Robert spoke about competing in previous tournaments. William listened while watching Pippa. Their humorous remembrances of a particular jester brought a smile to her face. It transformed her from a warrior to a young maiden. For an instant, he had a glimpse of the woman he gazed upon in the king's court with sparkling sapphire eyes ... breathtaking.

When the men ceased their reflections, he watched her relaxed countenance change. Her brows slanted above her eyes as if worry smothered out her joy. Her distraught expression caused a jolt to his heart like no other. He didn't love his wife and actually, held anger against her at times. Yet, his protective instinct bubbled up from his soul creating a yearning to destroy all reasons that caused her anxiety.

Ross nudged William's foot. "I'm turning in. Remember, Lady McKinnon furnished her coverlet for tha burial."

William looked at Ross. "I'm aware of it."

Ross rolled his eyes heavenward before settling back on William. "Cool air weel blow tonight. She weel need protection from tha chill."

William's stomach flipped when he realized the ramifications of Ross's words. His head turned toward Pippa who ambled toward the horses. Since he, too, retained no blanket, he would need to offer warmth from his own body. Could he cuddle her and remain unaffected? Debatable.

149

Ross's raised brows propelled him to action. He wiped his hands on his breeches and headed toward his wife. With the thought of embracing her for the night, his body betrayed him. This irritated him. By the time he arrived where she was brushing her horse, he wore a scowl.

"Wife?"

His gruff voice startled her. She whipped around with a knife in hand. After her initial surprise, she huffed. "Don't sneak up on me," she snapped. "I could have stabbed you."

He released a cynical laugh. "I think not."

She glared at him as she slid her knife into her waist band. Even though darkness reigned, the moonlight reflected her pinched mouth. "What is your purpose?"

His back stiffened. How could he have forgotten her straightforward, biting tongue? He forced his jaw to relax. "Forgive my intrusion. I desire a word with you."

"Yes?"

"Since, in kindness, you relinquished your blanket for my friends, I wish to provide you warmth for the night."

She tilted her head. "Oh? You possess an extra coverlet?"

"I possess my clan plaid and body warmth." He watched her eyes widen in fright. He wondered how his offer caused such a response. He observed different emotions skip across her eyes while she remained mute.

"Is there a problem with this arrangement?" he asked.

"No ... no problem except I have no need of your services."

"My services? Pippa, I fail to understand your hesitancy unless you are fearful of your response to my closeness." He expected his statement to present a challenge for her. If he knew anything about his wife, she never backed away from a challenge.

"My response?" She snorted. "Do not flatter yourself."

Heat skittered up his neck. "I have no time to brandish words with you. I need rest before my guard duty." He grasped her arm and hauled her toward the shelter.

"There is no need for this show of force."

He stopped midway to the covered lodging and whirled her around. Inches apart, William held fast. "When I release my hold, I expect you to walk beside me until we reach our abode. There we will spend the duration of the night side by side for your comfort and added protection. I require no further debate on the matter. Am I clear?" With impaired vision, he wasn't sure, but he thought smoke billowed from her nostrils.

"Of course, oh, mighty husband. How could I refuse your generous offer? Please lead on."

William counted to ten. He had always considered himself a calm warrior in the face of opposition and seldom allowed words to stir his wrath. It could prove deadly during an enemy encounter. However, when it came to his petite wife, she provoked his anger with ease. After a deep breath, he presented his elbow to her.

She hesitated.

He waited. A hand slipped through his crooked arm. They strolled up to the hollowed-out retreat. He hoped their heated conversation had gone unnoticed, and was thankful to find Ross, Edmund, and Robert resting against their saddles.

"I prepared our place here in the middle." The added grass and leaves further cushioned the hard-packed earth. When Pippa declined to answer, he sank upon the makeshift bed. He placed his sword and belt above his saddle and extended his hand toward his bride.

Again, she eyed him as if he might ravish her.

"Come, Pippa. You are safe with me."

Before lying down, she removed her knives and sword. She knelt upon the ground and laid her weapons to her side. "Where is my saddle?"

"You have no need of it. You will reside upon my breast with my arm securing you to my side."

"I like it not."

"I am weary. Come."

Pippa scooted nearer. With a slight tug to her hand, she tumbled upon his chest. His arm pulled her close to his side. "Snuggle under the plaid and get comfortable. We need our rest."

She squirmed and fidgeted until at long last her movement ceased. Her head found a home high on his chest under his jawbone. With a slight turn of his head, her hair tickled his face. When he breathed deep, the aroma of the palace soap attacked his nostrils. It was satisfying. In fact, her body next to his was quite pleasing—soft curves against hard muscle. After their heated words, he was surprised when contentment flooded his spirit. His body relaxed. Slumber soon claimed his mind.

A hand on William's shoulder brought him to high alert. He opened his eyes to see Ross.

"'Tis yer turn, m' lord."

Pippa roused. "Is something amiss?"

"No. 'Tis my watch." He eased out from under her weight and lowered her down. "You may sleep a bit longer. I'll awaken you when time to saddle up."

William gathered his weapons and secured them to his waist. Off to one side he noticed Edmund plunk down to nap a few hours before sunrise. He and Ross strode away from the sleeping men to where Robert waited.

"All is quiet at this time," Ross said. "The ridge is a good vantage point."

William clapped Ross on the shoulder. "Thank you. Get some much-deserved sleep. Robert and I will keep a watchful eye."

The two men trekked on light feet as they left camp. No chatter exchanged as they crept to their designated positions. Robert patrolled the ridge above their camp while William guarded the rise from the east. Each man knew to stay alert to unusual sounds, for an enemy could pounce at any time. Nighttime illuminated by a full moon meant their foe's vision was equal to their own. Vigilance was imperative.

In the wee hours before dawn, William stood to stretch. He waved a signal to Robert and received one in return. That's when he saw movement off to the east in the plains where the McKinnon men laid in eternal rest. He crouched down and pulled out his spy glass. He scanned the grasslands with a slow deliberate sweep. On his second pass, the moon peeped from behind the dark clouds and lit up the area. His heart pounded in his chest. The mercenaries had doubled back.

William raced down the hillside and gestured wildly to Robert who dashed from his spot to join William at the camp. Their pounding feet awakened the drowsy group. Each jumped to strap on their weapons and ready their horses. When William skidded into the busy campsite, he could have kissed Pippa. She had risen early and saddled half of the horses.

From William's urgency, all understood danger lurked. Pippa left Peter to finish preparing the horses and ran to meet William.

"The mercenaries are on the grasslands. We must make haste," he murmured.

"How many?" Robert asked.

"From my limited view, I guess about fifteen or more."

Curse words flew from Edmund.

"We should stand and fight." Edmund insisted.

"No. I will not risk our lives for no cause. One or more of us could be injured or killed. No ... we'll ride around this ridge and pray for a clear path to safety."

Pippa interrupted. "I know a place." She hurried on to say, "Not two miles from here is a concealed cave behind thick vines and brush. During the wet season there is a slight waterfall over the vines. If we stay far enough ahead, we have a fighting chance."

This time William didn't hesitate to trust his wife's advice. "Show us the way." He ignored the grumbling from Edmund. His youth and inexperience glared for all to see.

Speed and caution were of the essence. Pippa walked her horse around the jagged edge of the ridge before mounting to ride. William shadowed his wife while the other men followed single file with Henry as the rearguard.

Pippa stopped at the edge of the valley. Each man gathered close to hear her instructions in case of separation. She pointed northwest. "We ride across this vale and head northwest to the uprooted tree. From there we'll trot single file and weave through the dense forest." She made eye contact with every person. "Please, by all that is holy, don't separate from my path. Unless our enemy knows this forest well, they will easily get disoriented; and we will emerge victorious this day." They nodded in agreement.

William touched Pippa's arm. "Have a care, my wife."

She dipped her head in acknowledgement before spurring her horse onward. When they reached the open field, they road at full gallop. With daybreak, adequate light shone to help them perceive large obstacles; it was the concealed holes in the terrain that caused concern. A horse's stumble could break its leg. One downed horse could lead to the death of the rider or at best two riders on one horse, neither scenario desirable.

With less than two hundred yards to the edge of the forest, their enemies appeared from behind. Henry yelled, "We are discovered."

William looked to see at least fifteen soldiers riding at top speed toward their small band of warriors. The hair on his neck stood at the sound of their battle cries. He possessed full knowledge of their ruthless capabilities in warfare. "Hurry, Pippa, hurry!"

One hundred yards. Arrows whirred past missing their target. On a quick indrawn breath William yelled, "Longbows!"

All hugged their horse's neck. Not wanting to present a target, they crisscrossed the land. Henry's horse whinnied as an arrow grazed his flank. "Faster," Henry bellowed.

Dirt flew in the air as hooves pounded the earth. Additional arrows sailed but never found a mark. Fifty ... twenty ... ten ... .

Light was scarce when they entered the thick forest. Nothing slowed Pippa as she smashed through the underbrush. Her twists and turns made no sense to William as she crashed headlong into the unknown. With the thought of encountering mercenaries nipping at his heels, he considered praying. Alas, he denounced God long ago. No need to utter words to the wind.

His heart raced envisioning Pippa captured by these brutal men.

A shiver snaked down his spine. Why hunt his insignificant party? Would a possible suitor for Pippa hire mercenaries to seize the prize? Who revealed their whereabouts to these adversaries?

*Whack!*

The branch nearly unseated William. Blood trickled down his cheek as he crouched in his saddle. Now was not the time to ponder why they were being pursued. He needed attentiveness. Further loops and snaking curves. Horses heaved and snorted. Birds scattered upward as the noisy band plunged deeper into the woodland. Was his trust in Pippa misplaced? Did slaughter await them instead of safety?

# *20*

*God, help me! Lead me to the safe haven. Blind and confuse our enemy. Use Your wings to provide a hedge of protection around our small party ... especially Henry who watches our backs. May You send a league of angels to be our rearguard. Save us, Father!*

Pippa focused on every landmark. In her mind, there existed no room for error—it could mean their death—or worse, their capture. When she began to doubt herself, the final landmark came into view—a rock overhang. Relief swamped her. *Thank You, Father, thank You!*

Without a word, she jumped from her horse in midstride and grabbed the bridle. Each man followed her lead. Up ahead the waterfall covered the vine doorway to the cave. In her haste, she slipped on the wet rocks, but the firm grip on the bridle saved her from a fall. The roar from the falling water drowned out other sounds. She had no hint if their enemy had closed in on their position.

She blinked faster as the mist from the water clouded her vision. The trail behind the waterfall stayed hidden until Pippa located the boulder similar to a hog's rear end that directed her steps. She glanced around to see the row of men clustered behind her. Without delay, she funneled her way around the ledge and into the cave.

The opening permitted two abreast to pass through. She delved deeper into the hidden cavern allowing the others room to enter. Unfamiliar with the terrain, her warriors trailed her steps without variance. When she reached the first tunnel in the cave, she threw her reins to Robert and weaved her way back to the opening. There she found William and Henry hunkered on one knee.

She eased next to William. Her wild eyes looked from one to the other. She mouthed, "How close?"

Henry shrugged.

Sweat trickled through her hair and down her temple as her heart thundered. Had they reached their refuge unseen?

William unlatched his spy glass from his belt. He lay down on his stomach and crawled out of the cave. Pippa's brows came to a point between her eyes as she watched William leave the safety of their hideout. She glanced at Henry who kept watch on William.

After their eyes adjusted to the gloominess of the cave, Robert and Peter corralled the horses using a line of rocks across their path. Edmund and Ross soothed them with calming whispers and caresses while they all waited for William's report.

Pippa picked at her nails until Henry placed his hand upon hers. She snatched them free and closed her eyes. Her rapid breathing needed to cease to avoid dizziness. She concentrated. One breath in ... one out ... one in ... one out ... her head snapped up at a rustling. She looked over. Henry's knife parted the vines as his eyes stared ahead. Reaching down, she pulled her knife from her boot and scooted closer to the opening.

Henry glared at her and maneuvered his body to shield hers. Edmund and Peter crawled up beside her. She looked back to see the shadows of Ross and Robert with arrows drawn. Her heart hammered. When she thought she might faint from fright, William's head popped into view.

Edmund and Peter wiggled backwards and stood leaving her room to do the same. Once William scrambled inside, he moved toward the horses and motioned for them to follow leaving Henry as guard.

"Our enemy continues to thrash around in the brush. They beat and hack at the bushes as if perplexed. Their leader circles around and ends back where his men stand shaking their heads. I heard one say we were fairies and floated away."

A nervous giggle escaped Pippa. Her hand flew to cover her mouth as all eyes bore down on her. "Forgive me. 'Tis not humorous."

"Ah, Lass. Ye need nay ask for forgiveness," Ross said.

"We all understand the need for release," Robert said through a crooked smile.

Her gaze locked with William. Relieved to see no judgment, she asked, "How did the leader respond?"

"I willnae repeat his words, but one man came close to losing his head."

"'Twould be good. One less for us to kill," Peter said.

"I don't plan to engage in battle. For now, we'll stay hidden in hopes they think we escaped. I want two men on the outer ledge to serve as lookouts. Ross, you join Henry and take the first watch."

"Aye."

"Pippa, is there another way out?"

"Yes. It's a treacherous path—I've journeyed it once. We should secure the back opening to guarantee that the mercenaries can't attack us unaware."

"Show me which way to go, and I'll take Edmund along."

"No. I'll lead you. It has countless twists. You could easily get lost."

William's direct stare pinned her to the wall. "You will not endanger your life. Just tell me the way."

"No. I can't explain it but must feel for my landmarks. We are wasting valuable time."

William snorted. He pointed to Peter and Robert. "You two remain here. Edmund—with us."

"We'll need a torch," Pippa said.

"Hurry! Feel around for a solid limb," William demanded.

William's hushed, yet urgent voice sent a chill down Pippa's spine. She strode to the cave opening and pulled aside the vines just enough to let light shine deeper into the cavern. The men crawled while sweeping their hands across the floor searching for any object that would suffice. Robert located a small twig while Edmund found a larger stick against the rock wall.

"These are adequate," William said. "Peter, fetch my tinder box from my saddle bag."

Not far from the opening, Robert and Edmund scrapped their boots along the cave floor to prepare a place for William to produce a spark. William knelt and removed the fire steel, flint, and charred rags from his box.

"Robert, find two strips of cloth we can wrap around the end of our wooden sticks. Cut it from the horses' blankets if need be." William used the sharp edge of the flint to violently strike the fire steel at an acute angle in order to shave off small particles of metal. If all worked as planned, the oxidizing sparks would ignite the charcloth. After repeated tries, a spark landed on the cloth. William applied a small puff of breath to fan the flame.

Once Pippa saw the small flame, she released the vines and joined the circle of men. "I think it best to light one torch and reserve the other if the one burns low. Stranded in a dark tunnel without light is not what we desire."

William glanced up. "Aye. 'Tis sound judgment."

Pippa started down the dark tunnel while William followed carrying the torch. Edmund trailed behind carting the unlit torch. She slid her fingers along the slimy wall. Her first instinct? Jerk her hand away. However, the fear of death by a mercenary kept it fastened to the slippery wall.

The lone sound of their footsteps echoed off the stone until an occasional bat squeaked. The thoughts of a flying bat made her cringe. She didn't relish an encounter with those disgusting animals.

"Lady Fairwick, I wish to inquire of you," William murmured.

"Yes," she whispered as she continued to blunder through the shaft.

He came up close behind her. "Please enlighten me as to why two of your men deserted us."

She whipped around so fast, William grabbed her arms to keep from plowing her down. She stood on tiptoe as her hands braced against his leather chest armor.

"They didn't desert us. I sent them home to prepare for your arrival. My people weren't expecting me to drag home a husband." For a brief moment his grip tightened before he let go.

"Well, what did you expect to happen when you pleaded your case to our king?" His tight voice pinged off the cave walls.

She shoved out of his hold. "I didn't plead for you. I simple presented the betrothal for his inspection. Of course, you know the rest of the account. Excuse me, but we have an important task to complete." She whirled around and renewed her trek.

Twenty feet further William revived their conversation. "Forgive my accusation against your warriors—a misplaced judgment; however, you must see the wisdom in traveling with extra guards. We are now undermanned for battle against a foe who chases us with relentless determination."

Pippa rolled her shoulders before stopping again. She turned to face William and this time she raised her hand to stop his momentum. "I rode all the way from Fairwick castle to the king's palace with nary an incident." She cocked her head. "Since our wedding, we have been hounded by these men." Her eyes widened. *Gasp!* "They're not after me ... they're pursuing you!"

His neck stiffened as he reared back. His countenance grew thoughtful as he rubbed the back of his neck. He turned to her with a murderous expression. "I believe you are correct ... but why?" He searched the air for answers.

"Could they be connected to the disappearance of your father?"

His suspicious gaze fell on her upturned face. "'Tis possible. I need to widen my search once we evade these dunderheads and return you to Fairwick Castle."

She sucked in a quick breath and latched onto his arm with force. "There's more ... we captured a man who might shed light on your father's whereabouts."

"Why have you kept this from me?"

Her hand withdrew. With a slight grimace, she said, "I intended to offer the information as a wedding gift. 'Twas all I had to give."

"No matter. I can do nothing until we escape, and I speak with the prisoner." He shrugged. "'Tis a fine gift to receive."

Edmund cleared his throat. "Shouldn't we press onward?"

Both heads pivoted to stare at Edmund.

"Of course," Pippa said. "Of course, let us persist."

They trudged down two different passageways with urgency in every step. When Pippa's boot collided with a stone jutting out in the pathway, it caused her to trip. She groaned when her knee struck a sharp object on the cavern floor.

"Are you hurt?" William asked as he passed the torch to Edmund. He slipped his hands under her arms and helped her to stand. Over his shoulder, he said, "Edmund, light the second torch."

In their brief conversation, they had been courteous to one another and had struck a chord of agreement. Even in their dreadful state of uncertainty, the warmth of his embrace pleased Pippa. She chided herself for indulging in such a fanciful thought when possible death could lurk around the next turn. In the dim light, she saw genuine concern on William's face which served to fuel her irritation with herself. No need to engage in such whimsical notions. His care could turn to disdain in a flash. She took a moment to rub her injured leg and discovered it wet. Blood. Not wanting further sympathy, she said, "I'm not hurt. Come, let's be on our way."

The lie from her lips pricked her heart. She demanded truth above all else, and yet a lie rolled off her tongue like water. *Forgive me, Father.* It seemed her tongue became uncontrolled when encountering her husband. Once home a longer confession would be required.

After another fifty feet, she slowed her pace when she gauged the nearness of the back entrance. "If my calculations are correct, we arrived at the end of the tunnel," she whispered.

Dust swirled in the filtered light striking their boots. William grasped her arm and brought them to a halt. "I will take the lead. You move behind Edmund," he murmured near her ear. She might have enjoyed his warm breath on her neck if he hadn't sparked her irritation. With a firm clamp on her arm, he turned around. "Edmund, extinguish the light."

After he released his hold, she stepped to the rear. She refrained from stomping to her position since her knee ached. Well acquainted with warfare, she bristled at his highhanded manner. *Arrogant man!* Her penetrating stare bore a hole through his back while she drew her sword and slipped a knife from her boot. When free of danger, he would hear about the battles in which she had participated and commanded. *Humph!*

How could she hold fondness for him in one breath and in the next ... ready to smash his nose? She shook her head as they crept along. One fact was certain; she didn't understand her new husband.

William raised his fist bringing them to a halt. He crouched down as he peered through the thick vines. Edmund and Pippa stood with swords at ready. She prayed the mercenaries had retreated. To go back the way they had traversed without a lighted torch—impossible.

He edged backwards. "There is no sign of men or hoofmarks."

"Praise the Lord," she muttered.

"We will climb upward and skirt around the mountain's ledge headed east to the waterfall at a cautious pace. I will lead out with Edmund in the rear. Stay alert."

With each word William spoke, Pippa's heart increased in speed. To leave their sanctuary and put themselves in harm's way ... not a satisfying decision. The slightest reflection of sunlight on their swords could be their end. *God help us!*

# *21*

Daniel walked the length of his tether and back again. He worked the chain up and down to weaken the mortar around the ring that anchored the chain to the wall hoping to dislodge it. His agitated motions stirred the odor of his body. Nostrils flared at the nauseating smell.

"Cease," bellowed the guard.

"My legs need to move. Will ye not unchain me? I can do ye no harm in this room."

"'Tis me orders."

"By whom?"

Forced laughter floated under the door. "Ye willnae lure me to give his name."

"What does he hold over you to maintain your obedience? Money? Food? Does he threaten your family ... or are you afraid of him?"

The door crashed open as the giant guard stormed the room. He grabbed Daniel's neck chain and pulled him close. "Ye hold yer tongue. Ye know naught of what ye speak." Spittle flew into Daniel's face.

"Then tell me."

The guard shoved him away and turned to leave. Daniel's head banged against the stone wall as he scrambled to hold his footing. "Wait."

The old warrior stopped with hunched shoulders and head down.

"The man you serve is evil. Once he completes his wicked plans, your usefulness ends." When the man remained silent, Daniel continued. "My people are not slaves but free men. Once they've proven their worth, I offer a parcel of land to farm and to build their own hut. Can you say the same for the master you serve?"

The guard walked out and banged the door closed.

"I have much to offer, and I'm fair in my dealings." No answer. "Ponder it."

The man shuffled down the passageway until the sound of his footsteps disappeared. Daniel resumed jerking the chain up and down.

"What 're ye aboot?"

The quiet voice stilled Daniel's hand. "Sloan?"

"Aye."

Daniel waited. A scrapping sound crept through the window bars before the boy's head popped into view.

"Were you hiding nearby?"

"Aye. Bear dinna hear weel." His small nose poked through the opening as his hands wrapped around the bars. "What 're ye aboot?" he whispered again.

"I'm stretching my legs."

"I 'eard ye rattling tha chain."

"Are ye a secret keeper?"

A smile covered his face. "Aye."

"Is anyone close by?"

Sloan pulled his head away from the door and looked in both directions. "Nay."

"Unbeknownst to Bear, I plan to loosen my chains from the mortar."

Sloan's eyes grew round with fear.

"Escape is impossible tied to this wall."

"But ye might get slain for it!"

"Dinna worry."

Sloan's head pulled back. "I 'ear me mither." He hopped to the floor. With a bit of grunting, he shoved the stool against the wall with a crash. "I'll return. Fare thee weel." His pounding steps faded.

Daniel looked up. *Bless him, Holy Father. Keep him secure in Your protective grasp. And Father, might I ask a boon? Confuse my captors and cause dissention among them that I might see myself free from this confinement. Amen.*

---

"Lower the drawbridge," Pippa yelled as the weary band galloped closer to the castle. Wolf appeared from the nearby woods to run by her side. She had never been so happy to see her pet and her home. The journey to London and back again had been fraught with danger. As the warriors in the gate house released the iron restraints that raised the portcullis and lowered the bridge, relief engulfed her.

The horses thundered over the wooden drawbridge. Pippa led the group through the outer gate and into the courtyard. Cheers surrounded them as they trotted up to the keep. Malcom grabbed the reins of her horse as she jumped to the ground.

She raced up the keep steps to where her second in command awaited. "Walter, secure the castle."

"Straightaway, m' lady." He dashed down the stairs to accomplish her bidding.

"Malcom," she called out, "our mounts have proven their worth. See that they receive added care."

"Yes, m' lady." He whistled and headed toward the outbuilding with her steed. With two horses each, three stable boys guided the horses toward clean stalls.

She leaned down and hugged Wolf. Henry and Robert joined her but remained at a distance. No one came near when her pet wolf sat at her feet. The people stood silent with their eyes fixed on their lady.

William remained a statue at the bottom of the steps looking up at her. She extended her arm toward her husband. He climbed with slow deliberate steps. Wolf bared his teeth and growled.

"Hush, Wolf," Pippa commanded.

William took hold of her outstretched hand. When she raised their clasped hands into the air, the crowd roared with approval.

She smiled at her people. "It would seem they accept you."

"Once they know me, their cheers could change to heckles."

"Doubtful. In you, they see hope. Grand things can be accomplished with a hopeful people."

"We shall see."

"No matter ... but it would go a long way if you wore a pleased expression. If they sense you are disgruntled with our arrangement, they will question your authority. There is no time for a delay caused from distrust."

After several minutes of thunderous support, Pippa pulled their arms down. "Come, let's go inside." Before going inside the keep, she waved to all as she turned in a circle. Wolf looked up at his mistress. She removed a rope from her belt and looped it around his neck.

Upon entering the castle, Gwendolyn bobbed a curtsey. "Welcome home, m' lady."

"Thank you, Gwendolyn." She watched Gwendolyn's eyes dance with joy as Henry came through the door. "I will not need your assistance until the conclusion of the evening meal."

She turned to Henry. "Take your leave until the evening meal."

Henry nodded. "Thank you." He grabbed Gwendolyn's hand and stalked back out the door pulling his wife along.

Gathered in the main entryway Robert, Peter, Edmund, Ross and William looked to her for instructions. "I need to speak with the servants. Please await me in the war room."

She tied Wolf's rope to a sconce on the wall outside the war room. "Stay."

As she strode toward the grand hall, Patrick and John burst through the door. "Lady Fairwick," Patrick hollered as he ran to greet her. "We feared for your safety when you didn't return in a timely manner."

Overcome with joy at seeing her two men whole, her eyes burned. She grabbed their arms. "'Tis good to see your ugly faces once again," she said in jest. "Did you encounter any trouble on your journey?"

"No. We rode hard and stopped for nothing," Patrick said.

"Praise our Lord for your protection. There is much for you to know. You may join us in the war room for a brief discussion after I speak to the servants."

"We carried out your instructions. A feast and celebration await you at the evening meal," John interjected.

"Thank you, men. I had no doubt of your accomplishing my assignment. Now, if you'll excuse me."

"Yes, m' lady."

Pippa turned the corner and stopped before entering the great hall. She leaned against the wall and rubbed her eyes. The immense relief at seeing Patrick and John overwhelmed her. *Thank You, Heavenly Father of all that is good ... thank You for sparing my men. My command could have meant their death. I am most humbled by Your strong, protective arm.* Tears of joy threatened to fall.

"M' lady, is something amiss?" Merry asked as she descended from the second floor.

Pippa pushed away from the wall and pasted on a smile. "No, sweet Merry. All is as it should be. Is my parent's room prepared?"

"Yes, m' lady."

"Prepare a bath for that room as well as in my room. Moreover, please inform the cook we need refreshments sent to the war room, post haste."

"Yes, m' lady. At once."

"Thank you, Merry." Pippa heaved a sigh. There were no other urgent matters of which to attend. It was time to face her husband

and discuss their living arrangements. She looked up. *Give me strength, Father, give me strength.*

William drummed his fingers on the table at which he sat. Off to one side, Robert talked with Patrick and John. From their furrowed brows, no doubt Robert was describing the ordeal with the mercenaries. William took in his surroundings. The cold fireplace divided the wall in half with the table in the middle of the room. The chairs were worn but comfortable. No floor or wall coverings. Sparse but adequate.

"What think ye?" Ross asked.

William leaned his elbows on the table and turned to look at Ross. "Of what do you refer?"

Ross shrugged. "Tha greeting, tha castle, tha people ... all it entails?"

William flopped back in his chair and rested his clasped hands against his stomach. "Her people put much hope in a reformed mercenary."

"Aye. Their faith isn't misplaced."

*Humph!* He twirled his thumbs. "I waste time waiting on Lady Fairwick when I could be questioning her prisoner. My aim has not shifted."

Ross poised to ask another question when Pippa marched in the room trailed by her wolf. John all but tripped over a chair to move out of the path of her four-legged guard which snarled at him.

Pippa sat at one end of the table. "Please choose a seat, gentlemen, and let's discuss our tactics against this unnamed foe who plagues us. Lord McKinnon, what knowledge can you share about these men?"

William straightened in his chair surprised she directed the first question his way. "I know about one—ruthless in his attacks. Once I observed how he killed with abandon, I trusted him not."

"His name?"

"He never spoke his given name, but others called him Badger. He sells himself to the highest bidder whether they're in the right or not. With his lack of control, I wished to distance myself. Soon after, I left the cause and returned home."

"Do you think you are his target?"

"If I am, I can't comprehend why."

"Did you irritate the man?"

Pippa gasped. "Peter!"

"What about the young leader?" she continued.

"I have never seen him before the other day. When I saw him through my spy glass, he appeared older than I first surmised. I wager to say he's close to thirty plus years old."

Walter entered the room and took a seat. "The castle stands fortified. Is there pressing danger?"

"Mercenaries trailed our party. We know not of the reason or whom they seek to devour," Pippa said.

"If you will allow me to question your prisoner, I might piece together the facts for a possible conclusion," William said.

"You will get that chance before the night concludes."

"Walter and Robert, increase the men on the wall and send out scouts every hour. Keep the fires ablaze to chase away dark areas where our enemy might hide. Keep two guards at our postern gate and patrolling guards on the parapet as well as the grounds. I want guards at every entrance to the keep and one traversing each passageway. We will not be caught unaware this night."

Both men nodded their agreement.

"There is little else we can do at this time." Pippa stood. "We weathered much; let us rest and prepare for our upcoming dinner celebration." The men rose to leave. "Ross, a moment."

As the others lumbered from the room, William remained behind.

She directed her gaze at Ross. "Come. Merry will escort you to the room prepared for you. Please don't hesitate to ask if you have need for anything."

When she walked past William, he snagged her arm. At that instant, her wolf crouched in attack mode with teeth bared. "I need a word." He looked down at her wolf. "Call off your dog."

Pippa glanced at his hold on her arm. He removed his hand. Without hesitation, she said, "Wolf, lie down."

William gritted his teeth. The constant threat of her wolfdog proved wearisome. His thoughts churned devising a scheme to win the wolf's affection.

"Allow me to deliver Ross into Merry's care, and then I'll give you my undivided attention. Agreed?"

"I will wait."

# *22*

With squinted eyes, William watched steam wiggle through the air from the tub of hot water. He soaked his aching bones while he contemplated his wife. Somehow, she had managed to stall him from questioning her prisoner until after the night's celebration. *Ugh!*

He dunked his head. Under water, the muffled castle sounds soothed his tension as he calculated his next move. For now, he would observe the workings of the fortress and measure the devotion of her people. If he won their trust, their loyalty should shift to him. He rose out of his watery grave. Water sloshed over the side when he grabbed a drying cloth. *I will pursue her warriors and gain their trust beginning tonight.*

With quick, choppy motions, he dried off. He ran the cloth over his long, dripping hair, and then draped it over the tub's edge. He padded over to the four-poster bed where clean clothes lay upon the coverlet. *Who gave up their clothes so that I might dine in fresh apparel?* "Thank you, lady wife, that you didn't expect me to wear hose and pointed-toed shoes."

A loud knock at his door pushed him into action. With rapid speed, he pulled on his trousers. Before he had time to don his shirt, another banging occurred.

"'Tis I, Pippa."

Shirtless, William opened the door and propped his arm against the frame. "Yes?"

After gawking at his shirtless body, Pippa's face burned. She averted her eyes. "I came to fetch you for the banquet. I didn't realize you required additional time to prepare."

He looked behind her. When he saw no wolf, he tugged her into the room and shoved the door closed. His action caught her off guard, and she stumbled. With splayed fingers against his bare chest, she pushed. His arms wrapped around her waist and anchored her to himself.

"Where are you going? I thought you might like to gaze upon your purchase."

Her face wrenched upward. "I didn't purchase you."

His mocking smile reflected in her angry eyes. "Be that as it may, here I am." He freed her from his hold and stepped back. With arms outstretched, he turned in a circle. "Am I to your liking?"

She flipped around and presented her back. "It matters not."

"You look quite fetching in your green dress. The color suits you." He walked up and placed his hands upon her naked shoulders. "I might wish to view what I obtained through this marriage," he whispered near her ear.

She wiggled from his grasp and opened the door. Without turning around, she said, "I will await you in the passageway."

His laughter trailed after her.

With a satisfied grin, William finished dressing. Without grooming tools, he let his damp hair curl around his collar and used his fingers to smooth down his short beard. The scabbard around his waist cradled his sword while the belt provided a place for his knives. He viewed himself in the looking glass propped atop a small dresser. *When did those deep grooves form across my brow?* With a mental shake, he opened the door.

There under the wall sconce, Pippa leaned against the stone wall with eyes closed. The glow of the light encircled her head. For the first time since his life plummeted into pandemonium, he paused to study his wife. No longer was her hair red like a flame as in childhood but more like a smoldering, orange ember—quite appealing.

He cleared his throat. "Sleepy?"

Her lids popped open. "No." With a rigid back, she walked to meet him in the middle of the hallway. "Closed eyes shut out distractions."

"One caused by your husband?"

She rolled her eyes. "Hardly. It's not like I've never seen a man without his shirt."

For some reason her statement stung.

"I replayed our strange encounter with the mercenaries trying to determine the reason for their attack."

His wounded pride disappeared as he focused on that very question—why? "Did you come to a conclusion?"

She slipped her hand through the elbow he presented. "No." With slow steps, they made their way down the passageway toward the staircase. Pippa pointed out the significance of rooms that had served her family in the past.

Before reaching the end of the corridor, she stopped and turned to him. "We shall put aside the prior dilemma I mentioned and leave it for another time. Tonight, we celebrate our marriage."

She put her finger to his lips as he began to speak. His roguish nature reared up as he grabbed her wrist and kissed her finger.

She yanked her hand free and shook her head. "Please grant my people their merriment this eventide. Since the passing of my father, there has been little reason to rejoice."

He looked into her pleading eyes.

She continued. "Our wishes and desires are not what's important. The castle folk need to see a united front from Lord and Lady McKinnon. At the end of the evening, I will escort you to our prisoner ... if ..."

"If I agree to this farce of a marriage?"

She flinched. Hurt passed across her countenance. "The marriage is not a fraud, but perhaps your acceptance of it is a charade. Either way, will you agree to put on a face of contentment and cheerfulness for my people?"

His chest constricted at her wounded expression. He attempted to grin. "For *our* people."

She smiled. "You shall be rewarded."

He wiggled his eyebrows. "May I choose my reward?"

"The prisoner?"

"Ah. Of course, the prisoner."

At the bottom of the stairs, William stopped. Pippa's arm hung at her side while he dug into his waist pouch. He grabbed her left hand. With raised brows, she gawked as he slipped a sapphire and diamond ring on her third finger. He shrugged. "I picked this up in London."

Her heart fluttered. She blinked hard as she stared at her outstretched hand. "'Tis beautiful," she whispered. She wanted to ask if this meant he accepted his fate but didn't dare for fear of his answer.

"The sapphire reminded me of your eyes."

She glanced upward and caught his stare. "Thank you. It's a delightful surprise." After the forced marriage, his rage abounded; yet, he purchased a ring. Curious.

"You appear stunned."

"Forgive me. I fear I have nothing quite this grand to give you."

"No need." His face beamed. "You have a prisoner."

"Indeed, I do."

"Come, let us proceed."

It required all of Pippa's concentration to keep walking when the weight of her exquisite ring tugged for her attention. They lingered at the entrance to the grand hall and gazed at the festive room. The tables sagged under the weight of food, drink, and silver candelabras. In the midst of the beautiful scene, her heart grew heavy. She understood the sacrifice her people had made to present the prosperous feast.

William bent low. "You don't appear to be lacking in provisions."

"'Tis not as it seems."

When Henry noticed them, he signaled the musicians in the balcony. Trumpets heralded their arrival. All activity stopped and clapping commenced as the two strolled into the room. The smiles of her people were contagious.

A broad smile spread across her face. She peeked at William, who wore a crooked grin. "All are pleased," she said.

He nodded.

Pippa circled them through the crowded tables and greeted the excited group. She introduced William to the older warriors. Their warm welcome of her husband delighted her.

They stepped upon the dais and stood before the two family throne chairs draped in velvet. Pippa raised a hand for silence. "Thank you all for joining us at this extravagant banquet. The thunderous welcome warms my heart. Your hard work and diligence of caring for the castle in my absence speaks volumes about your loyalty—the loyalty I will share with my husband— Lord William McKinnon." She stepped aside and tilted her head toward William.

The men's tankards of drink banged against the tables while the women clapped. Loud guffaws filled the room as joy permeated the atmosphere. There seemed to be no end to the revelry until William raised his arms.

With his palms outward, he hushed the crowd. "Thank you for your heartwarming acceptance." He reached for Pippa's hand. With a firm grip, he raised them in solidarity. "Together, we can accomplish much."

The crowd roared.

"Let the festivities begin!"

After taking their seats of honor, Pippa leaned near and touched his arm. "Well done, husband."

"Thank you, wife."

Between them sat a trencher of food to share along with a chalice of wine. William wrapped his long fingers around the goblet and took a sip. "Mm ... fine wine indeed." He rotated the cup and raised it toward Pippa's lips. "I believe 'tis a tradition for the wedded couple to drink from the same spot on the chalice."

Their eyes locked. "Of course, it's as you say."

With a slow arm, he brought the cup forward. When her lips touched the rim, he tipped the cup. His gaze shifted to her lips as she licked a drop of sweet wine from her mouth. "Mm ... you are correct."

His hand went across his chest as he sighed. "I will store away this moment when we are in agreement. For I might need to draw upon this remembrance at a later time."

"Mayhap, we will agree often." She picked up the knife and began cutting their meat. "I hope you're up to a challenge."

"Oh?"

She looked up. "They expect us to lead off the dancing after the meal."

He plopped back against his chair as his head sunk to his chest. "Oh, no." He peeked at her. "Your feet will not thank you for requiring this of me."

William waited outside of Pippa's door while she changed clothes. She stepped out of her slippers as she knelt to open her trunk. There was no need to soil her one good dress in the nasty dungeon. Out flew her pants and pirate shirt—a gift from her Uncle Nicolas. She contemplated the night as she untied her dress.

Her husband's performance at dinner pleased her. He fooled everyone ... well not the men that had traveled with her ... but everyone else. No one suspected William anything but happy with their marriage arrangement. One hurdle down. *Thank you, Father.*

At a knock, she slid to the door on stocking feet. "Yes."

"Open the door."

She unlatched the door as she tucked her shirt in her pants. "I need to put on my boots."

William paused at the threshold and peered around the room. "No wolf?"

"No. He hunts outside."

He sauntered in and shut the door. "Oh, did you require additional time to prepare?"

Her head popped up to see his grin. She sat in the floor and laced up her boots. "I hope you gain further information from the prisoner. Duff tried his torture tactics but with little response."

"Who is Duff?"

"A giant warrior. His appearance alone scares most into confession, but not Errol."

A frown creased his brow. "You call your prisoner by his first name?"

She stood and reached for her knives. "Yes. Why would I not?"

"Calling them by name makes them distinct. You can't afford to feel sorry for them caused by familiarity. I wager to say you probably know all about his family by now. Is that not so?"

She ducked her head.

"I knew it." William slapped his glove against his thigh. "Let's get on with it." He walked into the hallway.

Her face scrunched with displeasure and mimicked his words while his back was turned. She knew her actions were childish but didn't care. With a skeleton key, she locked her door.

"You fear an intruder?"

She pocketed the key and turned. "I trust few." They walked side by side until arriving at the back stairway. "There is more you should know before questioning the captive."

William raised both brows. "Such as?"

"Not only is his name Errol, but it's Errol Elliot."

"Should I know him?"

"He is a cousin to Brodie Elliot ... the man who kidnapped your mother."

William's eyes became daggers—thankfully, not directed at her. He rubbed his forehead. "Let me see if I understand. In your

179

dungeon is a cousin to the vile Elliot Clan who almost killed my mother and probably is behind my father's capture?"

"Yes."

He bared his teeth. "Let me at him."

She grasped his arm. "You may not kill him."

"I have no intentions of such. I need him alive."

# 23

Per William's order, Pippa waited at the top of the stairs leading to the belly of the castle. She paced and snorted. Her resolve to stay put wavered as she contemplated her husband's manner. *Wait here,* she mouthed. Her fists clinched. Up until now, she had given commands for others to follow. Who knew the chain of command would shift the first night at Fairwick Castle? She liked it not.

The wall torch flickered as a draft wafted up from below. She squinted her eyes down the stairs. Clicking boots echoed louder with each step. At last, her mulish husband returned from the interrogation. He stomped up the steps. A thundercloud surrounded his face.

"What did you learn?"

He grabbed her arm. "Come. There is much to discuss."

She wrenched her arm free. "'Tis not necessary to drag me along. I'm not your prisoner."

He glanced at her as if seeing her for the first time. "We need to assemble your lead warriors tonight." His long strides ate up the floor.

Pippa jogged to keep up with him. "Is there imminent danger?"

"I will tell all in the privacy of the war room," he whispered.

She scanned the hallway. "Do you think an enemy lurks about?"

He failed to answer and kept walking as his eyes swept the area.

When they passed a guard, Pippa stopped. "Find Henry, Robert, and Walter. Send them to the war room, post haste."

"Yes, m' lady."

William lingered at the end of the passageway tapping his foot. Pippa hurried to meet him. They turned in unison to head toward the war room. "Charles will locate my warriors and send them to us."

Halfway down the stairs, William stopped. Pippa collided into his back. He caught her before she stumbled. "What are you doing?" she hissed. "You could have caused us to tumble to our deaths."

He held her close. "I wish Ross to be included."

"Of course." She peered up at him. "You may release me."

His eyes softened, but he didn't let go. "Forgive me. The facts I learned are most disturbing. When my mind's fixated on securing a castle, I tend to dismiss those around me."

"'Tis understandable." She squirmed. "Please free me."

"I rather enjoy your body next to mine, but this is neither the time nor the place for such affection."

Pippa sucked in a quick breath. Her husband's thought process confused her. Did he wish intimacy?

Her scabbard clinked against the stone wall as he pulled her back up the few steps. They continued down the next hallway at a fast clip until arriving at Ross's room.

Pippa huffed. "Was it truly necessary I accompany you?"

"Yes." William rapped on the door. "Ross!" he yelled.

With wide eyes, she shushed him. "The hour is late."

"It matters not. Ross!"

Pippa placed her hand against his mouth. "Lower your voice."

Ross opened the door. "Aye?"

With William grasping the wrist of her hand covering his mouth, she lowered her head in embarrassment.

"Ross, we have need of your services in the war room," William said.

She peeped at Ross to see him raise a brow. His eyes shifted from one to the other. "I will ready myself."

Hoping not to draw attention, Pippa tugged at William's hold. He held fast.

"My bride and I will await you." He lowered her hand, bent down, and delivered a slow kiss to her palm. Looking up, he winked. "Come, my sweet." He headed back toward the stairs.

A rush of heat consumed her. Since he held tight to her hand, she had no choice but to skip behind him—mortified! "Why did you do that?" she asked through clamped teeth.

"Because I wished it."

When they reached the war room, the room buzzed with speculation. All three waiting men spoke at once

"What's this about?"

"Did you learn more from the prisoner?"

"Do we need to sound an alarm?"

William pulled Pippa into the room and shut the door. He held his finger to his lips and walked around the room. The three men watched. Henry drew his sword with quiet intent. William motioned for them to gather in the middle of the room.

"We have one other in our midst who wishes us harm," he murmured softly.

"How did you extract that from Errol?" Pippa asked with a hushed voice.

All heads whipped around at the opening of the door. Ross joined the group. A collective sigh escaped.

"How is not important. The point is what I know."

"Who is it?" Henry demanded. "I will cut him from ear to ear."

"Errol didn't know a name but described him. He is a young man of powerful build with short brown hair. The two thieves were to deliver the castle plans to their leader ... again no name."

"Numerous boys fit that description," Walter said.

"Aww ... but this one has a facial scar from the corner of his eye to his ear."

"I will scour the grounds and bring him to you," Henry said in anger. He turned to go.

"No. Wait. We know not where he dwells among us. If he hears we guessed his plan, he will hide or disappear." William looked at each person. "I have a plan to catch him. From what Errol described, our young enemy thinks highly of his ability to blend in with our people and is quite proud of his strength."

"How does that help us?" Pippa asked.

William smiled. "We'll hold a special day of festivities in honor of our wedding. One of the activities will be a show of strength. Participants will be required to carry a huge log from one end of the field to the next. He will be unable to resist."

"'Tis not uncommon for men to wear hooded cloaks at this time of the year. What then?" Henry asked.

"Not only will we test their power, but part of the competition will be to measure their bulging muscles ... in other words shirtless."

"I don't see how that will entice him to participate."

All of the men stared at Pippa with unbelieving eyes. "Have no doubt; he will join in. His pride will demand it," William said. "Pippa and I will design the day's events and ready the provisions needed for the occasion. Rest well tonight, for tomorrow we need to observe all of the comings and goings of the castle. Go about your duties with sharpness. Resist the urge to engage our foe if spotted; instead, report to me of your findings."

"Should we not alert our night watchmen?" Pippa asked.

"Henry and I will handle it. I don't want the enemy to notice a difference in the nightly routines, but I will post men hidden around the grounds." His fisted hand slammed into his palm. "Nothing will escape us."

"Questions?"

Pippa looked at each man. A gleam of vengeance shown bright. In their midst hid a brood of vipers ready to strike innocent people without notice. Her heart pounded in her ears. *Thank you, Father, for William. He accomplished what I could not. I am forever grateful.*

She remained in the middle of the room and watched. William smacked each man on the back as they left—gleeful. Relief swept through her heart. She was no longer alone to face a concealed opponent. Her eyes closed as her heart began to slow.

"Wife? Are you sleeping?" He rubbed his hands together. "Come. There is work to do."

Her eyes popped open to see William's amused face. "I'm ready."

He stopped at the door and waited for her. He stuck out his elbow and latched onto her trembling hand as it slid through the crook. Leaning close he said, "Do not fear. All will be well."

She gnawed on her lip. "I've heard it said before."

"Come, my bride. Tonight, marks our official wedding night." He wiggled his brows.

A sharp breath caught in her throat. "What?"

He remained silent as they climbed the spiral staircase.

William escorted Pippa to her room. "I will await you while you gather your needed belongings for the night."

Her head whipped around. "Why should I collect those pieces of clothing?"

"Because tonight you will sleep in my room."

Her brows raised to the hairline. "I'm perfectly safe residing here." She looked up and down the passageway and leaned closer to William. "Remember, I have an escape route."

"I care not." He watched her eyes narrow. "Shall I choose your clothing?"

"No," she snapped. She extracted her key and unlocked the door. Smokey air hit their faces.

He grabbed her arm and prevented her from entering. "Who lit your fire?"

"Gwendolyn or Henry."

"How many keys float through this castle?

"Only two." She held up her key. "This one and Gwendolyn's."

"I like it not." He entered her room to look around.

"What are you doing? You said you would wait for me in the hallway."

"Nay. I said I would await you while you gathered your items. I never said I wouldn't come into this room."

Pippa huffed and stomped across the room to her wardrobe. William remained with his back against the closed door and surveyed his surroundings. The room appeared small but comfortable. Her rumpled bed glared at him, inviting his weary head to find rest.

"Where is your wolf?"

Glancing over her shoulder, she said, "He's allowed to run at night."

"Do you not fear he will kill your villagers' stock?"

"No. I trained him since a pup. Grave consequences arise if he even smells of our cattle or sheep. Besides, he's well fed."

"I wish you to bring him inside the castle and keep him by your side at all times."

She spun around clutching her night gown. "Why? Is there something you're not telling me?"

"Nay." He pushed away from the door and sauntered toward her. What a sight. The firelight danced across his warrior wife complete with sword, knives, men's trousers, and holding a dainty, white linen gown against her bosom—contradiction. "I cannot guard you at all times. I want to know your wolf will be at your side when I am not."

Her face relaxed. "I can take care of myself, or have you forgotten our altercation?" She smiled.

Her mischievous grin annoyed him. "Nay. I have forgotten nothing." His chest pushed against her hands with the gown between them. "Mayhap you have forgotten how I straddled you and pinned your body to the ground. Or do you remember it as a tryst instead of a conquest?"

She snorted. "A tryst? Surely you jest."

His fingers wrapped around her arms. "Nay. I do not jest." His breath caressed her ear. He watched her pulse race in her neck.

"Would you rather we dwell here tonight? It's small, but cozy for what I have in mind."

Her eyes darted to his face, and she trembled. "No. If you'll let me go, I'll collect my things."

Inwardly, he smiled—victorious. His fingers loosened as he stepped away. "Before we leave, you will show me your hidden passageway."

"The secret is known only to me. It's what my father wanted." She folded her gown and placed it in a sack with her brush and comb.

"Your father expected to guard you, but he is not here. At your request, I am your husband, and you will show it to me."

She snatched her dress from the hook and shoved it on top of the gown before pulling the drawstring tight. With hands fisted by her side, she said, "I will reveal it but under protest."

William raised a brow.

"Follow me." Pippa popped opened a door William hadn't noticed. He thought it a bookcase. She picked up a candle and lit it from the fireplace. With her hand cupped around the flame, she led him into a changing room complete with a table, a stool, and an extra wardrobe. She set the candle on a small table in the corner.

"Watch closely, for I will only show it once."

What a little imp, his wife. "Have no worries, I but need to see it once and will never forget."

She blew out a loud breath. "You must remove this stone. Inside dwells a handle. Do you wish to touch it?"

"Yes." He reached inside the hole and fumbled around until he felt a lever. "I found it."

"Pull it."

With a firm grip around the handle, he tugged. It necessitated great strength to move it. The wall began to slide open revealing a dark opening.

"Don't step through the doorway," she warned. She held the candle at the opening and pointed. "When you step on the stone in the floor, the wall closes leaving you inside the tunnel."

William studied the device and marveled at the ingenuity. "Quite clever, your father." He turned at her sigh.

"Yes, my father was many things." The sadness filtered through her soft voice. She stepped back from the tunnel. "To close it from inside, you will need to push the lever backward."

He grunted as he heaved against the lever. "Where does the tunnel lead and how long before you exit?"

"The stairs take you down under the castle. From there I walked until two torches burned low. The trapdoor is deep in the woods near a clump of trees west of the castle. There is thick soil and grass atop the access."

"'Tis good to know." They walked back into her room. "Where is the hidden latch for this bookcase?"

Her mouth formed a tight line. She pushed it closed.

"Did you think I didn't notice?"

Without answering, she grabbed his hand and ran it along the edge of the bookcase. "Feel the indention?"

"Aye."

"Push it."

With a forceful push of his finger, the bookcase opened with ease. "Ah. Another shrewd contraption. Who built these mechanisms?"

"The tunnel snakes underneath the castle and existed from the beginning. My father and my uncle added this hidden stairway and the moveable wall when they were young boys."

"Oh? Their father knew about this?"

"No. He was the one they wished to escape."

"Those who reside in the castle today know nothing of this escape route?"

She ducked her head. "Well ... Henry knows, but no other."

"Ah. Previously, you said no one knew but you. I will speak to Henry to verify he is the only one."

She frowned.

"Your irritation is unwarranted. It's for your own protection I ask these questions. Come." He held out his hand. "We have much to achieve this night."

# *24*

A clanking noise startled Pippa as a pain shot up her neck. Sleeping on the far edge of William's bed without turning over had proven unfavorable. Peeping from one eye, she saw her shirtless husband stirring the embers in the fireplace. She kept her breathing slow and steady. Not wanting to alert him of her awakened state, she kept her stiff body motionless.

Last evening proved stressful. Upon entering his room, she had feared he might demand his husbandly rights. That was not the case. Standing by the bed, he but required her promise to remain by his side all night. Without another word, he removed his sword, boots and shirt before crawling into bed to sleep.

This morning, behind her closed lids, she could still picture the rise and fall of his chest while he slept. No question, he was a fine example of a strong warrior. Unmoving, she had stood at the foot of the bed admiring his body waiting for her legs to stop shaking. At some point, she too slipped into bed—wearing clothes less her boots and knives.

"Wife, are ye awake?"

A soft sigh escaped her lips. "Yes." She rolled onto her back and moaned as she stretched her taut muscles. She propped up on

189

her elbows and peered over the foot of the large, four-posted bed. "Why do you continue to call me wife?"

"It helps to remind me that I am wed. There are times I think 'tis a dream."

He didn't sound angry, just resigned.

Pippa sat against the headboard and pulled her knees to her chest. Resting her chin on her knees, she watched her husband. Down on one knee at the hearth, his back muscles rippled with each log he added to the fire.

He looked over his shoulder. "Observing my work pleases you?"

Pippa shrugged and grinned. "'Tis nice to awaken to a roaring fire."

William stood and faced the bed. After replacing the poker and wiping his hands on his trousers, he walked to stand beside Pippa. "Did you sleep?"

Pippa looked everywhere except at William. "A bit."

His finger under her chin brought her focus to him. "Did you find sleeping in my bed a burden?"

"No," she whispered and looked away, "a bit awkward, I suppose." Her heart flipped at his nearness and began a rat-a-tat thump against her breast.

He sat on the edge of the bed. "Mayhap, you feared I would consummate our vows?"

Her head snapped up. The thundering of her heart doubled in time and pounded in her ears. "Perhaps." Her arms tightened around her knees.

William placed his hand upon her knee. His eyes softened. "Fear me not. I will never force myself upon your person. You have my word."

The warmth of his hand and the sincerity of his words worked to calm her runaway heart. Her fingers twisted together. "Thank you." She looked at his rugged face. His chiseled features were pleasing to gaze upon even with two days' growth of beard. The crackling fire and his closeness bolstered her courage. "Might I speak freely?"

His neck pulled back. "I expect nothing less than honesty."

In order to keep her concentration, she deemed it necessary to keep her eyes focused on his face and not gawk at his broad chest. "You have suffered much. This I know. Yet ... it has not brought you low. After the forced wedding, I expected you to hate me forever."

He opened his mouth to speak, and she placed a finger across his lips. He smiled beneath her finger. "When I stop your speech with aught but a finger, 'tis gratifying."

Grabbing her finger, he kissed it. "Don't expect it always to work."

The tingle from his kiss shimmied up her arm. She pulled her hand back to her knee. "Nonetheless, you find ways to lessen our burdens with lighthearted behavior. Of this, I am grateful. As my husband, last night you could have taken what rightfully belongs to you; nonetheless, you offered a reprieve."

"It was not without great willpower."

"I thank you."

He pushed to his feet and lifted her in his arms. Surprised, in order to keep her balance, she wrapped an arm around his neck while the other hand lay against his chest—noses inches apart. "Know this, Phillippe Emma Gail McKinnon, we will disagree on many fronts; however, we must covenant together always to be truthful with one another."

"I concur. Truthfulness is a great start," she said breathless.

He set her on her feet and swatted her bottom. She gasped.

"Time to dress as the proper wife of the lord of the castle. We have a competition to plan and an enemy to apprehend."

William hurried from the room afraid his wife's striking beauty might ensnare him. She had no idea the sway she could wield over him with one come-hither look from her stunning eyes. He needed to avoid the distraction—his father's life depended on it.

He surveyed the dining hall. Off to one side sat Henry and Ross, eating the morning meal. William strode over and plopped down on the bench beside Ross. "Good morrow, my friends."

Henry grunted. Ross nodded with a mouth full of thick stew. William glanced around until he caught the attention of the serving girl. She hustled from the room at his bidding.

"Ye seem quite chipper," Ross said. "Did tha night suit ye?"

Henry spewed his drink on the table.

William's lip twitched. "I think we fared quite well." He smiled broadly as she walked into the hall. "Ye might like to ask me bride."

Ross ducked his head. "I think not."

William stood when Pippa came to his side. "Allow me." He held her hand as she eased onto the bench.

She caught William's gaze. "Why sit here and not on the dais where the family takes the meal?"

"I want to discuss our tournament day."

"Of course."

The servant placed a platter of food before William. "I'll bring ye a meal, m' lady." The girl bobbed a curtsy and rushed out.

"Until she returns, I will share." William winked at Pippa.

She blinked several times. "Thank you, William."

Henry frowned as his eyes volleyed back and forth between the two. "What have you decided?"

William leaned close. "You and I will tour the courtyard and the outside grounds while I point out where I want extra guards. I plan to have games in the courtyard favorable for children." He looked at Pippa. "You may develop the details."

"This is uncommon. Children don't partake in this sort of event."

"I want them safe. If they remain inside the castle grounds, the guards have fewer people to watch."

She held his gaze.

"Do you have more to add?" he asked.

Her tight lips were her reply.

He refocused on the men. "The other strength events will take place in the lists. No outside seating will be required since no other clans or families are invited to attend. A few wagons and hay bundles will suffice."

"Will there be jousting?" Henry asked.

"Nay. The events will be simple and geared toward the peasant's participation. No knights may take part."

"I don't understand your reasoning," Henry said.

"Knights are stout and strong. Their presence would intimidate a common laborer. I want no reason for our enemy to decline the competition."

"This has never been done," Pippa said.

William turned to his wife. "I've seen it through my travels. 'Tis a good time had by your people and requires less outlay of coinage. As I said earlier, this is in celebration of our nuptials. They are to entertain us."

"I see."

"M' lady?"

Pippa leaned down to receive a hug from a little girl. "Hello, Catherine. Thank you for my sweet embrace."

Pippa turned to William. "Lord McKinnon, may I present Catherine?"

William nodded toward the small girl and smiled. "Lassie."

Catherine giggled. She bobbled her curtsey and grabbed William's outstretched hand to stay upright.

"Catherine is my helper," Pippa added. When the small child began to wiggle, Pippa offered her a piece of bread and cheese from William's plate. Catherine took the food and pulled Pippa closer to whisper in her ear.

"Excuse me, men. I'll leave you to your plans. My attention is required elsewhere." Pippa lifted her husband's trencher as she stood to leave.

"What are ye about?" William frowned.

"You may eat my portion when it arrives." Catherine clutched a fist full of Pippa's gown as they traipsed from the room.

William stared after his wife. The sway of her hips caught his attention. The long braid swished below her waist with each step. He preferred her hair loose and flowing, although a braid bested a wimple. His head jerked back when Ross cleared his throat.

"She likes it not you rule the castle," Henry murmured.

William glared at Henry. "'Twas my understanding that that is the exact reason she sought me out."

"She wanted a partner, not a sovereign lord."

William's back stiffened. "'Tis the way of things. By her own hand, I am the lord at Fairwick Castle. She will grow accustomed to her new position as Lady McKinnon."

With fingers wrapped around his cup, Henry's knuckles turned white.

While William held Henry's stare, the serving girl placed hot food before him and scurried away. "Do not concern yourself." He picked up his eating knife. "Can I depend on your loyal service? One who will follow my directions without question?"

Henry remained silent while he drank his ale. His tankard clanked on the table as he swiped his mouth with the back of his hand. "Yes, but this you should know; she has a fiery temper when crossed."

William laughed. "'Tis no secret." He began to cut his meat. A masculine clash had been averted. "Let us proceed with our plans. A man thinks better with nourishment."

"What if the boy doesn't show himself?" Ross asked.

"All guards will be privy to his appearance. If he sneaks into the castle while the games occur, he will not be alone. Every possible development must be considered."

"Could we not release tha prisoner?" Ross asked.

William stopped eating and turned to his friend. "I'm listening."

Ross leaned on his elbows with his head low. "Fabricate a story for Errol and give him false drawings of tha castle to deliver." He nodded toward William. "I'll leave tha story for ye to devise. Mayhap, tha two would rush from here. Our mon would follow." Ross shrugged. "Me thinks we'll be led to yer enemy's camp."

William smacked Ross on the back. "Well done, my friend. 'Tis a grand scheme. With the games and an escape in the works, either way, our enemy will make an appearance." Satisfied with how the plans came together, William ate with gusto.

For two days, tightened security reigned. Preparing for the day's events, Pippa wove a ribbon through her hair. "Any word?"

"No sighting of the young man. However, today, Errol will *escape* with the false drawings of the castle, but not before the tournament." William buckled his scabbard and slid his sword into place.

He glanced up. "You look quite fetching." He walked up to his wife and ran his fingers through her hair. "I like it when your hair flows free. 'Tis becoming."

She held her breath.

"Wife, fear shines in your eyes. Are you fearful I'll overpower you and have my way with you before the day begins?" He grinned as he released her hair.

Her nails bit into her hands. She had worried two days with that precise thought. "No, I but dread this day. What if your plan fails, and he vanishes?"

He picked up one of her fisted hands. "Have faith. We will win the day." After prying open her fingers, he bowed and kissed her red palm. "Come, Lady McKinnon. Let us play our part."

*What does he mean? What part am I to play?*

He kept hold of her hand and walked to the door. "When we step through this portal, we are nothing more than a wedded couple off to delight in entertainment provided by our people. Do not covertly attempt to locate the enemy. Eyes will assess our behavior. Leave the spying for our capable protectors." He stooped to eye level with Pippa. "Do I have your word on this?"

Disappointed, her huff blew one of her curls. "I do not like it."

"Wife?"

"As you wish. You have my word."

"What word?"

She rolled her shoulders. "My word I won't go hunting for our enemy."

"And?"

She closed her eyes.

"Wife?" he said with more force.

She peeped at his face so close to her own. His warm breath had skipped across her lips giving her a shiver of pleasure. "I will act as if this is a grand day and will not look about for the enemy. Now ... are you satisfied?"

He grinned. "Most assuredly."

They strolled down the hallway toward the winding staircase. Pippa looked at William from the corner of her eye. Self-assurance exuded from his being as he walked with confidence. Having him by her side bolstered her hope for the future of Fairwick Castle and the villagers.

"Have you looked your fill?" he asked with amusement.

She sucked in a quick breath. "What mean you?"

"Ah, wife. We said we would speak truth in all things." He stopped at the end of the passageway. "Do you wish to say anything different?"

Treatment as a wayward child didn't sit well; yet, that's precisely how she had responded. She tilted her face upward. "You are correct. It would seem I need to perfect my veiled observations." Her mouth twisted. "I know exactly what you meant." She took a deep breath. "I gaze upon you to familiarize myself with my husband." Her eyes squinted "You puzzle me."

He smiled. "I hear a bit of mystery is good for wedded bliss."

*Humph.* "I already regret agreeing always to speak truth."

William's laughter echoed down the stairs.

# *25*

Henry strode up the keep steps to William and Pippa when they exited the castle. "All is set in place."

"Well done, Henry. Pippa and I will observe the children's competition for a time. At half past the hour, we will join you in the lists. The main games may begin when we are present and not before."

Henry bowed and took his leave.

"I thought you wished to go straight to the men's events." Pippa whispered.

William patted her hand resting on his arm. "We must not appear in a hurry. This is a day of leisurely amusement. The Lord and Lady need to talk with those in attendance. Our man dares not leave without his prize, and Errol won't be released until late in the day."

Together, they strolled around the courtyard. Women bobbed a curtsey and congratulated them on their nuptials. Several little girls ran around them singing their made-up songs while the boys tussled in the dirt.

William stopped Pippa. "Why do you give your food to these young children? Do they lack food?"

Her smile drooped. "There are many needs going unnoticed. Much of our money goes to fortify the castle walls damaged by our enemies. Hopefully, since I'm wed, suitors will cease to bombard the battlements." She sighed. "Since my father's death, we experienced a drought, and then pestilence ate much of what was on the vines." Unshed tears formed. "With shrinking funds ... well ... that is that as they say."

William's thumb wiped a lone tear that escaped. "You have a heart for your people."

"Our people," she sniffed.

"Cease to fret. After today, I will see to their hunger and the castle repairs. I have ample coinage for both."

She squeezed his arm. "Thank you, William." A crooked smile shaped. "And I will help you find your father."

William's mouth opened for a reply, but Gwendolyn approached. "Lord and Lady McKinnon, the children are prepared to show off their talents if yer ready."

"By all means," William said.

"Your place of honor is there." Gwendolyn pointed to a rickety wagon filled with fresh hay.

They maneuvered around groups of children toward their royal seat. William's hands spanned Pippa's waist as he lifted her onto the back of the wagon. He hopped up and joined her. Grasping her wrist, he raised their hands in the air. "Let the games begin!"

They clapped and cheered for the small competitors. First, the boys held a foot race. Between tripping each other and rolling on the ground, it was hard to determine the winner.

William bounced off the wagon. "Come, boys. Let's try this race again. Only, this time, we divide into smaller groups. All boys younger than seven, line up with me."

He removed his belt and handed his sword to Pippa. "Will you see to the safety of my favorite sword?"

She beamed. "Indeed, 'tis safe with me."

The children's large eyes stared at their lord. "Are ye runnin' wiff us?" Timothy asked.

"Aye. I am. Can you beat me?" William asked.

"Yea. I'm fast."

"Let's see how fast."

Merry held up a ribbon in the air. "Get ready ... go!" The ribbon floated to the ground as the young boys sprinted toward the line of hay bundles. William trotted with the little one in last place. "Hurry, my friend."

The boy pumped his arms faster. "We are last."

William encouraged him. "No matter. We are strong."

With Lord McKinnon in the foot race, the boys completed the course without incident. He continued to run with each new assembled group.

Ross ambled up to Pippa. "Lord William entertains tha wee ones."

She laughed. "Yes. The boys are particularly pleased. Look there." She pointed. "Lord McKinnon has gained a friend forevermore—sweet Timothy." The young girls squealed with delight as William pursued them around the courtyard. "Even the girls are enchanted by his charms."

"Are ye content with yer hoosband, as weel?"

Pippa tilted her head as she gazed at Ross and smiled. "He'll suffice."

Ross grinned.

"We have much to learn about one another."

"Ye have a lifespan."

"Yes ... yes, we do"

William ran over and swept Pippa off the wagon. "Come, wife. You shall be my prey. Run!" Over his shoulder he called to Ross. "Guard my sword."

Pippa raised her dress and ran from William shrieking like the others. It didn't take long for all the children to stop and shout as their lord chased their lady.

"Catch her!"

"Look out!"

"He's behind you!"

She dodged around the hay bundles, wagons, and children.

"She went the other way!"

William ended their play when he snagged her around the waist and lifted her against his chest.

Pippa squealed. Even though the captive arms of her husband held tight, they reminded her that all of her troubles were now halved. To retain the option to share her burdens with another relieved her once troubled heart.

"I have you, my pretty!" He held his squirming wife and nuzzled her neck.

The wind stole her gasp.

The children erupted in cheers and laughter. The women smiled and nodded as they watched the interplay. Laughter floated down from the castle walls as guards looked on.

"Time for us to move to the lists," he murmured behind her ear.

"You must give way," she said breathless.

His firm grip loosened as he set her on her feet. Surrounded by children, they bid their farewells.

"Thank you for a rousing competition," William boomed. "I see future warriors and servants in our midst. However, Lady McKinnon and I must move to the next round of challenging games."

Husband and wife joined Ross at the wagon. "'Twas a lively shew with tha lads and lassies," Ross said.

William reattached his scabbard and sword. "Yes. A nice diversion."

Pippa smoothed her hair from her face and caught William's look. "You made friends this day ... all be it, young ones, but friends nonetheless."

Ross laughed. "A mon canna have too many allies."

"You are correct, my friend." William reached for Pippa's hand. "Let's go catch an adversary."

During William's play with the children, the change in the position of the sun had heightened his awareness of the dangerous task before him. Was the man he sought the one who murdered his father's guards? His boot heel dug into the ground with each step.

A strong tug at his arm by his wife brought him to an abrupt stop which caused Pippa to stumble. If not for his quick hand, she would have fallen to the ground. "Wife, what are ye about?"

Ross walked away from the two.

Righting herself, she adjusted her headpiece. "Can you please shorten your step or slow down? Remember, I'm in a dress today."

He gave himself a mental shake. So focused on apprehending the enemy, he had disregarded the wife by his side. "Yes ... of course ... forgive me," he mumbled.

Her eyes darted about before settling on William. "We all desire the same thing; but as you said, we must not appear hurried."

William breathed deep. "You are correct." He rolled his neck and shoulders.

"Paint on your smile. We're a happy couple, remember?"

William's lips twisted in an attempt.

Pippa giggled. "Alas, you have failed. It looks more like a sneer."

He gazed heavenward. Looking back to his wife, he sighed. "Is this better?"

She grinned. "Those teeth look like Wolf's, but they could work to my advantage if the enemy chases after me."

*Humph!*

Arm in arm they turned toward the lists. Loud grunts and howls of laughter drifted on a breeze. "Sounds as if the men are ready to begin. No doubt they are impressing the few maidens lining the area," William said.

Stopping at the edge of the warrior's training range, William surveyed the land. He spotted the five hidden guards placed where he had suggested. Henry and Robert stood off to the side observing the wrestling match. Glancing upward, more guards walked the parapet as if watching beyond the castle walls.

His eyes scanned the crowd. Henry caught his attention and nodded toward a group of young men—all shirtless. Wanting to rub his hands together in triumph, William refrained. "Lady McKinnon, I believe our throne awaits us for the viewing."

"Another wagon of hay?"

"I believe this hay is softer and piled higher."

"You jest?"

He chuckled. "Aye."

They threaded their way through the groups of men. William lifted Pippa onto the back of the open wagon. He climbed atop the wheel and waved his arm.

"The royal couple has arrived. 'Tis time for the competition to begin." He jumped in and rolled to Pippa's side. On his back, he yanked her down beside him.

She shrieked. "What are you about? This is unseemly."

The rowdy group of men guffawed at the scene. With one arm preventing her escape, his other hand drew her face close. "He's here," he rasped.

Her eyes widened. "Truly?"

"Aye." He kissed her forehead and sat up. "Now, we are ready," he announced to all within hearing. He pulled her to a sitting position and plucked straw from her hair. "You are a mess."

She moaned as she shook her head at William. The men clapped their approval having no idea it was a contrived tender moment. "From the roar, it seems the men commend my actions."

She ducked her head. "Please, get on with the contest."

William stood in the wagon and silenced all with his upstretched arms. "Lady McKinnon and I welcome you to our first annual laborer competition. May the strongest man win!"

"I will win!" one shouted.

"No, I."

"Malcom, yer wyff is stronger than ye."

The crowd erupted in boisterous laughter as Malcom grinned a toothless grin and scuffed his boot in the dirt.

"Stop with the boasts and show us your might," William shouted with merriment. "The winning side receives unlimited ale for two days."

Men pushed one another in revelry while others threw loose straw in the air—all claiming victory.

Edmund and Peter separated the men into two teams. The groups huddled and discussed their strategies. Each man would be paired with a man from the opposing team. Equal size was important if they wanted a chance to triumph.

William leaned back on his hands while Pippa swung her legs off the end of the wagon. Behind her, he watched as the breeze blew her long curls. The yellow ribbon woven around her crown enhanced the contrast between her few sun-kissed tresses and her flaming locks. He once thought his preference was golden hair like his mother's, but Pippa's auburn color suited him.

A brawny young man looked his way causing him to sit up. His eyes narrowed as he stared first at William and then at Pippa. William's hands fisted as he glared back. He made note that the lad joined Peter's team. Peter yanked on the boy's arm to draw his attention back to the group.

Unable to see if the young man possessed a scar, William's teeth ground. Waiting for the action to play out involved great effort.

"Is something amiss?"

Pippa's breath tickled his ear. Startled, his head whipped around at her question. The uncertainty in her eyes, stirred him. "I thought I saw the perpetrator but am unclear. 'Tis difficult to wait for our enemy to pounce. I'm accustomed to pursuing until my foe is defeated." His gaze swung back to the crowd. How could he concentrate on his enemy with the sweet fragrance of his wife surrounding him?

"I've heard, patience is a virtue."

"'Tis a quality I lack." To gain distance from her delightful scent, he jumped to the ground and leaned against the wagon with arms crossed over his chest.

At long last, the first competition began. One man from each team carried two heavy logs to the end of the lists and dropped them. This repeated until all the logs accumulated at the other end of the lists. Next, they rolled a barrel down, filled it with three logs and dragged it back. Each time the barrel rolled to one end, more logs were added. The last man's task proved strenuous.

The shouted cheers were deafening as each team struggled to finish first. Edmund's strategy worked. He placed Duff as his final competitor. Duff was massive. He silenced the competition as he sat atop his barrel waiting on the final challenger from Peter's team.

William followed Henry's eyes to view the rage of one man who kicked logs and smashed a couple of hay bundles—his enemy. It was plain to see, losing didn't set well with him. William's grip tightened on the hilt of his sword. It required great fortitude to refrain from engaging the adversary.

"Duff is quite proud. Look at his smile—it's broader than the night sky." Pippa clapped with the crowd.

William was aware when her clapping ceased, and she leaned near.

"What think you, husband?"

He heard the smile in her voice. "Aye ... proud."

"You seem distracted. Do you see him?" she whispered.

The warmth of her nearness made his head spin. He looked back at his wife and offered a weak grin. "I'm assessing all who participate today. Excuse my rudeness."

"You've spied him," she hissed, "and didn't plan to tell me."

He straightened from his slouched position. "The less you know, the better."

She reared back from him. "I understand. You're afraid I will act in a suspicious way and alert him." Her tightly grasped hands sat in her lap as her face turned from him.

Walter announced man-to-man competition. Those who wished to compete stood to one side. Walter paired them according to size, age—not considered. William honed in on his enemy and hoped to observe him without notice.

Distracted when Pippa jumped down and stalked off, William watched her a moment. When he looked back, his foe had disappeared.

# 26

Pippa stomped through the courtyard. First, her husband demanded her promise not to impede the capture of their enemy, and then he acted as if she were untrustworthy. Her fisted hands swung by her side. She plowed a path through the celebrating peasants and stopped near the gatehouse.

She glanced over her shoulder. No one appeared to witness her irritation. Aggravated with William, she decided to release her frustration out of eyesight. With a slower pace, she exited the castle and crossed the drawbridge.

A shrill whistle from her lips brought her wolf to the edge of the woods. "Hey, boy." She walked closer to the trees and knelt. Her wolf trotted up to her outstretched hand. She hugged him close and ruffled his fur.

His excited answer knocked her to her bottom. "Are you happy to see me, sweet boy?" She failed to prevent the lick to her face. "Ech! You know I'm not fond of your kisses on my face."

"Then, where do you prefer kisses?"

Pippa twisted around, scanning the trees from whence came the voice. Wolf crouched low and growled. She grabbed a hunk of fur to hold him. "Whoa, boy. Stay close," she whispered.

She stood but kept a hold on Wolf. "Who's there? Show yourself."

A man walked to the fringe of the dark forest. The hood of his cloak hid his face.

"Do I know you?" An uneasiness covered her.

"Nay. I know yer hoosband."

"Ah, Scottish. Did you wish to speak with Lord McKinnon?"

"Nay. Ye weel suffice."

Her breathing grew faster. "Why lurk in the trees?"

"'Tis my way."

Pippa narrowed her eyes. "You may join our celebrations and then talk with my husband."

"Nay!"

She flinched at his forcefulness. Wolf growled and bared his teeth. How dare he come on her property and scare her with his sinister attitude. Anger simmered close to the surface.

"What is your purpose?"

"All weel be revealed in due time."

"Lady McKinnon," Henry yelled.

Pippa turned to see Henry running her way. When she looked back toward the trees, her mystery man had disappeared. Her eyes roved the tree line to no avail. She stamped her foot in frustration. "'Twas no doubt an enemy, Wolf, and now he's gone."

Henry's sword clanked against his belt as he approached. "What are ye about? You exposed yourself to danger without a guard."

Wolf changed his aggressive stance toward Henry. "I think not. Wolf protects my side."

Henry huffed. "We lost sight of our foe. He vanished before the games concluded. He is a potential threat."

She turned back toward the woods. "I spoke to him."

"What!" Henry came in front of Pippa and glared. "You jest."

"We conversed until you shouted my name."

Henry drew his sword. "What direction did he flee?"

"He will return. Of this I'm certain." Pounding hoof beats drew their attention. William, Walter, and Ross galloped their way.

William leapt from his steed and rushed to Pippa's side. "What happened here?"

Henry and Pippa talked at once; nevertheless, Henry's booming voice won out. She squatted down and placed her arm around the neck of her pet. "Men are quite troublesome," she whispered in his ear.

"Wife, your actions are irresponsible!" He reached for her arm and Wolf lunged. Pippa's strong hold prevented a nasty bite. "Call off your wolf. Now!"

Pippa's brows rose to her hairline. "When you lower your voice, Wolf will ease his attack stance." She watched as the other three men backed away to allow them some privacy.

The tic in William's cheek caught her attention. He might be furious with her leaving the castle, but she was equally angry with his actions. This was one stare down she refused to relinquish.

"Lady McKinnon, please accompany me on my horse back to the safety of the castle walls. Your pet may run alongside if it pleases you."

He didn't fool Pippa. She knew beneath his false calm prowled an angry lion. "I prefer to walk beside you while I inform you of my findings."

The bridle reins slapped against his leg. His lips formed a thin line. "As you wish." He circled his hand signaling the men to ride guard around them.

"Wolf, come." Her pet trotted between her and William. "Ever my protector."

With hands behind his back and his horse trailing along, her husband waited. Each breath sounded like a snort.

She tried to remain unaffected by his obvious ire. "While talking with Wolf, a man emerged from the forest." She hurried on to say, "I was not in immediate danger. Wolf kept him in his place."

William grunted.

"His hooded cloak kept his face from my sight. He said he knew my husband."

William stopped. "And?"

"His brogue was Scottish; so, I asked if he wished to speak with you. He replied nay with vehemence. When I asked his purpose, he said all would be revealed in due time."

"Nothing more?"

"No. Henry scared him away. He disappeared amongst the trees. We must be ever vigilant this eventide. I expect his return."

"We need to hurry. He might well have doubled back and reside inside the walls. I postponed the release of Errol until I knew of your whereabouts. Please, ride with me."

His slight reprimand didn't go unnoticed by her. "Certainly. Give me a boost."

William spurred his horse and the others surrounded them. His arm secured her against his chest. "We will resume our discussion about the disregard for your safety when we reach the privacy of our room."

Pippa steeled herself for the showdown to come. He might be her husband, but she had a mind of her own and planned to use it.

"Lower the portcullis," William called out once they rode past the barbican. His rear guard followed to the keep steps. There, he assisted her from his horse and claimed her hand. "Ross, see my horse retuned to the stable. Ask Malcom to bed him down for me."

"At once, m' lord."

Pippa raised her hand to her wolf. "Stay."

"Henry ... Walter, I'll meet with you in the war room once I see to my wife's safety."

Standing to his side, Pippa rolled her eyes heavenward. She attempted to remove her hand from his hold, but he held tight. Without another word, he marched up the steps dragging her along. She dared not rebuke his actions or endure further embarrassment.

He bypassed the dining hall and headed for the stairs without pause. She grabbed a handful of her dress and raised it high above her boots. No doubt he would drag her up the winding staircase if she tripped on her dress.

Once reaching their bedchamber, he flung her into the room and slammed the door with a kick from his boot. With both hands, he

scrubbed his face and then rubbed his forehead. At last, his arms
fell away, and he stared at her standing in the middle of the room.

"I should turn you over my knee and give you the beating you
deserve."

She leveled her eyes at him and glared. "I advise it not."

"Not only did your actions jeopardize our efforts, it put you at
risk of capture ... or death."

"I was in no danger. Wolf provided my protection."

"You knew not if other men hid in the forest for the moment to
capture you. Tell me, how many men can Wolf take down before
he's slit open? In the meantime, you are whisked away never to be
seen again or slit open like your wolf and left for dead." His voice
raised with each statement.

Pippa gasped at the horrific scene he painted.

"Did you possess your sword or your bow with arrows? Or your
knives hidden beneath your dress? Mayhap you would have talked
the enemy into submission?"

"Stop!" Her hands trembled. Fear mixed with her anger
produced a volatile state.

William rubbed the back of his neck and leaned against the door
with closed eyes. His breathing slowed with each breath.

Pippa watched as he gained control from his outburst—grateful
he refrained from thrashing her backside. She would have fought
him, but he would have won with his brawny strength. "You didn't
trust me," she whispered.

He opened his eyes and frowned. "Of what do you refer?"

"You spied the enemy and feared if you told me the *truth,* I
would foil his capture." She flounced over to a chair by the cold
fireplace and plopped down. "One moment you trounce
truthfulness; and the next, you hold the truth from me. You can't
expect me to agree with your mingled signs. Either you're truthful
or you're not." She turned to look at him. "Which will it be?"

William leaned his head against the door and looked up to the
rafters. With a heavy sigh, he pushed away from the door and
ambled to sit in the opposite chair. He crossed his boots at the

ankle and rested back in the chair. After a moment of silence, he looked at her.

"As you know, I chose soldering as a profession."

"A mercenary."

"Aye. Not my proudest moment. During that time, my contacts consisted of men with disreputable reputations. I found few trustworthy comrades."

"I am not ..."

He held up his hand. "Let me finish. It didn't take long to realize this occupation attracted evil scoundrels. Dishonest men full of deceit swarmed around me. Men who slept soundly were ill fated—murdered in their sleep for their portion of the gains. It sickened me. I distanced myself from them and hired out to protect titled men who paid me well for my services."

"Why tell me this?"

"You need to know my background, so you can traverse our future. Trust of another comes hard for me. Not to mention, the women in my life have proven deceitful and cunning. All except my mother and oldest sibling, Emilia."

Pippa picked at her fingernails as they both sat silent. *How can I convince him of my honesty?* She stilled her hands. "From our previous encounters, you know I am straightforward. Rest assured the words from my mouth are truthful. I strive to respect what my parents taught me—honesty and honor. The art of cunning deceitfulness belongs to a socialite which we both know is a ludicrous picture of me. View me more like your mother."

William's booming laughter broke the seriousness of the moment. His feet flew apart as he leaned his arms upon his knees. "I cannot think of you like my mother."

Warmth spread from Pippa's chest to her face. She resisted the urge to cover her flaming cheeks with her cool hands. "I see nothing amusing about what I said."

"Ah, Pippa. I'm pleased conceit never tainted your soul. You know not the affect you have upon me." His gaze swept over her form. "One day I will tell you, but not today. You are not ready to hear it."

He stood and pulled her to her feet. His hand buried in her thick hair and tilted her face upward. "I will work on trusting you; this I pledge."

Flutters rippled through her stomach. When she thought a kiss was forthcoming, he freed her hair and stepped away.

"I wish you to remain in our room while I talk with Henry and Walter. Your wolf may reside with you." William strode to the door.

"He might attempt to bite you."

"I bite back."

Errol's feet crunched on dried leaves. "Finlay ... Finlay," Errol's hushed voice called.

With the swiftness of a mountain lion, Finlay grabbed Errol and laid a knife against throat. "Where have ye been, ye vermin? I have waited weeks for ye."

"They held me captive in their doongin."

Finlay whipped Errol around with the knife point in his side.

"How did ye escape? Did ye lead them to me, ye fool?"

The point drove deeper in Errol's side. "Nay... nay, I sware. We moost hurry from here. They wilt coom."

"Did ye git tha maps, ye useless mon?"

"Aye. Here." Errol shoved the pouch at Finlay.

"Coom with me. 'Tis too dark to see." Finlay prodded Errol with the tip of his knife.

The two men picked their way across the forest floor. Errol stumbled numerous times to keep the pace Finlay demanded. They worked their way west of Fairwick Castle toward the boundary line between England and Scotland.

"Stoop," Finlay whispered.

Errol froze.

"Wait here. Ye better be here when I return." Finlay crept northeast of their position with the pouch strapped to his back.

Errol sat with his back to a tree and waited. His eyes strained to see through the dark mist of night yet failed to identify any object more than two feet away. At one point, he reasoned Finlay had abandoned him.

Rustling leaves sent Errol scrambling to his feet.

"Count yer no-good-self blissed. I found nary a mon trailing us."

"We moost hurry. They weel look for us."

The black of night slowed their progress. Even though the moon peeked out on occasion to give light for the journey, they traveled several hours to reach the campsite in Scotland.

Finlay stopped short of the campsite and whistled his arrival. When he received a whistle of like kind, they approached the camp.

"We verra near gave ye up," Raven snapped.

Finlay smacked Errol in the back of his head. "This galoot is tha reason for our delay."

Raven's frown was immediate. "Is he a traitor? Do we need to slay him?"

"Nay. He redeemed himself. He turned o'er tha maps to tha castle." Finlay removed the maps and spread them out near the firelight.

Raven and Finlay poured over the drawings while Errol sat between two guards on the opposite side of the fire. Errol's knee jiggled up and down while he bit his nasty fingernails.

"Ye appear fearful," one guard said.

Errol snatched his hand down. "I feared for me life in the doongin. No doubt, we weel be hunted."

The guard laughed. "Let them coom. I'm lusty for a fight."

Raven and Finlay murmured low about the castle map until Finlay reared back with force. "There is something amiss here." He pointed to the map and looked back at Errol with a scowl. "Bring him to me."

# 27

The next morning, Walter came to the dining hall to report their findings. He strode up to the dais where Pippa and William finished their meal together.

Walter crossed his chest with a fisted hand and bowed his head in respect. "M' lord and m' lady."

William stood. "Lady McKinnon, please lead us to a private room."

"Follow me."

He and Pippa left by way of the door behind their chairs. Walter followed them down a short hallway and up three stairs to a secluded room where the clerk worked on the accounts.

The room stood empty at the early hour. William arranged three chairs close together. Pippa sat on the edge of her seat. After Walter closed and latched the door, he joined them.

"What have you learned?" William asked.

"It was as you suspected. The young man, named Finlay, led us to an encampment across the border line. According to Henry, it lay within a few miles of your family estate."

William burned from within. "I imagine Finlay is responsible for the torching of the castle."

Pippa and Walter regarded William.

"Ignore this bitter man. Continue your account," Pippa said.

"Finlay and Errol joined five men at the camp. Finlay and a man named Raven scrutinized the map you provided. At one point, Finlay said there was something wrong with the map. Errol came over to observe and denied any errors. At that time, Raven said they would present the map to the master and let him verify the drawing."

"Did he name the master?" Pippa asked.

"Yes. His name is Eugene."

William looked to Pippa. "Is the name familiar to you?"

"No."

"It's known to me," Walter said. "When your mother, Lady Brigette Fairwick McKinnon lived here as a young woman ..." He paused.

"What troubles you?"

"The story is not mine to reveal. 'Tis your mother's."

"My mother would want you to tell all if it means getting my father home. I will bear up under any tale."

Walter glanced at Pippa before continuing. "A man named Eugene lived here at Fairwick Castle. He and your mother devised a wicked plan to capture and dispose of Lady Isabelle Fairwick, her brother Nicolas's wife. At some point in the scheme, your mother had a change of heart. She wished to be done with Eugene. However, he proceeded in an attempt to kill Lady Isabelle with an arrow and nearly succeeded."

Pippa sucked in a breath as her hand flew to her mouth. "Oh, dear. I've heard bits of this story. I thought it was nothing but a tale among servants."

"Eugene expected Lady Bridgette Fairwick to wed him and escape the heavy hand of her brother, Nicolas."

"Was he a knight?" William asked.

"No. Nothing more than a guard in Lord Fairwick's service. Some thought him to be deranged. Lady Isabelle refused to allow death as his punishment. She hoped for his salvation."

"Did he escape?" William asked.

"No. Lord Fairwick released him in Scotland with no weapons. It was understood that Lord McKinnon, your father, would see to his demise."

William shot to his feet. He paced the room as his anger built. "I will tear him apart!" He spun around. "Where is Eugene?"

"Henry and his men trail the seven men to their destination. He will report back as soon as possible. The group headed further north into Scotland. The arrogant men never suspected we followed them."

"My men are excellent trackers," Pippa said.

William's mind whirled with possibilities. Relieved for the information, he wondered if his father lived. "Well done, Walter. If there is nothing more, you may take your leave."

"Thank you, m' lord." Walter unlatched the door and closed it behind him.

"What's our plan?" Pippa asked—eyes bright.

William looked into her expectant eyes and saw hope. He knelt beside her chair and took her hands into his own. "I ride south for needed coinage. I will update my mother and bring the needed funds back for your people. Then I ride north into Scotland to locate a few friends. They are exceptional in black powder warfare."

Her eyes lit up. "I've not experienced the power of the black powder, but I've heard about its destructive capabilities."

"It's a fragile element and requires expertise in its mixture."

"Fascinating!"

"I hope you have no reason to gain such knowledge."

Her lips pouted. "What do you require of me?"

Thankful she didn't ask more questions, he continued. "I wish you to oversee the wall repair. I desire the castle fortified and impenetrable; not to mention, winter will soon be upon us. Do you own adequate supplies for mortar to begin the rebuilding?"

"Yes. I retain spare coins if needed. I set aside the monies to restock our winter food supply."

"Use it if required. I will replenish it." He rubbed his thumb across her hand. "Don't take unnecessary risks. We know not who

Finlay left behind to wreak havoc inside our walls. Be on guard and keep Wolf by your side at all times. Sleep in your childhood room where an escape route exists. I care not if you wear trousers with your knives readily available." He grinned. "Loose ones. I don't wish a guard to fall from the wall because of distraction."

"How soon until you depart?"

"Once needed items are packed."

"'Tis time for my morning vespers. Prayers for your safe travels shall grace my lips ..." She placed her hand atop his. " ... as well as your father's return."

His eyes gravitated to her mouth. *I can think of a better use of your lips.*

"Prayers are wasted on me." He let go of her hands and stood. "Come. There is much to accomplish."

They hurried toward their room. In William's mind, he pictured his father in good health. It was the best way for him to focus on his next action.

Pippa slipped her hand into his and squeezed. "You will find your father. Now, to make my way to the chapel."

"Wait." He opened the door to their room and whistled. "Take Wolf."

Wolf trotted up to William and stopped. He petted his head and glanced at Pippa.

Open mouthed, Pippa stared.

With a crooked grin, William said, "We've arrived at an understanding."

She snapped her teeth shut and looked from William to Wolf. "I see. Come, Wolf." She bent low and whispered, "Traitor."

William longed to follow her to see she arrived safely but refrained. Instead, he packed a change of clothes and a few coins in his travel bag. He sent the guard to inform Ross they were taking a trip. Next, he moved his wife's garments and additional weapons to the room where she would reside in his absence. When he finished, he headed toward the chapel to bid her farewell.

Stopping right inside the door, he scanned the room. Ever vigilant, wolf guarded halfway down the aisle. He glanced at

William yet stayed in place. Alone at the altar, Pippa's voice echoed off the stones. How long would she remain on her knees?

"Bless his journey ... may it be free of peril ... may he find his mother in good health as he delivers an encouraging word. Oh, God, my help in ages past, deliver my husband from his bonds of slavery."

His head jerked as if struck. *I'm not enslaved.*

"Touch his heart with Your loving hand and give sight to his blindness."

*What is this prattle? Blindness?*

"Give him wisdom and bring him back to me, Oh, God, my Lord and Savior ..."

Prayers were pointless. Hadn't he witnessed enough carnage to believe God gave no thought for His people? Innocents died alongside evil ones. Where was God's justice? His heels scraped along the stone as he walked toward Pippa kneeling at the altar.

She tilted her head at the sound but continued to murmur her prayers. When she finished, she looked to the cross above the altar. "Thank you, Father."

Standing beside her, William offered a hand up. His large, roughened hand engulfed her delicate one. "Walk with me."

He drew her hand through his arm. "Remember all I have voiced. Your safety is utmost in my mind."

"Rest assured, I will follow your commands. Especially the one where I'm to wear trousers. 'Tis my favorite demand of all." Her impish smile caused a longing to swell in his chest.

"'Twill do my heart good to know my wife obeys my commands."

Wolf fell in behind the couple.

"Who travels with you?"

"Ross, my faithful companion."

"He is a good friend. You are most fortunate."

"Aye." He heard longing in her voice. "Who do you call friend?"

She squeezed his arm. "We'll save your question for a fireside chat once you return. At present, let us go to the kitchens to collect food for your travels."

The cooks were delighted for their lord and lady to make an appearance. They loaded William with breads, meat pies, cheese, and fresh roasted venison. His flask spilled over with ale. "Ladies, 'tis more than enough. Thank you for this tasty fare." In the doorway stood his wife smiling as the women pampered him. His ears heated when he caught her looking his way. "Enough, good ladies. Ross and I will savor and enjoy this fine meal on our journey. For now, I must be away."

Pippa and William dashed from the kitchens. "Honored that you came to the lowly kitchens, they wanted to please you."

"I never considered the kitchens lowly. I spent many a day hiding amongst barrels of milled wheat waiting for the right moment to steal a pastry."

"Childhood antics ... not a care ... what happy memories."

"I'm placing Duff as your personal guard."

She frowned at him. "There's no need."

"Please question me not." He raised his hand. "Before you say it, I know you can defend yourself. Think of it in this manner. 'Twill lessen my guilt at leaving you in possible danger."

Her sigh was audible. "As you wish."

Outside the keep, he turned to Pippa. "I will return post haste."

Her folded hands rested against her stomach. "I look forward to news of your family." She cocked her head. "Have a care, my husband."

He bowed and jogged down the steps. Ross sat atop his mount holding the reins to William's horse. He vaulted into the saddle and looked up at his wife. She appeared small and delicate; yet in his heart—fragile—she was not. "Fare thee well."

Pippa watched as the two horses thundered across the drawbridge. Would her new husband return as he promised? Did his enemies plot evil against him even now?

*Remember him, my Lord and Savior. Beset him behind and before and place Thine protective hand upon him. Whither he goes, may Your presence go before him. Capture his soul, oh mighty God, and hold it until the day of Your deliverance.*

Fearful for his journey, she blinked away gathered moisture.

Walter joined her. "What is your desire for this day?"

She looked to see the day peep on the horizon. "We best get started mixing mortar. What think you?"

"Yes, m' lady. I'll make ready the lime kiln and see the materials are gathered." Walter left to ready the tools.

Pippa hurried inside to change her clothes. Wearing a dress restricted her movement. It would be delightful to go about her business without the constraint of a dress and undergarments. With Wolf at her heels, she climbed the circular stairs and headed toward the room she shared with her husband. When she arrived, she noticed her items were absent. *Who moved my clothing?* Standing in her parents' room brought a pain in her breast. Would the heartache lessen with more time? Doubtful.

She whirled around and bumped into Duff when she exited the room. "Pardon me, Duff."

Wolf growled.

"Stop, Wolf. Duff is my friend."

"My apologies, Lady Fair ... McKinnon." He ducked his head.

"Hearing Lady McKinnon is foreign to my ears, as well. No apologies necessary."

She listened to Duff's steady footsteps as she walked to her childhood room. She welcomed sleeping in her own bed. To dwell in a bed with William was discomforting. His nearness made her crave his touch which left her irritated. She lived unencumbered for years only for her knees to go weak with one look from her husband. Inexcusable! She would do well to remember she forced him to wed ... well, with the king's help.

A tapping on the door brought her from wool gathering. "Enter."

"M' lady."

"Gwendolyn, what is it you require?"

"Am I to see to the cleaning of this room or the larger room down the hallway?"

"The servants are to keep both rooms prepared. In my husband's absence, I reside here. 'Tis cozy and warm."

Gwendolyn stepped inside and shut the door with a click.

Pippa raised a brow. "Is something wrong?"

"Why dress thusly?"

Pippa glanced at her trousers and shirt. "My husband commissioned it." She grinned. "I think I might keep him."

Gwendolyn gasped. "M' lady!"

She put a knife inside her boot, and one attached to her belt. "I promise it's true. He asked me to oversee the repairs to the wall curtain. Like I said, he authorized my attire ... not as if I need anyone to tell me what to wear." A frown formed between her eyes. "Gwendolyn, you worry too much of things that matter not."

Gwendolyn held her ground. "You are the wife of a Scottish Laird in his own right. There is proper decorum to follow. I fear for your reputation."

"Enough. No more discussion on this subject. Men await my direction." Pippa stomped from the room leaving Gwendolyn in the middle of the room wringing her hands.

When William had asked of her friends, Gwendolyn sprang first in her mind. They weren't of equal peerage, but Gwendolyn saw her through many an escapade. She kept a look out when Pippa embarked on misdeeds. In the end, both girls reaped punishment from her mother. A sad smile formed.

Pippa shook her head. No need to favor self-pity. She would change nothing of her childhood ... except one—to postpone her parents' deaths. She possessed few women she called friends, but adventures were still plentiful.

Without turning around, she asked, "Duff, how did you get the honor of following my every step?"

"I volunteered, m' lady."

She looked over her shoulder. "There's none better to guard my back. I thank you."

He nodded.

Once outside the gate, Pippa, Duff, and Wolf walked to the southeast wall. Catapulted boulders damaged the outside wall leaving the rubble core exposed. They needed to shore up the stone wall and then pour in the binder to help stabilize the fortification.

"Walter, give me an accounting."

"Men are crushing the limestone to process through the kiln. Once the quick lime forms, we will mix it with the sand and water. If need be, I will add animal lard to strengthen the mortar."

"Are there enough cut stones for the outer repairs?"

"No, m' lady. I need coin to purchase Ashlar from the village. I will see to the purchase of the stone while you continue here."

Pippa and her men worked all through the day. In the beginning, there were few clouds. As the day progressed, darker clouds rolled across the sky. The outer barricade was completed. The binder between the inner and outer stone walls was all they lacked.

A large drop of rain struck Pippa's cheek drawing her face upward. The black clouds threatened to open wide. "Walter, what is needed to finish the filling?"

"Peter. He is the lightest one among us to pour in the mortar from atop the wall walk. A line of men will pass the buckets of mortar to Peter while he pours it in. The newest placed stones are inadequate to hold one heavier than Peter."

Rain pelted harder as he spoke. "There's no time. I'll go up."

"No, m' lady. 'Tis too dangerous! The wall could give way if the rain weakens the mortar around the new stones. I cannot sanction such an endeavor."

Pippa ran toward the outer stairs. When she reached the top, she grabbed the wall to steady herself. She closed her eyes against the ground far below. *God help me!* Her hand touched the stones as she scooted her feet toward the opening between the walls. No time to stagger from fear.

Thunder rolled. Rain stung her face. She leaned her back against the inner wall and peered down the hole. "Hurry men. Get the binder to me," she shouted over the storm. She yanked her foot back when it squished in the new mortar. "Hurry!"

The fresh mortar lacked adequate time to harden completely. Stray hairs plastered to her face and neck. She wiped rain and hair ringlets from her eyes. At last, a bucket of binder arrived. She received it with one hand and braced herself against the wall before dumping the first batch. After repeated times, she saw the hole filled up with the lime, water, and sand.

While waiting for another bucket, the ground trembled from a lightning strike nearby. The loud clap caused her to jump. Her foot slipped into the hole. The suction of the filling pulled her downward. Her body collapsed upon the walkway.

"Duff!" she screamed as her fingers scratched the stone walkway for a solid hold. The forceful pull was that of quicksand.

A firm grip grabbed one arm and yanked. She cried out in pain. Duff then clutched both of her hands and pulled. With a slow, agonizing drag her legs broke free from the grip of sure death. The rain continued to batter Pippa and her men. Even when the mortar released her feet, her heart pounded like a hammer against an anvil.

Before she caught her breath, Duff scooped her into his arms and ran toward the steps. Pain shot through her shoulder with every footfall. Walter barked orders. "Patrick, alert Gwendolyn. Lady McKinnon needs a hot bath. Edmund, get the village healer. Quickly!"

As her head flopped against Duff's chest, the rolling black clouds blurred.

*Papa.*

# 28

"We barely escaped with our lives!" William declared as they galloped down the road.

Ross chuckled.

William looked over at Ross. "'Tis true, and well you know it. My sisters are heathen beasts—not fit for human companionship."

"One day a mon weel wed tha lassies and rejoice in it."

William doubled over in laughter. "Oh, Ross. If it happens, I'll dance unclothed through the village. For Gillian to get chosen, the doomed man would have to be a saint or daft." He hooted at his own wit. "I pray I live to see such a wonder."

Ross shook his head.

The men road half of the day before reaching the crossroads. William pulled up. His mount pranced in a circle. "Should we continue to Fairwick castle or inspect the McKinnon castle ruins?

"It weel be dark soon."

William's smile disappeared. "Aye. Ye are correct. Home it is."

The men turned east and headed to Fairwick Castle in England. William mulled over the word *home.* The thought of his childhood spent in Scotland was bittersweet. His father had been strict but fair. The day his father married Lady Brigette Fairwick from

England, at five years old, William thought his life perfect. As his mind conjured up a picture of his beloved home sitting in ruins, a knife twisted in his heart. *I will avenge this atrocity, my father. On this ye can rest assured.*

As twilight flickered on the horizon, William and Ross viewed the burning torches atop the battlement at Fairwick castle. What an eerie yet picturesque sight for William's bone-weary body.

"'Tis a welcoom sight," Ross said.

"Aye. Freedom from this horse will be a refreshing change. A tasty meal followed by a piping hot bath ... all beside a roaring fire ... nothing can compare."

A shout went out from the gatehouse guard to herald their arrival. "Mayhap, ye'll be met by yer bonnie bride."

William smirked. "I'm not counting on it."

The horses rumbled across the drawbridge and into the courtyard. The crashing sound of the portcullis dropping into place for the night alerted all to the conclusion of another day. William guided his horse to the nearest stable and climbed down. Removing his saddle bag, he threw the reins to Malcom. "Give these two steeds an added amount of special care. They earned it."

As the men rounded the front corner of the keep, Walter waited atop the steps wearing a frown. "What could cause such a scowl in four days' time?" William asked.

"Need ye ask?" Ross replied.

William jumped the steps two at a time. "What ails ye, my friend?"

"There was an incident."

When Walter wasn't forthcoming with an explanation, it caused concern. As William followed him inside, he looked to Ross. "Eat and retire for the night. You deserve a respite. I'll call upon you if need be."

Ross nodded. "As ye wish."

Halting outside the entrance to the grand hall, William waited for Walter to tell his news. He watched the servants scatter when they saw the two men. The hair on his neck prickled.

"We worked on restoring the damaged wall when ..."

Walter's long pause unnerved William. "Out with your report!"

"Lady McKinnon took a nasty fall during the repairs."

His heart raced. "Does she live?"

"Yes, confined to her room."

Not waiting for further account, William dashed up the stairs. He envisioned his wife with bloody wounds and possible broken limbs. The fault was his. He told her to oversee the renovations never expecting her to participate. Foolish of him to not anticipate her actions.

With clammy hands, he opened the door to their bedchamber and dropped his bags. A cold, dark room greeted him. Where was she? He surged into the hallway. "Walter!" William jumped at Walter's nearness.

"She's in her room, down the passageway and around the corner." Walter walked beside William. "Her injuries are not grave; however, we thought it best for her to rest and refrain from strenuous activity."

William's galloping heart began to slow at Walter's reassurance. "Explain."

"She stood atop the wall pouring the binder inside the wall when a clap of thunder shook the ground and her foot slipped into the filler. It sucked her down."

He reached out and stopped Walter. "Why was she chosen to do this dangerous task?" Sweat formed above his lip.

"No one chose her. It began raining, and the wall was in danger of collapsing if not completed before the storm. She deemed it necessary for her to climb atop the wall since Peter was not close at hand. Due to the instability of the wall, it required one of less mass. He's the lightest of our men."

They arrived to find Henry outside of Pippa's door. Before Walter concluded his explanation, William burst into Pippa's room. His gaze landed on the bed where he expected to find her resting. "Wife?"

Wolf raised his head for a quick look but didn't growl. Pippa peeked around the chair where she sat by the fireplace. "I'm delighted you returned unharmed." She stood and smoothed the wrinkles from her robe. "They kept me a prisoner for days. At last, freedom."

Confused, William scowled. "Why are you not abed?"

"I'm recovered. There's no need for more rest."

William noticed Gwendolyn sat on a stool at the foot of Pippa's chair. Henry and Walter had stepped inside the room as well. "Everyone out!"

Laying aside her needlework, Gwendolyn jumped from her seat and scurried out the door. Henry and Walter backed away closing the door in the process. Pippa's back stiffened as she held onto the chair. Wolf plunked down by her side.

She glared at William. "What is the meaning of your outburst?"

William walked over to his wife dressed in her night clothing and robe. He pulled her away from the chair into the middle of the room. Other than a perplexed look, her face appeared unscathed. Walking around her, his eyes traveled up and down her form. Wolf shadowed his steps. "Are your wounds hidden?"

Her head twisted and turned to keep up with his movements. "My shoulder is a bit stiff, but that is the extent of my injuries."

He stopped in front of Pippa with arms crossed and Wolf at his feet. "Walter states you were atop the wall instead of Peter. Putting your life in jeopardy was unwarranted."

Her face turned red. Stepping back from him, her hands flew to her hips. "You told me to oversee the repairs and that's exactly what I accomplished."

His arms flung wide in frustration. "I told you to direct the work, not to perform the labor."

Her lips thinned. "This exchange is pointless. I'm unharmed. The wall is mended. You returned safe and whole. Have you eaten?"

The change in the direction of their conversation disoriented him. Excessive fatigue muddled his mind. "What?"

"You look quite weary. I will send a meal to your room and request a bath prepared."

With no time to gather his thoughts, she and Wolf disappeared. Standing in the middle of her room, William stared out the door.

226

His young, petite wife had seized their argument and escaped the room. How had he lost the upper hand?

He plopped into the vacated chair and rested his head in his hands. The thought of her sucked into the center of the wall sat like a stone on his chest. She would have suffocated. He slumped in the seat and his chin dipped. Relief covered him. She was unharmed ... but what about the next time? Possessing a wife was turning out to be a challenge of a different kind.

Shaking his head, he pushed to his feet and marched out of the room. When he turned the corner, he saw maids hauling water buckets into his room. Pippa's bossy voice bounced down the hallway as she instructed the women. A mouthwatering aroma reached his nose causing his ravenous stomach to grumble. Reaching the doorway to his room, he propped himself against the stone wall and waited for the women to complete the filling of his steaming tub.

With his legs crossed at the ankle, he folded his arms and closed his eyes. Weariness washed over him. Certain a relaxing bath and meal would refresh him, he withheld the tongue lashing Pippa deserved. When Walter had started the dreadful tale, an overwhelming sense of failure had weighed on him. Unacceptable. It surprised him when the responsibility of a wife proved tougher than facing an enemy. An enemy possessed certain predictable traits, a wife ... not so much.

Pippa walked into the hallway. "Your meal and bath await you."

Unfurling his stiff body, he opened his eyes. He latched onto her hand. "You will assist me." It pleased him when she offered little resistance to his tug.

As he laid the safety bar in place, he noticed her bright eyes stood in contrast to her pale complexion. "Fear not. I can bath myself; nonetheless, you remain here and give a full accounting of the episode."

Her mouth opened to reply and then snapped shut.

He began to remove his boots. "You may open the folding screen to protect your delicate sensibilities."

"As I've said before, an undressed man does not concern me."
The screen stayed folded against the wall.

"Very well. Begin your telling." He noticed she chose the chair
facing away from his tub. He grinned. Coward.

"Wolf, come." He trotted to Pippa's side and lazed beside the
stone hearth. Stroking his head, she launched into her tale.
In his opinion, her details lacked substance. No doubt, Walter
would fill in the gaps of her story. He knew enough to realize how
close she came to death. A tremor ran down his back as an
overwhelming need to protect jabbed his heart. He liked it not.

Water sloshed to the floor when he stood to dry off. "The fault
is mine. The chance to repeat this incident is forbidden. You are
henceforth restricted to running the castle from within."

Pippa jumped to her feet and turned. "What? You can't mean
it?" Wolf whined.

"Believe it." He padded over to the fireside chair and plopped
down wrapped in nothing more than a blanket.

She held her fisted hands at her side. "We shall see." When she
attempted to evade him, he grabbed her arm.

He looked up. "Pippa, this is non-negotiable. Until our enemy is
put to rest and my father found, you will obey me in this. I can't
afford the distraction of your safety while I search them out." He
released his hold and lowered his head. "My conscience couldn't
bear your death," he whispered.

She walked away. "I'll prepare your meal." The clinking
utensils gave proof of her intentions.

Watching the flames lap at one another, William transported
back to when he helped torch an enemy's wooden castle. He closed
his eyes in hopes to erase the memory. The cries of the people left
homeless just because they served an evil lord ripped his flesh to
the bone. Screams of those on fire as they ran from the burning
building sent a shudder to his toes.

When Pippa placed his trencher on a small table, he eyed her.
"Sit with me?"

With her hand on the table, she tilted her head. "Provided our
chat is to my liking."

228

His bitter laugh enveloped the room. "You, of all people, should know that nothing turns out as we hope or desire."

She sat back in the plush chair and pulled her feet under her robe. "You discount God when you make such a statement. He can turn our hopes and dreams into reality if we trust Him."

His head flopped against the chair, and he stared upward. "I'm too weary to brandish words about God. It might comfort you to put your faith in Him, but I trust my sword along with my capabilities to forge my own destiny. Let us speak upon a more pleasing subject."

A moan escaped as he savored his bite of pastry. "Excellent cooks work here."

Pippa's tight grip on the arm of her chair slackened. "They will be pleased at your assessment. It seems they enjoy spoiling you."

William looked at his wife. The paleness of her skin made the dark crescents under her eyes shimmer like a moonless night. Her near-death experience carried a toll she wished to ignore. "Are you confident your injuries have healed?"

She sighed. "Yes. I told you. Henry and Walter confined me to my room four long days. I did nothing except rest ... and pace. My shoulder had ample time to mend. The problem existing is the stiffness from inactivity."

William wiped his hands and pushed aside his near empty food platter. "Tomorrow, I plan to ride into Scotland and inspect the ruins to see if any activity transpired in my absence. Might a short journey loosen your taut joints?"

A smile crept across her face. "I'm most certain an outing on Romeo would bring me to full health provided I'm allowed to travel in suitable clothing."

"You may choose your own attire." He studied her. One moment they entertained a heated discussion; the next, she spoke with composed kindness. "Your ability to grant forgiveness is admirable. 'Tis a quality I struggle to attain."

"I crave the life my parents lived. To achieve it, I must make concessions. Of course, I pray you will do likewise."

"Commendable." He rubbed his chin. "I will endeavor to return in kind."

He rose and sauntered over to the clothing hooks. Her gasp reached his hearing when he released the blanket to don his breeches. Her interest delighted him. Living in precarious times heightened his longing for a willing wife to produce an heir. He pulled a shirt over his head without tying it closed. The time to retire was upon them.

He came to her chair. "Since I have returned, you will reside in this room ... with me."

He touched her cheek with his thumb. His fingers caressed her chin and then forced her to look up. "'Tis time to turn in if we wish to leave early on the morrow."

She gripped his outstretched hand and rose. Her body trembled as he untied her braids to allow her hair to cascade over her shoulder. He stepped back and swept his gaze over her form.

Her pulse jumped in her neck as her eyes darkened. It was all the invitation he needed. His fingers combed back her hair. As he dipped his head, her eyes closed. A craving hummed through his body. His lips grazed hers before moving to the pulse in her throat and tasting her there.

When her arms inched around his neck, desire rippled through his frame. The kiss intensified. She pressed her body tight against his own. Breaking free, he allowed his lips to caress her curls. His low voice growled. "If we continue, I won't wish to stop."

Her hands embraced his face near hers. "Our day-to-day survival is uncertain. For whatever reason, God spared my life upon the battlement." Her eyes sparked. "Do not stop."

His heart pounded with anticipation.

# 29

Daniel remained chained to the wall. All attempts to free himself failed. Without a confrontation with his captor, his unknown enemy continued to vex him.

Keys jangled in the iron door. His jailer walked in. "Today is yer lucky day. Ye are summoned by tha master."

Daniel said nothing as Bear unlocked the chain from the wall but left his ankles shackled. The iron band around his neck stayed in place, yet no longer was he tethered to the wall.

Bear yanked his neck collar. "Coom."

On stiff legs, Daniel tried to keep the pace. He stumbled through the dark tunnel, but Bear's firm grip held him upright. "Are we going outside?"

Bear grunted and kept walking.

Sunlight reflected on the damp stone the closer they came to the entrance of his underground prison. From what he saw, the opening to the outside contained no gate. Bear dragged him up four steps and outside before throwing him to the hard ground. Daniel rolled and sat up, shielding his eyes from the brightness. He breathed deep of the fresh air, filling his lungs to capacity.

A gravelly voice came from behind. "Well, if it isn't the mighty McKinnon."

Daniel pushed to his feet and turned. All around him lingered six men with crude swords and shields. "Who do I have the pleasure to meet?"

A hooded man broke through the circle to stand in the middle. "You don't remember me?"

"I might recognize you if I saw your face." His eyes shifted. Two men drew their swords.

The one called master raised his hand, and the swords lowered. "I have waited years to meet you face to face." Leaning on a walking stick, he limped around Daniel with his face hidden. He smashed his staff into the back of Daniel's knee causing his leg to buckle. "You look a bit weak."

Daniel grimaced and struggled to right himself.

The man halted in front of Daniel. "Have you not benefited from our royal treatment?"

The six men laughed and jeered. Daniel stayed mute.

"Do you remember a woman named, Isabelle?"

"Aye."

"Did you not abduct her?"

"She visited my castle. Later I released her into her husband's hands. Unharmed."

"Liar!" He smacked Daniel's face. "You kidnapped her. Admit it!"

The jarring from the stick couldn't compare to the anger boiling inside of Daniel. Thinking the man daft, he decided to play along. "Aye."

"See ... truth is best."

Daniel spied Sloan peeping from behind a tree. He averted his eyes. If this mad man caught Sloan, Daniel feared for the boy's life.

The crazed man walked away. "Bring him to my throne."

The six men followed their leader in single file while Bear tugged on Daniel's chain. He observed his surroundings as he staggered along behind his jailer. He smelled sea water and heard gulls flying overhead. The so-called castle proved nothing more than ruins buried in a hillside—vines overtaking it. Several grass huts dotted the landscape with a thin line of smoke furling from their smokestacks. Makeshift accommodations.

The leader sat upon a fallen log at the edge of the forest. "Kneel before me."

Bear pulled on Daniel's collar until he knelt upon the ground. "This is as it should be." He flipped off his hood, dipped a drink from a water bucket, and wiped his mouth on his sleeve.

It required great fortitude for Daniel to remain silent. The man's deformed face lacked an ear and exhibited a sunken hollow instead of an eye. His burned face prevented Daniel from recalling their acquaintance.

"Once I, too, resided in horrid chains such as you, but not in Scotland—England. Do you remember the tale?"

The demented man provided few clues to his identity. Daniel simmered at the game. "Nay. If you speak your name, perhaps I'll recall it."

"What say you men? Should I reveal my name?"

"Juist kill him." One man hit his club in his hand.

"Nay. Drag him to tha sea."

"Let me stab him with me dirk."

The gruff laughter bounced off Daniel's back.

The master held up a gnarled hand. "Cease." His dark eyes stared at Daniel. "My name is Eugene from Fairwick castle. Lady Brigette's lover."

---

The crisp morning found Pippa astride Romeo. Puffs of mist swirled as he snorted and pawed the ground. As William imparted final instructions for the castle's protection, her eyes followed his movements. Her stomach fluttered at the remembrance of their night together. Quite delightful. Who knew a husband could bring such pleasure?

He swung into his saddle and glanced her way. Even though embarrassed, she held his stare with a raised brow. He smiled and then led their small party out the gate. She sighed. Perchance, one day his heart would follow his carnal lusts and offer her affection if not love.

Peter, Edmund, Patrick, and John surrounded Pippa as the five trotted behind William. All were young, agile warriors with accurate aim. William had chosen his defenders with care. Pippa would miss talking with Ross—one of her favorite escorts. He stayed behind to disperse the coins needed to purchase the winter food from a nearby city.

William turned in his saddle. "Shall we pick up our pace?"

Pippa bent low over Romeo and nudged him in the flanks. The cool, fresh air stung her eyes as they sped down the road. Her braid flopped against her shoulder with wispy curls dancing across her face. She had missed this—a carefree day of riding.

After an hour, they came near the border into Scotland. William slowed his horse to a walk. "We will soon cross into Scotland. At this point, my father's castle stood as the first defense. Without him in residence, there could be trouble stirring. Keep watch."

Pippa remembered this section well. Not too long ago she presented the betrothal. Much had transpired since that day—inconceivable events.

"Follow me. I wish to show you my favorite watering hole. In fact, Pippa, your uncle Nicolas and my father often played here as boys ... without their father's knowledge, of course." His horse plunged into the forest without hesitation.

Pippa gazed in wonder. There nestled, hidden in the trees rested a small paradise. Water trickled off the small hillside rocks into a pool of clear glass. Sun filtered through the leaves and shimmered across the surface of the pond.

"How beautiful."

Her husband's face beamed at her praise.

He allowed their horses to drink but didn't dismount. "It's not much farther to my family's home. If time permits, we can stop here again on our way back to Fairwick castle."

Not to sit by the pond and enjoy the tranquility disappointed Pippa. Maybe when danger no longer roamed, she and William would spend a day lounging in the serene setting. As they rode back through the trees, she yearned for peaceful times.

William set a slower tempo for the remainder of their ride. She observed the countryside as they plodded along. The rolling hills dotted with sheep—breathtaking. She longed for a day to explore the area with her husband. No doubt, he knew fascinating places to investigate.

She trotted up to her husband and pointed. "What is the white bloom covering the hillside?"

"Ahh. 'Tis heather." He sat up straighter. "The majority of heather is purple in color. There is a legend attached to the white heather."

"Do tell."

Peter groaned.

"Hush, Peter. I wish to learn about it," Pippa reprimanded.

"Legend has it that in the 3rd Century AD, Malvina, the daughter of the legendary Scottish poet, Ossian, was betrothed to a Celtic warrior named Oscar. Tragically, Oscar died in battle. When Malvina heard the news, she was heartbroken. The messenger who delivered the bad news, also delivered a spray of purple heather Oscar had sent as a final token of his undying love for her. It's said that when Malvinas' tears fell onto the flowers in her hand, they turned white, and this magical occurrence prompted her to say: *'although it is the symbol of my sorrow, may the white heather bring good fortune to all who find it.'*"

This time both Patrick and Peter groaned.

William laughed.

Pippa scowled at the pair. "'Tis a fascinating folklore."

The last hour soared by as Pippa studied her husband's homeland. To know him better, she needed to understand his origins. The picturesque land kept her entertained for the duration of the journey.

William halted the group and spoke in a low voice. "The castle sits around this turn in the road. Proceed with caution. I know not what vagabonds inhabit the vicinity."

They broke from the road and picked their way along a narrow path leading up to the castle. The six swept the area for danger. Pippa grasped her loaded bow—ready for a skirmish. Low hanging branches and thick underbrush aided in their concealment.

When they reached the edge of the tree line, William motioned for two to circle east and two to circle west. He and Pippa rode up the middle toward the ruins. Flapping wings of startled birds caused Romeo to jerk his head up and down. The peek-a-boo sun rendered shifting shadows as if ghosts floated among the stones. The overall eeriness triggered a chill up her back.

The cutting wind whistled through the remains flinging sounds all around. If a foe lurked out of sight, it was hard to determine. With each step Romeo made, pebbles tumbled alerting anyone to their presence. Having left off her chainmail, Pippa wondered if it had been a mistake.

They stopped in what resembled the courtyard. She peeked at William and saw pain etched in his face. To fathom his grief of losing his home and father at the same time escaped her.

He dismounted and walked up to Romeo. He extended his hand. "Allow me to show you my home."

His despondent voice pricked her heart. She disengaged her bow and placed the arrow in her quiver. William's hands clutched her middle and lifted her down. Their four men rode into view as they picked their way through the rumble.

"No one in sight," Peter reported.

"Nothing untoward from our direction," John said.

"Stay alert," William directed. "Continue to scan the perimeter while Lady McKinnon and I examine the remnants." His arm extended forward. "My home."

His soulful eyes punctured her heart. "Please. Give me a tour."

His lips twitched. "I'm flattered, m' lady, to have you in my home." He reached for her hand.

His lightheartedness charmed her. She placed her hand in his and smiled. "Lead on."

"Be careful up these stairs."

Her smile widened at his playful attempt. No keep steps existed. They picked their way through the debris and into the grand hallway.

William turned in a circle. "This part is boring. I ate here and often was caught hiding under the tables with the dogs."

She cut her eyes at him and grinned. "A mischievous boy who annoyed his mother."

His hand covered his heart. "You wound me."

She snickered. "My apologies."

"Follow me up this winding staircase to the second floor where my naughtiness abounded. I oftentimes played hide-n-seek with my mother. She seldom found me before I jumped out to scare her. Even though she promised I would turn her hair gray, I waited and watched to see the spectacle—it never happened."

Pippa's laughter echoed. "What a rascal. I pray our children don't treat me in like manner." Her smile faded at the implication of her accidental statement.

His eyes held hers as he pulled her into an embrace. "Perhaps you carry my son even now." His hand found its way to her stomach.

Her breath hitched. A ripple of delight filled her belly.

When they moved apart, he captured her wrist. "Even though our marriage did not start as a love match, I'm confident our affection will grow in the right soil. You shall have no reason to fear me. I might have served as a mercenary; nevertheless, I follow the Knight's Code of Chivalry—courtesy and honor.

Her heart beat a tattoo under the skin. With their gazes locked, he raised her hand and pressed his lips to her thudding pulse. He could charm apples from a tree, but it was his words that created an ache of longing in her chest.

With a firm hold on her hand, he pulled her down his imaginary passageway. "Our portraits hung in this room." He released a shaky breath. "One painting showed my father, my birth mother, and me." He chuckled. "My new mother, Lady Brigette Fairwick, didn't appreciate the portrait in the bedchamber she shared with my father. He had refused to remove it after my birth mother's death." William shook his head. "Not long after the wedding, my mother painted a new portrait and removed the old one. Only this time it contained her in the center."

"Lady McKinnon a painter. How extraordinary!"

"Yes, she is quite exceptional. Her presence brought joy back to our home. My father adores her." A cloud formed on his face. "I've reminisced long enough." He kicked the remains of a rotting log. "For a short while we can hunt for salvageable items. Then we must return to Fairwick castle."

Disappointment struck. Pippa relished his stories. His voice inflection and nuances opened a gateway into the core of his being. She hoped it was the beginning of other revelations to come.

The toe of her boot struck a shiny object covered by layers of mud. Bending down, she used her nails to dig around the item. To complete the unveiling, she needed a sturdy stick. Spotting one, she snatched it up and raked with fervor. "William. I found something of interest."

He strode over just as she pulled out a jeweled chalice. She wiped it on her tunic and handed it to her husband.

"'Tis my parents' wedding goblet." His eyes sparkled. "Thank you, wife. Ross and I combed this area and found nothing." He pulled her up. "All it required was a woman's keen eye."

She smiled. "Let's keep searching."

Before William responded, John's horse thundered up the small rise. "M' lord. Come quickly. Evil men are near."

Both William and Pippa dashed to their horses. By the time they mounted, Patrick and Edmund arrived.

William's face was a mask. "Where is Peter?"

"He watches the scoundrels. We desired no surprise attack."

"Are they riding this way?"

"No. They camp not far from here."

"How many?" Pippa asked.

"We counted five. There could be scouts."

William's eyes narrowed. "Let's see what they are about."

# *30*

Once John described the location of their enemies, William showed them a hidden path behind the castle ruins. It led to the fringe of the forest behind large boulders embedded in the hillside. William and John dismounted and crawled along the rim of the rocks. They saw Peter below concealed in the brush, his horse nowhere in sight.

John whistled a low bird call. Peter glanced upward and acknowledged the two. He slithered under the thick foliage and headed their way.

William retrieved his spy glass from his belt. With the sun directly above, he hid in the shade of a bush. He counted seven—not five. He lowered the glass and pinched the bridge of his nose. Did he dare engage his adversary with Pippa along? He peered behind when grunts floated upward. Not long afterward, Peter's head appeared. He clawed his way over the ledge.

"What have you learned?" William murmured.

"I couldn't get close enough to hear. Two more joined the group. There are seven."

"I counted the same. What think you men? Dare we risk stealing closer to hear their exchange? I don't wish to endanger Lady McKinnon."

Peter cut his eyes toward John. "Our lady would be insulted to hear you ask. No doubt, she would wish to lead the scouting expedition," Peter whispered.

John grinned and nodded in agreement.

"Where is your horse?"

"Not far from here. I tucked him away on the other side of this hillside."

The three crept back around the hillock and joined Pippa, Edmund, and Patrick.

"What say you?" Pippa asked.

"We face seven adversaries camped on the other side. They lounge about drinking and waiting ... on whom is what concerns me."

Pippa's eyes brightened. "I say slip closer and listen in on their conversation. They might provide the leads you need to find your father."

"They outnumber us. Are you recovered enough to fend off an attacker?"

All gazes swung toward Pippa. Her eyes sparkled.

"Undeniably." Her hands rubbed together. "What's the strategy?"

William ignored a pesky notion to leave Pippa behind. Confident her skills matched that of a warrior, he yielded to her wish to partake. "I need Peter and Patrick to head west. Lady McKinnon and John will ride east with me. Edge near enough to hear but stay well hidden. Don't take any unnecessary risks. I plan to dismount and crawl closer to view their faces—see if any look familiar. If they become suspicious of our presence, depart and rendezvous at the castle ruins. Several concealed tunnels exist under the debris and can provide a place for us to disappear."

"Can we release their horses?" Patrick asked.

"No. If possible, I desire to slip in and out unnoticed. However, if they left weapons attached to their saddles, 'tis acceptable to relieve them of those armaments."

The men beamed.

The two groups headed out in opposite directions under the cover of the forest edge. William kept his company at a gentle trot. Any faster risked alerting his enemies to their approach. The three wove among tall shrubs and clumps of trees. When the camp came within sight, he slowed to a walk. Unless the men drank too much, the sound of snapping twigs and crunching leaves would warn of intruders. The slightest warning would doom their mission.

William found an area with thick vegetation and stopped. "You two stay here on your horses." He slid off his mount and handed the reins to Pippa. He peered into her tight face and wiggled his brows. "I'll return shortly." He crouched low and disappeared.

On his stomach, he slithered within fifteen feet of the campsite. When he counted six men, he dropped his head to his arm. One missing man meant trouble. He glanced around and saw no trace of the vagabond. Wiping the sweat from his brow, he strained to hear their exchange.

"I miss me bed. 'ow long moost we linger here?"

*Belching.*

"Until tha master gits tha cub."

"'e 'as tha bear. Me thinks 'tis enough."

"Ye galoot." A thrown cup crashed into the man's skull. "Tha McKinnon is old. His lad weel one day rule. When he shows oop, we'll stick a dirk in his black heart and depart for home."

"I miss Mara," a young man said.

"Ye juist want 'er to warm yer bed."

"Aye."

"Ye aught to share 'er." Gruff laughter floated through the trees.

"I want to arrive home before tha first snow. I don't relish a boat ride oop tha coast," an old warrior said.

"Ye can travel on land. 'Twould take ye a few extra days' time."

"Nay. Too 'ard on me bones. Of all tha places, why Coldingham Shore? 'Tis spooky."

Raucous laughter erupted. One drunken man fell off his log in uncontrolled hilarity. "Robin, ye believe in ghosts. What a fopdoodle."

William's mind whirled ... Coldingham Shore? He knew the area. On the clifftop of Kirk Hill sat the abandoned ruins of the Aebba monastery—a perfect place to hide. His heart drummed in his chest. At last, an indication of his father's whereabouts.

A twig snapped. "Weel, what have we here?"

William rolled into the underbrush and bounded to his feet on the other side. The once missing guard lunged with his sword. William dodged the attack. He heard swords slide from their sheaths as the encampment heard the scuffle. Not wanting to involve Pippa, he threw his favorite dirk into the man's neck and ran. He jumped fallen logs as he crashed through the undergrowth.

"Make ready," he shouted.

His excitement of the pertinent information spouted from his foes nearly got him killed. Pippa and John rode toward him. He leapt into his saddle and prodded the horse into action.

"Follow me!"

The three raced into the open field. "Is this wise?" Pippa shouted.

"Trust me!"

The horse's hooves thundered across the field churning up clods of mud and grass. Each pressed close to their horse's neck. They headed west toward Patrick and Peter. William glanced back to see five men in pursuit. The absence of two didn't bode well.

As they ate up the distance of the meadow, Peter and Patrick waited at the forest border. When he reached them, he issued orders.

"Peter, Patrick, ride south and cut over to the ruins. We'll divide their party."

Peter and Patrick galloped south. Two enemies broke from the five and followed his warriors. Three pursued William's party, but what of the other two? He examined his surroundings hoping to discover the missing men's whereabouts.

Leading Pippa and John into the woods slowed their retreat. He picked through the timberland with one destination in mind—the swinging bridge. Hoping the bridge still existed, he charged ahead.

After several minutes in the dark forest, they broke free into another wide-open meadow. As his heart pounded in his ears, it almost overrode the horse's thunderous hooves. He chastised himself. Pippa's safety depended on secure passage across the deep ravine below the bridge—the bridge he constructed with his father when a wee lad. Would it hold?

"They're getting closer!" Pippa shouted.

William veered right. They sped around the base of a knoll. On the other side of the hill, he maneuvered them inside a cave. He leapt from his horse and guided him down a darkened tunnel.

Pippa jumped from Romeo. "They will follow us." she whispered.

"Shh. I know a way out. Grab my horse's tail and stay close."

"Go ahead. I'll defend our position," John said.

"No. Grab Romeo's tail and protect Pippa's back."

The three shuffled along. The hooves squished in the soft earth and slushed out with each step. The suction echoed. When they reached twenty feet down the passageway, they heard an enemy enter.

"Ye are trapped."

William kept them moving. What a fool he was to have placed them in harm's way. He gained valuable information, but at what cost?

"Coom out, little cub. It weel go better if ye do."

William wanted to turn around and confront the assailants. His fury burned like a roaring fire to know they imprisoned his father. Obtaining the location, he no longer needed these dunderheads to point the way. Still, he continued down the next tunnel without hesitation.

He and his father had played in this cave so near to their home. It resided on his family's land, and he had traversed it often. The farther they traveled, the more inaudible his antagonists became. Behind him, he heard Pippa whispering prayers. Mayhap God would hear her today and answer.

He questioned the tunnel he selected when a tiny light filtered between the stones up ahead. "Stop."

"What is it?"

"I see the outlet. Wait here. Pippa, hold my horse."

She hugged the damp wall and reached for the bridle. "I've got it. Be watchful."

"Aye."

*Swish.* His sword blade glistened. On occasion it clinked against the stone wall as he crept near the opening. If met by an enemy with arrows, the fight would be short lived leaving Pippa and John at the mercy of murderers. *Almighty Father, if ye care for yer people like Pippa says, hear my earnest plea. Shield us from our enemies.*

William edged closer to the gap in the cave. Tall shrub blocked the doorway. He used his sword to part the greenery and peer out. No one in sight. He pushed through and stepped outside the opening. The thick foliage hid him well. A few birds chirped but he detected no threatening sounds. He ducked back inside the cave and trotted to retrieve Pippa and John.

He heard the horses pawing the ground before he reached the two. Sliding his hand along the wall, he stopped near his horse. "The way appears clear."

Pippa puffed. "Thank you, Oh Holy God."

"After we leave the cave, we will head northwest toward the edge of my family's property. There is another way out of this dilemma. Stay alert. Our hunters will not give up easily."

"I didn't have time to ask. Did you gain any relevant news?"

"Aye. They hold my father at Coldingham Shore."

She squeezed his arm. "Praise God from whom all blessings flow. Once we evade our tormentors, we'll head up the coast."

"Aye. For now, we focus on our task at hand."

"Indeed."

The three mounted and trotted northwest. Each stayed vigilant. William crisscrossed the land in hopes of leaving an unclear trail. While the three rode abreast, William issued instructions. "Not far from here, there is an open field. On the other side is a place to shelter until our enemy leaves or darkness falls—whichever comes first."

"What if they refuse to concede?" Pippa asked.

William caught her gaze. "I have a reserve plan. It involves a bridge."

She frowned. "Why not take the bridge while our enemy lags behind?"

"It's an old bridge. I know not its condition. We will use it if necessary."

William caught John's eye and nodded. John moved behind Pippa. The exposed grassland would make them vulnerable for attack. William wished he could reopen the day. He would have altered his choices.

To ride across an open field was not desirable. Instead, the three skirted the edge of the forest. Birds flew tweeting their displeasure from the disturbance of the riders. William watched for any sign of the enemy—a glint from a sword or the sudden flight of a flock of birds. The sun rested at midafternoon. Its warmth faded as gray clouds drifted by and covered the burning sphere.

"Look!" John pointed. South of their position, a group of pheasants soared high above the trees. "The enemy."

William could no longer avoid riding in the open pasture. It was the quickest route to safety. "Time to outrun our adversary."

Their horses launched from their covering and bolted across the countryside. Their hooves pummeled the earth and churned up clods of soil.

"There are five!" Pippa cried.

William looked over his shoulder. The two missing soldiers had reunited with the three. Bearing down on them were five outraged warriors. Their swords flashed as they twirled them over their heads.

"When we reach the other side, John rides off with our two horses in hopes to divide the five. Pippa and I will elude them at the bridge."

"Are you sure you want to split us up?" Pippa asked.

"Yes. Alone, John can outrun them and join forces with Peter and Patrick."

Far enough in front of the men, William felt confident they had time to throw the reins to John and all escape. He looked at Pippa's determined face. "Be ready to jump and run."

She nodded.

The forest trees grew larger the closer they came to the end of the open field. William's blood rushed through his body and pounded in his temples. His rapid breathing matched that of his horse. Steady ... steady. "Now!"

William and Pippa leapt from their saddles. John grabbed both horses and continued to gallop south. Their pursuers split but not as William had hoped. One followed John and four stayed after them. He grabbed Pippa's arm and tugged her into the cover of the trees. "We must hurry."

"I fight better on Romeo."

"Trust me." They zigzagged southwest and deeper into the woodland.

Pippa kept looking back. "Will those men not follow us across a bridge?"

"Not on horseback. 'Tis a special bridge." He stopped at slight gap in the trees. "We made it!"

Their arrival came none too soon. The warriors crashed through the trees just north of their location.

"Hurry!" William started across the swinging bridge expecting Pippa to shadow his steps. He stepped with care and tested each board with quick precision. A rope bracketed each side to add stability. Halfway over, he glanced back. Pippa had a white-knuckle grip on the rope. She remained frozen two steps in—her mouth open and her eyes wide with fright.

He started back toward her. A flash caught his eye—an archer. "Pippa, look out!"

246

An arrow sailed and found its mark in her back. The force of the strike jolted her forward. Her look of panic seared his mind. She plunged over the rope.

"No!" Terror tore at his throat as he watched her plummet to the water below. If the arrow didn't kill her, the fall might.

*What have I done?*

His tortured heart brought him to his knees. The shaking of the bridge snapped him back to the danger at hand. Three warriors holding the ropes, stalked their prey.

William's eyes burned as his fury choked him. He stumbled to the other end of the bridge.

"Ye 'ave nay where to go. We weel kill ye juist as we slew yer woman."

William drew his sword and struck the knotted rope. With speed he chopped and hacked until it frayed loose. Then he started on the rope holding the other side.

"Turn back! Turn back!" yelled the warrior in the front. "Tha bridge weel fall." His foot slipped as the bridge tilted. One man shrieked as he tumbled off the bridge. The other two grabbed for the rope and scrambled for solid footing.

The stranded men looped their arms around the taunt rope while their legs dangled over the ravine. William made quick work of the rope railing all the while searching the water below for a glimpse of his wife.

"Death awaits you!" On one knee, William struck the final blow to the tattered rope. His enemies plunged to a sure demise. He watched as their heavy chainmail sucked them under the rushing water.

"I weel coom for ye."

His head jerked to gaze across the ravine. Standing on the other side was Badger. William's rage ignited like a black powder fire. "Badger!"

The man saluted and ran in the opposite direction.

For a moment, William froze, his mind whirled. After one last look over the edge for Pippa, William sheathed his sword and sprinted toward the ruins. This day, his poor decisions had triggered a series of horrible events. Had she survived the fall? Tormented with visions of Pippa's dead body washed up on shore, his legs wobbled. Once again, his prayer for protection went unanswered.

Who had hired Badger to hunt him down? And why? While he ran, questions swirled in his head. In the midst of his personal examination, the realization that Pippa was caught in the middle fueled his anger at his unknown enemy ... and at himself.

Hot wrath burned through his body. Powered by his need for vengeance, William's strength revived. He hoped his men left one prisoner for him to vanquish. On that thought, his arms and legs pumped with force.

# 31

"Coom, Albert. We moost find wood." Rhona attached the sling to Albert's halter and arranged it on the ground behind his back legs. He stamped his front hoof in displeasure. "If ye wish to stay warm this winter, then ye weel help me." She shuffled toward the stream's shore tugging Albert's rope.

She left behind the two-room cabin nestled among the tall trees. A thin line of smoke wiggled out of the chimney. The thatched roof sagged from neglect. No matter. She had called it home for over fifty years.

"Albert, is today tha day of me birth?" She gazed toward the sky with a frown. "I think we wilt celebrate." She had forgotten her age long ago. No need to keep tally of such nonsense—her weak body was a constant reminder. After a rain, the soggy ground made it difficult to haul firewood without Albert's help. "I was tha first wee lassie of six, and look at me. I'm tha one survivor." She chuckled.

"Stoop, Albert." Rhona bent to pick up a twig. Her boney fingers stuck out from underneath the worn stockings used for gloves. Fresh mud gathered under her long fingernails as she dug.

249

No stick was too tiny for her pile. The small twigs were for kindling while the larger logs kept her fire roaring most of the day. "Well, tha hole in me apron pocket let me sticks slip oot." *Hump.* She retrieved the twigs and walked around Albert to lay them on the cloth sling he pulled.

With her hands at the small of her back, she stretched and looked about. "Look thither. Four good size logs." She tugged at Albert's lead line. "Ye ornery ole donkey. Git up with ye."

The farther they ventured from the cabin, the cooler the wind. "Do ye smell tha river? Mayhap, we'll find a trinket or two washed ashore. If ye oblige me, I could sell 'em in tha village." The closer to the water's edge they came, the harder Albert pulled against her hold.

"What's tha matter with ye?"

With his teeth bared, Albert brayed.

"Ye git more stubborn ever' day." Rhona pushed aside the branches on a bush and spied a shiny object along the shoreline. "What have we here?"

She squinted her eyes. Albert tried to back up, but Rhona held fast. She tied him to a low-hanging branch and lifted a club-size log from the cloth. "Nary a need to go aboot unarmed." She sloshed to the shores edge and squatted. Using her nails, she uncovered a jewel-handled dirk. Washing the knife in the water, the ruby shone bright. "My, my, Albert." She slid the dagger into her waistband. "'Tis a good day for finding treasures."

She ventured farther along the river's edge as her eyes scanned the soil. When Albert brayed again, she decided to return. The suction of the mud pulled at her dilapidated boots. "Albert, ye bletherin' old fool. Stoop yer hollerin'. I'm a coomin'." With her eyes trained on the shore, she hoped to discover other items of worth.

Through the years, the lapping water had comforted Rhona. It proved steady and true—never failing. Others had forsaken her, but not the river. When she turned to head up the slight incline, she noticed a muddied shoe by a boulder. With club in hand, she crept closer. She sucked in a quick breath—a body.

She lay aside her club and knelt. The person was wedged between two rocks and lying on one side. A broken arrow shaft jutted from the shoulder and blood seeped from the wound. With one last look around, she pulled the body over. "A wummon!" When the woman moaned, Rhona fell back on her haunches. She scrambled to her feet and hurried to get Albert.

"Albert! Albert, I need ye." The donkey neighed. She scurried to the sling and started unloading her wood. "There's a lassie by tha waterside." She came around and grabbed Albert's halter. "She's wearing breeches!" She rubbed his nose. "Forgive me for tha scolding. Ye were trying to warn me." After her announcement, she finished emptying the cloth. "Coom. We have work to do."

She led the reluctant donkey to the shoreline. With him facing the water, she could position the sling to receive the body. Rhona removed a belt, a sword and a shield from the woman and placed them beside the body. Then she grabbed the two legs and pulled. Rhona grunted. "Yer small shape deceived me." She tugged again. "Ye're heavy."

After she freed the woman from the rocks, she rolled her to the sling. The woman cried out when the arrow shaft jabbed further into her skin, yet her eyes never opened. "Sairy, m'lady. 'Tis tha only way." She pushed, shoved, and rolled until the woman lay upon the sling. She recovered the weapons and put them beside the woman.

When satisfied with the placement, she wiped her brow with the back of her arm. "My, my, Albert." She picked up the lead rope and began the slow walk home. Albert tried to run, but Rhona pulled back. "Slow down. Ye canna git away from tha lassie. 'Tis been a while since we had a visitor." They trudged onward without a word from their cargo. Rhona giggled. "'Twill be a welcome change if she lives."

William bent over with his hands upon his knees. His sides heaved. The castle ruins were within sight. The run from the bridge had been painful. All the while visions of Pippa had tormented his mind. The thoughts of vengeance had strengthened his body and powered his legs. He straightened and hurried on.

At the fringe of the ruins, he whistled low and precise. An answering shout confirmed his men's presence. With little energy left, he tramped into sight. Ross stepped from hiding and ran to embrace him. "I thought ye were lost, boy." He looked behind William. "Where is Lady McKinnon?"

He gulped air. "She plummeted from the bridge."

Ross guided William to a fallen log. "Catch yer breath and tell all."

Peter brought a canteen of water. William guzzled until he choked. "We must mount a search party."

Patrick and John joined the group.

Ross shook his head. "Darkness is upon us. We'll leave at first light."

William jumped to his feet. "Nay. We must go post haste."

Ross placed a hand on William's shoulder. "Nay."

Tormented, William turned to face Ross.

"There is nary enough light. On the morrow."

William's face fell. He turned to gaze across the land. "She trusted me." He pinched the bridge of his nose. "I failed her."

"When we parted, you said you had an escape." John scowled. "What happened?"

"Coom to tha fireside. Recount tha story and we'll form a rescue plan," Ross said.

Peter, John and Patrick glared at William from across the fire. Ross stood close by keeping watch over the landscape. William looked at Ross. "What are you doing here? I left you at the castle."

"After yer tale."

William rubbed his scratchy eyes. "We arrived at the bridge. I tested each step as I hurried across." He shook his head. "I thought she trailed behind me. She did not."

Peter vaulted to his feet. "A bridge? She's afraid of heights!"

William's heart thumped. "What? I knew this not!"

Peter growled. "You are her husband. You should have known!"

William bounded to his feet. "I cannot know if she keeps it hidden."

"You know her not because you care not." He lunged at William.

The two men scuffled in the dirt. Ross and John pulled them apart but not before a few well-placed punches by both.

Ross struggled to restrain William. "Cease!"

William tugged from his hold and wiped his bloody mouth. John released Peter.

"This accomplishes nothing," Patrick said. "Peter, we have known our lady far longer than her husband. You are unfair in your assessment."

Ross stared at each one. "We moostn't fight amongst ourselves. There is a devious enemy aboot."

Peter snorted. "I'll take the first watch. I've heard enough." He marched off into the night.

When William started to call him back, Ross said, "Let him go."

William's stomach burned. "I didn't know of her fear."

Patrick threw a stick into the fire. "'Tis not your fault. Our lady keeps her worries to herself. She's done this since her father's passing. Without Henry's presence, Peter assumes the role of protector of our lady. He lashed out from guilt. Please, finish your account."

William plopped onto the ground and pulled his knees to his chest. His stomach rolled. "An archer released his arrow before I could rescue her." His voice faltered. "She tumbled over the side and into the water. I lost sight of her." He continued in a monotone. "Next, the warrior chased after me. I ran across the bridge and watched three of them step onto the bridge. Once they were halfway across, I used my sword to chop the anchored rope. The three plunged to their deaths. Regrettably, one who failed to step on the bridge, escaped."

"Are you certain the three died?"

"They wore chainmail with heavy shields strapped to their backs. I watched. None of them surfaced after hitting the water."

John perked up. "Lady McKinnon wore no chainmail, and she knows how to swim."

William's frown relaxed. "'Tis a relief to hear." He glanced around the campfire. "Two enemies pursued you; where are they?"

Patrick cut his eyes toward John before answering. "They are dead."

William surged to his feet. "I needed one alive!"

John stood. "I rode hard and led them to the ruins. Patrick and Peter were waiting." He ducked his head and glanced at Patrick. "I called out before reaching the castle." He shrugged. "I didn't wish Peter or Patrick to mistake me for an enemy. They stepped from their hiding places with arrows ready for flight. Once I passed their location, they released ... and found their mark."

Patrick rose. "It was fight or be killed. We had little choice."

William's fists clinched and unclenched as he paced by the fire. He stopped with his back to the men and rolled his shoulders. With his head down, he walked back to face the two. "I'm well aware of split-second decisions for preservation. You made a wise judgment. Forgive my outburst."

"With my boot on his chest, one man coughed out two names before succumbing to death."

William's eyes widened with interest. "Aye?"

"He said the young leader's name is Finlay of the Elliot Clan. The other is Raven."

William rubbed his hands together. "Good work, men. Good work."

Ross ambled over to the fire pit.

"Ross, I'm sending you on a most important errand on the morrow."

"Ye don't wish for me to search for tha lassie?"

A pain shot through William's chest. "Nay. We will find her. I need you to take a message to my friend in Midlothian. His name is Ranulf Scott."

"Of tha Scott border family?"

"Aye, the verra same. Tell him I'm collecting his debt. He needs to round up the other five and bring the black powder to Fairwick castle, post haste. Take John with you."

"We'll leave at first light."

"Who's leaving at first light and why?" Peter came into the circle of light wearing a scowl.

The hair on William's neck stood to attention. He balked at Peter's disrespectful tone. "Ross and John."

"Are we not all searching for m' lady?"

He ground his teeth. "Ross and John are on a different mission as are you. You will ride to Fairwick castle and bring back additional warriors to search for *my wife*."

Peter's eyes narrowed. He crossed his arms over his chest. "Why wait? I'll leave now."

William refused the bait. He had no time for an altercation with one of Pippa's guardians. "Nay. You run the risk of injury to your horse which would impede your journey. I want to know I can count on your speedy return." He strode over to Peter—inches from his rigid body. "You will obey my command. Is that clear?"

Standing taller than Peter, William waited.

"Yes, sir." Peter flung his arms down and stalked away.

Ross came close. "He weel follow yer order."

William looked into the area where Peter had disappeared. "He's young and hot-headed."

"I knew one such mon."

William's grim expression turned to Ross. "I haven't changed much, have I?"

"Ye are becoming a fine leader. Trust yer instincts."

"My instincts might have killed my wife."

"Tha lassie is in God's Holy hand. He hath tha power to save her. Juist trust Him."

William wanted to believe it. He watched Ross stroll into the darkness.

*Does He, Ross?*

# *32*

Pippa's shoulder burned like fire and her head pounded. Behind closed lids, her eyes roamed to and fro following the sounds around her. Her nose wrinkled at the smell permeating the air. It smelled of a wet, dirty dog.

"Albert, git back."

Pippa stiffened. She didn't recognize the raspy voice. Her breathing grew more rapid which caused pain to radiate through her body. Was she in danger? The clanging sounded like a blacksmith striking iron. To find out, she must open her eyes. With great effort, she pried her lids apart and scanned the room through mere slits.

A stooped woman wearing ragged clothing stood over a black pot sitting over a fire. Her white hair and wrinkled skin indicated an advanced age. However, the appearance of a donkey's face near her own caused her to gasp.

The old woman left her spoon and waddled over to Pippa. "Albert, I told ye to git away." She swatted at him. "Are ye awake?"

Pippa stared.

"I daresay ye're thirsty. Let me git ye a sip of water."

Her gaze followed the woman as she pushed the donkey out the door. Leaving the door propped open, Rhona tied the donkey to a hitching post and picked up a pale of water. When the bucket bumped Rhona's leg, water sloshed over the edge. The burning pain in Pippa's right shoulder grounded her. Otherwise, she would declare it all a dream.

She noticed her naked shoulder protruding from under a worn blanket. A wet cloth covered part of her upper frame. The excruciating throb reminded her of her misfortune. Wonder of all wonders, she had tumbled into the river and lived.

"Here ye be, lassie." The woman tipped the dipper to Pippa's lips.

The dribble of water soothed her parched throat. "Thank you."

"Me name's Rhona. Me and Albert found ye." She smiled a toothless grin.

Pippa strained to answer. "Thank you, good woman."

Rhona set aside the ladle and pulled a stool next to the cot. "'Twasn't sure ye'd live. Ye washed ashore with an arrow in yer back. Nasty wound. I used yer dirk to dig it out. Ye'll wear a scar. Sairy I am for it."

Pippa struggled. "Ye are in danger."

*Pishah.* "I fear no mon. The Almighty is me hoosband. He protects me."

Pippa lacked the energy to explain their predicament. All she could do was shake her head.

Rhona pulled back the blanket and peeped under the damp compress. "It still seeps. Tha honey weel help." She replaced the covering. "Ye rest. I'm cooking oop some haggis to give ye strength." Humming a tuneless melody, she rose on wobbly legs and shuffled back to the pot.

Did William live? Was he searching for her ... was the enemy? She willed her eyes to stay open, but they snapped shut like a rabbit's snare. Troubled, she drifted off.

William spent the remainder of the night pondering Ross's words. With a humbled heart, he admitted God alone possessed the power to protect Pippa. His recent decisions caused nothing but harm. The burden he carried for Pippa's calamity weighed on his mind. Shamed at his pride, he sought out Peter and made peace. No need to add to his guilt with an unsettled quarrel.

While the last of the darkness blanketed the ruins, the men mounted. Sitting tall in his saddle, William issued his last order. "Go with God, my friends."

Ross and John left for Midlothian while Peter galloped toward Fairwick castle. William, shadowed by Patrick, turned west and headed toward the entrance to the ravine. Until the sun peeked on the horizon, a slow pace prevailed.

William and Patrick picked their way down the rocky slope. The rushing river flowed on their right with thick forest coverage on their left. "Be on guard. Our enemy still lurks about."

After arriving at the river's edge, they looked for any evidence of Pippa or her armor. Their entry point was miles from the site of the bridge. He hoped not to find any sign of Pippa. The river's bank consisted of sand and mud which sucked at their horses' hooves. "Stay close to the rim. We want the hoof prints to wash away with the ebb and flow of the water."

Patrick brought his horse beside William's steed. "Look." He pointed across the river at a body half in the water. The soldier's legs swirled in the river.

"'Tis one of our enemy. Perchance, we'll see two more."

"Lady McKinnon is a strong swimmer."

William looked at Patrick's hopeful face. "I'm sure you're correct."

The tedious search continued. After looking along the river's border, they ventured into the forest to hunt for human tracks. When none appeared, they returned to the river. As they traveled around a bend, William's horse reared.

With expert horsemanship, he brought his stallion into submission. The reason for his horse's distress lay before him ... a dead warrior.

"Be on guard."

Patrick drew his weapon but remained astride. William dismounted and approached with sword in hand. He bumped the man's arm. No response.

"Is he dead?"

William probed him with his sword. "Aye." He bent on one knee to assess the remains and weapons. Rubbing the shield attached to the man's back yielded a clan emblem. "'Tis Clan Elliot."

He shoved the man over to view his face. The sightless eyes were frozen in fright. "I dinna recognize him, but it appears the water terrified him."

"For good reason."

When William's examination produced no other hint about his attackers, he confiscated a knife, but left the crude sword. "Let's keep going. There is nothing of import on the man." He straddled his horse and applied a soft kick.

Patrick kept his voice low. "Do you think someone searches for these men?"

"Nay. There is no honor among outlaws. If they search for anyone, it's for me or my wife. With her in their grasp, they control me."

The two persisted in their quest. The sun shining high overhead proved deceptive. Crisp air danced through the trees. When William waded into the river to retrieve a piece of cloth, the cold water snatched his breath. Could anyone survive long in the icy water? Doubtful.

Patrick leapt from his horse when he happened upon an arrow. He picked it up and examined the feathers. Looking at William he said, "'Tis one of m' lady's."

William's heart plunged to the bottom of his ribcage. "Are you sure?"

"She makes her own arrows. There is no doubt."

"We'll walk from here." William stepped down. He perused the sandy area looking for footprints. Not far beyond the discovery of the one arrow, Patrick spotted part of an empty quiver.

William's legs buckled. A firm grip on the horse's halter is all that held him upright. He knelt in the mud next to Patrick. They dug with both hands to uncover the quiver. "What think you, Patrick?"

Patrick ran to the water's edge and rinsed off the leather quiver to reveal the Fairwick emblem. "'Tis hers." He walked over and showed it to William.

Sitting back on his haunches, the cries of Pippa as she fell from the bridge echoed in his ears and pierced his heart. He propped his hands against his legs and squeezed his eyes shut.

*Almighty God, help me.*

Patrick wandered the terrain, eyes focused on the ground. "Lord McKinnon, come hither."

William jumped to his feet and hurried toward Patrick. "What did you find?"

"Look. A disturbance among these boulders. It appears as if something was dragged." He glanced up. "The indentation disappears into the forest."

William's heart thumped. "Let's follow this trail." He rushed toward the trees pulling his horse behind him. The depressed ground contained an unusual pattern through the woodland. It seemed to track around fallen logs and large rocks giving him hope someone towed a live person—not an animal dragging its prey.

On occasion the two men stopped to survey their surroundings. The dense area gave nothing away. No signs of human life. Thankful the trail persisted, a chill crawled over William's skin. If he sees the obvious tracks, the enemy would see it as well. Had Badger beat him to the scene? His steps quickened.

The trail seemed unending and less clear the farther inland they tracked. The dense vegetation allowed little light to filter through the tree branches. Would the trail grow cold?

A donkey brayed with force.

William's and Patrick's heads jerked at the sound as they looked at the other. William mouthed, "a donkey."

Patrick nodded in agreement.

Both men scanned their position. No one in sight.

Patrick wrinkled his nose. "Do ye smell it?"

William sniffed the air. "It smells of smoldering wood."

Patrick pointed high above their heads. "'Tis a thin line of smoke."

"Be wary. It might be a trap."

The two stepped with care until they came to the tree line. William used his hand to move aside a branch to view an open gap in the otherwise continuous forest. A tiny cabin sat in the small area. The smoke twisted from its roof.

Patrick exhaled in William's ear. "Do you see anyone?"

"Nay." He gazed around the house. "Tie our horses here. We'll advance from opposite directions. Whistle if trouble emerges."

Patrick secured their mounts and headed west. William headed east to encircle the hut. Each step on dried leaves sounded like a crackling whip. There was no denying his approach. With sword in hand, William proceeded. After a slow progression around the cabin, he met up with Patrick.

Patrick shrugged and shook his head, no. All appeared clear. William motioned for Patrick to follow. They jogged back to their horses and mounted. "Wait while I ride to the front of the house. You retain a better lookout advantage hidden here."

With his hand upon the hilt of his sword, William walked his horse to the front of the house. Standing on a small patch of grass, the donkey eyed William and displayed his teeth. He was thankful the beast refrained from alerting the owner by neighing.

"Greetings to the house." His thumping heart increased.

Right before he planned a more forceful tactic, the door creaked open. Out shuffled an old woman. Her deformed back kept her from looking him in the eye. "What do ye here?"

"Good woman, I'm searching for my wife." Before he added details, the woman spoke.

"I'm Rhona ... tha only one here."

William had no time to match wits or play with words. "I followed your trail from the river's edge. You hauled something quite heavy. I hope you carried m' lady. She is injured."

"Ye could well be an enemy." She twisted her head. "What kind of wound?"

William left his horse and rushed to the woman's side. "An arrow pierced her back. Her thick braid is the color of a sunset, and her eyes are like a sapphire. Does she live?"

"Aye."

William waited no longer. He burst through the door without thought that his enemy resided within. Once his eyes adjusted to the dim room, he spotted Pippa. Her ashen face and still form caused his heart to stop. In two strides he knelt by her side.

"Pippa?" When she failed to answer, he looked to the woman blocking the doorway. "You said she lived?"

"Aye. She drank a potion."

He vaulted up and shook the woman. "What have ye done? She barely breathes." When he realized the sharpness of the woman's bones, he released her as if cut and stepped back. "My apologies."

The woman rubbed her arm. "'Tis like ye men. Quick to judge. Tha wound is grave. Rest is vital. I had to stoop her thrashing aboot."

William turned back to his wife and crouched beside the cot. His shaking fingers stroked her hair. "Pippa, can you hear me? Wake for me." Her shallow breathing added to his remorse.

He dared to lift the blanket to view the damage. What he saw caused him to choke on his breath. The gaping hole in her skin shone bright red as fresh blood oozed. His eyes closed at the sight. "Is the entry wound as large as this exit one?" He turned to look at the woman.

"Nay. I nudged it out with tha dirk at tha outlet."

Taking a risk, he rolled his wife to her side in order to see the entry. There on the cot puddled more blood ... fresh ... red. The likelihood of her survival—poor. He eased her down and rested his head on his fisted arm laying at the edge of the cot. Helpless!

A boney hand touched his arm. "Ye canna do more. Tha lassie's in tha hands of our Holy Savior."

# 33

Pippa's head lolled from side to side. The heat burned her skin. She needed cool water or perish. What prevented her from escaping the heat? She attempted to call for help; instead, a groan escaped her lips.

William tumbled off the edge of the cot. "Pippa?"

The familiar voice brought her comfort. Yet, she failed to discern who spoke. Her muddled mind refused to form a clear thought. She attempted to open her eyes, but heavy stones kept them shut

"Pippa, 'tis me, William. Open your eyes."

His silky tone caused her stomach to quiver. *William*? She drew her brows into a frown. A drop of cold water touched her lips. Her parched tongue darted out to catch it.

"That's it. Drink."

There it was again—the gentle voice. A roughened hand cupped her face while a finger caressed her cheek. Why did her eyes refuse to open?

"Her eyes roam behind her lids. Can she hear me?"

"Aye. 'Tis the mixture. It jumbles tha mind. Keep watch. She'll look at yer bushy face soon enough."

*Another drop of water. Oh, so good.*

"She drinks."

"'Tis good. Verra good."

*Who owns the raspy voice?*

"Her eyes flickered."

A scraping sound drew closer. "I need to look at tha wound."

Cool air wafted across her chest. Who touched her? She concentrated on opening her lids. Fluttering, they allowed a stream of light to filter through. At last, they unlocked. A tousled head of hair and deep brown eyes stared back. William.

"Pippa!"

Her memory returned in spurts as her eyes traveled to the old woman. The bridge, an arrow, water, pain. Details flooded her mind faster than she could process. She flinched as Rhona smeared a sticky substance on her wound. Her eyes locked on William. "What goes on here?" Her croaky voice sounded strange to her ears.

"Good woman, Rhona, found you by the riverside and brought you to her cabin." He picked up her hand. "I searched for you. Well, Patrick helped me." He kissed her hand and clung to it while Rhona applied a new dressing. "You scared me." His eyes grew misty. "I thought you perished."

"Thank you."

He grimaced. "The fault is mine. I didn't know you feared heights." His head lowered.

"No one's fault. Share the blame." Her eyes drooped with each clipped sentence. "Home."

"I'll take you home when you're stronger."

She peeked. "Today."

William glanced at Rhona. She shrugged.

"I brought a cart filled with fresh hay and blankets for your comfort. When the time is right ..."

"Now."

"Take her. She'll heal faster at home."

266

William ran a hand across his scruffy face. "I like it not. In her weakened state, the journey could ..." His sentence trailed off as his eyes fastened to Pippa.

"Help me to sit."

William braced her back with his arm. With great care, he lifted her shoulders. She trembled with the effort. He scooted behind her back to support her weight and hold her upright.

"My woozy head blurs my sight."

Rhona stopped washing her hands. "'Twill pass soon." She laid aside her rag. "Warm broth awaits ye. See if ye can eat. I'll be outside if ye need me."

Pippa's eyes followed the woman out the door. Her head leaned against William's chest. "Who is she and where am I?"

"After you fell from the bridge, you washed ashore not far from here. Rhona found you when she searched for firewood. Her donkey transports her wood on a sling. She placed you upon it, and Albert dragged you here."

"Albert?"

"Aye. Her donkey."

Pippa squeezed her eyes shut and rubbed them with her left hand. The over-warm room suffocated her even though she shivered. "Take me home. Please."

William rubbed her exposed arm. "First, you must sip the broth. You are quite weak from this ordeal. Allow me to prop you against the wall and let your legs dangle off the cot."

A slight nod was all she could muster as her right arm lay limp by her side. Her eyes roamed the small room. A roaring fire produced more than adequate heat, a crude table with a chair rested by the hearth, and the cot upon which she sat rounded out the furnishings. A broom hoovered in the corner below wall hooks for a cloak. Simple, yet, sufficient.

With a cup of broth in his hand, her husband knelt on one knee in front of the cot. He set the cup on the floor. "It needs to cool."

It looked like black soot under his eyes. Deep lines grooved his whiskered cheeks while red-rimmed eyes gazed at her. Thankful her sight had cleared, she offered a small grin. "You look dreadful."

His eyes widened before he looked away. When he looked back, his tenseness diminished. "Forgive my untidiness. Much to Rhona's dismay, I refused to leave your side. I feared you ..."

She finished his sentence. "Might die?"

"Aye."

When she extended her trembling hand, his face snuggled into her palm. With her voice a bare whisper, she said, "Even though you are a strong and mighty warrior, you cannot direct my fate. God alone controls my destiny and breathes His breath into my body. When He ceases, I return to dust. As of today, the Almighty permits me to live."

He blinked several times. His face twisted into thought. "Your broth is cool. 'Tis time to eat." He tilted the cup to her cracked lips.

"Mm." Her stomach grumbled.

"Sounds as if your belly approves."

She smiled and continued to drink. She left nary a drop.

"Does enough time exist to get home before dark?"

"Aye. You roused at sunrise."

"Please ask Lady Rhona to assist me."

William's chest puffed out. "I'll give you aid."

She rolled her eyes. "I think not. Call her."

William's face heated. "Aye."

Pippa wondered at the wisdom of traveling in her condition. Weak as a newborn kitten, she questioned her judgment. She reasoned that remaining here put all in danger, even Rhona.

Rhona ambled through the door. "Yer going home?"

"Yes. You have been most gracious with your hospitability. Thank you, Lady Rhona."

Rhona cackled. "Lady Rhona, indeed."

Pippa patted the cot blanket. "Join me?"

Rhona sat on the droopy cot. "What's amiss?"

Pippa covered one of Rhona's withered hands with her own. "I thank you from my heart. You could have left me to die, and none would have questioned you for it."

"Ah. The good Lord brought ye here. I had to obey."

"You are a grand soldier in God's mighty army. I wish you to join us on our journey. Come and live out your days at Fairwick castle." When Rhona started to speak, Pippa squeezed her hand. "You will want for nothing. No more searching for firewood or scavenging for food. What say you?"

Rhona's eyes filled with tears. "Ye are too kind. Me and Albert weel stay here."

"Albert is welcomed, too."

"It's me home." She patted Pippa's hand as a tear slipped down her cheek. "Ye have a pure soul; but nay."

Pippa's own eyes blurred with unshed tears. Not wanting to leave on a sad tone, she blinked them away. "Then I will leave you with a gift." She glanced over in a corner where her belongings huddled. Nothing but muddy clothes until she spied the tip of her knife. She perked up. "I gift you with my ruby-handled dirk."

After a quick glance toward the knife, Rhona shook her head. "'Tis too mooch."

"No. I insist. It pleases me to give it."

"'Tis a treasure."

"It's settled. You may keep it." Pippa stretched her good arm around Rhona's scrawny shoulders. "You are the treasure."

"Ye are a sweet lass." She sniffed and pushed off the cot. "I'll help ye dress."

With great difficulty, Rhona steadied Pippa as she used the slop jar before getting dressed. Sharp pains raced with every movement. They labored together to complete the task. Pippa cringed each time she heard creaking bones.

"Leave my boots for William. You have done enough."

Rhona shoved to her feet and smiled. "Me and Albert weel miss ye."

"When I'm recovered, I'll come for a visit and bring a meat pie and an apple tart for your pleasure."

Rhona smacked her lips as she opened the door.

William stumbled where he leaned against the door.

Pippa's brows raised.

He blushed.

"I need you to put on my boots and lace them up."

With gentle hands, he slid her shoes over dirty but dry stockings. Using meticulous precision, he laced each boot. When he glanced up, longing swelled in her chest. Would she survive long enough to enjoy a life with her new husband?

"Your carriage awaits. Are you ready?"

"Yes."

He scooped her into his arms and held her close. "I fear you might break."

"We Fairwicks are stout. You cannot be rid of me that easy." She saw hurt form in his eyes.

Flustered, he stammered. "I would never wish your death."

She sighed. "I'm glad to hear it."

The blustery wind smacked her in the face and stole her breath. He turned to shield her from the strong breeze as she snuggled into his neck. It was the roar that chilled her to the bone. Peeping out, she met the gazes of fifteen Fairwick warriors dressed for battle. All cheered for their lady with swords waving in the air.

Walter, Peter, and Patrick stood among the group. Tears stung her eyes. "Where are Ross and John?"

"They're on another mission. These men camped here for three days to escort you home."

The scene overwhelmed her. No longer able to control her emotions, tears spilled over the rim. Her body quaked with sobs of thankfulness and relief that she still lived.

William crooned in her ear. "'Tis alright. Do not cry." He strode over to the cart. "Let's get you settled and go home."

The journey to England proved long and difficult for Pippa. She slipped in and out of awareness. William fretted at her groans. He worried the jostling wagon would reopen her wounds. Fresh blood stained her bandage, but the holes in her skin held together. Rhona insisted on sending honey for the wound and sleeping potion to ease her pain. He planned to deliver extra grain and lard to Pippa's rescuer to help her through the winter months.

Pippa roused the last five miles of the trip. "How much farther?"

Her weak voice tugged at his heart. "Two, perhaps three miles more."

He rode the entire trek with her nestled in his arms hoping to lessen the jolts from wagon wheels plunging into holes. No matter. The trip had strained her already battered body.

"I like it not that Rhona refused to come with us."

"I, too. She remains in danger as long as our enemy prowls about."

Pushing her hair behind her ear, he stroked her face. "When I witnessed your fall, I prayed for God to protect you."

A tiny smile formed. "Thank you, husband. He heard and answered."

"You kept a devastating secret from me."

Her eyes scrunched in concentration. "Oh?"

"You are afraid of heights."

Her face relaxed. "Ah. 'Tis true." She closed her eyes. "I allowed my pride to rule my head. I feared you might think me weak."

He touched her cheek, and her lids opened. "Weak? The last word to describe you. As I searched for you, I mentally berated myself for my poor decisions that put you in danger. Reliving our short time together, these words came to mind: strong, fearless, determined, courageous ... and beautiful."

Pippa snorted and rolled her eyes.

"Let me finish. Your beauty starts from deep within by how you care about your people, how you honor your men, and how you put all others before yourself." A slow grin spread across his face. "That you are pleasing to look upon is an added boon."

Pink tinged her pallid cheeks. "Surely, I'm near death for you to spout such nonsense."

He smiled. "Once you are recovered, I hope to prove my admiration in other ways."

From the front of the procession, Walter signaled to William.

"Lady Wife, we have arrived."

She wrenched her head around and grimaced. "Help sit me up. I don't wish to appear a feeble, young girl."

William shook his head as he assisted Pippa. His arm supported her as his lips grazed her temple. "Young girl? Nay." His husky voice dropped low. "A tempting woman? Aye."

# 34

Days later, sitting in their solar, William clutched a clump of his hair while looking over the account books. The people at Fairwick castle should have perished from starvation long ago.

"Is there a problem with the books?"

William let loose of his hair and turned to gaze at his wife. Sitting by the roaring fire wrapped in a fur blanket, her delicate face peeped out. From across the room her sapphire eyes stared back at him.

"Nay." He stood and walked over. "Refreshed after your nap?"

Her brow raised. "'Tisn't polite to draw attention to my slothfulness."

He squatted beside her. "You are far from lazy. Your body is working hard to heal." He gave a slight tug to her thick braid.

She reached to smooth his ruffled hair. "I tire of this new duty."

He captured her hand and kissed a path up to her ring. "Once you mend, we will find more enjoyable ways to spend our afternoons." He grinned as she blushed to the roots of her hair.

"You seem different." She tilted her head. "In a pleasing way."

With one foot, he pulled the stool near and sat down. Still holding her hand, he caressed her wrist. "While you remained

273

missing, I spent time examining my dark soul. During that time, our sweet Savior pointed out the error of my ways and my arrogance." His looked at their intertwined hands. "It took me several days to accept His findings." He peered into her face. "The Almighty reminded me that He controls the universe, and I am but a servant."

Her eyes softened. "I'm happy you've made peace with God."

"A fiery woman from Fairwick castle pointed me onto the proper path."

She grinned. Her enchanting smile created a longing in his chest to start over. "When you become stronger, we will plan a proper wedding. One at the kirk with the McKinnon Clan and all of Fairwick kingdom in attendance."

She pulled her hand free and cupped his face. "That sounds delightful."

He kissed her palm and breathed deep of her scent. Standing, he placed his hands upon the chair arms and leaned in. Her lids slid shut when a knock sounded on their door. Nose to nose, her eyes popped open. He grinned and pressed a kiss against her forehead. "Wait for me."

William walked over and cracked the door.

Merry bobbed a curtsy. "Ross and John have returned."

"Thank you, Merry. Serve them a repast, and I'll be right down." William retrieved his weapons near the door and buckled on his sword.

Pippa's head peered around the chair. "Is anything wrong?"

"Nay. Ross and John returned with a report."

"Bring me news?"

He walked to her side. "Of course." His lips captured her mouth in a searing kiss. He pulled back before he caught fire. "I shall return."

He nodded at Duff as he strode down the passageway and ran down the spiral staircase. His heart thumped with anticipation. Arriving at the grand hall, he spotted Ross and John off to one side eating alone. His friends nowhere in sight. Disappointed, he stepped into the room only to be grabbed from behind and lifted off his feet.

"Lord Willy!" A burly man squeezed him tight and then dropped him.

William spun around. "Ranulf!" The two men embraced and slapped each other on the back.

"I hear ye have need of me services."

William shushed him and dragged him by the arm over to where Ross and John sat grinning. Ranulf plopped down by Ross with his back to the doorway. William sat with John across from the two.

"How dost m' lady fair?" Ross asked.

"I'm thankful to report, she heals. 'Tis a slow process."

Ross smiled.

Ranulf nodded. "Sairy to hear aboot tha misfortune."

"I thank thee, my friend. God was merciful." William's eyes traveled the room. "We must keep our voices low." The four hunkered and leaned close. "The location of listening ears is unknown." His intense gaze caught Ranulf's eye. "Where are the others?" Ranulf's wicked grin sent chills down William's neck.

"Roamin' aboot."

William grimaced. "John, see to their whereabouts and place a guard on each one ... to help them find their way while visiting our fine castle, of course."

Ranulf howled. "Where's tha fun in that?"

William ignored his comment. "Did you bring the black powder?"

"Aye." Ranulf rubbed his hands together. "Ross told me aboot yer fither. What's tha plan?"

"We head up the coast toward Coldingham Shore. If our information can be trusted, he's imprisoned at Kirk Hill where the Aebba Monastery ruins reside."

"'Tis a ghostly place, indeed," Ranulf whispered.

William gave Ranulf a pointed look. "The sinister people who reside there have skin, and one goes by the name of Eugene." William hesitated. "However, we can use the ghost legend to our advantage. I know for a fact, one of their warriors feared the unseen spirits at the ruins."

Ranulf guffawed. "I like yer thinkin'. I know tha area. 'Twill be easy to fool tha dunderheads."

A ruckus erupted when John and Peter brought the missing five into the great hall. Relieved to see his supporters, William rose to greet the warriors. Each possessed their own form of expertise. Eunan dished out horror to his uncooperative victims. The tallest and strongest warrior was Marcus. He banged heads together without use of his sword. The flaming redhead was Reid. With nothing but a few components, he could start a blazing fire. Kester plotted devious ways to torture an enemy for information. Cameron or Cam owned the handsome face. He could charm food from a beggar.

"Sit my friends. Merry, please bring more ale."

Before sitting down, Cam eyed her. "She's quite fetching."

William scowled. "Cam, our aim is to retrieve my father."

Unrepentant, Cam said, "Nay harm in admiring one bonnie lass."

"You take the place by Ross."

While the men strategized, John ran to obtain maps of Scotland along with writing tools. William spread the map out and pinpointed Coldingham Shore. He dipped the quill pen in the inkhorn and sketched their plan of attack on the parchment paper.

"I will requisition a boat from my Uncle Nicolas. Eunan, Cam, Ross, and John will sail up the Berwickshire coast and dock on the south side of the Head at Horsecastle Rocks. Ross and John will remain with the boat while Eunan and Cam come ashore and meet the rest of us on the other side of the cliffs." He looked at the four seamen. "Be mindful of the craggy rocks jutting from the inland. Sail out far enough to avoid running aground."

"What of their horses?" Peter asked.

"For those of us traveling over land, we'll bring extra mounts and supplies. I know not the condition of my father. Most likely he will return by boat."

After refining their scheme, William sent Peter and John to secure the needed supplies for the long trip. The others dispersed to their rooms except for Ranulf.

"Ye propose a grand undertakin'."

William rubbed his neck. "Aye."

The weather would be a big factor in their timetable. With winter close at hand, travel on the water concerned him. *Am I sending my men to a watery grave?*

He looked at Ranulf. "My father's life hangs in the balance. We must succeed."

Pippa heard the door open and close with a soft click. Still ensconced by the fire, she waited. Earlier she had brushed out her braid and allowed the hair to flow freely. Her heart raced in anticipation. One boot thumped to the floor followed by the other. On stocking feet, her husband slid soundlessly across the floor.

William poked his head around the chair. She grinned. "I'm awake."

"So, I see." He stoked the fire and sat down in the opposite chair. He stretched out his long legs and crossed them at the ankles. With clasped hands on his belly, his head leaned back. He observed her through hooded eyes. A deep sigh escaped.

"I'm not sure about your sigh. Are you tired or uneasy?"

"Both."

Her fingers curled into a fist under her blanket. She had hoped to wait for him to speak but couldn't contain her curiosity. "Well? Tell me the news."

With a sad smile, he sat forward and rested his arms on his knees. "My six friends arrived. They are anxious to execute my rescue plan."

She examined his face "You seem unsure. What troubles you?"

His hands dangled between his knees as he watched the flames. "I'm sending four men up the coast. 'Tis a precarious time to travel by boat. The way is fraught with dangerous jagged rocks. They could meet with tragedy."

The deep lines across his face spoke of his agonizing decision. He risked many lives to save one. She longed to comfort him, but how? The silence stretched. Unfurling her legs, she pushed from her chair leaving the blanket behind. It was a mere two steps to his side.

Startled, he glanced up. His frown deepened as he grabbed her around the waist. "What are you about?"

"I need to sit in your lap."

Even as he settled her on his legs, he issued a slight reprimand. "You shouldn't be up without your wrap."

"I trust you to keep me warm." With her injured shoulder facing the fire, she squirmed.

"Stop this movement."

She smiled. "I desire to snuggle close and need to get comfortable."

"'Tis dangerous."

She arranged her head under his chin. "You will be gone overlong?"

He stroked her flowing curls. "If the winter snow holds and we meet with no other difficulties, I predict two, perhaps three weeks."

After she pulled her feet onto the edge of the chair, William tugged the gown over her exposed toes. An ache formed in her throat at his thoughtfulness. "Thank you." His short beard tickled her nose. "Are your friends mighty warriors?"

"Aye. The only mercenaries that I trust with my life. Their leader, Ranulf, is from a prominent border family. He is well versed in numbers and literature; yet, for a brief time chose the life of a mercenary."

Her eyes closed as his lips caressed her hair. This is what she longed for as warmth swirled in her stomach. Her voice was barely above a whisper. "What of the others?"

"Reid has red hair much like your own." He raked his fingers through her thick mane. "No. His hair consists of tight, springy curls while your tresses are as soft as a baby lamb's wool." He sniffed her hair.

"Are there not six?"

He let go of her hair and with both arms wrapped around her, he pulled her closer. "Marcus is strong, Eunan and Kester can extract information out of a mute man, and Cam ... well Cam is charming. Stay far from him."

She giggled. "Rest easy, I wish not to meet Cam." She nuzzled his neck. "I have a husband."

William moaned. "You must stop weaving this spell on me. I am defenseless against your wiles."

She kissed his neck. "I like you defenseless."

His groan rumbled against her ear. "You are injured."

"I am stronger than you think." She wrapped her left hand under his ear and stroked.

He kissed her pulsating wrist and blew his warm breath across her skin. Chills formed on her arm. She was almost dizzy with want for her husband. A near-death experience changed how she viewed her husband and their life together.

"At night I still hear your shrill cries. They pierce my heart over and over again."

She twirled his long hair at the base of his neck. "Life is uncertain. All the more reason not to waste a day."

With one finger, he turned her face. Unhurried, he traced each brow, down her nose, and across her lips. "So soft." His mouth lowered to her delicate eyes—kissing each one. Then he moved to the corners of her lips that parted in readiness. When his kiss was not forthcoming, she peeped. His eyes revealed a turbulent storm raging from within. His hunger for her showed as clear as the crisp morning air.

"Test me. I will not shatter." She tugged his hair and claimed his mouth with her own.

William deepened the kiss. Pippa's pulse drummed in her ears. She broke the embrace and gasped. "Take me to the bed."

Breathing rapidly, he leaned his head against hers. "'Tis not wise."

"Trust me."

# 35

Lying in their cozy bed with her eyes closed, a warm exhale skimmed across Pippa's bare shoulder. She dared a peep. With his head propped on his knuckles, her husband's sad eyes stared back at her.

"Husband, what is amiss?"

He used his free hand to trace a circle around her wound. "Your angry, red scar shouts at me."

She reached to cover it with the blanket, but he stilled her hand.

"'Tis a good reminder of my foolish judgment. The guilt from your near-death experience haunts me."

She caught his squirming finger and held it against her heart. "You will not take all the credit. I hesitated on the bridge and allowed the arrow time to find its mark."

"I'm the one who chose the bridge as our escape." He pulled his hand free and flopped onto his back. "For years I considered no one when making my decisions."

Pippa eased to a sitting position using the blanket to cover her naked body. She peered down at her husband. "The accident stays in the past. We all err at times. I'm confident even I have made

281

errors in judgment." With a finger on her chin, she looked upward. "However, not a one comes to mind."

William chuckled.

Her attempt to lighten his disposition worked. He opened his arms, and she nestled close to his heart. "Remember, my husband. None are perfect save one—our Lord and Savior Christ Jesus."

His finger tapped the end of her nose. "Aye. How did you become so wise?"

She opened her mouth to answer, but snapped it shut when a knock came on their door.

William patted her bottom. "Enter."

Pippa gasped at her husband's nonchalant manner. Mortified, she scrambled under the covers.

Merry stepped inside and bobbed a curtsy. "My Lord. Henry has returned from Scotland. He says it's urgent."

"Thank you, Merry. Tell him I'll come down straightaway." William hopped out of the bed before the door clicked shut and pulled on his pants.

Pippa flipped the coverlet off her head. Her heart picked up speed. "Why was Henry in Scotland?"

"I sent him on a scouting mission." He looked about. "Where's my shirt?"

She looked up and pointed.

His shirt dangled from the bedpost. Their gazes collided. His wicked grin sent quivers spiraling through her body. "For an injured warrior, you were quite enthusiastic." He snatched it down and tugged it over his head.

His playful banter failed to hinder her questioning. "Do you fear our enemies remain close?" Pippa started to get out of bed but stopped short remembering her bare state.

He buckled his belt. Sitting on the edge of the bed, he tugged on his boots. "I will report to you as soon as I hear Henry's news." He stood and sheathed his sword.

On her knees, Pippa sat back against her heels. "I'm coming with you."

He walked toward the door. "There is no need."

She swung her legs over the edge. After a deep breath, she stood and walked to her armoire wearing naught but a smile. She dared not turn to look at her husband.

His quick breath confirmed he watched. "Pippa!"

Perhaps he would forget why she needed to stay abed. "Please help me with my clothing. I can't lift my arm high enough."

His groan reached her ears. "What a tempting vixen."

She glanced over her shoulder and smiled. "If you assist me, the sooner we leave."

His cheeks puffed as he blew out his breath. He stomped across the floor. "This is not wise."

"Duly noted."

Together they managed to get her dressed in pants and a loose shirt. She sat on the stool and shoved her foot into each boot while William knelt at her feet.

"Thank you, husband."

He helped her stand. His eyes sparked as he dug his fingers through her hair. The act caused her head to tilt upward leaving her lips exposed. "You will obey me when we leave this room. Understood?"

"I will try."

He moved his lips closer to hers. "You will or you stay here."

She chewed on her lower lip.

"Henry awaits."

His breath brushed across her lips. If she didn't relinquish, no doubt he would lock her in the room. "As you wish."

His lips broke into a slow grin. "Now that wasn't so hard."

When his lips claimed hers, she melted into him. It seemed, ever since her mishap, her husband had endeavored to adjust to their marital status. It pleased her and provided her hope for their future together.

After a few moments, William broke the heated kiss and untangled his fingers from her hair. "Henry awaits."

Relieved that William yielded, Pippa gladly headed out the door. Grant it, her step was slow and cautious. Aggravated at her weak legs, she leaned into William as he supported her with his arm around her waist. Tired of staying in their room during her recovery, she anticipated returning to her normal duties.

As they walked down the hallway, her eyes soaked up the surroundings—thankful for a reprieve. A few servants nodded when they passed the couple while going about their early morning duties.

Pippa yawned.

William squeezed her waist. "Did you not get adequate rest?"

She disregarded his lure to discuss their evening activity. "You failed to tell me why you sent Henry to Scotland."

"All in due time. Patience, young wife."

When William opened the door to the war room, they found Henry pacing the room. He looked at them stunned. "Lady McKinnon, should you not be abed?"

Pippa rolled her eyes. "No." She eased into the closest chair and William sat beside her.

Henry's wide eyes swiveled from William to Pippa and back. "I didn't expect Lady McKinnon to join us."

"Henry! Whatever the report, I'm privy to it."

Henry sighed. "As you wish." He stalked over to the table and yanked out a chair. "We did as you suggested."

"Wait," Pippa interrupted. She turned to William. "'Tis time to tell me what's transpired while I've been locked away."

Henry grunted. "Locked ..."

William raised his hand before Henry finished his statement. "I sent a contingent of men to take food to Mistress Rhona and to see how she fared."

A smile spread across Pippa's face. "Why, thank you, husband. How thoughtful. I planned to visit her once my wound healed." She looked between the two men. "What are you not telling me?"

William's fingers tapped on the table. "Let Henry finish his report, and we'll both know the outcome of his mission. Please, continue. My wife will refrain from further questioning until you've concluded." His narrowed eyes caught her gaze.

She nodded in agreement.

"Before we even came to her cabin, we smelled smoke and saw it billowing upward. We first thought a roaring fire blazed; but at the edge of the forest, we saw her cabin burned to the ground."

Pippa gasped as her hand flew to her neck. William put his arm around her shoulders.

Henry gulped.

She couldn't stand the suspense. The ache in her heart stole her breath. "Is she dead?"

"No. She lives."

Pippa sagged against William. "Thank you, Holy Father."

William frowned at her. "I should have followed my instinct. You are not ready for such news. It's vital you return to our room."

"No." Cowering from her responsibilities suited her not. She had endured worse. "Please?"

William heaved a sigh. "Resume."

"Bloody donkey parts littered all around her smoldering cabin. At first, we feared to find her body under the ruble. I called her name over and over while two men kept guard. We knew not if the ruffians hid nearby."

Pippa whimpered.

"Wife, this is too much for your delicate situation."

She sniffed. "No. Please, I must hear all."

"Hurry this along, Henry."

"Patrick found her off to the side where we stacked her winter wood. Even though badly beaten, she lived."

Pippa's back stiffened. "Where is she?"

"We brought her here. The village healer attends her."

"I must go to her."

"Now, Pippa ..."

Her voice strengthened. "Take me to her."

"Henry, go break your fast while I take my wife to see Rhona. I'll meet you here afterwards."

"Yes, m' lord."

Once Henry walked out the door, Pippa burst into tears. William's arms tightened around her while her body shook with sobs. "This is my fault," she cried.

"Nay, wife. "'Tis the evil men for whom I search. The blame lies at their door."

"Find them!"

Once convinced Rhona received the best of care, William insisted Pippa return to bed. He allowed Wolf to stay by her side. Stroking his fur often calmed her. Gwendolyn brought her morning meal to the bedchamber and promised to sit with her while William met with Henry.

He was thankful his days as a mercenary taught him self-control. Otherwise, his burning fury at such an injustice would escape. The loud click of his boot heels ricocheted off the walls with each step. He never understood how anyone possessed such a wicked soul as to harm children and women. The vile act reeked of Badger's depravity.

William stormed into the room where Henry waited. He slammed the door. "Give me the details."

"The scene was gruesome. 'Twas easy to find the woman. Her bloody trail led to the head of her donkey thrown in the wood pile. Poor mistress wailed over leaving the animal. Most disturbing."

Henry breathed deep. "Nothing left to salvage." His eyes narrowed. "How did you know a cart would be needed?"

William shook his head. "The day we left mistress Rhona at her cabin, an uneasiness invaded my spirit. My regret is I waited too many days to follow up."

"Her injuries are grievous. I dare say, the healer hid most of the damage under a blanket so as not to shock m' lady. The wounds spoke of torture."

William scoured his face as his heart pinged against his ribs.

"She told us they kept asking her about the buried bodies—who buried them, and what happened to the woman. Her lies about m' lady's whereabouts ensured her brutal punishment. Those cruel men were relentless."

William pounded his fist against the table. When he stood, he bumped his chair back and tramped to the window. He whirled to face Henry. "I can't wait for Pippa's total healing. I leave on the morrow." He roamed the room ticking off the men he required to accompany him. "Ranulf, Cam, Eunan, Reid, Kester, Marcus, Ross, John, and Peter." He put his hand on Henry's shoulder. "You will oversee the castle in my absence. Protect her well."

"Indeed, m' lord."

"Make the necessary arrangements for our travel. We need enough provisions to last three weeks. Remember, I hope to add one or more to our travels home once I find my father. The winter weather is upon us. Provide adequate blankets."

"I understand your needs. Fear not. All will be ready."

William looked at Henry's tight expression. "Of course. It is as you say. I trust you. Since I've made my decision, my mind whirls with thoughts."

"You fear Lady Phillipe."

A slow grin formed. "Aye. She is, shall we say, formidable."

Henry laughed. "You mean difficult. This I know." As he left, his laughter floated out the door leaving William to sort out his own dilemma.

In the quiet of the war room, William contemplated the clash to come. He had to inform Pippa the upcoming battle with the enemy didn't include her. How should he approach the subject? His sluggish feet carried him out the door and up the stairs. All the while he disregarded each idea that formed. No doubt, she hoped to capture or kill the adversary singlehandedly. He shook his head in wonder at his fearless wife.

When he started down the passageway leading to their room, he noticed the guard no longer stood outside the door. Now what? He withdrew his sword as he jogged the remaining steps. The door stood ajar. Pushing it open with the tip of his blade, he approached with caution. He scanned the empty room. "Pippa? Gwendolyn?"

He stepped back into the hallway and looked both ways. A servant girl toting a slop bucket walked in his direction. She ducked her head when she came abreast of his position and dipped a curtsy.

"M' lord."

"Do you know the whereabouts of the guard for Lady McKinnon?"

"'e's outside the chapel."

"Thank you, miss." William sheathed his sword and headed down the corridor. His long stride ate up the distance to the chapel housed in the other wing. Before he reached the special room, he saw a lighted torch blazing outside the doorway—the guard at his post.

"Duff." William nodded. "Gwendolyn."

"M' lord," they said in unison.

"Is my wife inside?"

Duff deferred to Gwendolyn. "Yes, m' lord."

William reached for the door.

"She convinced me to carry her sword to the chapel and issued orders not to disturb her," Gwendolyn whispered.

His brows rose. "Is that so? Wait for me here." With a gentle touch, William opened the heavy door and slipped inside. His wife knelt at the altar with Wolf halfway down the aisle. Wolf raised his head and looked at the interloper before turning back toward Pippa. Motionless, William waited against the back wall.

"I praise Ye, O Lord, my Rock and my Redeemer. I praise Ye for my countless blessings bestowed upon me by You, my Heavenly Lord. I give thanks unto You, Lord, for Your mercy endureth forever. Your name is great and greatly to be praised. If I could sing, I would sing Your praises." She looked upward shaking her head. "You realize my singing makes even the deaf to cringe."

She heaved a deep sigh and bowed. "Father, I beseech You. Please bestow Your mighty strength upon my husband. He goes forth into battle." She sniffed. "I fear for his safety. The way is treacherous with danger at every turn. You and You alone must surround him with your protection. Blow away the ungodly foe as if chaff in the wind. Unto Thee I lift up mine eyes from whence comes my help and the help of my husband."

She hesitated. William thought her finished until she stood to her feet with her eyes focused on the cross.

"Lord, if You tarry, lend me Your ear for a personal request. I would be forever grateful if You saw fit to impart Your divine healing touch to my shoulder which hinders my fighting ability. Then I could offer my aide and battle by William's side. Hear my cry for Your power and deliverance from this affliction. Amen and amen."

Curious, William watched as she reached for her sword laying at her feet. With both hands she gripped the hilt. A cry tore from her throat when she attempted to raise it. Instead, it clattered to the stone floor.

William rushed forward with Wolf at his heels.

"Pippa!"

He lifted her body as she slumped against the altar steps. She turned her face against his tunic and cried. Wolf whimpered and nuzzled her hand. William sat down on the front bench with his wife in his lap.

"What is the meaning of this weeping?" He tried to look into her face, but she scrunched further into his shirt.

He held her tight and stroked her hair. "There is no need for such tears."

She arched backwards as her flushed face met his gaze. "I'm unable to lift my sword! I'm of no use against the enemy if I fail to mend before your journey to Scotland."

Her purpose was clear. His fingers brushed the hair from her face and then captured her chin. Her desperate eyes speared his heart, but he refused to allow her distress to dissuade his decision.

"I'm sorry, but I leave on the morrow."

# 36

William stood on the keep steps while the men loaded the horses with the final supplies. They worked with urgency in light of the information on the latest enemy attack against Rhona. As the crisp air stung his eyes, he glanced over and observed his regal wife standing erect watching the warriors. Even though he thought it unwise, Pippa had insisted on dressing and coming to see him off. Her hooded cloak hid her face from his view. He didn't have to see her to know how she regretted missing out on the battle to come.

He stepped closer and snaked his arm around her waist. The action brought her head around. Her tormented eyes caused a pain in his heart.

"Wife, why such anguish? I return in less than one moon."

When she failed to respond, he decided on a different tactic. He leaned close to her ear. "Have you grown so fond of your husband that you'll yearn for our bed sport?"

Her nose lifted as she turned back to watch the men. "I'll simply return to my life before a husband. I need no man to fulfill my existence."

She didn't fool him. He knew underneath her superior tone lurked a frightened young woman. She feared for him and for all of the men riding into harm's way. He refused for a stilted exchange to mark his farewell.

He grabbed her hand. "Come with me." He marched them back inside the castle and straight into the war room. "Explain yourself."

Pippa stepped down the two stairs into the room and turned to face him. "Of what do you speak?"

His eyes narrowed. "You know exactly of what I speak ... your last remark."

Her back stiffened. As her chin raised, the hood fell backward. "Before you, I ruled unaided. Once you leave, I will resume my usual responsibilities until your homecoming ... or perchance, forever alone if you fail to return."

With slowness, William stepped down to her level—within inches of his trembling wife. He witnessed sadness pass through her eyes before she quenched the emotion. He stooped low to gaze directly into her face. "You fool me not."

Redness rimmed her eyes.

Her chin rose as she stepped back from him. "What do you expect of me? I've lost both of my parents. This could well be my last day to speak to my husband." Tears gathered. "If you abandon me through death ... I have no words."

At last, she spoke truth to him. He stepped toward his fragile wife. Her arm whooshed out to warn him away. He grasped her hand and tugged her into his hold. She dissolved in his embrace and cried. With a gentle sway, he rocked her.

After her head nestled under his chin, his lips grazed her soft, frazzled curls. "Oh, my wife. You are correct. There are no guarantees in this life; but I know a wise woman who once said and I quote. 'God alone controls my destiny and breathes His breath into my body. When He ceases, I return to dust.'"

She snuffled. "Don't use my words against me."

His arms tightened.

She wiped her nose on his cloak and laid her cheek against his leather jerkin. "Forgive my flood waters. I've been quite volatile since my mishap."

He reached up and cradled her face in his hands. "I always welcome tears born of truth. For you, I bequeath a pledge. I promise to use caution when I engage in battle and take no unnecessary risks." He kissed the tip of her nose. "My life is in God's hands."

"Yes," she whispered.

"I entrust you with my last request."

She raised one brow. "Oh?"

"Rest, heal, and pray for me."

A sad smile split her lips. "I heard three requests ... but I will endeavor to complete all you ask." She bracketed his whiskered face. "Come back to me."

His gentle kiss turned into one of desperation. Her fingers slipped under his jerkin and dug into his back as she clasped him tightly to her bosom. He ravished her lips before trailing delicate kisses across her velvet cheeks. Breathing heavily, he ended their intimate moment with a tender hug.

"I must depart."

Hand in hand they walked outside. Fairwick warriors lined the parapet while castle folk crowded the courtyard. All of William's men held their horse's bridle, ready for his signal. With Pippa snuggled close to his side, he raised a fisted hand. "We go forth to vanquish our foe."

Deafening cheers erupted.

He kissed Pippa and bounded down the steps. Well-wishers smacked his back before he leapt into his saddle. With his final gaze upon his wife, he waved farewell and guided the procession out the gate.

***

The men road hard for two days before resting at Ayton Castle, not far from Eyemouth, Scotland. After a short reprieve, Ross,

Eunan, and Cam split off and headed toward Sanddown Castle. There they boarded a boat owned by Nicolas Fairwick and sailed north for Coldingham Bay.

William and his men escorted the extra pack horses and wagon filled with two barrels of black powder. Rainy weather slowed their progress when the cart wedged in muddy ruts along the road. Ranulf and Marcus heaved on the wagon wheel buried in the mud while William and Peter tugged the cart-horses' halters. Off to the side, Reid and Kester secured the other horses. Reid goaded the men.

William grunted as his foot slipped in the mud. "Stop your nonsense. It helps nothing."

Reid winked at Kester. "I hear an annoying sound. Dost ye hear it, Kester? 'Tis like a pest boozing in me ear."

"Aye."

As the wheel lurched out of the hole, mud flung onto Marcus and Ranulf. Covered in slimy muck, Ranulf's face wore a thundercloud as he slung mud from his hands. Reid snickered.

"Ye dunderhead!" Ranulf ran at Reid and launched a handful of wet sludge hitting Reid in the mouth.

"Why ye scoundrel!" Reid wiped his face and drew his sword.

Tired and wet, William had heard enough. "Cease!" He marched up to Reid who eyed Ranulf with anger. "Put away your sword. We have no time for your childish display."

Reid's eyes of fire turned on William. "I've kilt men over less."

William stared back. "Remember whom you challenge."

Reid stomped down the road as he sheathed his sword.

Ranulf walked up to William while he watched Reid tramp away. "His temper matches his hair."

"Aye." William turned to Ranulf. "You know his temper is easily ignited. Do not engage him again."

Ranulf's mouth pinched together. "Because ye are me friend, I will let yer slight pass."

"You owe me a debt. Until it is paid, I am in charge of all the happenings with this traveling party. Is that understood?"

"Aye." Ranulf trudged to his horse and snatched the reins from Kester.

William caught Kester's notice and shook his head. No need for Kester to explode. Glad he averted a useless killing, William realized he best not forget their hotheaded personalities again.

"Mount up." William heaved a sigh. He needed Ranulf's precise measurements for the black powder and couldn't afford to lose him before reaching his father. How soon he had forgotten the mercenaries quarrelsome behavior—much like children except more deadly.

After four additional hours of slopping through the muck, they arrived on the outskirts of Coldingham. William led them deep into the forest. "We camp here for the night." Groans of relief reached William's ears. "Kester, Reid, forage for fresh meat. Don't stray too far from the camp. Marcus, Ranulf, secure the wagon and powder. Peter and I will brush down the horses and hobble them while we eat and discuss our strategy."

Peter walked beside William. "Do you think they will slay one another during the night?"

William glanced at the retreating backs of the other men. "I pray not. Their typical style is to attack like angry dogs and then calm down to civil creatures. My guess is they have stewed over an issue for weeks before their outburst. After a restful night, I expect them to behave in a manner befitting their status, both highly educated men spawn from noble families."

"I believe the saying."

"What saying?"

"Red-headed people possess powerful tempers. I've witnessed it in m' lady a time or two." His eyes grew round. "Forgive me, m' lord. I spoke out of turn."

William laughed. "'Twas just the amusement I needed." He scuffed Peter's back. "Thank you."

Kester and Reid brought back two rabbits and three quail to roast over the small cooking fire built by Ranulf. Marcus pulled a loaf of bread and a chunk of cheese from their supplies to add to the meal.

"We drink water tonight. I need all of us at our peak performance tomorrow." The men grumbled, but none challenged William's announcement.

While the men devoured their meal, William used the time to explain their next strategy. "Peter, you and Marcus ride into Coldingham and locate the nearest tavern. There you will enter, and each buy one tankard of ale. Drink slow while you listen for news about the happenings at the ruins on Kirk Hill. As visitors to the place, don't stay overlong."

Kester grumbled. "Don't ye need anither pair of ears?"

William grinned. "Nay. The rest of us need to plan the attack of the lingering ghosts."

Ranulf laughed. "Tha what?"

"Ghosts of the nuns and monks killed in a fire at the monastery will reappear to haunt the evil men shaming their memory."

Reid rolled in laughter. "This sounds more excitin' than sipping ale."

Marcus and Peter hurried through their meal and left for the fishing village of Coldingham. William used his boot to smooth the dirt near the fire. He knelt upon one knee and spread out his maps.

Using a stick, he pointed. "Here is the location of Kirk Hill and the ruins. There exists an underground channel starting at Castle Rock and tunneling under the monastery. Eunan and John will traverse this passageway and produce a few sporadic chilling sounds."

Reid clapped his hands. "I love it."

"I've brought white linen cloths to attach to ropes tied between several trees near the site. We will fill a section of the cloth with grass and leaves; then, tie it off to represent a head. A pulley system between the trees allows our ghosts to float back and forth—high enough for obscurity, yet visible. Marcus, Kester, and Peter will manipulate the *spirits*."

Reid leaned close. "What aboot me?"

William sat back against his boot heel. "You, Ranulf, and I will work our way closer to the actual ruins with a trail of black powder. With our enemy distracted by the phantom spirits and spooky noises, if careful, we should go undetected."

Ranulf rubbed his hands together. "This area seems familiar. I believe bats roost nearby."

Kester's eyes sparkled. "Splendid. We could stir them up with tha ghosts. Between ghosts and bats, the sairy lot weel scream for their mithers."

"What weel Ross and Cam do?"

"They will safeguard the boat moored in the bay. Any other questions?"

"Nay. When dost we start?" Ranulf asked.

William rolled up the maps and stood. "Tonight, after I scout out the perimeter of the ruins. Ranulf, you're with me. The rest of you clear away the remnants of our meal and gather your needed supplies. We'll return within the hour."

William and Ranulf saddled their horses.

Ranulf looked up when he finished. "Dost ye think it weel work?"

William stepped in the stirrup and swung into the saddle. "It must succeed." He nudged his horse and headed northeast.

# *37*

William and Ranulf dismounted far in the forest and left their horses tied to a tree branch. Their quiet stealth afforded them safe passage through the underbrush. The two crawled on their bellies the last few feet reaching the edge of the forest near the ruins. They encountered no guards and saw no tracks of man.

William withdrew his spyglass and poked it through the bushes while Ranulf watched his back. With a slow steady pace, he swept the glass from one end of the compound to the other. A thin line of smoke trickled out of two small huts off to the left of the main ruins. It appeared a strong storm could knock them flat. Two guards patrolled the grounds with nothing more than clubs.

A shout caused him to sweep far right. Some type of disturbance sent the two guards running. He kept watch at the entrance to a crumbling wall of the ruined monastery. A man in chains stumbled out, and a burly guard shoved him to the ground. When the man raised his head, William hissed. His father!

Tears formed in his eyes. He yanked away the glass and swiped his sleeve across his face to clear his vision. He took a deep breath. *Praise God, he lives!*

With quick speed, the lens moved back in place when a whip cracked. A cloaked man wielded the whip against his helpless father.

He growled. "I will kill him."

Ranulf peered through the bush. "What's taking place?" he asked in a low voice.

"An evil man beats my father while he is chained."

Ranulf grabbed William's arm and shook his head.

It took great effort for William to concentrate when he wanted to storm the place and rescue his father. He held up three fingers and pointed right. Then he held up two fingers and pointed left. One finger pointed upward. He handed the spyglass to Ranulf and waited.

William rested his head against his arm and listened. His father received ten lashes, and then the flogging ceased. He heard no sound from his father's lips during the entire beating. Relieved when it stopped, William took back his lens and looked. Two guards lifted his father and dragged him back into the dark ruins. The hooded man limped away while the two guards with clubs headed back to their posts.

He swept the area one last time before signaling a retreat to Ranulf. The men scooted backward until safe to stand. They ran to their horses and mounted in haste. William urged his horse into a gallop and headed back toward their camp with Ranulf by his side.

Once they traveled over a mile, Ranulf broke the silence. "We weel slice them up and leave nary a survivor."

The thoughts of the battle to come soured in William's stomach. His fury built with each hoof beat. He desired for the enemy to suffer, but he no longer possessed the enraged vengeance that once drove him to kill. It mattered not. He planned to destroy any who stood between him and his father's rescue.

Their horses skidded to a halt at the camp. Both men jumped down. Kester grabbed the halters and led the horses away. William stormed over to the men sitting on logs under the trees.

Marcus handed each man a cup of cool water. William drank his in one gulp and gave the cup back. "What did you and Peter learn?"

"There is mooch talk aboot tha ruins and evil happenings."

Peter frowned. "An anxious man at the tavern is one of the guards—a young one named Raven. He failed to produce the young cub ... you. I believe he feared showing up without you. His lips loosened with each tankard he consumed."

"Aye. Six guards, three women, one boy and one evil man named Eugene."

"I think Raven makes the seventh guard, but I'm not sure. He became quite drunk."

William's breathing slowed. "Their plans?"

"To kill all prisoners once they capture you."

William rolled his tight shoulders. "One I didn't see—Badger, the mercenary. If he remains with the group, beware; he carries massive weapons and uses them with deadly accuracy."

"I remember 'im," Reid said. "'e's merciless."

"Aye." William looked around the circle of men. "Do not harm the women or the child. We came to extract my father and any other prisoners held by this evil monster in whatever manner you deem necessary."

Ranulf stepped forward. "We need to ride. Nay mooch daylight."

"Agreed. I ride to Castle Rock to assure the arrival of Ross and his men. Then I'll join Ranulf and Reid." Watching the men mount up, William's stomach ached. Who would survive?

"Go with God."

William broke from the group to ride east toward the shoreline while the others rode north to the fringe of Kirk Hill. He expected each man to execute his task with excellence—professionals at their trade. His heart thundered with the anticipation of the difficult battle they all faced.

*I'm coming father.*

His horse slowed to a walk when he encountered the rocky ridge. The treacherous path wove downward around the cliff. The cold, salty breeze from the North Sea whipped around the stony bluff stinging William's eyes. When he rounded the last edge and saw a ship moored in the distance, a wave of relief rippled through his body. Encouraged, he watched for signs of Ross and his men. Before venturing out on the sandy beach, he whistled.

The shrieking wind made it difficult to distinguish the sounds bombarding his position. The cutting breeze scampered down his neck, chilling him to the bone. He wiped his lips and whistled again. This time a beautiful ringing floated to his ears—Ross's tiny bell.

William spurred his horse to walk at the edge of the sand near the cliff. Ross emerged from the entrance to the channel and motioned for William to enter the sanctuary. He hopped off and walked his horse through the opening. A small fire greeted his shivering body.

"Where have ye been, boy?" Ross asked.

"Ross, what are you doing here? I said to wait on the boat!"

"Nay need. Lord Nicolas Fairwick awaits on tha ship."

William blinked hard. "Lord Fairwick?"

"Aye. He insisted on bringing a few of his warriors. Ten men weel coom ashore a fore daybreak to assist in tha battle. He said they wear tha Fairwick coat of arms." Ross chuckled. "He feared ye might mistake him for tha enemy."

William smiled as his body relaxed. His uncle was a ferocious fighter. A good man to have at his back. "'Tis good news, indeed." He peered down the dark tunnel. "Is this passageway clear?"

Ross grinned wide. "Aye. Eunan and John await me signal."

"Remember to sound off the spooky sounds intermittent."

"Aye." Ross chuckled. "Tha excitement of tha lads alarms me."

"I'm reassured to know you are here overseeing this end of the plan. It brings me peace."

"I won't fail ye. Go find yer fither."

"I saw him, Ross. Eugene delivered ten lashes while he stood chained." He ground his teeth. "Coward."

A frown deepened on Ross's face. "Then we need to hurry, lad."

The warmth of the fire satisfied William's shivers; but to chase away the chill in his spirit, he needed his father's embrace. "I'm on my way." Compelled by an unknown force, William turned back and hugged Ross. "Have a care, my friend."

William trotted up a small incline near Kirk Hill just as the sunset glowed on the horizon. He remained hidden in the woods, picking his way through thick underbrush to the rendezvous point.

"You made it." A quiet voice floated on the breeze.

William twisted in his saddle to see Peter dangling high in a tree. He bracketed his mouth with both hands and spoke low. "Well done, Peter. I failed to hear you or spy your perch."

"The black hood covered me face. Merry's a master seamstress."

"Aye, she is. What of the others?"

"Here," Marcus murmured a few trees away.

"Kester hangs further down the row where you'll find Ranulf and Reid." Wearing a childish grin, Peter pointed. "Our system is quite impressive."

William smiled and saluted. Afterwards, Peter disappeared behind a branch. William dismounted and walked his horse the remainder of the way. From his position, the ruins stayed hidden from his sight which meant he, too, traveled unseen. He found Ranulf and Reid sitting on the cart guarding the explosive powder. Ranulf hopped down and approached wearing a frown.

William reported. "Our men arrived on shore. They slithered under the monastery waiting for the darkness of night. We also garnered the support of Fairwick warriors. My uncle brought ten soldiers to aide our cause."

"'Tis good." His frown deepened. "Badger arrived."

William rubbed his neck. "He yearns to slay me."

"He weel fight to tha death."

"Aye. He will sniff me out. When he does, I will lure him near the black powder ..."

Ranulf interrupted. "I'll shoot a flaming arrow."

"... and then ... I'll run."

They both grinned like young lads.

"Reid tied together tree branches to wear on our backs while we crawl along tha ground. We'll go unnoticed. Moreover, those scared fopdoodles weel stay close to tha ruins for fear of ghosts."

"Not everyone will cower. Vigilance is imperative. Since all is at ready, I'm going to scout for activity."

"Aye."

William crouched low and made his way to the edge of the forest. Positioned on his stomach, he unhooked his spy glass. Darkness engulfed the ruins. Torches along the outside stone wall emitted the only light. He spotted two guards walking the perimeter as far as the light's range when a yell came from within.

The two guards sprinted toward the entrance of the monastery. William beamed. No doubt, ghostlike sounds from John and Eunan had begun. Eugene's head popped out from one of the huts at the commotion. Guards came running from the other side of the forest.

"Thank you for revealing your whereabouts," William muttered.

Additional light shone from within the ruins. It was easy to watch the pathway of the guards. Light glowed through each tiny gap in the mortar and each barred window as they ran down a passageway. William saw three possible portholes that might house his father. Narrowed bars covered their openings. The secure monastery protected the nuns and monks from possible invaders. Now, it shielded him from reaching his father.

William remained at his location for about a half hour. Watching. He heard rustling behind him. Easing his glass to the ground, he rolled withdrawing his sword as he bounded to his feet.

Lord Nicolas Fairwick stood in full armor. "Greetings, young one."

"Uncle!" William sheathed his sword. "Ross said you awaited on the boat."

Nicolas grinned. "I didn't wish to miss a virtuous battle. In addition, the faster I get your father home to your mother, the better. Her constant weeping has become intolerable."

Inwardly, William smiled. He knew his Uncle Nicolas loved his sister even though he accused her of theatrics. "Thank you for coming. Our chances for victory increase with your aide."

"Enlighten me on the situation."

William retrieved his lens and hooked it on his belt. The two walked away from the ruins and toward the encampment. "Earlier, Ross and his men created quite a stir with their ghostly sounds. They continued for over a half hour. Now, we let our adversary calm and believe all is secure." William stopped when they reached the cart where Reid stood guard.

"Where is Ranulf?"

"He gathers berries."

William's brows shot to his hairline. "In the dark?"

"He says he smells 'em."

"The purpose?"

In the moonlight, Reid's teeth gleamed bright. "'e plans to droop them on or near tha guards. Bats love 'em."

Nicolas covered his laughter with his hand. "Splendid idea."

"'e says it adds to tha eeriness of tha night."

William nodded. "I agree."

"If ye guard tha keg, I'll take tha wind chimes to Peter and Marcus. It's near time to add more disorder."

"Aye."

Nicolas leaned against the cart and crossed his arms. "Do you plan to scare your enemy to death?"

William's amusement disappeared. He didn't appreciate his uncle's tone. "You stand in Scotland not England. I know what I'm about."

Nicolas's arms fell loose at his sides. "I trust you do. I meant no disrespect."

"Since you are unaware of the legend, I'll educate you. Because mystery surrounds the monastery, many in this region believe the nuns and monks haunt these ruins after the fire. I heard one enemy guard voice this very fear when I crept near his camp. I hope to disorient the guards using their fear as a tool."

"Creative."

"Besides, it gives my men a purpose through the night. They function best when executing a task ... and it provides them amusement."

Ranulf burst through the trees. Nicolas snatched his knife in readiness. "'Tis me. Put away yer knife."

William huffed. "Ranulf, ye know to tread with a tender step."

He dumped his bag into the cart. "Look at me berries."

Ranulf's enthusiasm caught on. "Ye acquired a powerful stash. 'Tis time for you and Reid to plant your black powder." William looked at Nicolas. "Are you game for some sport?"

"Point the way."

# *38*

After a night of spine-chilling shrieks, ghostly figures soaring, and hungry bats plummeting the guards, the enemy jumped at every noise. During the night, William observed them almost attack one another in their fear. Tensions ran high as they blamed each other for one debacle after another as they tripped and stumbled through the night.

The foes' torches burned low until Ranulf sprinkled a bit of black powder on the flame from his post on the roof. The powder caused the flame to burst forth and die away. The guards' frightened state made them dull-witted. Not once did a one of them check the roof for an adversary.

With darkness as his ally, William decided to attack before dawn. At one point, Eugene and his wicked men had banded together and encircled the ruins. No other way existed to rescue his father except through bloodshed.

Nicolas stood beside William. "The men await your signal. I plan to keep Eugene in my sights at all times. He will not escape."

"We begin with bows. Strike hard and fast. Keep them occupied while Marcus, Peter, and I make our way to the other side."

"How will I know you have arrived?"

"I have a pouch of black powder. You'll see the eruption of the flame when I throw it at the torch."

Nicolas clasped his hand around William's forearm. "I cannot face my sister if death takes you."

"I won't allow it."

William, Marcus, and Peter rode undetected through the trees until they reached the border of the open plain near the rear of the monastery. William's heart drummed against his ribs as he secured his horse. He pulled his dirk and held up three fingers aiming his knife at the guards. Marcus and Peter did likewise. They crouched low and crept closer to the rubble of the building.

From behind, Peter and Marcus sliced the throats of two men hovering near the edge of the wreckage. They dragged the men into woods. The three scooted into the shadow of the wall. Marcus boosted William onto what remained of the roof, and then he and Peter retreated to the safety of the forest. William lay on his stomach and inched his way toward the front. At one point, his boot knocked a loose stone to the ground. He froze. He saw one enemy guard whip around with a sword in hand.

"Who's There?"

William followed the guard's movement until he got too close to the stone wall and disappeared from his sight.

"Show yerself."

William grinned. How absurd.

"If yer on tha roof, coom doon."

William held his breath. 'Twas too soon to get discovered.

"Finlay, did ye see anythin'?"

Approaching footsteps were heard from William's hiding place.

"Ye reek of ale, ye galoot. 'Tis yer fear of spirits making ye lose yer courage. Where's Gavin and Garroway?"

"They vanished," the guard whispered.

"Go find them!"

One set of feet faded away. One remained. William feared Finlay might hear the loud hammering of his heart.

"Finlay, where's tha guards?"

William recognized the voice—Raven.

"Gavin and Garroway are missing."

"Keep alert. These eerie sounds dinna belong to ghosts."

The two men walked away from William's section. He needed to reach the edge of the roof in order to drop black powder on the torch flame. His weapons grazed the stone as he advanced. He dared not remove them. After agonizing moments, he achieved his goal. He withdrew his pouch of powder and poured a generous amount into his palm. Extending his hand over the roof's rim, he released the powder.

*Boom!*

William scrambled backward as he heard running feet nearing his position. Before the guards arrived, Ranulf released a flaming arrow which hit one of their small buckets of powder out in the field between the ruins and the forest.

*Boom!*

Eruptions of the powder continued as more burning arrows hit their targets.

"We're under attack!"

Confusion reigned as the enemy clambered for safety. The blasts awarded William a few precious moments to get inside the monastery. He jumped to the ground and met Peter and Marcus. "Kick in the rear gate!"

With one well-placed boot, Marcus bashed in the fragile gate. Out poured two guards swinging their swords. "We'll finish these two," Marcus shouted.

William sidestepped the melee and stepped into a darkened passageway. Frantic screams filtered through the walls from the battle raging outside. Swords clashed as explosions continued. He crept toward the first doorway.

"Duck!" Marcus yelled.

William hit the floor and rolled. Swords clanged together over his head. He jumped to his feet to deflect a downward thrust from an enemy. Marcus entertained one man while another slashed at William. The guard was intent on winning the day when William swept his boot under the man's feet causing him to stumble. William ran him through as he staggered to stand. Sliding his sword clear, he whacked the knees of Marcus' man. As his knee slammed to the ground, Marcus finished his enemy with one swipe of his sword.

Peter hollered from the doorway. "Between the exploding powder and Lord Fairwick's men, the enemy stays occupied."

"Grab a torch and help us search!"

Without adequate light, the quest remained treacherous. When Peter appeared with fire, it changed the hunt. William kicked one door open. "Peter, hold the torch, but guard our backs while we comb the area."

They worked their way down the long hallway. Peter picked up a rag and wrapped it around a club left by one of the guards. Using his torch, he lit the rag and handed it to William.

"Thank you, my friend. Check each room!"

As William edged down the corridor, he heard a moan. He glanced around before rising on his toes to peer through bars into a cell. A man lay on a cot against the wall. "Father?"

The man stirred and groaned. "Who's there?"

An Englishman. "'Tis Lord William McKinnon. Hold. I'll get you out."

"No need." *Coughing.* "I'm near death. Rescue the other."

William didn't plan to leave any behind. He put his lips to the bars and spoke in a hushed voice. "Who controls the keys?"

"The one ... they call ... Bear." The man panted. "Be careful. He requires no weapons."

"I'll return for you."

When William came to a bend in the walkway, he halted and signaled to Peter and Marcus. They moved in close. William poked his head out and drew back rapidly. A huge man stood guard at another door. He handed the torch to Marcus. As he contemplated his next move, a shout filtered through the passage.

"Bear! Bring the prisoner!"

"Aye."

William listened to rattling keys. He peeped again. The guard focused on unlocking the door. William waited until the prison door creaked open. Then he barreled toward the cell praying his father was within. The running feet alerted the watchman, who spun around and leapt sideways from William's sword.

"Father?" William yelled.

"William?"

"Aye." Light on his feet, William dodged Bear's fists.

"Bear, don't harm my son. Stay alert, son. He's quite fierce."

Bear grunted and lunged toward William. William dropped in a roll and ended up behind Bear. He gave a mighty shove to Bear's back sending him sprawling to the stone floor. With haste, William jabbed his sword point into the back of Bear's neck.

"Don't move."

"Beware, son. He's cunning."

Bear still gripped the keys in his beefy hand. "If you wish to live, I advise you to stay motionless. Toss the keys aside." Reaching into his waistband, William removed his dirk. With his boot on the man's back, he placed the knife tip on the exposed neck and used his sword to reach the keys. Raking the keys along the ground, he drew them to his boot and picked them up. Numerous keys swayed on the ring.

William exhaled with force.

"Hurry, son."

Marcus entered and blocked the doorway.

"Marcus, bring the torch, and restrain this guard if he dares to move."

Marcus raised his sword. "I'll juist end his worthless life."

"No!" William's father's voice was weak but determined.

William stared at his father. Bear stirred. Before William could respond, Marcus boxed Bear's ears.

William grabbed the arm of Marcus. "Cease!"

His father struggled to stand. "Bear aided me. Harm him not."

William tried each key until one unlocked the first mechanism. "Father, can you walk?"

"I'm stiff, but I'll try."

"Bear?" A voice shouted from further down the passageway.

"Son, you are in danger."

"I have help."

Peter looked in. "A man with a limp is headed this way." He grinned. "Greetings, m' lord."

"Meet Peter, one of the men from the Fairwick Castle. Marcus, see to our visitor. Peter stand guard over our captive." At last, William managed to free his father from the neck collar. His father winced. William put an arm around his waist causing his father to cry out. "I witnessed your beating. I regret your pain, but speed is essential." Almost lifting him from his feet, William half dragged his father through the doorway.

Peter remained by the prison guard.

"Wait." His father glanced back. "Bear, do you wish to accompany me?"

William blinked. "Father?"

His eyes pleaded with William. "Bear?"

The big man rolled onto his back and sat up. "Leave me. Scotland is me home."

"We have no time to waste, Father." William forced his father away. They headed toward the back entrance. "Peter, did Marcus return?"

"No. He ran after the man."

"Eugene," his father said.

When they walked past the room containing the man on the cot, William stopped. He leaned his father against the wall. "Wait here. Peter, stay with him." He ran back to retrieve the keys from his father's cell. Bear stood in the doorway.

"I don't wish to harm you for my father's sake, but I won't hesitate if you give me reason."

Bear held forth the ring of keys.

"Thank you." William grabbed and ran.

Shouts sifted through the loose mortar. The battle raged on. William trotted back with great concern. Because he was too weak to stand, Peter held up William's father. "I promised to rescue another imprisoned man."

Wheezing filtered under the door. "Leave me, I say."

Marcus appeared at the end of the tunnel. "William! We have need of you!"

Bear walked toward the group. Peter chanced a glance at William. "We can take him down."

"Nay," his father said. "Bear will open this door. Hurry, Bear."

Torn, William looked at Marcus and then his father. "Father, can your guard be trusted?"

"Aye."

"Then I must leave you in Peter's capable hands."

His father's grip was strong. "Spare the young lad named Sloan."

"My men were commanded to spare all women and children. Fear not. Now, go. I'll meet you at the boat." He hugged his father's neck and ran out the back doorway.

"Bear, bring him out," William's father commanded.

Bear walked in and scooped up the man as if he were a child. When he carried him out, Lord McKinnon gasped.

Peter allowed no exchange between the men. He offered a steady arm to William's father and prodded the men forward. "We need to escape before our way is blocked."

"Aye."

Once they reached the opening, Peter peered around the corner. "The way is clear. We will run for those trees. Horses await us there." He looked at Bear. "Do not lag behind."

When William turned the corner, fires blazed from the explosions. Enemies on horseback battled against his men on foot. One horseman raced toward his position. William hurriedly looked about and spied a burning piece of wood. He ran and grabbed it. When the enemy got close, William held his torch out from his body and threw a handful of black powder through the flame as he tossed the torch. The explosion frightened the horse and unseated the rider.

As the rider fell from his mount, he lost his shield. William plunged his sword through the heart of his enemy. With swiftness, he turned and faced a foot soldier. He blocked the downward thrust of the sword with his own. When the enemy raised his arm for the next blow, William, using his other hand, threw his dirk into the man's belly. As he doubled over from the stabbing, William finished him off with his sword.

William picked up the flame and ran toward the wall. There he grabbed the bow and arrows from a dead enemy. With the wall at his back, he knelt on one knee and aimed for the enemy. He released three arrows that hit their targets.

A movement caught his eye. Badger. He loomed within fifteen feet of William's spot. William rose with a tight grip on his sword.

"What have we here?" Badger took two steps his way.

William glanced all around. He noticed the big barrel of black powder up against the wall several feet from where he stood. Holding his sword at ready, he backed toward the barrel. With his father out of harm's way, there was no reason to wait.

"Where are ye headed?" Badger's steps increased. "Have ye lost yer courage?"

Without further delay, William ran toward the barrel with Badger in pursuit. He jumped atop and scrambled for the roof. Badger grabbed for his foot. William smashed his other boot into Badger's face and managed to pull himself over the roof's edge. He stood.

"Ranulf! Reid!"

Badger was strong but bulky. He attempted to climb onto the barrel to pursue William.

Ranulf emerged from his hiding place in the trees with a flaming arrow poised and ready. "Aye!"

"Release! Release!" William ran along the roof in the opposite direction of Badger.

Reid lit the trails of powder leading to small buckets filled with the explosive. Ranulf shot his flaming arrow straight at the barrel of black powder. The flare sailed past the fighting men and struck the barrel. The massive explosion propelled Badger upward and splintered the wood fragments outward. The roof and stone wall crumbled. The force of the blast threw William off the roof and face down on the ground.

Climbing to his feet, he shook his head, but couldn't stop the ringing in his ears. Men sprawled all around him. Helmets, shields, and bucklers scattered the ground. Without thought, he stumbled toward the enemy to ensure their deaths.

He used his boot to shove over the first man. Dead. Circling the field of bodies, some lived. "Ranulf, Reid, Marcus, Kester, come forth!"

Lord Fairwick and his men assisted William as he searched among the slain when the ground began to quake. They looked up to see Fairwick men on horseback.

William stared in unbelief. "Now they choose to join us?"

Lord Fairwick walked over to William. "Their presence means your father is secure aboard the ship."

William's head whipped around. "Where is Eugene?"

"We will find him. He won't get far." Lord Fairwick shouted orders to five men on horseback. "Ride the perimeter and search for a man with a pronounced limp. Bring him to me at once."

"Lord Fairwick, if you will see to these prisoners, I'm going to search the ruins and behind the monastery." William scanned the men. "Marcus, with me."

William headed toward the cliff at the back of the monastery. He and Marcus stepped over piles of rubble as they hunted for evidence of Eugene or his dead body.

"Look there!" Marcus pointed to an object off in the distance. "'Tis a mon."

A flowing robe flapped in the wind as the man hobbled away. William and Marcus took off at a run. "You circle right, and I'll circle left. He must not escape!"

Kirk Hill was a rocky mound bordered by the black sea. William knew caverns and tunnels hid along the hillside. If Eugene reached one, he might evade capture. William's arms pumped at his side as he sprinted north while keeping him in his sights.

He climbed over boulders and jumped underbrush for speed. At close range, he noticed Eugene slipped on a rock and sank to his knees. William arrived within thirty feet of the man.

"Stop!"

Eugene glanced his way with angry eyes. "You will not capture me." He pushed to his feet and continued.

"You can't outrun me. Stop at once!"

Eugene stopped and turned toward William.

William stopped twenty feet from Eugene. "Why have you pursued my family?"

A harsh laugh echoed on the sea breeze. "Lady Brigette Fairwick was mine. Your father stole her from me."

"She married my father, and she loves him."

"No! She promised me her affection. Lord Fairwick thrust her upon your father. Then your father ordered his men to slay me." Eugene snickered. "I failed to die."

William's anger flared. "Were you behind my mother's abduction?"

"No! I planned to save her from the vile Elliot clan who took me in when your father left me for dead." His deformed face twisted into a snarl. "Instead, I received burns when your father ordered the Elliot castle burned to the ground as he whisked Lady Fairwick away from me."

"Did you think if you killed my family, you would acquire my mother?"

"I no longer want the filthy woman. I but wished to make her suffer by disposing of all those she loved dearly—those who caused my torment."

"You are a foolish man." William advanced on Eugene. "You caused your own affliction."

"Come no closer." Eugene backed up. His foot slipped near the edge of the cliff.

William saw Marcus creeping closer from the other side. He extended his hand toward Eugene. "Stop. Your foot nears the edge of the bluff."

"I will not go with you." Eugene glanced behind him. He stretched to see over the rim.

William and Marcus rushed forward. Eugene sneered. "Farewell." He turned and jumped off the hill. His scream bounced off the rocks.

316

The two men stared down at the rocks below. Eugene's body lay sprawled and broken on the jagged stones.

Marcus sheathed his sword. "He dinna survive tha fall."

"Praise our Lord and Savior, it is finished."

# 39

.

"M' lady, a messenger arrived." Merry stood at the threshold of Pippa's bedchamber.

"Offer refreshments, and I'll be down straightaway." Pippa closed the account books and locked them away in the trunk. She smoothed the front of her dress with trembling hands. As she passed the mirror, she noticed wisps of frazzled hair had escaped her braid. With no time to tidy the mess, she unleashed her hair and used her fingers to comb through it. Placing a circlet around her head, she left the room.

She prayed the messenger brought news of her husband. Weeks had passed without a word. Her heart drummed with trepidation. Had he succeeded with his quest? Was he injured ... or ... ? She forbid her wayward thoughts to go any further. They served no purpose except to bring her discontent.

Her hurried steps skimmed across the stone floor. The unbound hair fluttered behind her. She slowed her pace when she reached the stairs. No need to trip and fall to her death. With caution, she made her way to the grand hall. Her pounding heart drowned out all other sounds.

She spotted the messenger sitting off to one side drinking his ale. After a deep breath, she clasped her hands at her waist and glided over to the courier.

"I'm Lady McKinnon. You have a message for me?"

He stood. "Aye, lassie." He presented her with a rolled, sealed parchment. "It demands a reply."

She reached for the message. "If you'll excuse me, I'll return in a moment with an answer."

Walking on shaky legs, Pippa left the room. She dared not travel far for fear of collapsing. Instead, the war room provided the privacy she required. After closing the door, she looked at the wax to see the Fairwick seal. Her heart plummeted. Why not the McKinnon seal?

Pippa plopped in a chair near the window. An ache formed in her throat as she broke the seal. Unfurling the page, she read the salutation. *Lady Wife.* Tears of relief flooded her eyes. Clutching the missive, her head leaned against the chair. He lived! With eagerness to read all, she rubbed her eyes clear.

*Lady Wife,*

> *I wish to report a successful quest.*
> *My father is safe in the arms of his adoring wife.*
> *I pray you will permit my absence a few more days*
> *while I visit my family. I have much to share with you.*
> *Lord William McKinnon*

After reading the note several times, Pippa laid it in her lap and closed her eyes. *Thank You, thank You, thank You! My gracious, Heavenly Father, Your mercy has no bounds. Your protective arm secured my husband during his difficult battle. You saved him from the Valley of Death.*

She wiped her nose on a handkerchief pulled from her sleeve. *Thank You is so inadequate for all You have accomplished with and through my husband. My heart overflows with gratitude. Now, may You bless him with a safe journey home. Amen and amen.*

Joy gurgled up as she jumped to her feet and twirled around the room. A knock startled her and brought her victory dance to a close.

"Enter."

Merry popped her head around the door. "The messenger wishes to leave, m' lady. Do you have a reply?"

"Yes." She bounded up the two steps and hugged Merry. "I have a most joyous reply." Pippa ran to her room for her writing material.

> *Lord husband,*
> *Your message brought me great joy.*
> *I rejoice at the safe return of your father.*
> *Indeed, I grant you time to dwell with your family.*
> *Give them my best. With great anticipation,*
> *I await your return.*
>                                    *Lady Philippa McKinnon*

Using the McKinnon signet, Pippa pressed it in the hot wax sealing her reply. She kissed the wax. "I have much to share with you as well, my husband."

William placed his belongings in the saddle bag and collected his weapons. Even though reuniting with his father and his extended family had brought him great delight, it was time to return home. As he had conversed with his parents and Aunt Isabell and Uncle Nicolas the previous night, an empty longing overtook his heart. At one time, he had thought a path to great wealth would satisfy his secret yearnings. As a man grown, he realized neither wealth nor family sufficed when it came to inner peace.

He was eternally grateful for his wife's insights. She had proved influential in pointing him toward God. He discovered that putting his faith in the one true God provided him deliverance from his inward wickedness and granted him the peace that had eluded him in the past. He smiled.

Now, for a final conversation with his parents to find out the authenticity of his betrothal to Lady Philippa Emma Gail Fairwick McKinnon. When he opened his door, Ross rested against the outer wall. He joined William as they headed toward his father's room.

"What say you, Ross?"

"Are ye homeward bound?"

"Aye." From the corner of his eye, he looked at Ross. "Ross, might you consider remaining here for a time?"

Ross's brow rose as he cocked his head toward William.

"I wish for you to watch over my father; and on occasion, bring me word of his recovery. What say you?"

Ross put his hands behind his back as he continued walking. "I weel do as ye command."

William put a hand on Ross's arm to stop him. They faced each other in the hallway. "No. I give you permission to do as you want. All my life you protected me with no time to call your own. I'm offering you a reprieve from those duties. Mayhap see if a pretty lassie catches your eye."

Ross laughed. "I'm past tha prime of such undertakings."

This time William hooted. "No man is ever too old unless he's dead." He glanced around as servants scurried about their duties. "Stay here for a while; and if no one catches your eye, come to Fairwick castle for a look."

Ross just shook his head. "I'll watch over yer fither for a time."

"Thank you, my friend. I'm on my way to see Father. I'll inform him of our decision."

William walked with purpose. His eyes roamed the dark corners expecting his aggravating sisters to pounce. Perhaps they were still abed. Upon reaching the family wing of his uncle's castle, he rapped his knuckles on his parent's door.

It surprised him when his mother opened the door.

"William!"

Her genuine smile warmed his heart.

"Come in. Your father asked for you early his morn."

"Is something wrong?" He stalked inside the room.

"No, son." His father's voice drifted from the direction of the window where he lay upon a divan. "The way you talked last night, I feared you might leave before dawn."

William sat in a nearby chair. "Father, I would never leave without saying my farewells. How are you today?"

"Each day I get stronger. The healing balm and your mother's touch is all I need for a full recovery." He smiled at his wife as he grasped her outstretched hand.

Their intimate gaze at one another caused William to look away. He felt like an intruder on their private moment.

"I'm glad to hear it, for today I journey home."

His mother grinned. "'Tis time. You've been away from your young bride far too long."

He glanced between his parents. "Might I inquire of you before I leave?"

"Of course, son. You seemed unsettled when last we spoke. What troubles you?"

"Did you possess a betrothal between Philippa Fairwick and myself?"

His mother sat on the edge of the divan. "I told your father of our earlier conversation about this very matter."

Staring at his father, he waited.

"Your mother knew nothing of the betrothal." He grinned. "She can't keep a secret." He kissed her hand and winked. "Anyway, after Lady Fairwick was born, her father and I drew up a betrothal with a stipulation. If for any reason we felt the match to cause distress to either child, the betrothal would be null and void."

"Did her father reject me?"

"No. When you left to pursue a different path ..."

"To become a mercenary?"

"Aye. I informed Phillip if another asked for his daughter's hand, I would relinquish the betrothal."

"Why didn't you tell me?"

"In your last years at home, you seemed agitated and restless. I hesitated because you lacked maturity for such an undertaking and

Philippa was extremely young at the time. The night you informed your mother and me of your decision to leave our home, I planned to tell you. However, in light of our disagreement, I chose otherwise."

William clinched his teeth as he listened to his father's explanation. Afterward, he stared at his hands for a long moment before looking at his father. "I like it not, but you were correct. I would have refused you outright causing a violent rift between us."

"Your father knows you well, my son."

"The betrothal document, no doubt, burned in the fire. If you are terribly unhappy with the arrangement an annulment can be arranged."

"'Tis too late for an annulment."

"Oh?" His mother's big eyes twinkled.

William felt the heat rise in his neck at his parent's perusal. "The marriage remains unbroken as long as we both shall live. An accurate account is all I desired. Thank you for clarifying your motives."

He stood. "I found a small, locked chest. What dwells inside?"

A sweet smile broke across his mother's face. "It contains some of my most prized possessions—locks of our children's baby hair."

William grinned and shook his head. "Now, I take my leave." He hugged his mother and grasped his father's arm. "In all my travels, my love for you never waned."

His mother sniffed as tears formed. "Safe travels my son."

"By the by, does my baby brother have a name?"

Both parents laughed. His mother rolled her eyes. "Not yet. We can't seem to agree."

With his hand upon the door latch, William turned. "Ross remains here for a time. He is to report your progress to me ... and I charged him with the task of finding himself a wife."

His mother clapped her hands. "Oh, I'll be happy to assist in the matter."

"Now, my sweet ..."

William laughed and walked out the door leaving his father to manage his mother's matchmaking.

William traveled with Peter and John toward Fairwick castle. He left his Scottish friends at Sanddown castle where they continued to enjoy entertainment and to receive frequent accolades for their part in the rescue. He encouraged Lord Fairwick to throw them out at an appropriate moment; otherwise, they might stay the duration of the winter.

After hours of travel, the men crossed over into England. The familiar landscape brought a ripple of gladness to William. "Not much farther." Even his horse seemed to realize the closeness of home. His stride stretched longer as his muscles bunched under William's leg.

The moment he left Sanddown castle, his thoughts turned to his wife. He relived their stormy first encounter and smiled. Her bravery and liveliness drew him like a dog after a spirited fox. Her flaming hair matched her fiery boldness.

"Look!" Peter shouted. "Home!"

The castle sat high on the horizon and looked magnificent to William. Peter and John laughed like young lads with their first taste of freedom. William found their enthusiasm contagious. Free from the weight of finding his father alive, he allowed himself to imagine blissful winter days.

When they rode within shouting range of the guards, William noticed a movement to his right. There stood Pippa and her wolf at the edge of the forest with Duff close by. He broke from the men and rode straight toward his wife. His heart clanged inside his chest at the sight of her. The closer he came, the faster his breathing became. He pulled his horse up short and jumped from the saddle within a few feet of Pippa. Her face glowed with her smile. `

He dropped the reins.

She stepped forward, as did he. Without a word, he pushed back her hood. Her eyes darkened.

"I missed you husband."

His fingers dug into the thickness of her hair. Her lips parted as he lowered his head. His tender touch turned intense when she wrapped her arms around his back and drew him close.

As his pulse thrummed, he reared back to gaze at her. "After I found my father, my days lacked purpose without you by my side." He hugged her and breathed deep of her pleasing scent. "Come. Let us ride home together."

Without releasing her hand, he walked to his horse and boosted her into the saddle. Swinging up behind her, he grabbed the reins, bracketing her body with his arms. She cuddled back against him. He whispered in her ear.

"I have much to tell you."

Pippa relished her husband's embrace. He nuzzled her ear as his horse walked at a slow pace. When his lips caressed her hair, anticipation swirled in her stomach. Her fingers dug into his arm. "I'll call for your bath when we arrive."

He chuckled. "Will you assist me?"

"If you wish it."

When he spoke, his voice was hoarse. "I wish it."

As they passed through the gate, a roar erupted. Cheering warriors and servants lined the courtyard and parapet. William waved his hand in victory. Pippa's chest swelled with pride for her husband. She had worried how he might act toward her upon his return. Inwardly, she smiled, thankful her concerns were for naught.

He rode to the keep steps and dismounted. She slid off the horse into his capable hands. Instead of putting her on the ground, he carried her up the steps and turned to face the people. "My father recovers at Sanddown castle. I'm grateful for your prayers and support while I've been away. It appears my wife is hearty and well." His arms dipped as if the weight was too much for him. The crowd howled. "Now, if you will excuse us. My wife says she has much to tell me."

Pippa gasped. "M' lord!" He whipped around and marched inside the castle and directly to the stairs.

"Every man and woman within hearing are aware we have been parted for over four weeks." His smile spread across his face. "We do have details to discuss and a bath to receive."

She buried her hot face in his shoulder.

Once reaching their bedchamber, he set her on her feet and kicked the door closed before removing his weapons. It pleased Pippa when a knock on the door produced a tub and steaming water. Her servants anticipated their needs to perfection. Ten servants traipsed in and dumped hot water into the tub. After she ushered out the last maid, she turned to see William ease into the water.

"Wife, I need assistance."

She removed her cloak and threw it aside. Her heart beat a frantic tempo as she approached the tub. She squared her shoulders and knelt on the rug. With soap and rag in hand, she began with his face and neck. His head rested against the rim with his eyes closed. Her gentle touch lathered the soap and soothed away his worry lines.

"Mm. 'Tis nice."

Once she rinsed away the foam, he stilled her hand. "I will bath myself." He flashed a wicked grin. "I wished to see if you would perform the task."

"Why, you ..." She splashed his face and stood. "Perhaps, I'll watch."

"Be my guest." He laughed when she stomped away. "You recline by the fire, and I'll entertain you with my travels. Will that please you?"

She looked over her shoulder from where she stood by the chair. "Yes. Don't leave out any details."

William launched into his tale. Fascinated, Pippa asked questions about the black powder and how much danger surrounded him. She longed to see his expression as the story unfolded and was thankful when he joined her by the fire.

He picked her up and sat down with her on his lap. "Can you guess the best part of my journey?"

"Well, of course, finding your father alive."

"No. It was realizing that My Heavenly Lord, God controls my destiny, not me. When I admitted this truth, then I knew locating my father was up to God's intervention in my life. It was a relief."

Pippa cradled his face. "What a blessing." She gave him a tender kiss. His warm breath tickled her nose.

"There's more. My father explained the marriage betrothal."

Her eyes softened. "I knew the truth about it long ago."

His neck stiffened. "You did?"

"Yes. My father told me all of it. It mattered not." She ducked her head. "I wanted no other."

His finger lifted her chin. "Our fathers chose wisely." His finger trailed down her neck and arm. He raised her hand and kissed a path from her elbow to her wrist.

Only his eyes looked up. "Your pulse races."

"Yes," she murmured. Her eyes halted on his lips.

From her wrist, he kissed a path to the ring on her finger. Flames erupted from all the weeks of missing him. Her stomach fluttered in pure agony waiting on each delayed touch.

When he stood with her in his arms, her contented sigh escaped. His hungry eyes heightened her senses as he walked toward the bed. Placing her on her feet, he unpinned her loose braid and stepped back. His gaze swept up and down.

"You are breathtaking." His hands traveled up her bare arms. "What did you wish to share with me?"

"It can wait." She grabbed his hands and pulled backward. They fell upon the bed in a tangle of lovemaking.

# Epilogue

*Five Months Later*

"William, sit down and be patient. This pacing around our bedchamber distresses me."

He stood with his hands on his hips. "I have waited five months to reveal my surprise for you. Just leave your hair flowing."

Pippa looked up at Gwendolyn. "Pay him no mind. Finish pinning my curls." Holding up a hand mirror to gaze at her husband who stood behind her, a sly smile spread. "I commissioned a wedding gift for you, as well. Would you like to receive it now?"

His hands hung by his side as he walked over to Pippa sitting on a short stool. Kneeling beside her he placed two hands upon her extended belly and leaned close. "Please, no twins."

Gwendolyn giggled. Pippa bopped his head. "William!" She sighed. "We will graciously receive whatever the good Lord provides. Moreover, the babe is not your surprise."

He plopped on his bottom and looked up at her. "Praise the Lord Almighty! The horror of my twin sisters still haunts me. I couldn't bear to produce two who behaved thusly."

"I'm finished, m' lady."

"Thank you, Gwendolyn. You may go."

Pippa rose and stared down at her husband's boyish face. She granted him a sweet smile. "Our twins wouldn't dare act unseemly."

He fell over onto his back. "Oh, no! Please, don't even jest about such a thing."

Pippa shook her head and retrieved his gift wrapped in a purple velvet cloth and tied with a ribbon. "Only a man full grown can receive this precious gift."

Her husband bounded to his feet wearing a mischievous grin. He bowed low. "As you wish, lady wife." Straightening to his full height, his eyes sparkled.

With the gift nestled in both hands, she presented his wedding gift. When he reached for it, she held tight. "Promise to use it wisely?"

His grin widened. "Aye." He untied the bow and unrolled the cloth to find a jewel-handled dirk.

"Since you lost yours in battle ..."

"'Tis a stunning knife fit for a king." He lifted his head and revealed his flashing eyes. He turned it over in his hand rubbing a thumb over the shinning jewels. "You did well, my wife." He slid it behind his belt. "Perfect."

Willingly, she stepped into his embrace. After a lingering kiss, he continued. "I could have never imagined all God prepared for my life. He blessed me with a beautiful warrior bride who cares deeply for me and has taught me how to love others with an unselfish love." His hands cupped her face. "With all that I am, I love you, Philippa Emma Gail McKinnon. You are my most precious gift from above."

His tender kiss brought her to tears.

He wiped her cheeks. "Why this waterfall?"

She shrugged. "'Tis touching. I used to envision my life married to you, but those dreams were nothing compared to the genuine joining of a man and woman. My love for you runs deep. Your devotion and commitment to me far exceeded my imaginings."

With a crooked grin, he fingered one of her loose curls. "My admiration for you began the day you stormed into my life and demanded I honor the marriage betrothal." His head cocked to one side. "My respect for you grew into this all-consuming love that oft takes my breath when you're near."

"Your words soothe my spirit like a healing balm. After my mother's death, I tried to please my father and be what I thought he wanted. Now, I see all he wished for me was happiness."

He tweaked her nose. "Are you happy?"

"Extremely."

He presented his arm. "Shall we get married?"

Pippa rolled her eyes and put her hand around his elbow. "We are married."

"Today, you receive the wedding day you deserve."

"'Tis improper for a woman great with child to partake in a wedding ceremony."

William's laughter echoed down the hallway.

William and Pippa repeated their vows on the steps of the village church for the people. As the local villagers and castle folk cheered, William rubbed his wife's huge belly. He feared she might faint from embarrassment, but the people treasured the moment with applause and chants of fondness for their lady.

"Come, wife. We'll hold our private ceremony inside the church.

"Don't you dare shame me in front of your family by rubbing my stomach." She pulled him to a halt. "Is that understood?"

He hung his head. "If you insist." His head popped up. "The people loved it."

His wife moaned. "You are impossible."

"But you love me anyway?"

"You still live, do you not?"

His hand went to his heart. "You wound me right before seeing my family." He stopped her in the vestibule. "My gift for you resides inside the chapel."

"Getting to see your family is such a valuable treasure."

He fidgeted. "A more precious gift than my family awaits you."

She laughed. "Then do not delay. You have piqued my curiosity."

Two men opened wide the vestibule doors exposing the people inside the chapel. William attempted to walk his bride toward the front of the church, but she stopped at every bench to greet kinfolk.

In the back sat his mother nursing his baby brother. William averted his eyes and saw his sisters clustered together—his father oblivious to their scheming. Gillian directed her wicked grin his way. *God preserve me!*

Lord and Lady Nicolas Fairwick packed two benches with their crew of children. His Uncle Thomas dozed against the far wall after an all-night trip from service to the king.

"Oh, William, how sweet of you to include Rhona." She turned adoring eyes on him.

Unbeknownst to Pippa, off to one side sat a gentleman in the priest's chair. When the bride and groom approached the priest, the man stood. Pippa didn't notice him until William nodded to the right. "Look Pippa."

She smiled at William and turned to look. Her grip tightened around William's hand. "Papa?"

"My daughter."

Pippa sagged against William and burst into tears. William steadied her as she walked to her father. "Papa! You're alive!"

The two embraced. Sniffling and outright crying filled the small church. William watched as Pippa clung to her father and wept tears of joy.

"I thought you died in a carriage accident. Oh, Papa!"

The priest eyed William with raised brows. He smiled back and shrugged. "One can't rush a reunion such as this."

Phillip rubbed his daughter's back. "The carriage misfortune was no accident, but I'll tell more after I witness the joining of my sweet daughter to Lord William McKinnon." He looked between them. "It appears some joining has already taken place."

Pippa gasped. "Father!"

He winked. "We'll speak again after the ceremony."

Once Pippa collected herself, they proceeded with the ceremony. After the vows, chatter erupted in the chapel. It sounded as if a swarm of bees had invaded the place. With much ado, William ushered the lively group into the grand hall of the castle for the wedding festivities.

Instrumentalists played as the family ate the wedding feast and talked of times past. Pippa's father reclined at the wedding table holding his daughter's hand all during the meal.

"Father, why didn't you come home?"

William's heart ached to hear the distress in his wife's voice.

"Oh, my sweet Pippa. After the carriage left the road and crashed at the bottom of the ravine, soldiers dragged me free and tied me up. I never knew the fate of my traveling companions." His face contorted in pain.

Pippa patted her father's hand. "I'm sorry to report, they perished."

"After the rough treatment I received, I presumed them dead." His downcast countenance ripped at William's gut. He looked out at his own father who bore scars from the horrific imprisonment. "Tell us where you were taken and by whom."

"The culprit was Eugene. If you remember the story, he had attempted to kill Lady Isabell to prove his love for my sister, Brigette. When all failed, my brother, Nicolas, deported him to Scotland and left him for Lord Daniel McKinnon's men. We all thought him dead when in actuality, the Elliot clan rescued him. They planned to use him against our family since he had knowledge of our castle."

He gulped his ale and continued. "After the capture of Brigette by the crazed Brady Elliot, Eugene thought he would save her and keep her as his own." He leaned around Pippa to look at William. "I'm forever grateful to your father for saving my sister."

"My father would have moved heaven and earth to get his bonny bride home."

"After winning the battle against the Elliot Clan, Nicolas burned the Elliot castle to the ground to flush out Brody. In the process, Eugene received severe burns. He fled the area with Brody's son, Finlay, who was nine at the time—the very boy who confronted Daniel and vowed to kill him one day for the murder of his father."

Pippa frowned. "Such a complex tale."

William squeezed her hand. "Killing children is not my father's way, but he deeply regrets not taking the child's threat seriously."

"Eugene and Finlay met up with an evil man, Raven, who led a group of wicked warriors. They delighted in delivering vengeance on others. They hid out at the old monastery where we were taken to wait our fate of death." He glanced at William and then back to Pippa. "Your husband was the final prize to gain."

Pippa hugged and kissed the weathered cheek of her father. "Praise the Lord of Heaven, He spared your life."

"Your husband's wisdom and cunning saved us all."

Pippa beamed at William. "He is my perfect warrior husband."

The talk turned to more pleasant topics after Phillip recounted his experience. Pippa seemed content to hold his hand and admire the entertainers. Not long afterward, Phillip kissed his daughter. "I must retire. Enjoy your wedding night."

Since he remained fragile from his injuries, Thomas aided his departure. At her father's insistence, he had taken Pippa's childhood room instead of his own. He had wanted no part of the room he once shared with her mother.

The celebration continued until the wee hours of the night. Not wishing his wife to overdo, William carried Pippa up to their room. She laid her head upon his shoulder.

"'Twas a most glorious day and night." She yawned.

"I fear you are overtired."

"No." She yawned again. "I'm in awe of my beloved husband who gave me a priceless gift—my father." She nuzzled his neck.

His body tingled from her actions.

Once inside their room, William undressed his exhausted wife and removed her shoes. He pulled her gown over her head and sat her upon the bed. Joining her on the mattress, with deliberate slowness, he unpinned her hair and watched as the curls bounced free. For a brief time, he ran his fingers through her hair and massaged her scalp. When he finished, he gazed upon her beauty.

He took her hands in his own. "When I calculated my future, it included no one else. But, alas, God had greater plans for me." He kissed her left palm. "His ways are not my ways." He kissed her right palm. "He blessed me with a wife worth far more than rubies or gold." William lowered his mouth to her parted lips for a tender kiss. "A wife who captured this heart of stone."

# Reading Group
## Discussion Questions

1.     Which character in the novel did you most like?
What qualities made them your favorite?

2.     How did William's mood color his response to Pippa's
betrothal document?
Do you allow your attitude to affect the way you treat other
people?

3.     Did Pippa's impatience cause her to rush God's timetable
when she petitioned the king about her betrothal?
What happens when we get ahead of God?

4.     Can you pinpoint when William and/or Pippa made unwise
decisions and the results caused by those decisions? Share a
time when you made an unwise decision and the lessons
God taught you through the process.

5.     How hard was it for Pippa to relinquish her rule at Fairwick
castle?
Do you have an area in your life that you need to surrender
to God? Why do you insist on holding on to it?

6. Do you agree or disagree with Pippa's statement? Explain.
   *"God alone controls my destiny and breathes His breath
   into my body. When He ceases, I return to dust."*


7. In the beginning, William had a revengeful heart. At what
   point did his heart begin to soften? What event or person
   aided his change? How?


8. Tell about William's journey to understanding God. Who
   influenced your view of God? A father, a mother, a
   preacher, a teacher? Has your view changed over the years?


9. Did any character or happening in the novel surprise you?
   How so? Did you enjoy the revelation at the end?


10. What interesting facts did you learn about Scotland?

# Author's Note

As I map out each novel in my mind, there are times when I need certain land markers to fit into the storyline. At that point, my research becomes fascinating. With this particular plot, I needed an obscure place where wicked men could hide while plotting their evil deeds. It didn't take long to locate Coldingham Shore. Later in the 19th century, it was renamed St Abbs in honor of the legend of Aebba by a local laird, Mr. Andrew Usher.

Aebba was a 7th century abbess of a nunnery founded on Kirk Hill, just north of the village of Coldingham. Legend says Aebba was a daughter of King AEhelfrith of Bernicia, the first leader of a unified Northumbrian kingdom. When her father was killed, she fled north into the Scottish kingdom of Dalriada, where she converted to Christianity.

Decades later her brothers re-established themselves on the Northumbrian throne, and she was free to found a monastery on the clifftop known now as Kirk Hill. This abbey housed both monks and nuns for about 40 years. The monastery is thought to have been destroyed by fire in 683 A.D. I intentionally left the date out of my story. The ruins remaining after the 683 fire would have been insufficient to accomplish what I needed for my story in the year 1627.

Certain characteristics of the Middle Ages captivate my imagination: castles, knights, and mighty conquerors. With the average male lifespan of only 33 years, one married young to produce children they prayed lived to adulthood. Even though our lifespan has increased, Pippa's and William's story of tragedy and triumph still rings true today. Have we all not faced difficulties and disappointments? We wonder if God truly hears our cries of distress, and if so, why He remains silent.

God loves you and wants a relationship with you. Whether a Christian or not, He will orchestrate events in your life to draw you to Himself. Whether you struggle through fears, sorrow, or pain, God's unlimited resources await your prayers. Come to His Word for the strength to carry on, and He will supply the power to traverse the turbulent storms ahead.

*Ps. 18:2*
   *The Lord is my rock, and my fortress, and my deliverer; my God, my strength, in whom I will trust; my buckler, and the horn of my salvation, and my high tower.*

*Ps. 46:1*
   *God is our refuge and strength, a very present help in trouble.*

 Teresa Smyser lives in Northern Alabama with her minister husband and her mom. They have two married children, two grandsons and two granddaughters. She graduated from Eastern Kentucky University and now works as an accountant and divides the rest of her time between family, friends, church activities and writing. Teresa's prayer is that not only will her novels entertain, but they will point people to the love and the hope found in her Lord and Savior, Jesus Christ.

For more information about Teresa and her books, visit her at www.teresasmyser.com or www.facebook.com/teresasmyser

She loves hearing from her readers. Send questions or comments to authorsmys@gmail.com

*Thank you for reading the third book in the Warrior Bride Series. If you enjoyed the read, please take a moment, and leave a review on Amazon or Goodreads. It would be greatly appreciated!*

Capture a Heart of Stone - Kindle edition by Smyser, Teresa. Religion & Spirituality Kindle eBooks @ Amazon.com.

Capture a Heart of Stone (Warrior Bride #3) by Teresa Smyser | Goodreads

# If you enjoyed

# CAPTURE
## *a heart of*
# STONE

## then read:

## *Warrior Bride Series: Book 4*
### *Find out what happens to Gillian*

# COMING SOON!

Made in the USA
Columbia, SC
25 February 2022

56458411R00207